The Delhi Directive

The Delhi Directive

Once You're Marked, There's No Escape

Anirudhya Mitra

JUGGERNAUT BOOKS
C-I-128, First Floor, Sangam Vihar, Near Holi Chowk,
New Delhi 110080, India

First published by Juggernaut Books 2025

10 9 8 7 6 5 4 3 2

P-ISBN: 9789353459352
E-ISBN: 9789353452513

This is a work of fiction. Any resemblance to actual persons, living or dead, or to actual events, is either coincidental or used fictitiously for narrative purposes. The intent of this work is not to depict factual accounts or to harm, defame, or misrepresent any individual, group or institution.

Typeset in Adobe Caslon Pro by Mukul Chand

Printed at Thomson Press India Private Limited

To my late father, Anil Mitra, and my late mother, Nilima Mitra, whose love and values shaped everything I write.

And to all those men and women who serve this nation from the shadows. The nameless, faceless spies, operatives, assets and handlers who live and die for the country without ever being known. They work like ghosts. No medals, no applause. Many of them are erased from files, their names blacked out from official records.

A former intelligence chief once said that a spy agency is known by its failures. Maybe that is true in the eyes of the world. But those who have seen them work know that their successes are far greater and far more frequent. Only, they cannot be spoken of.

This book is for them, the invisible protectors of India, who remain in the dark so that the rest of us can live in light.

Contents

Preface

Writing about extrajudicial killings is like walking a tightrope suspended over an abyss of denial and secrecy. No nation openly admits to carrying them out, and yet the shadows of such actions are cast across the world. Consider the assassination of Osama bin Laden in Pakistan: a surgical operation by the United States that was broadcast to the world with pride. The motives were clear – to avenge the humiliation of 9/11 and to restore America's image as an unassailable superpower. It was a rare moment when the cloak of covert action was cast aside for all to see. But such moments are exceptions, not the rule.

India's story is different. Traditionally, Indian governments have cloaked themselves in deniability, their silence as calculated as their actions. This strategy began to shift in 2014, when a new government rose to power, emphasizing nationalism and decisive leadership. Covert operations, long shrouded in secrecy, began to take on a different hue. Public celebrations of the surgical strikes after Uri and the airstrikes after Pulwama marked a dramatic shift, with the narrative amplified at political rallies to project strength. Statements like '*Ghar mein ghus ke maare hain … ghar mein ghus ke marenge* [We entered their homes and killed them … we will do so again]' became rallying cries before elections.

This was not to suggest that earlier governments were passive. On the contrary, India's intelligence agencies have a long history of taking decisive covert actions. For instance, in 1986, Prime Minister Rajiv Gandhi's government established a specialized division called 'J' within R&AW to tackle cross-border terrorism. Extrajudicial killings were not unheard of during that era, but they were decisively brushed under the carpet. The difference today is stark: covert actions are often presented as overt, repackaged to gain political mileage on the domestic front.

Meanwhile, when allegations about India's role in these actions have arisen, whether from adversaries like Pakistan or even from Western allies, the responses have been calibrated. Leaders have publicly denied any involvement, maintaining diplomatic decorum. But the juxtaposition of these denials with the celebratory political rhetoric has painted a complex picture. India, it seemed, was rewriting the rulebook of covert operations balancing denial with a visible narrative of strength that resonated with its domestic audience.

In June 2023, the Canadian prime minister's claim of a 'credible allegation' linking India's spy agency, R&AW, to the assassination of Hardeep Singh Nijjar, a Canadian Sikh, set off a geopolitical firestorm. Overnight, the narrative changed. Suddenly, the world's gaze turned sharply towards India. Pakistan's long-ignored allegations found a new audience. Security agencies in the UK, the US and Australia raised alarms, concerned about the implications for mutual trust. And though the American government remained measured in its public rhetoric, whispers began circulating about a failed attempt on Gurpatwant Singh Pannun, a Khalistani leader in New York. The shadows that India had so carefully navigated were now starkly illuminated.

The media pounced, eager to connect the dots. Yet the details were frustratingly scarce. The killings, whether in Pakistan, the UK or Canada, followed a near-identical script: masked assailants on motorbikes, swift and brutal, vanishing without a trace. Social media erupted with speculation, every night bringing a new name to the rumour mill. Was Masood Azhar eliminated? Was Dawood Ibrahim poisoned in Karachi? Was Syed Salahuddin shot? The truth remained elusive, but the list of confirmed killings grew steadily, reaching over twenty-five by the end of 2023.

This was the world I found myself drawn into. Having left investigative journalism in 1994 for a career in television and films, I thought my days of chasing such stories were behind me. But the fascination of these mysterious operations proved irresistible. I called up old contacts, digging for answers, but hit a wall of silence. 'You know how it works,' they told me. Those who spoke did so off the record, warning of the risks of exposing such secrets. Even my most trusted sources were unwilling to confirm anything outright.

The deeper I dug, the more I realized how extraordinary this story was. Not just because of the killings themselves, but because of what they revealed about a shifting global order. India was no longer playing by the old rules. It had become a force to reckon with, a nation that could act decisively and, apparently, with impunity. This was no longer the India of the 1980s or 1990s. This was a new India, unapologetic in the pursuit of its interests.

But how could I tell this story? With no proof, no on-the-record statements and a thousand potential landmines, I knew a direct account was impossible. That's when the idea struck: what if I told it as fiction? A fictional truth, inspired by real events but unconstrained by the demands of evidence. When I proposed this to a few insiders, there was a long silence … and then, slowly, they began to talk. What followed was a journey into a world of covert operations and geopolitical chess games, a world both exhilarating and deeply unsettling.

The Delhi Directive is the result of that journey. Writing it was not just an exploration of geopolitics but a deeply immersive experience. The story reflects the complexities of modern espionage, blending real-world inspiration with a gripping fictional narrative that feels both authentic and urgent.

Among the characters, the one who captivated me the most was the national security director (NSD), the chief architect and mastermind behind the plan. For decades, even after retiring as the head of the Intelligence Bureau (IB), he meticulously kept track of the whereabouts of India's most wanted. His resolve never wavered; the targets remained firmly on his radar. All he needed was the political mandate to execute his vision. Enter Awasthy, whose vast organizational network across the globe turned the NSD's blueprint into reality. With his sharp foresight and relentless determination, Awasthy ensured no one strayed from the mission's path.

But at the heart of the story is Aditya, the protagonist, who fights a dual battle. One against the enemies of the state and the other against the fractures in his personal life. His journey is not just about the missions he undertakes but also about the emotional and psychological toll of living in the shadows. Aditya's internal conflicts, his sacrifices and his resilience make him a character who lingers long after the story is told.

Equally compelling is Mridula, whose ethical stand in a world of disinformation and lies brought a unique tension to the narrative. Her struggle to uphold her principles in the face of overwhelming pressure highlights the moral cost of espionage. She is a reminder that even in the shadowy world of covert operations, conscience can be both a guide and a burden.

The narrative plunges you into high-stakes confrontations: a failed attempt on a Khalistani leader in New York, a dramatic standoff in Surrey and a network of spies unravelling in Germany and Australia. It delves into the corridors of power where decisions are made and secrets buried, from the clandestine operations of R&AW to the calculated moves of intelligence agencies in Washington, London and Ottawa. You will meet characters forced to choose between loyalty and survival, and duty and humanity, their choices shaping a volatile global landscape.

In this novel, I have tried to capture the fine line between national interests and international norms, inviting readers to reflect on the moral ambiguities of extrajudicial actions. It explores not just the missions but also their ramifications, the power dynamics, the quiet ruthlessness of backroom decisions and the humanity behind the shadows.

This is not a story of heroes and villains. It is a story of shadows, where light and darkness blend, and where every choice carries a cost. As you turn the pages, you will encounter layered intrigue, strategic plotting and high-stakes drama. A mirror to the fractured world we live in.

The war in the shadows has begun. Will you step into the light?

Prologue

The Zabeel Palace loomed in the heart of Dubai, a fortress of luxury and power, crowned with golden domes. The residence of the prime minister of the UAE stood as a legacy of wealth and authority, where decisions that shaped the region were made within its ornate walls. Below, the city lights shimmered like a sea of jewels scattered across the desert, their glow softening the edges of the otherwise silent night.

The desert heat clung to the air, wrapping the palace in a blanket of stillness, broken only by the occasional murmur of distant traffic and the whisper of a warm breeze. It was a night like any other, a façade of tranquillity.

In a particular wing of the palace, the lights began to dim, one after another. This was where the ruler, the prime minister, withdrew for rest, and with each light extinguished, the end of the day approached. The rhythm of the palace's slumber was almost ritualistic, a slow surrender to the night's silence.

Yet, in the heart of this serenity, something stirred beneath the surface. The stillness wasn't peace. It was a mask.

The waters of the Arabian Sea stretched endlessly, reflecting the pale glow of the moon as it hung like a sentinel in the sky. The soft lapping of the waves against the hull of a sleek yacht created a rhythmic, almost hypnotic sound. Far from the bustling shores of

Goa, the yacht drifted silently in the international waters in the vast expanse of the ocean.

On the front deck, two figures huddled beneath oversized hoodies, their faces shadowed in the night's cool breeze. One of them was Princess Habiba, daughter of the prime minister of the UAE. She was a striking contrast to the luxury and opulence she was accustomed to. Just thirty-two, she was petite, with a loose ponytail that danced gently in the breeze, and eyes that were dark and intense, holding a fire of defiance. Tonight, she was not the princess of one of the world's richest families but a woman on the run.

Beside her sat Tiana George, a sturdy, no-nonsense Finnish martial-arts instructor. Years of training had sculpted her body into a weapon of strength, and her sharp gaze was ever watchful. She wasn't here for luxury or pleasure. Tiana was the one person Habiba trusted with her life, and that trust was about to be tested to its very limits.

For years, Princess Habiba, daughter of the prime minister of the UAE, had nurtured a secret. A secret if exposed, could shake the very foundations of her family's power. She had crafted the plan with precision, laying the groundwork step by step. What began as whispers of rebellion in her mind evolved into tangible action – training in extreme sports to build her endurance and agility, securing a fake passport that would carry her far from the grasp of her father's influence, and carefully smuggling cash to a shadowy network of conspirators who supported her in her desire for freedom.

By the time she entrusted her plan to Tiana George, her martial arts instructor and closest confidante, it was almost complete. Habiba had already arranged for a yachtsman, a discreet and loyal mercenary, to pick her up under the cover of night off the coast. His mission: to sail her away from the suffocating control of the UAE, to the shores of India or Sri Lanka, where she would disappear into the crowds. From there, she would take the final step of flying to the United States, the land where she could claim asylum and finally live on her own terms.

Every piece had been meticulously placed, but as the yacht sliced through the waters, Habiba knew that the most dangerous part of the journey still lay ahead. This was her one chance for freedom. A chance she would not squander.

Habiba tapped swiftly on her phone, her fingers moving with a confidence that had been absent for years. She sent a message to a trusted friend: 'I really feel so free now. A walking target, yes, but totally free.'

Above her, in the captain's cabin, the middle-aged yachtsman stared intently at the GPS, his grizzled face illuminated by the soft green glow of the screen. He murmured to himself, 'Forty more miles, and we're home.' His voice carried a mixture of relief and caution because he knew the waters they navigated were fraught with risks.

One of the crew, perched with night vision binoculars, interrupted the captain's momentary respite. 'Captain, look,' the man said, pointing toward the sky. The captain followed his gaze, narrowing his eyes as he spotted the faint silhouette of a plane in the distance. Its quiet hum barely cut through the sound of the waves.

Meanwhile, on the front deck, Habiba tucked her phone into the pocket of her shorts and turned to Tiana with gratitude welling up in her eyes.

'I can't thank you enough for this, Tiana. I owe you my life,' Habiba said.

Tiana, ever composed and unflinching, gave a small smile. Her sturdy frame seemed even more reassuring in the moonlight.

'Habiba, I helped you escape so you could finally see the world for what it is without bars around you. I'm excited it's all coming together.'

'Promise me you'll stay with me, all the way to freedom?'

'Promise,' Tiana said. She yawned slightly, her exhaustion starting to catch up. 'But right now, it's time to catch up on some sleep. Come on.'

Habiba smiled, the weight of the world momentarily lifting from her shoulders. She lay back on the deck, gazing up at the stars, the endless sky a stark contrast to the gilded cage she had been trapped in for years.

'Let's fall asleep stargazing, just this once?' Habiba pleaded.

Tiana chuckled and reached down to pull her friend up.

'I'm tired, and there will be plenty of time to see the stars, believe me,' she said.

'Yes, but this time I won't be silenced,' Habiba replied. 'I'll wake up knowing I can do whatever I want, go wherever I want.'

Tiana gently pulled Habiba to her feet, her voice steady but kind:

'And you will. But for now, we need to rest.' The two women shared a quiet, understanding look before heading inside.

Just as they descended to their cabin, a sudden roar broke the peaceful night. A spotter plane from the Indian Coast Guard flew low over the yacht, its presence unmistakable. Inside, unaware of the danger closing in, Habiba brushed her teeth in the cramped bathroom, the noise outside muffled by the yacht's walls.

Beneath the surface of the sea, commandos emerged silently from the dark water, their eyes fixed on the vessel. The night was no longer just Habiba and Tiana's; it belonged to someone else now.

As Habiba stepped out of the cramped bathroom, the air exploded with a deafening burst of blasts. Above, feet landed on the deck in quick, wet thuds. The soft rubber soles of boarding boots slapped against metal as the commandos moved fast and low, water streaming off their suits.

'Tiana? What was that?' Habiba's voice trembled, her eyes wide.

'They've found us,' Tiana hissed, shoving Habiba back into the bathroom. In one smooth motion, she drew a gun from her waistband.

'No!' Habiba screamed, grabbing Tiana's arm and yanking her back inside before slamming the door shut. Her hands trembled as she frantically typed out a string of SOS messages on her phone, but deep down, she knew it might already be too late.

Smoke began to pour in through the air vents and light fixtures, creeping into the small space. The air turned thick and suffocating as they both struggled to breathe, each breath coming more painfully than the last.

'I'm sorry, Tiana,' Habiba sobbed, her tears falling fast. 'I'm so sorry ...' Tiana pulled her into a tight hug, her voice soft but resolute. 'We'll fight till the end, baby.'

With that, Tiana stepped forward and flung the door open, gun raised high. The darkness outside was instantly cut through by the sharp red lines of laser sights, crisscrossing through the air like deadly webs.

Tiana fired, her hand steady, but not with the precision of a professional. The bullets sprayed wildly, hitting nothing but shadows. She emptied the magazine far too soon, the echo of her last shot lingering in the air.

In a heartbeat, masked men stormed in, seizing both women with brutal efficiency. Their hands were bound tightly, their struggles meaningless against the overwhelming force. Dragged out to the deck, Habiba's eyes darted to the captain and crew, beaten and bound, their blood smeared across the wooden floor.

They forced her down, her hands tied cruelly behind her back. But Habiba fought, kicking, screaming, clinging desperately to the gunwales as they tried to haul her away. 'Shoot me here!' she shouted, her voice cracking. 'Don't take me back!'

It was pre-dawn, the usual time for the NSD, Bhuvan Rawat, to wake up and begin his morning yoga. The stillness of New Delhi at this hour always offered a sense of calm before the day's storm of responsibilities. But today was different. Today, his focus wasn't on tranquillity. It was on a princess caught in a dangerous game.

Standing by the window, he held his phone to his ear, his tone measured yet authoritative. 'Alright. Keep her safe on the Coast Guard ship. See if the princess needs any medical help.'

He hung up, his mind racing through the next steps, and immediately dialled another number. Moments later, the anxious voice of the prime minister of the UAE came through, barely masking his fear.

'Any news of my daughter?'

The NSD's voice was calm, assuring. 'No need to worry, Mr Prime Minister. The princess is in the safe custody of our forces. A doctor is attending to her, making sure she receives all necessary care after the rough ride at sea.'

Relief flooded the UAE prime minister's voice. 'Thank you so much. I can't express my gratitude enough.'

'You're welcome, Prime Minister. Rest assured, your daughter will be handed over to your forces at a designated point in international waters.'

There was a pause before the prime minister spoke again, this time his tone more composed. 'Is there anything I can do in return? For India? For you? For the honourable prime minister?'

The NSD's lips curled into a subtle smile. 'For now, your daughter's safety and well-being are our priority. When the time comes, I will not hesitate to ask.'

The phone call ended, but the seed had been planted. What seemed like a favour in the heat of the moment would have rippling consequences – consequences the prime minister of the UAE could not yet foresee. When the time came, the NSD would call in his favour, and it would be a request far more significant than anyone could have anticipated. The princess's rescue was just the beginning of a much larger game, one that would soon unfold in ways neither country could predict.

1

Of Milk and Blood

14 February 2019.

The morning sun struggled to pierce through the dense fog that wrapped itself around the small rural town just outside Kanpur in Uttar Pradesh. Inside a cosy home, the warmth from the hearth painted a stark contrast to the biting chill outside. A young mother moved quietly through the room, careful not to wake her sleeping son, Babloo, just yet. His small form was buried under a quilt, his innocent face peeking out as he dreamed in the comfort of their modest home.

She approached him with a glass of milk in hand, gently shaking him awake. 'Come on, Babloo,' she coaxed, her voice filled with the sweetness only a mother's love can hold.

Babloo stirred but didn't open his eyes. 'Get me Bournvita in the milk, or I won't get up,' he mumbled, his voice groggy with sleep.

The mother, with a smile, walked over to the cupboard only to find the Bournvita jar empty. 'Looks like a thief has polished off your Bournvita,' she teased, hoping to stir him out of his stubbornness.

Babloo pouted from beneath the quilt. 'Then I don't want it.' He pulled the quilt over his head, refusing to budge, much to his mother's growing frustration.

Her gaze flickered to the clock on the wall. 'Babloo, I just don't like your attitude,' she scolded gently, though there was still warmth in her tone. 'The van rickshaw to take you to school isn't going to wait forever.'

She set the glass of milk aside, sighing as she glanced out the window, the fog creeping closer, swallowing the morning whole.

At the same time, hundreds of kilometres away, in the heart of Jammu and Kashmir, the atmosphere was far from cozy. In a secluded hideout nestled in a remote village, the chill of the air seemed to seep through the very walls, mirroring the grim intent of the men inside.

Shakir Bashir, a hardened member of a terror group, sat hunched over a table, his face bathed in the dull glow of a solitary lamp. He stared at the maps spread out before him, the weight of the urgent message he'd just received heavy on his shoulders. The news was clear that the convoy of CRPF vehicles was scheduled to pass along the NH44 near Kakapora in Pulwama.

Time was running short.

He surveyed the map, eyes narrowing as they traced the routes leading to the highway. Only one path seemed viable: an unmonitored slip road, poorly guarded and easily accessible. He marked it carefully, circling the spot with precision.

Across the room, a young boy, Adil Dar, listened intently, absorbing every word as Bashir laid out the plan. The cold in the room wasn't just from the weather, it was also the chill of impending violence, and both of them knew the magnitude of what was about to unfold.

Back in the quiet village in Uttar Pradesh, the mother sighed as she scrolled through her phone and dialled her husband Suresh. The morning wasn't going as smoothly as she'd hoped, and Babloo's refusal to get out of bed was only adding to her frustration. Suresh, a CRPF officer travelling in a convoy from Jammu to Srinagar, picked up her call with a broad smile, the familiar sound of his wife's voice warming his heart.

In the distance, Babloo sensed his mother's distraction. 'Are you calling Pappa?' he asked, peeking out from beneath the quilt.

Suresh could already see his wife's grumpy expression through the phone screen. 'Why do you look so upset this early in the morning?' he teased, the playful tone unmistakable.

'Because your pampered son doesn't want to go to school!' she retorted, pointing the phone towards Babloo. 'Now, talk to him.'

Suresh chuckled, his voice softening. 'Relax, sweetheart. Do you know what today is? Valentine's Day. Lovers aren't supposed to fight on this day.'

Babloo's face lit up at the sound of his father's voice, and without hesitation, he threw off the quilt and jumped out of bed, racing toward his mother to grab the phone. His mother made a mock annoyed face at her husband, but there was warmth in her eyes as she handed Babloo the phone.

'Pappa!' Babloo squealed, his excitement spilling through the small room.

Suresh grinned, flipping the phone's camera to show Babloo the long convoy stretching ahead of him. There were 78 vehicles winding through the rugged terrain. The atmosphere among the jawans was light-hearted, despite the long journey. Some were playing cards; others were glued to their phones, sending messages to loved ones; others were cracking jokes. Laughter echoed through the bus as someone threw out a witty remark, sparking new jokes from his comrades.

Babloo's eyes grew wide with curiosity. 'Pappa, show me your gun!'

Suresh, always the playful father, lifted his AK-56 rifle into view, the gleam of the weapon catching the light. Babloo clapped his hands in delight, bouncing on his toes with excitement. 'Pappa, you're the bravest and most powerful man on earth!'

The young boy's imagination was already running wild, and a new idea sparked in his mind. 'I'm going to paint a picture of you with your AK-47 and send it to you!' he declared, full of pride.

Suresh smiled at his son's enthusiasm but gently shook his head. 'Don't send it just yet, son. I'll be relocating to a new address soon. I'll visit home soon, and then I'll see your painting in person.'

The promise hung in the air, filling the small room with hope, as Babloo's mother watched her husband through the screen, her heart swelling with both love and worry.

In the cold, desolate landscape of Jammu and Kashmir, Shakir Bashir and his young accomplice, Adil Dar, stood side by side, eyes scanning the Bolero SUV in front of them. Inside, carefully stacked and hidden beneath innocuous cargo, were the explosives and detonators that would soon bring chaos to the highway. The preparations were complete; there was nothing left to check.

The weight of the moment hung heavy in the air. Bashir, with years of hardened resolve, looked at Adil, the younger man's face a mask of grim determination. Adil wasn't just a boy anymore; he was about to become a weapon in their larger cause. There was no turning back.

Bashir reached out, pulling Adil into a tight embrace. 'This is it, brother,' he whispered, his voice low but steady. 'May Allah be with you.'

Adil returned the embrace, his heart pounding, his mind a mix of steely resolve and resignation. He nodded silently, stepping back as Bashir's eyes bore into his. Bashir would not be going with him. This was Adil's journey to complete.

Without another word, Adil slid into the driver's seat, his fingers gripping the wheel with a new intensity. He started the engine, the low hum of the vehicle blending into the quiet of the rural road. Bashir stood motionless, watching as the Bolero rolled away, dust rising in its wake. He didn't move until the vehicle had disappeared from view.

Adil's hands tightened on the steering wheel as he drove down the narrow rural road leading to the highway. His breath came in steady, controlled bursts.He knew the pistol lay under his seat, a quiet reminder of the violence to come. With each passing second, the CRPF convoy drew closer. He knew the exact point where he would merge onto the highway, where his vehicle would blend into the rest of the traffic, just another SUV amidst the chaos of daily life.

As he neared the highway, his eyes flicked to the rear view mirror, and he leaned over to catch a glimpse of his own reflection. His face was set in a grim mask, the determination etched deep into his features. There was no hesitation in his movements; only the cold, mechanical rhythm of a man who had accepted his fate.

The slip road appeared ahead. He merged onto the highway smoothly, his Bolero falling into line with the other vehicles. The convoy wasn't far now. In the distance, he could make out the dull gleam of the military trucks, the chatter of the soldiers likely filling the air inside. His heart beat faster, but his grip remained steady. Each second brought him closer to the inevitable.

The convoy loomed larger in his sights, and the weight of what he was about to do pressed down on him. But his resolve didn't falter. His mission was clear. The moment of reckoning had come.

At that very moment, Babloo's eyes were still glued to the phone screen, watching his father's face framed by the familiar background of the convoy. But suddenly, the screen flickered. In an instant, an orange flash filled the display, and then it turned black. The sound of muffled screams broke through the fading connection, leaving Babloo frozen, the phone slipping slightly in his hands.

'Mamma …?' he whispered, trying to make sense of what he had just seen. His small fingers frantically tapped at the screen, trying to reconnect. But nothing happened. His father's voice, the cheerful chatter of the soldiers – it was all gone. The signal had disappeared into an eerie silence.

Back on the highway in Pulwama, the world had been transformed into chaos. A massive explosion ripped through the CRPF convoy with devastating force. Vehicles were tossed like toys into the air, crumpling and shattering as fire and smoke swallowed the road. Flames licked at the twisted metal, black smoke billowing towards the sky, a thick, choking cloud that darkened the morning sun.

Adil's mission had reached its horrific conclusion.

Amidst the wreckage, where once there had been camaraderie and laughter, now lay the aftermath of unimaginable destruction. Bodies littered the ground, some thrown from their vehicles, others still trapped in the mangled remains of the convoy. Shouts of anguish and disbelief filled the air, but they were drowned by the roar of fire and the sickening crackle of burning debris.

In the midst of the wreckage, Suresh's body hung from the window of a shattered bus, his life brutally cut short. His uniform, once a symbol of bravery, was now torn and bloodied, his upper body draped limply from the twisted frame. His hand, still clutching the phone he had used to speak to his son just moments before, dripped blood onto the ground below, an agonizing reminder of the conversation that had been cut off in the blink of an eye.

The warmth of his voice, the joy in Babloo's excited squeal, were silenced forever.

~

An hour later, the shockwaves of the Pulwama attack reverberated across India. In homes, offices and crowded streets, phones rang and notifications lit up. On screens large and small, a chilling video began to circulate, shared across social media platforms, forwarded from one group to another with growing disbelief. It was the final message of the suicide attacker, Adil Dar.

In the poorly lit frame of the video, a young man sat at the centre. His face was fair, his expression cold and resolute. A stubble covered his jaw, and his short hair cast shadows across his brow. He held an M4 carbine in his hands, its menacing form gleaming in the low light. On either side of him, a deadly arsenal was arranged: an AK-47 assault rifle on his left, a sniper rifle with a night sight scope on his right. Ten grenades lay at his feet, alongside an equal number of magazines. Behind him, a stark black banner of Jaish-e-Mohammed loomed, its bold script a haunting reminder of the terror group's reach.

Adil Dar began to speak, his voice steady and emotionless, carrying the weight of his deadly mission.

'My name is Adil,' he declared, staring into the camera with a chilling calmness. 'I joined Jaish-e-Mohammed a year ago. After a year's wait, I have finally been given the chance to do what I joined Jaish for.'

His words were a dagger to the heart of a nation in mourning. As he spoke, the reality of his actions began to sink in for those watching. Families, students, workers and people from all walks of life listened in horror as he continued.

'By the time this video reaches you, I'll be in heaven,' he said, his voice resolute. 'This is my last message for the people of Kashmir … Jaish has kept the flame alive and stayed put in adverse circumstances. Come, join the group and prepare for one last fight.'

The video ended abruptly, leaving a stunned silence in its wake. But the damage was done. Adil Dar's message had spread like wildfire, igniting anger, fear and sorrow across the nation. His chilling words, delivered with such conviction, left a nation reeling in the aftermath of his horrific actions.

Across India, the Pulwama attack dominated every news channel, every social media feed and every conversation in homes and offices. The nation was gripped by shock, anger and grief. Televised debates flared as spokespersons of the ruling party vowed swift and stern action against those responsible, while Opposition leaders sharply criticized the government's handling of security. The country, already reeling from the tragedy, now found itself facing not just a crisis of safety, but a crisis of leadership, laid bare before the cameras.

As twilight settled over New Delhi, casting the city in a slowly darkening crimson light, the military wing of Palam Airport became the solemn heart of the nation's mourning. Forty-two coffins, draped in the Indian tricolour, were displayed in neat rows, each bearing the remains of the brave soldiers who had perished in the attack. The air was suffocating with sorrow and rage, a potent mix that mirrored the darkening sky above.

Under the weight of grief, the prime minister of India stood alongside the three military chiefs, the NSD, heads of security agencies and key members of his cabinet. His eyes, moist with unshed tears, betrayed the depth of his sorrow. Yet his jaw remained visibly clenched, a confirmation of the anger simmering beneath the surface.

The silence around him was palpable as he stepped forward to address the gathered assembly, his voice steady but laden with emotion.

'We must get to the bottom of the incident,' he declared, his tone firm despite the weight of grief. 'Leave no stone unturned and find out the perpetrators of this ghastly crime.'

A heavy silence followed his words, the weight of the loss pressing down on everyone present. The prime minister's gaze shifted to the NSD, standing just behind him, his expression unreadable but his presence commanding.

The NSD stepped forward, his voice low yet resolute. 'Let us fix the images of these forty-two coffins in our minds and keep them there until we've delivered a fitting response to the architects of this massacre.'

The words hung in the air, heavy with the promise of retribution. The solemnity of the moment was punctuated by the soft strains of the national anthem as it played in the background. The flags stood at half-mast, fluttering gently against the deepening crimson sky, a silent reminder of the blood that had been spilled.

As the ceremony drew to a close, the prime minister gave one final, lingering look at the rows of coffins before turning to leave. His heart heavy, his mind already focused on what had to come next. It would be an unyielding pursuit of justice, no matter the cost.

The prime minister's convoy sped through the streets of New Delhi, the flashing lights of security vehicles reflecting off the sleek, dark cars. Inside the PM's vehicle, the atmosphere was heavy with silence, the weight of the evening's events pressing down on everyone present.

At exactly 6.46 p.m., the prime minister's fingers hovered over his phone as he composed a message meant to unite a grieving nation. His mind replayed the images of the coffins, the tearful families, the shattered lives. His heart ached with sorrow, but beneath it all, a steely resolve began to take root.

With a final glance at the words, he tapped the screen, sending the message into the digital world: 'The attack on CRPF personnel in Pulwama is despicable. I strongly condemn this dastardly attack. The sacrifices of our brave security personnel shall not go in vain. The entire nation stands shoulder to shoulder with the families of the brave martyrs. May the injured recover quickly.'

As the message began to spread across social media, shared by millions in a matter of minutes, the prime minister turned his gaze out of the car window. The city lights blurred into streaks of white and yellow as they passed, a sharp contrast to the darkness that weighed heavily on his mind. His face, reflected faintly in the glass, was a mixture of determination and grief, mirroring the mood of a nation that mourned its fallen but demanded justice.

He knew this attack had struck at the heart of India, and there would be no going back. The weight of leadership bore down on him like never before. The decisions he made in the coming days would shape not only the country's response but its position on the global stage.

The blur of the city lights continued, but in the prime minister's mind, things were becoming painfully clear. The time for words would soon give way to action.

Next day, as the city of New Delhi settled into an uneasy quiet, the Prime Minister's Office was anything but calm. The lights inside the grand building remained bright, and the air was heavy with tension. The prime minister had convened an urgent meeting of the Cabinet Committee on Security Affairs, and around the large conference table sat the most powerful figures in the government including ministers of defence, home, finance, foreign and legal affairs, along with the NSD.

The gravity of the situation weighed heavily on each face. The usual formality of such gatherings was overshadowed by a shared sense of determination. This was no ordinary crisis. The Pulwama attack had shaken the very foundations of the nation, and every individual in that room understood the gravity of what was at stake.

The NSD, standing at the head of the room, began his presentation with cold, clear efficiency. Reports from the preliminary examination of the blast site lay before him, and as he spoke, the entire room seemed to lean in, hanging on every word.

'It is clear,' the NSD began, his voice steady but laced with the seriousness of the moment, 'that the Pakistan-based terror group Jaish-e-Mohammed is behind this heinous attack. While Pakistan is attempting to claim that the suicide bomber was a local Kashmiri, the social media post we've recovered directly implicates JeM in this unforgivable crime.'

The ministers exchanged dark looks as the implications of this statement sank in. The NSD continued, unfazed by the tension.

'We are already in talks with our allies in the US and other western nations, asserting our right to self-defence against cross-border terrorism. Our intelligence is working tirelessly to trace the network that supported this attack, and we've made it clear that this cannot be tolerated.'

The prime minister, seated at the head of the table, nodded, his expression grim but resolute. 'Yes,' he said, his voice breaking the silence that followed. 'Both the US and the UK have already offered their full support to India in bringing the perpetrators and their backers to justice. They understand the gravity of this situation as well as we do.'

The room fell silent again, the weight of the prime minister's words settling over them. Every individual present knew this wasn't just about retaliation; it was about reshaping India's position on the global stage, reaffirming the country's stance on terrorism, and demonstrating that such an attack would not go unanswered.

The NSD glanced at the assembled ministers before continuing. 'Our forces are on high alert, and we are preparing for all possible scenarios. We have also initiated diplomatic channels to ensure the international community supports any actions we may need to take. But the final decision, of course, lies with this committee.'

The prime minister's gaze swept the room, taking in the hardened expressions of his cabinet. He could feel the shared determination, the understanding that this moment was pivotal as not only for the country's immediate response but for the future of its security and geopolitical standing.

'We must be clear in our intentions,' the prime minister said, his tone unwavering. 'The time for mere words is over. We will act.'

The room remained silent, but the resolve was palpable. This night would mark the beginning of India's journey toward justice, whatever it took.

In the stillness that followed the urgent meetings, the weight of the night's events hung heavily in the air. The bustling energy of the cabinet ministers had faded, and now only two figures remained in the conference room. They were the prime minister and the NSD. The large space, once filled with voices and urgency, now seemed eerily quiet. Both men, though exhausted, remained alert, their minds far too burdened to rest.

The prime minister stood by the window, gazing out at the darkened city beyond. The streetlights cast faint halos of light across the quiet streets, and for a moment, the world seemed peaceful in a stark contrast to the storm brewing in his mind. Behind him, the NSD, equally weary from the night's discussions, stood silently, a shared understanding passing between them. They both knew the gravity of the decisions that lay ahead.

In a voice much gentler than the one he had used during the meetings, the prime minister broke the silence. 'Go and have some rest,' he said, his tone calm but resolute. 'We have to start early tomorrow.'

The NSD, his face lined with the weariness of both the day's events and the burden of his role, shook his head slightly. 'You too need some rest,' he suggested, though he already knew what the prime minister's response would be.

The prime minister turned slightly, his expression soft but unyielding. 'I cannot sleep,' he said quietly. 'This is my time with myself. I need to think, to reflect on what lies ahead.' A faint smile crossed his lips. 'And 4.30 a.m. is my yoga time.'

The NSD couldn't help but smile slightly at the familiar discipline of the prime minister, but the smile quickly faded as the weight of the conversation returned. He cleared his throat, his voice steady but filled with the seriousness of the situation.

'You ordered a surgical strike across the Line of Control last September after Uri,' the NSD began, his tone measured but firm. 'We took 23 lives, and the action was meant to signal to the world that India would not shy away from punitive action.' He paused, the weight of his next words hanging in the air. 'Yet the neighbour didn't care. And now, we have Pulwama.'

The prime minister's eyes, still fixed on the city lights, darkened with understanding. The NSD's words echoed the unspoken truth they both had been grappling with.

'It's time for a bigger step,' the NSD continued, his voice low but charged with conviction. 'A more significant response. We've shown restraint, we've sent messages. But this time, the message must be unmistakable.'

The prime minister remained silent, his thoughts racing. He knew the NSD was right. Despite the surgical strike and the countless diplomatic overtures, Pakistan had continued its provocations, pushing India to the brink once again. Pulwama was a stark reminder that the stakes were higher than ever, and India's next move would need to reflect that reality.

The NSD straightened, sensing the prime minister's internal struggle but knowing he had to give him space to process it. He offered a small nod, a gesture of both respect and understanding. 'Good night, sir,' he said quietly before turning to leave.

As the NSD left the room, the prime minister stood alone, the city's quiet night unfolding before him. His mind churned with the weight of leadership, knowing that the decisions he made in the coming hours would not only define the immediate response but would shape India's future in the region.

In the quiet of his solitude, he braced himself for what was to come. The nation's resolve would soon be tested, and this time, there would be no turning back.

∽

The streets of the capital lay draped in pre-dawn quiet, the city still holding its breath before the rush of a new day. The NSD's black SUV, accompanied only by a lone security vehicle, sliced through the stillness, the hum of the engine a faint intrusion on the tranquillity of the hour. The lights of the city blinked faintly in the distance, but for now, the world seemed paused, hovering on the edge of awakening.

As his convoy approached a traffic light, the NSD, seated in the back of the vehicle, gestured to his driver. 'Stop here,' he said, his voice soft but commanding. The driver pulled over without hesitation, and the NSD leaned forward, peering out at the quiet scene unfolding before him.

At the side of the street, under the muted glow of a streetlamp, a group of newspaper vendors worked with swift precision, sorting bundles of the morning's news. The rustle of paper filled the air as they prepared the day's editions, each headline a window into the world's stories. A few early morning joggers passed by, their rhythmic footfalls barely audible against the backdrop of the city's silence.

Without a word, the NSD stepped out of the vehicle, the crisp morning air hitting him as he approached one of the vendors. The man looked up, startled at first by the unexpected figure, but quickly handed over the fresh newspaper. The NSD nodded in thanks, slipping a note into the vendor's hand before returning to the car.

Once inside, he unfolded the newspaper, the bold headlines immediately catching his eye. 'Pulwama Attack: A Nation in Mourning' screamed from the front page, accompanied by images of devastation and grief. His eyes scanned the articles – reports of the carnage and promises of retribution, and political commentary on the government's next steps. Each word seemed to carry the weight of the lives lost, the gravity of his responsibilities pressing down on him with renewed force.

As the streets slowly brightened with the coming dawn, casting the first light of day across the silent city, the NSD continued reading, his thoughts racing ahead to the decisions that would need to be made in the coming hours. The world was waking up to the news of the attack, and with it, expectations were rising.

He folded the paper carefully, setting it aside as the SUV resumed its journey through the capital's waking streets. The headlines, though now hidden from view, remained imprinted in his mind. A constant reminder that the hours ahead would shape the course of the nation.

The days following the Pulwama attack were marked by a flurry of high-level meetings in the corridors of power across New Delhi. The PMO, the Cabinet Secretariat in South Block and the ministries of home and defence in North Block, became the epicentres of urgent discussions. The air inside these buildings was heavy with the momentousness of the decisions being made, each conversation carrying the weight of national security and retribution.

In one of the most critical meetings, India's top defence strategists and military officials sat in a room filled with quiet tension. At the head of the room stood Ashok Awasthy, the head of the Research and Analysis Wing, the man tasked with presenting the options for India's next move. His presence commanded attention, and the room fell into a focused silence as he prepared to speak.

Using a sleek iPad-like console, Awasthy tapped the screen, and a large, detailed map of the Indo-Pak border appeared on the wall-sized screen behind him. His finger hovered over one section of the map before pressing down, and the city of Bahawalpur, just across the border in Pakistan, lit up in bright red.

'We strongly suggest dismantling JeM's infrastructure,' Awasthy began, his voice steady but charged with the significance of what was to follow. 'Bahawalpur, Sawai Nallah and Balakot,' he said, listing the targets with precision.

He gestured to the map, highlighting Bahawalpur once again. 'Bahawalpur is the hub of Jaish-e-Mohammed's operations,' he explained, his finger tracing the routes leading in and out of the city. 'A strike here would disrupt the group's leadership and its propaganda capabilities.'

The men and women around the table exchanged glances, the implications of the suggestion sinking in. But Awasthy wasn't finished. He swiped his finger across the screen, and another location, Sawai Nallah, lit up.

'Sawai Nallah,' he continued, 'is strategically located near the Line of Control. It serves as a crucial transit point for militants infiltrating into India. Dismantling this location would severely hamper their ability to send operatives across the border.'

The room was utterly silent, the tension palpable as Awasthy moved to the third and final target. His finger tapped the screen one last time, and the map zoomed in on Balakot, nestled deep within Pakistan's Khyber-Pakhtunkhwa region.

'Balakot,' Awasthy said, his tone more deliberate now, 'is their main training and indoctrination centre. It is remote but critical to the operational importance of JeM. Striking here would deliver a decisive blow to their ability to train and deploy militants.'

The room remained still, each official and strategist weighing the gravity of what they were being asked to consider. These strikes, should they be approved, would send a powerful message, one that would be heard not only in Pakistan but across the world.

Awasthy lowered his iPad, his eyes scanning the room. 'These are the targets we recommend. The decision, of course, lies with this committee.'

For a moment, no one spoke, but the room was charged with the enormity of the choice before them. India's response to Pulwama would be more than just a military operation – it would be a statement of the nation's resolve.

The second important meeting took place in the oval room of the PMO, where the air was filled with anticipation. Ashok Awasthy stood alongside the Army chief, surrounded by top military and intelligence officials. Spread out before them were detailed maps and satellite imagery of each JeM camp spread across Bahawalpur, Sawai Nallah and Balakot. The images glowed faintly on the large screens, each location under careful scrutiny.

The conversation in the room was hushed, but from the focused actions of the participants, it was clear that they were preparing for something monumental. The quiet intensity of their movements, as they gestured over the satellite images and pointed to strategic routes, left no doubt that a military strike was in the works.

The Army chief, a man of few words, broke the silence, emphasizing the need for precision in the strike. His voice was steady, each word carefully chosen.

'The strike we recommend is surgical,' he said, his gaze moving across the room. 'Our aim is to minimize collateral damage while effectively crippling JeM's operational capabilities. We cannot afford mistakes.'

Heads nodded in agreement. The objective was clear: send a message, cripple the enemy's infrastructure, but do so with the utmost precision, respecting international law and avoiding unnecessary casualties.

A few days later, a critical meeting took place in the PMO conference room. The tension was palpable as India's senior-most security officials completed their presentation before the prime minister. The Army chief, Air Force chief and Navy chief sat alongside Ashok Awasthy of R&AW and the NSD. The plans for the Balakot strike had been laid out in meticulous detail. Satellite images, operational routes and contingencies had been reviewed. Now, all eyes were on the prime minister.

A heavy silence filled the room as they awaited his decision. The prime minister, his hands resting on the polished table, took a deep breath before speaking.

'Go ahead with Balakot strike,' he said, his voice calm but resolute. 'Ensure maximum precision and minimal harm to civilians, keeping in mind the ethical considerations that guide India's military actions. Our response must be proportionate, targeted and in line with international law.'

The room remained still for a moment as the gravity of the order settled over them. Then, one by one, the officials stood up, saluting the prime minister before filing out of the room.

But the prime minister noticed something. Throughout the entire meeting, the NSD had been unusually quiet, his normally sharp input absent. As the room cleared, the prime minister waved him to stay back.

When the last person had left, the prime minister turned to the NSD, his tone gentler but probing. 'You've been unusually quiet of late. Don't you agree with the action being planned?'

The NSD looked at him, pausing slightly before responding. 'Of course, I am in agreement with the action being planned,' he said, his voice calm but with an edge of thoughtfulness.

He hesitated for a moment before continuing. 'Look, if this is an act of revenge or to teach our neighbour a lesson, I can tell you our soldiers are trained well enough to return victorious, hundred on hundred. But,' his voice lowered, filled with a hint of resignation, 'if we are assuming this is going to stop terrorism or prevent future attacks on India, then we are expecting too much. I believe there will be terror attacks on us in six months' time.'

The prime minister leaned back slightly, taking in the NSD's words. He could sense the weight of the unspoken concerns but wasn't ready to delve deeper just yet. He chose a lighter tone to ease the tension.

'*Arrey, yeh Balakot toh pehle ho jaane deejiye, bhai. Phir dekhenge.* [Oh, let this Balakot happen first, then we'll see],' the prime minister said with a faint smile. 'Unless you have doubts that you're not sharing.'

The NSD shook his head, his expression resolute. 'I have no doubt that your decision to strike Balakot will blow away the myth of Pakistan's nuclear blackmail.'

The prime minister nodded, understanding the NSD's position. The Balakot strike was just the beginning, and while they both knew the road ahead was fraught with uncertainty, for now, the decision had been made.

~

26 February, morning.

Inside the NSD's office, the air was heavy with anticipation. The NSD sat in front of a large screen, his eyes fixed on the television as the morning news broadcast filled the room. The images of Balakot were fresh: plumes of smoke rising in the early light of day, the terrain scorched from the precise strikes that had targeted JeM's terror camps.

A news reporter stood on the screen, speaking directly to the camera, his voice confident, carrying the weight of the morning's events.

'In the early hours today,' the reporter began, 'the Indian Air Force launched a precise strike on Balakot, successfully destroying the JeM terror camps. The operation resulted in the elimination of a significant number of JeM terrorists, achieving a critical blow to the terror network.'

The NSD watched for a moment longer, absorbing the news and the significance of the operation's success. The weight of the past few days, the meetings, the decisions, the planning hung in the air, but the mission was now complete. A quiet satisfaction settled over him.

He reached for the phone, dialling the direct number to the prime minister. The line connected after a single ring.

'Congratulations,' the NSD said, his voice steady but laced with relief. 'The strike was precise and executed just the way you wanted.'

On the other end, the prime minister's voice was filled with a quiet sense of accomplishment. 'Congratulations to you, to all of us,' he replied. But then, after a brief pause, his tone shifted slightly, more thoughtful. 'Now let's see how they respond.'

The prime minister's words hung in the air for a moment before he added, 'Hiten will give you the time to come to my office.' And with that, the call ended, the prime minister hanging up.

The NSD lowered the phone slowly, his mind replaying the prime minister's second line: Let's see how they respond.

He leaned back in his chair, thoughtful. The operation had been a success, no doubt. But now came the part that was beyond their control. How would Pakistan react? Would there be retaliation? The airstrike had struck a critical blow, but it was also a step deeper into uncharted territory.

As the morning light filtered into the room, the NSD understood the prime minister's unspoken thoughts. The Balakot strike wasn't the end. It was the beginning of a new phase, one that could escalate into something far greater.

He exhaled slowly, the weight of the responsibility settling on his shoulders once more. The game had shifted, and now all eyes would be on what came next.

The day after India's bold strike on Balakot, the nation was electrified with a mix of pride and anticipation. Newsrooms hummed with activity, their feeds flooded with updates. Television screens across the country flickered with breaking news banners, their anchors speaking rapidly, trying to keep up with the developments that were unfolding at breakneck speed.

The morning had brought news of India's triumph, but as the day wore on, the tension began to mount. Pakistan had decided to retaliate.

The footage on television screens shifted rapidly with grainy images of fighter jets streaking across the sky, plumes of smoke rising along the Line of Control. The air felt heavy with the tension of battle. Various news channels cut between reporters and field correspondents, their voices urgent, almost breathless, as they delivered the latest updates.

An Indian news reader, his expression grave, stared directly into the camera as he relayed the latest shocking development.

'The Pakistan Air Force has engaged in a fierce battle with the IAF along the Line of Control. During this confrontation, one of our Indian fighter jets was shot down. We have received confirmation that IAF pilot Abhinandan has been captured by Pakistani forces.'

The words sent shockwaves through the nation. In living rooms, cafes and office spaces, people stared at the screens, their hearts racing, their breaths held in unison. The triumph of the morning had given way to dread.

The camera switched to a foreign television network, the anchor's voice colder, more detached, but no less alarming.

'The capture of fighter jet pilot Abhinandan has escalated tensions between India and Pakistan, pushing both nuclear-armed nations to the brink of a potential full-scale war. The international community is deeply concerned, fearing that this conflict could develop into a catastrophic confrontation in South Asia.'

The tension was palpable, and across the world, leaders scrambled to contain the situation. But in India, the weight of the moment was heaviest of all. Night fell over New Delhi, but inside the PMO, the lights blazed with urgency. A critical phone call was taking place. It was a conversation that could tip the scales of war.

That night, a crucial talk between India and America took place.

The prime minister sat behind his desk, his eyes fixed on the secure phone line in front of him. The tension in the room was thick, the air barely stirred as his advisors waited anxiously for what would come next. On the other end of the line was the president of the United States, his voice crackling faintly over the connection.

'This is the time I need my American friend's help,' the prime minister said, his voice low but firm, cutting through the stillness.

The president, ever the pragmatist, replied with cautious interest. 'Like how?'

The prime minister wasted no time. 'I urge you to speak with Pakistan's prime minister. Tell him to return my pilot immediately.'

There was a pause on the other end of the line, and then a hint of amusement slipped into the American president's tone. 'And what if he doesn't comply ... at least for the moment?'

The prime minister's gaze hardened, his jaw set with the resolve of a man with no other options. 'Then you tell him this ... if the Indian pilot is not returned within 24 hours, India will have no choice but to escalate this situation into a full-scale war against her neighbour.'

The American president let out a soft chuckle, the sound almost incongruous with the gravity of the situation. 'Wow! I like that.' But then, in an instant, his tone shifted, the humour draining away as he became serious. 'Let me think about it, my friend.'

The line went quiet, and the prime minister leaned back in his chair, the weight of the moment settling over him like a heavy cloak. The stakes couldn't be higher as India was on the brink of war, and the next 24 hours would determine the course of history.

As dawn approached, the world watched and waited. India and Pakistan stood on the edge of a precipice, the shadow of nuclear conflict looming ever closer. In living rooms and offices, and across the airwaves, people held their breath, knowing that what happened next could change everything.

The tension between India and Pakistan had reached a boiling point, and the world watched anxiously as diplomatic efforts moved into high gear. From Capitol Hill in Washington, DC, a crucial phone call was taking place between the US Secretary of State and the prime minister of Pakistan. The stakes were high, and every word carried the weight of two nations on the brink of war.

The Pakistani prime minister, his voice tight with frustration, defended his country's actions. 'We acted in self-defence,' he said firmly. 'It's India who provoked Pakistan with an airstrike that was completely uncalled for.'

The US Secretary of State, seated behind his desk in Washington, kept his tone measured, diplomatic. 'I see your point, Mr Prime Minister. But we believe that releasing the Indian pilot would help reduce the current tension and de-escalate any further action.'

There was a pause. The Pakistani prime minister, bristling, pressed on. 'Nobody wants a war, but I wonder if have you asked *India* why they acted irresponsibly?'

The Secretary of State leaned forward, his voice remaining calm, though the urgency in his words was unmistakable. 'We're not here to judge anyone, sir. We simply feel that it is in everyone's interest, including Pakistan's, to immediately return the Indian pilot. The geopolitical dynamics have shifted acutely, and this action would send a clear signal of your willingness to de-escalate.'

The Pakistani prime minister's voice grew firmer. 'I want to talk to the president.'

The Secretary of State didn't flinch. His response was swift, cutting through the tension like a blade. 'Mr Prime Minister, what I am conveying to you was dictated to me directly by the president's office, hence there is no need for further discussion.'

There was silence on the line, a moment of quiet that seemed to stretch infinitely. The weight of the ultimatum hung in the air. The prime minister of Pakistan knew that his next move would be critical.

In no time, the world was taken by surprise as news broke that the captured Indian fighter pilot, Abhinandan, was being returned to India. The cameras zoomed in on the border as the handover took place, and the pilot, bruised but unbroken, crossed back into his homeland. His return was met with relief, celebration, and a collective exhale from a nation that had been teetering on the edge of war.

The chapter of retaliation and escalation had closed, for now. But as the dust settled and the soldiers returned to their posts, it was clear that the future still held untold challenges, and the spectre of conflict was never far from the horizon.

2

Diplomacy of the Dark

28 February 2019.

Two days after the Balakot airstrike, the atmosphere inside the PMO was one of subdued jubilation. A meeting had been convened to formally congratulate the heads of India's top security agencies. The mood in the room was buoyant, since the operation had been a success, a strategic blow to JeM's terror infrastructure. There was a sense of accomplishment in the air as the prime minister moved around the room, shaking hands with each of the officials, offering words of praise.

'Congratulations to each of you,' he said, his tone filled with gratitude. 'You've all done the country proud.'

He watched over the informal gathering, ensuring that everyone had tea or coffee in hand, the table spread with an assortment of snacks. It was a rare moment of ease in the PMO, a fleeting pause before the next wave of challenges would inevitably arrive.

But as the heads of the agencies began to take their leave, one by one, the NSD lingered. His face was calm, but there was a sharpness in his eyes that hadn't been present earlier. The prime minister noticed, sensing that something more pressing was on the NSD's mind.

Just as the last official stepped out of the room, the NSD approached. 'Do you have time for a short chat?' he asked, his tone respectful but with a hint of urgency.

The prime minister, already suspecting that the conversation would shift from the light-hearted mood of the moment, nodded. 'By all means. Need you ask?'

The two men moved toward the centre of the room, the prime minister settling into his chair, while the NSD remained standing, as though he had been preparing for this conversation for some time. The atmosphere shifted instantly; the sense of celebration evaporated, replaced by something far more serious.

The NSD took a deep breath, choosing his words carefully. 'Do you remember,' he began, 'that I mentioned before the Balakot strike that these surgical strikes alone may not be enough to deter future terrorist attacks from Pakistan?'

The prime minister's expression darkened slightly. 'I do,' he replied, his voice now more measured. 'But are you asking for more actions by our armed forces? Because that would lead to a fresh war.'

The NSD shook his head. 'No, not in the conventional sense,' he clarified. 'Let me explain.'

He swiped across the screen of his iPad, opening up a page filled with documents and images. 'I propose that we take action against terrorists who have harmed India, but who are now living comfortably under the protection of other countries.'

He paused for effect, his eyes meeting the prime minister's. 'Take Osama bin Laden, for example. He was hiding in a safe house in Pakistan. Did America spare him?'

The prime minister held up his hand, interrupting. 'India cannot do many of the things that America does,' he said firmly. 'We are bound by different geopolitical realities.'

The NSD's expression didn't waiver. 'I believe India can, under your leadership,' he replied, his tone unwavering. 'But our approach doesn't have to mirror that of the Americans. We won't act overtly. Our men will engage in one-on-one combat, eliminate these individuals in their safe havens, wherever that may be – Pakistan, Afghanistan, the UK, Canada, the US … wherever.'

The prime minister leaned forward, his gaze intense. 'Such a move would have far-reaching consequences. Even if just one of our men is caught, it would directly implicate India. It seems our "covert" operation strategist has become very "overt" in his thinking.'

The NSD didn't flinch. 'Let me assure you,' he said quietly, 'none of our strikers will know who they are working for. There will be multiple layers of cut-offs, leaving no traceable link to India. I've been working on this plan since 2014.'

The room fell silent, the gravity of the proposal hanging in the air between them. The prime minister's mind raced as he considered the implications. This wasn't just a covert operation. It was a paradigm shift in India's approach to counterterrorism. One that, if successful, could change the rules of the game entirely.

But the risks were immense. And so was the responsibility.

The NSD reached into his folder and pulled out a single sheet of paper, handing it to the prime minister. The list was brief but damning. It was a timeline of some of the worst terror attacks on India. At the top was the 1985 Air India Kanishka bombing, followed by more recent attacks that had left deep scars on the nation. Each attack was paired with the current location of the individuals responsible for planning or funding, men who were now living under the protection of foreign governments, far beyond the reach of Indian law.

The prime minister scanned the paper, his expression hardening as he read each line. He understood the NSD's argument all too well. These men, these ghosts from India's painful past, had to be brought to justice. But the timing … the timing was everything.

The prime minister set the paper down on the table, taking a deep breath before responding. 'I understand your points,' he said, his voice steady but carrying the weight of political realities. 'But right now, we cannot afford any distractions.'

The NSD frowned slightly but said nothing.

The prime minister continued, his tone more decisive. 'Let the elections get over. I cannot focus on anything else right now.'

The NSD nodded slowly, though inside, he felt the subtle sting of disappointment. The prime minister's response, though couched in practicality, was an indirect rejection of his proposed strategy. At least for now. The elections, with all their noise and complications, had taken priority, and the NSD knew that this delay could cost the nation valuable time.

But there was nothing more to be said. He had made his case, and the decision had been deferred.

The prime minister stood, signalling that the meeting was over. The NSD gave a respectful nod and quietly left the room, the weight of the conversation hanging heavy on his shoulders. As he walked down the softly lit corridor of the PMO, his footsteps echoed faintly, each one a reminder of the delicate balance between India's political realities and the urgent need for security.

Just weeks earlier, the prime minister had told him, 'Let the Balakot strike be over.' And now it was, but still the delay came: 'Let the elections be over.'

The NSD's mind raced. He understood the necessity of political timing, but he also knew that the threat wasn't waiting. It was out there, lurking, preparing for the next moment to strike. And each delay only gave India's enemies more time to regroup, to plan, to move further out of reach.

As he stepped into the night air, he took a deep breath. He would wait, just as the prime minister had asked. But he knew this wasn't over. Not by a long shot.

∽

A week after the resounding victory of the ruling party in 2019, in the heart of New Delhi's diplomatic enclave, tucked away behind the grand façades of embassies and consulates, the Krishna International Foundation hummed with the energy of intellectual exchange. The foundation, established in 2009 by the NSD himself, was a sanctuary of ideas, a place where the country's top minds often gathered to discuss the challenges and opportunities facing India.

On this particular afternoon, the atmosphere was light, informal. The NSD sat among old friends and colleagues, sipping tea, the warm, familiar scent of cardamom filling the air. The conversation flowed freely, marked by the ease of long-time associates, men who had worked together through thick and thin.

One of his former colleagues raised his glass in a toast, congratulating him. 'With the PM's resounding victory,' he said with a grin, 'it looks like your next term could be even more eventful!'

There was laughter around the room, but the NSD shook his head, a wry smile playing at the corner of his mouth.

'Nah,' he said, his tone surprisingly casual, but with a hint of something deeper. 'I've had enough. I'm planning to resign. It's time for me to travel with my family … spend time with my grandchildren.'

The room, once filled with easy laughter, fell into a sudden silence. The weight of the NSD's words hit everyone at once, the reality of his declaration sinking in. These were not empty words, not the idle musings of a tired man. They all understood what his departure would mean; this was the man who had been at the centre of India's security apparatus, a close confidante of the prime minister and a figure instrumental in shaping the country's geopolitical strategies.

His colleagues exchanged uncertain glances, the gravity of the moment stifling the light heartedness of their earlier conversation.

Sensing the shift in the room, the NSD spoke again, his voice more resolute this time. 'I appreciate your good wishes,' he said, offering a reassuring smile. 'But I'm serious. Enough is enough.'

The silence deepened. Even those who had known him for decades were caught off-guard. Among the group was Sachidanand Murthy, a member of the foundation who was known for his close proximity to the prime minister. He watched the NSD carefully, sensing the underlying exhaustion, perhaps even a trace of pain, in his declaration.

Sachidanand Murthy leaned forward, his voice gentle but probing. 'Come on,' he said, trying to lighten the mood. 'I'm sure the PM cannot afford to let you go. There must be many unfinished tasks for you in his head. Don't you agree?'

The NSD met his gaze, his expression softening for a moment. But then he shook his head. 'Forget it, Sachi. I've crossed 75. I need some rest, too.'

The finality in his words settled over the room like a heavy cloud. His decision was made, and no amount of persuasion seemed likely to change it. The conversation faltered, the usual banter replaced by a collective realization that the NSD, that their leader, their mentor, was ready to step away from the arena that had defined his life for so many years.

The room remained quiet, the camaraderie now tinged with a sense of loss, as the NSD took another sip of his tea, resolute in his choice.

Later that night, the portent of the NSD's words lingered heavily in Sachidanand Murthy's mind. In the quiet of his hotel room, far from the light-hearted banter of the afternoon, he found himself deeply moved by the NSD's firm and emotional declaration. The room was lit by only a bedside lamp, the hum of the city outside a distant backdrop to his thoughts. He paced slowly, replaying the conversation over and over in his head.

The NSD's resignation wasn't just a personal decision. It would have profound consequences for India's national security, for the delicate geopolitical balance the NSD had helped maintain for years. Murthy could sense the weight of this moment. The prime minister had to know what was at stake, and he couldn't afford to let this issue wait until tomorrow.

Feeling the urgency of the situation, Murthy sat down at the desk, pulling out a notepad and pen. The scratch of the pen against paper filled the silence of the room as he began writing a note in longhand to the prime minister. Each word was carefully chosen, the tone respectful but urgent.

He emphasized the NSD's pivotal role in shaping India's security policies, from covert operations to international alliances, and the critical need for his continued presence. He underscored the profound impact the resignation would have – not only on the nation's security apparatus but on the prime minister himself, who had relied so heavily on the NSD's counsel. The note wasn't just a plea to keep the NSD in office; it was a call to action, urging the prime minister to intervene before it was too late.

Sachidanand Murthy re-read the note, his heart racing slightly with the weight of what he had written. He folded it carefully, sealing it in an envelope. The decision had been made – this message had to reach the prime minister as soon as possible.

Without hesitation, he picked up the phone and called his secretary. 'I need you to deliver a sealed envelope to Mr Hiten Dave at the PMO first thing in the morning,' he instructed. 'It's important.'

The secretary, recognizing the urgency in Murthy's voice, assured him it would be done. With that, Murthy hung up the phone, staring at the sealed envelope on the desk. The message was clear, and by morning, the prime minister would know the weight of what was at stake.

The sprawling gardens of the NSD's residence in Lutyens' Delhi were bathed in the soft, golden hues of late October of 2019. The leaves, crisp with the early hints of winter, crunched underfoot as the NSD, wearing a light jacket, stood in the middle of his neatly manicured lawn. His grandchildren, Abhishek and Priyanka, laughed and shouted with excitement as they prepared for a game of cricket. The chill in the air was no match for the warmth of their playful energy.

The NSD's usual stern, composed demeanour was gone, replaced by a smile that radiated pure joy. He was in holiday mode now, focused on spending time with his family, particularly his beloved grandchildren. These moments, far from the world of politics and national security, gave him the rare opportunity to unwind and embrace the lighter side of life.

'Alright, team,' he said cheerfully, setting up the wickets with a wink, 'let's see if Grandpa still has his bowling skills!'

Priyanka, her eyes shining with determination as she gripped the cricket bat, grinned back at him. 'Be easy on me, Grandpa!' she pleaded, but the twinkle in her eyes revealed that she was ready for the challenge.

'Go full speed, Grandpa!' Abhishek chimed in, bouncing with eagerness. At just 10 years old, his enthusiasm knew no bounds, and he wasn't about to let Priyanka get an easy pass.

The NSD chuckled at their contrasting attitudes, his heart warmed by their sibling rivalry. He started bowling gently to Priyanka, his movements measured and encouraging, giving her just enough challenge to test her skills. The soft clunk of the ball against the bat echoed across the garden, and although Priyanka missed the first few swings, the NSD's smile never wavered. His eyes sparkled with pride as he watched them play, this quieter, softer side of him rarely seen by anyone outside his family.

Abhishek, however, couldn't resist teasing his older sister. 'Come on, Priyanka! Even Grandpa's easy bowls are too much for you?'

Priyanka, her brow furrowed in concentration, tried again. The ball sailed past her, and Abhishek's laughter grew louder. 'It's not funny, Abhishek!' she snapped, and banged the bat on the ground in frustration. 'He's not bowling easy!'

Abhishek's grin widened, his teasing becoming more pointed. 'Maybe we should get you a basketball, one you can't miss!'

That was enough to tip Priyanka over the edge. With a huff, she angrily threw down the bat. 'I don't want to play anymore!' she declared, crossing her arms in defiance.

The NSD watched the exchange, his usual calm character momentarily shifting. He understood the sibling rivalry well, but instead of his typical role as mediator, he decided to take a different approach. He bent down, picked up the bat Priyanka had thrown, and smiled mischievously.

'Alright,' he said with a playful gleam in his eyes, 'how about we change the game? Let's see if you two can catch Grandpa instead!'

Before the children could respond, the NSD took off across the garden, surprising them with his agility. His light-footed dash across the lawn, dodging imaginary fielders, waving the bat in the air, was a sight to behold. The seriousness of the moment faded, replaced by confusion and then pure delight as Abhishek and Priyanka burst into laughter and chased after him, their earlier frustration melting away.

In this moment, the NSD wasn't the powerful figure responsible for India's security. He wasn't a man embroiled in political intrigue or covert operations. He was simply Grandpa, revelling in the joy of his grandchildren's company, making memories that would stay with them long after the last cricket ball had been bowled.

'Grandpa, you can't be serious!' Abhishek shouted between giggles, struggling to keep up with the NSD's unexpected burst of speed.

Priyanka, now catching up, laughed breathlessly. 'This is not cricket!'

The NSD, still running ahead, grinned to himself. He knew the game had taken an unexpected turn, but it was all part of his plan. He wasn't just running for the fun of it – he was teaching them something valuable in the most subtle way possible. As they darted through the garden, dodging bushes and skirting around trees, the NSD was instilling a lesson about unpredictability and adaptability.

After a few more rounds of playful pursuit, the NSD, now slightly out of breath, stopped in the middle of the garden. His grandchildren skidded to a halt beside him, panting and grinning from ear to ear.

'You see,' he said, catching his breath and looking at them with a twinkle in his eye, 'sometimes, life throws you a curveball. Instead of giving up or getting mad, you find a new way to play the game.' He placed the bat next to the stumps.

Abhishek and Priyanka, still breathing hard from the chase, exchanged a curious glance. They weren't sure where their grandfather was going with this, but they listened closely.

'In my job,' the NSD continued, his voice now a bit more serious but still warm, 'things rarely go as planned. We often have to think on our feet, just like we did just now. And what's important is how we adapt and keep moving forward together.'

The children were silent for a moment, absorbing what he was saying. They could see their grandfather wasn't just talking about cricket anymore. There was something deeper in his words, a lesson they hadn't expected to learn in the middle of a game.

Priyanka, now standing a little straighter, nodded. 'So, it's like making up new rules?'

The NSD smiled at her insight. 'Exactly. But the golden rule always remains the same – we support each other. Whether we're making new rules or following old ones, we do it together.'

Abhishek and Priyanka, catching their breath and feeling a newfound sense of understanding, looked at each other with respect. Their playful rivalry was now replaced by a shared bond, strengthened by their grandfather's wisdom.

And just when they thought the lesson was over, the NSD grinned mischievously. 'But,' he said, his eyes twinkling once again, 'catch me if you can!'

With that, he took off running towards the house, his grandchildren's laughter trailing behind him as they gave chase once more, their earlier frustrations forgotten. The playful shouts of 'catch me if you can!' echoed through the garden as the NSD made a dash for the front door.

As he slipped inside the house, the warmth of the game and the lesson lingered in the air, leaving Abhishek and Priyanka with a memory they would carry with them for years to come – a lesson about life, teamwork and the importance of adapting to the unexpected.

The chase continued inside the sprawling residence, with the NSD using his intimate knowledge of the house's many rooms and corridors to slip away from his grandchildren's sight. He darted through the hallways with surprising agility, leaving Abhishek and Priyanka to search for him in the maze of rooms. Their excited giggles echoed through the house, the earlier tension between them now forgotten in the thrill of the game.

Abhishek and Priyanka quickly realized they would have to split up to find their elusive grandfather. Abhishek took the left corridor, while Priyanka headed right, both calling out for him as they checked behind curtains and peeked into closets.

Panting and slightly out of breath, the two eventually found themselves in the study, a room filled with books, medals and official documents – a space both familiar and mysterious. It was their grandfather's sanctuary, the place where he transformed from the playful grandparent they adored into the formidable figure responsible for India's security.

Abhishek looked around the room, checking behind the large, heavy curtains. 'He's not here,' he said, his voice slightly breathless. 'Did we miss him?'

Priyanka, equally puzzled, glanced around. 'He's too good at this!'

Exhausted, they collapsed onto the sofa, their earlier excitement giving way to amused resignation. The room grew quiet, save for the sound of their heavy breathing. As they started to relax, their eyes scanning the room for any sign of their elusive target, something shifted.

A seemingly innocuous shawl, draped over the computer table, stirred slightly. Before they could react, the NSD, who had been hiding under the shawl the entire time, emerged with a triumphant grin. His clever camouflage had worked perfectly, and he stood before them, beaming with pride at his successful evasion.

Priyanka jumped, startled, but quickly dissolved into laughter. 'Grandpa, you're the best at hide and seek!'

Abhishek, still catching his breath, looked at his grandfather with admiration. 'How did you even think of hiding there?' he asked, clearly impressed.

The NSD chuckled, but before he could respond, a sharp beep interrupted the moment. It was his smartwatch, the unmistakable signal that duty was calling. His expression shifted, the carefree joy of the game giving way to the familiar seriousness of his role. He glanced at the display, noting the time.

'Ah,' he said, his voice softer now, 'looks like duty calls again. I've got a meeting in five minutes.'

Priyanka, understanding all too well, gave a knowing nod. 'It's okay, Grandpa,' she said, smiling. 'We're used to your message beeps. But we had fun, Grandpa. Love you.'

The NSD's heart warmed at their understanding, a mix of affection and regret crossing his face. He knelt down beside them, ruffling their hair gently. 'Thank you, both,' he said, his voice filled with tenderness. 'We'll definitely continue this game soon. Make sure you practise until then!'

He walked them to the door of the study, pausing for a moment to take in their smiling faces before they headed back towards the garden. Their laughter and chatter echoed faintly as they disappeared down the hallway, the joy of their game still hanging in the air.

But as the NSD pulled the curtains shut and returned to his desk, the weight of his other life settled back onto his shoulders. The room felt different now, quieter, the playful grandfather slipping away as he once again became the NSD, a man whose every decision carried the weight of a nation's safety.

He sat down at his desk, his eyes scanning the documents waiting for his attention. But in the back of his mind, the memory of his grandchildren's laughter lingered, a reminder of the delicate balance he constantly walked between family and duty.

The room was bathed in very dim light, the soft glow of a solitary desk lamp casting shadows across the walls. The bluish hue from the large indigenously made computer screen flickered gently, creating a subdued yet focused atmosphere. The blinds were tightly drawn, adding to the feeling of seclusion, as if the room had been deliberately shut off from the world outside.

The slide on the screen retracted with a quiet hum, revealing Ashok Awasthy, his face showing a blend of professional urgency and personal respect. Despite the nature of the discussion, the rapport between the two men was evident, a bond forged through years of trust and cooperation.

'Good evening, sir,' Ashok said, a warm smile softening his otherwise serious expression. 'How are you holding up today?'

The NSD, leaning slightly back in his chair, returned the smile. 'Evening, Ashok. I'm keeping well, thanks. How's Anita doing? All good?'

Ashok's face relaxed further, the tension in his shoulders easing slightly. 'Much better, thankfully. Your help with her treatment in London was a godsend. We owe you one.'

The NSD waved the comment away, his tone casual yet affectionate. 'Don't mention it, old friend. Glad I could help.'

He paused, his gaze shifting to the screen. 'So, what's on your mind today?'

Ashok's smile faded, replaced by the focus of a man who had come prepared for a difficult discussion. 'It's about Malik, sir …'

As Ashok spoke, the computer screen before the NSD split vertically. On the left, Ashok's face remained, while on the right, a dossier filled the screen with details of Ripudaman Singh Malik. The NSD's eyes scanned the file, his mind already working through the implications of what Ashok was about to propose.

'Malik is ready to publicly back our peace initiatives with the Khalistani groups in Canada,' Ashok explained, his tone measured. 'But there's a catch – his name is still on that old blacklist, along with 312 others. Some of them are key figures who plan to accompany him.'

The NSD, now fully engaged, raised an eyebrow. 'So, he wants a clean slate for himself and the others, huh?' He paused, considering the ramifications. 'But you have to make sure this turns the tide in our favour.'

'Exactly, sir,' Ashok replied, nodding. 'If we remove their names, it sends a powerful message. Malik believes it will strengthen our position, showing that we're serious about peace.'

The NSD's gaze lingered on the dossier for a moment longer before he spoke, his tone thoughtful. 'Okay, so what are you expecting from me?'

Ashok sensed an unusual reticence in the NSD's voice, a subtle shift from the proactive stance he was accustomed to. It was as though the NSD was holding something back, and it was unsettling.

'The entire strategy of bringing Ripudaman Singh Malik into the fold,' Ashok continued carefully, 'using him to counteract the militancy of Khalistani groups from Canadian soil, had been orchestrated under your meticulous guidance. We cannot fathom achieving our objectives without you at the helm.'

The NSD maintained his composure, though he was acutely aware that Ashok was inching closer to a truth he wasn't ready to reveal. Diplomatically, he steered the conversation towards a more bureaucratic path. 'Ashok, you know as well as I do that the removal of names from the blacklist is in the domain of the Ministry of External Affairs.'

Ashok, however, wasn't easily dissuaded. He pressed on, though his tone remained respectful. 'Sir, we will follow regular channels. But I would request your good offices to take it up with the PMO.'

Realizing that Ashok was trying to push for a level of involvement that he wasn't yet willing to commit to, the NSD carefully chose his next words. 'I will do everything in my capacity, Ashok,' he said, his voice steady but non-committal. 'Rest assured. But you must follow up through the regular channels. Protocol is crucial.'

Ashok, sensing that the NSD wasn't ready to engage more deeply on the matter, shifted gears. He didn't want to push too hard, not when something clearly weighed on the NSD's mind. 'That goes without saying, sir,' he replied, his tone lightening.

After a brief pause, Ashok added, 'Sir, there's one more thing … Anita and I have been planning to invite you and ma'am over for dinner at our place.'

The NSD's smile returned, warmer this time, as he appreciated the change in topic. 'Happily,' he said with a nod. 'We'd love that.'

As the conversation wound down, Ashok logged off, leaving the NSD alone in the room. The air felt heavier now, the weight of both the professional and personal hanging over him. He glanced at the dossier on the screen, his mind already calculating the potential outcomes. But for now, he pushed it aside. There were more pressing matters to deal with.

The NSD sat back in his chair, the light from the screen reflecting off his glasses as he quietly contemplated his next steps.

In the first week of November 2019, the air in the PMO was heavy with the weight of the moment, a seriousness that underscored the importance of the discussion that was about to unfold. The prime minister, seated at his desk, motioned for the NSD to sit. He slid a single sheet of paper across the table, the rustle of the paper the only sound in the otherwise silent room.

'Remember this?' the prime minister asked, his voice calm but charged with meaning.

The NSD, slightly taken aback, glanced down at the paper. It was the document he had shared with the prime minister months ago; a proposal that had outlined his bold plan for dealing with India's enemies hiding abroad. He blinked, a moment of confusion crossing his face. 'Yes, but …'

Before he could continue, the prime minister spoke again, his tone firm. 'This is the time for you to accomplish your mission.' He paused, then added, 'I am extending your term by another five years.'

The words hung in the air, sinking in slowly. The NSD stared at the prime minister, the realization dawning on him. The hesitation he had sensed earlier, the delays that had left him questioning the prime minister's commitment to his plan. It had all been a misunderstanding.

'I understand now that I got you wrong,' the NSD admitted, his voice filled with newfound clarity.

The prime minister raised an eyebrow, curious. 'What do you mean?'

The NSD gestured toward the paper on the desk. 'I thought you weren't in favour of my plan when I shared this with you,' he said, his voice steady but laced with the vulnerability of someone who had misread the situation.

The prime minister burst into laughter, a sound that broke through the tension in the room. '*Arrey bhai*,' he said, smiling broadly, '*Aap toh jaante hain ki* James Bond *bhi apne pradhanmantri ka intezaar nahi karta, hai na? Hamare apne '007' ko kaise lag sakta hai ki vo alag hain? Chunavon ka intezaar tha bas, main toh hamesha saath tha. Chaliye, ab kaam par lag jaate hain, kya kehte hain?* [Oh, brother, you know even James Bond does not wait for his prime minister, does he? So how can our own '007' feel he is any different? We just had to wait for the elections, that was all; I was always with you. Come, now let us get to work, what do you say?]'

The NSD couldn't help but smile at the prime minister's words, feeling a renewed sense of purpose. The doubts he had harboured, the uncertainties he had grappled with, faded away. The prime minister had always been on his side; he had simply been waiting for the right moment to act.

As the meeting came to a close, the NSD stood by the large window in the PMO, his gaze sweeping across the sprawling expanse of Lutyens' Delhi. The city stretched out before him, vast and complex, much like the mission that now lay ahead of him. The prime minister's words echoed in his mind, and with them, the realization that his journey was far from over. The next chapter of his career, and his life, was about to begin.

He took a deep breath, feeling the weight of the responsibility settling onto his shoulders once more. But this time, there was no hesitation, no doubt.

It was time to get to work.

3

The Avenger

A month later, in December, the Delhi winter had tightened its grip as Aditya's fingers traced the coarse texture of the khaki envelope. His intuition, a silent guardian, hinted at the envelope's origin and purpose even before it was opened. Inside, predictably, was nothing but a void that spoke volumes to those skilled in the art of hidden messages.

With a practised motion, Aditya transformed the envelope into a single sheet of paper, revealing an address and a time scrawled in a hurried hand. To anyone else, it might have seemed an ordinary note, but to Aditya, it was a summon back into the shadows from which he had been temporarily exiled.

The message, though cryptic, was clear: it was time to re-enter the game, to dance once more with danger and deception. The thrill of the chase beckoned, irresistible to a spirit as restless as his.

As the paper lay discarded, Aditya committed the address and time to memory, aware that his life was on the cusp of change. The call to action was undeniable, and Aditya Singh was ready to answer it, stepping back into a world where every shadow held a story, every whisper a clue. The game was on, and he was its principal player.

Aditya Singh, at 35, was a blend of youthful vigour and impulsive idealism, traits that marked his tenure as a R&AW operative. Grounded after an operation in Mizoram failed due to his overzealous actions, the summons now in his hand didn't pique his curiosity as one might expect. Instead, it threw him into a quandary, clashing head-on with the day he was to appear in a family court for the final hearing of his divorce. Faced with the crossroads of duty and personal turmoil, Aditya found himself weighing his commitment to an organization that offered a glimmer of redemption against the unresolved ties to his soon-to-be ex-wife. This internal conflict presented him with a crucial choice: pursue the faint promise of professional salvation or close a painful chapter of his personal life.

The cryptic nature of the message hinted at something beyond routine; it reeked of the clandestine and urgent. Aditya, though sidelined and stuck in a professional limbo, had continued to receive his salary punctually, a ghost operative with no missions to his name. Counselling sessions had become his new norm, an attempt by the organization to temper his fiery approach, which they deemed too reckless for covert operations. Aditya, however, harboured no regrets for the incident that had branded him with infamy, seeing it not as a failure but a necessary act of zeal. His superiors disagreed, insisting on a tighter leash until he proved capable of measured restraint.

This sudden summons, then, was unexpected. It suggested a shift in the organization's stance, perhaps a readiness to overlook past transgressions in favour of his skills that, despite everything, remained in high demand. Aditya sensed that the winds were changing, possibly heralding his return to the shadowy world of espionage that had always been his true calling.

Skipping court could jeopardize everything Aditya had been working towards on the personal front, a fact he was painfully aware of. In a decision that felt both desperate and calculated, he turned his thoughts to Meera Desai, the woman who, despite the chasm of estrangement between them, might be his only hope in navigating this precarious juncture.

The clock had just struck 6 a.m., and Aditya, fresh from his morning jog, still felt the cool morning air clinging to his skin.

His dedication to physical fitness was unwavering, a silent protest against the organization's judgement of his mental and emotional readiness. Preparing his morning tea, he adhered to the ritual that connected him to a semblance of normalcy amidst the chaos of his life. The flicker of the gas stove brought a momentary light to the kitchen as he placed the steel saucepan on the flame, the water inside poised to boil.

With a glance at the khaki paper that had brought so much turmoil into his already stormy life, Aditya made a decision. The paper, a messenger of potential redemption or further downfall, had served its purpose. He held it over the flame, watching as the edges caught fire, the inked instructions curling and blackening into oblivion. This act of destruction was a part of his life's unwritten protocol, a necessary erasure that kept the clandestine nature of his work sealed away from the world.

As the paper turned to ash, Aditya's mind raced through the impending phone call to Meera. It was a bridge he hadn't crossed in a long while, and as the water began to boil, signalling the time to steep the tea, he steeled himself for what was to come. The conversation ahead would require all his diplomatic skills, a negotiation of personal and professional stakes that he couldn't afford to lose.

Meera's refusal to manipulate the court schedule came as a blunt refusal to Aditya, her logic unforgiving and her stance firm. Her interpretation of Aditya's request was layered with scepticism, seeing it as a tactic to buy time, a luxury she scarcely had. The looming possibility of the court's summer recess further tightened the noose, making the prospect of a new date a gamble.

Meera, with her arms crossed, eyed Aditya disbelievingly across the café table. 'So, you're telling me you need to reschedule our court date for … what, some secretive meeting?' Her tone was laced with disbelief.

Aditya, trying to keep his frustration in check, replied, 'It's not just some meeting, Meera. It's important … more than you can imagine.'

'And you think my moving to Mumbai with Ameera isn't important?' Meera retorted sharply. 'What could possibly be so crucial that it can't wait? You're not meeting the prime minister!'

Aditya sighed, the weight of the conversation and the secret he couldn't share heavy on his shoulders. 'If you only knew,' he murmured under his breath, a hint of weariness betraying his otherwise stoic demeanour.

Meera leaned in, her voice softening but her words cutting deeper. 'Family should be your priority, Aditya. Not these endless cloak-and-dagger games. Can't you ask your boss to reschedule? Or is he too as busy as the prime minister of the country, so he can't care about us?'

The repeated mention of the prime minister struck a nerve, unknowingly echoing the seriousness of Aditya's situation. He clenched his jaw, the reality of his duty and the sacrifices it entailed crystalizing within him. 'It's not that simple, Meera. And it's not just about asking. It's about duty.'

'Duty over family, always, isn't it?' Meera's voice cracked, a mix of anger and sadness. 'Fine, Aditya. Go play your spy games. Just remember, Ameera and I are not just another mission you can postpone.'

With that, she stood up, her chair scraping against the floor loudly in the quiet café. Aditya reached out, a futile gesture as she stormed off. 'Meera, wait …'

But she didn't look back. Aditya sat back, the cold realization settling in that his dedication to his duty had once again cost him more than he was willing to admit. The waiter approached with a sympathetic glance, placing the bill on the table. 'Sir, you've already taken care of this,' he said, gesturing to the pre-swiped card.

The evening air, heavy with the onset of Delhi's unforgiving summer, did little to soothe Aditya's tumultuous thoughts as he returned home through the city's pulsating veins in an autorickshaw. The heat, a mere backdrop to the storm brewing within. His mind was a battleground, torn between the duties of his covert profession and the personal demons he now faced. The fear of losing Ameera, his beacon of innocence in a life shrouded in shadows, was a wound deeper than any he had encountered in the line of duty.

Ameera, the thread that connected Aditya to a world beyond undercover operations and clandestine meetings, represented a love untainted by the complexities of his work. The possibility of her moving to Mumbai with Meera, a city that would distance him from his daughter's laughter, her inquisitive eyes and the comfort of her presence, the smell of baby powder from her body, was a scenario he had never prepared for. The battlefield had always been external, a domain where he could manoeuvre, predict and control. But this, this was a war of the heart, with stakes that left him vulnerable and exposed.

The weekly visits, a negotiated peace in the tumult of separation, were his lifeline, a connection to Ameera's world that he cherished above all. The thought of those moments being snatched away, relegated to memory by miles and legalities, was a fear that gnawed at him more fiercely than any threat he had faced in the line of duty.

As the autorickshaw weaved through the city, the cacophony of Delhi's nightlife a stark contrast to the silence that enveloped him, Aditya realized that the hardest missions were not always in the shadows of enemy lines but in the quiet battles fought within the realms of love and loss. The uncertainty of his future with Ameera, amidst the complexities of his impending divorce, was an indication of the fact that some battles, particularly those entwined with emotion, bore no clear path to victory.

Stepping out of the shower, the chill of the air conditioning was a stark contrast to the lingering warmth of the water, refreshing Aditya's senses as he briskly dried off. Catching his reflection, he couldn't help but notice the familial traits mirrored back at him – the image was not an exact replica of his father, but the resemblance was undeniable. It was a connection that went deeper than appearance, a shared legacy of service and sacrifice that had always been a silent bond between them.

His father's framed photograph on the wall caught his eye, a poignant reminder of the man who had shaped his early world. Aditya often wondered if his father would have approved of his choices, of the path that seemed predestined yet fraught with shadows far deeper than those his father overcame. The thought was a fleeting visitor, interrupted by the unexpected sound of the doorbell.

With a practised motion, Aditya reached for a second towel, draping it over his shoulders to conceal the scars that marked his body, silent testimonies of his life's more perilous moments. The bullet wounds, each a story of survival and sacrifice, were not for the world to see. They were personal, a part of him that few could understand, and even fewer could accept without the shadow of pity or discomfort.

Moving towards the door, the weight of his history felt both a shield and a burden. Each step was a reminder of the journey that had led him here, to this moment of pause in a life otherwise marked by constant motion and hidden battles. Who awaited him beyond the door was a question that momentarily pushed aside the reflections of his past, focusing his mind on the immediate, the now.

The doorstep, devoid of any visitor, presented a puzzle in the form of a small sticky note. The simplicity of the message, bearing only the name of the café where, earlier in the day, his confrontation with Meera had unfolded, was cryptic. Yet, to Aditya, the meaning was as clear as the dawn that would break over the city in a few hours. He was no stranger to the language of silence and suggestion; his career had honed his ability to deal with the unsaid, to read between the lines where intentions and truths lay hidden.

In the quiet of his apartment, the sticky note was a whisper from the shadows, a nudge towards a meeting shrouded in the casual anonymity of public spaces. The absence of a specified time did little to deter Aditya's resolve. His instincts, sharpened by years of decoding the unspoken, led him to conclude that the rendezvous was intended for the coming morning. It was an inference drawn from the habits of those who walked the tightrope between visibility and secrecy, those who found solace in the predictable patterns of their daily routines yet operated within the unpredictable realms of covert operations.

The decision to arrive early at the café, under the pretence of an ordinary morning's start, was strategic. Lodhi Garden, with its sprawling expanse offering both solitude and the semblance of normalcy, was a common enough starting point for the day for many in the city, including those whose lives intersected with Aditya's in less ordinary ways. He anticipated his contact, perhaps someone who sought the clarity of thought that only a morning walk could provide, would prefer the seamless transition from solitude to the subtle dance of clandestine meetings.

As the night deepened, Aditya's mind raced through the possibilities of the next day's encounter. Each scenario was played out, analysed for its potential outcomes and pitfalls. In a world where trust was both currency and contraband, he prepared himself for the myriad ways the morning could unfold. The café, a stage set for the next act in a drama woven with secrets and strategies, awaited its players. And Aditya, ever the adept protagonist, was ready to play his part, guided by instinct and the shadows of a life that thrived on the unseen and unsaid.

Aditya's realization that he was under surveillance was not one that came lightly. The seamless alteration of meeting timings to accommodate his court date was an anomaly in the ruthless efficiency of his professional world, where personal lives were often collateral in the grander scheme of operations. This deviation from the norm underscored the significance of the impending meeting, marking it as a pivotal moment that could very well reshape his current professional standstill.

His attempt to reach out to Meera, although met with silence, was indicative of the tangled web of his life. The unanswered call, followed by a text message, was a bridge over turbulent waters, an olive branch extended in the midst of chaos signifying his willingness to reconcile the conflicting demands of his duty and his disintegrating family life.

The text, left unread, floated in the digital ether, a silent plea for understanding and perhaps forgiveness, a signal flare in the dark, signalling his intent to fight not just for his country but for what remained of his family.

In the shadowy realm where Aditya lived, such moments of clarity were rare. The acknowledgement that someone, somewhere, was manipulating the strings of his life with a degree of empathy was both unsettling and strangely reassuring. It suggested a level of personal investment that went beyond the impersonal machinations of espionage and covert operations. Now, in this moment of vulnerability, Aditya found a sliver of hope, a possibility that amidst the chaos, there might be a path that led to reconciliation and redemption, both in the eyes of his country and those of his estranged wife.

Aditya's steps faltered as he entered the café, his eyes locking onto the figure seated in the far corner. A short man, perhaps in his sixties, wearing a grey T-shirt over black track pants and white jogger's shoes, innocuously blending with the café's morning crowd. He was absorbed in the day's newspaper, an image that contradicted the high-stakes nature of Aditya's mission. He had expected to meet a superior from his own organization, R&AW, someone familiar with the coded language of their covert communications. Instead, he found himself staring at the NSD of India, Bhuvan Rawat! The realization sent a jolt of surprise through him, his mind racing to process the unexpected turn of events.

For a moment, Aditya hesitated at the threshold, uncertainty gripping him. The possibility that Rawat might be there for unrelated reasons, perhaps a casual morning read over tea, crossed his mind. The thought of approaching the NSD unannounced, potentially interrupting matters of national importance, was daunting.

However, it was the NSD who bridged the gap. Looking up from his newspaper, he caught Aditya's eye and, with a nod and a wave, beckoned him over as if they were old acquaintances. The gesture was simple, yet it carried the weight of authority and assurance, dissolving Aditya's hesitation.

As they shook hands, Aditya couldn't help but marvel at the ease with which the NSD operated. There was no air of formality, just a firm handshake that seemed to acknowledge Aditya's past services and the criticality of the meeting.

'Please, have a seat,' he said, his voice calm, welcoming.

Aditya complied, taking the seat opposite the man who was a legend in the intelligence community, his mind still reeling from the surprise. The waiter's prompt arrival offered a brief reprieve, during which Aditya ordered a black coffee; the NSD was having mint tea.

'I must admit, I wasn't expecting you, Mr Rawat, sir! I thought I'd be meeting someone from my office,' Aditya confessed, his voice steady despite the inner turmoil.

The NSD smiled, a gesture that seemed to cut through the formalities. 'I understand. The reason behind today's meeting required my presence.' The café around them buzzed with the morning rush, a cocoon of normalcy around their secluded bubble of conspiracy and national security concerns. Aditya leaned in.

'Sir, I'm listening,' he said, signalling his readiness to dive back into the deep end, the weight of their first-ever meeting now a catalyst for the mission that lay ahead.

The NSD slightly leaned in, his approach shifting to one of serious intent. 'Listen ... well, what can I tell you? I don't even know if you're the right man ... We'll have to find out. But if you are, your country needs you.'

Aditya, taken aback by the directness, nodded slightly, an unspoken gesture of respect towards a man revered by the nation and feared by its adversaries. The unexpectedness of the meeting, the weight of the words spoken, all seemed surreal. Aditya, who had been in the shadows, now found himself in the light of day, face to face with a figure whose presence was a rare occurrence, even for the highest echelons of his former agency.

'Do you have an answer?' The NSDs question cut through Aditya's thoughts, demanding immediacy.

'Yes, sir, yes, sir...' Aditya's response was quick, albeit tinged with hesitation, '... does my office know about this meeting, or do I have to ...?'

'You don't worry about that,' the NSD reassured Aditya, his voice carrying the assurance of authority. With that, he stood, signalling the end of their clandestine meeting with a wave to the waiter for the bill. 'The job would be fascinating and very important for the country,' he added, a final note that left Aditya grappling with the magnitude of what was being asked of him.

As the NSD settled the bill with precise cash, Aditya observed the man's meticulousness, a trait that perhaps defined his career. They then moved towards the exit, the mundane action contrasting sharply with the extraordinary nature of their encounter.

Outside, the NSD's black SUV waited, an unspoken proof of the consequence of the man. The NSD paused, turning to Aditya with a finality that seemed to encompass both an end and a beginning. 'Let me know by tomorrow.' The request was more of a directive, leaving no room for doubt about the urgency of the matter.

Aditya watched in silence as Rawat climbed into the vehicle, a part of him still processing the surreal nature of the meeting. He didn't have the NSDs number, nor did he know the exact path forward. Yet, by the certainty in the man's voice it was clear that contact would be made and decisions expected.

As the SUV merged into the traffic of Lodhi Road, Aditya stood rooted to the spot. The world around him hummed with the morning rush, yet he was encapsulated in a moment of profound solitude, the weight of the impending decision pressing down on him. The red tail lights of the NSD's SUV disappearing into the distance were a metaphor for the path he was about to embark on – a journey back into the depths of national security, where the line between friend and foe blurs, and the stakes are as high as the nation's well-being.

As Aditya made his way toward the taxi stand, the cacophony of the city's hustle melded with the turmoil in his mind. He dialled the garage, his voice steady, in contrast to the storm within. The confirmation that his car was ready seemed to offer him a brief respite, a semblance of control in the chaos that was his life. Changing course, he decided to retrieve his car, seeking solace in the familiarity of its confines.

The drive to the garage was automatic, yet his thoughts were anything but. The temptation to reach out to Meera was a gnawing presence, an itch he longed to scratch. With a deep breath, he resisted the urge to call, instead opting to check for a sign of her in the digital world they now seemed to inhabit more than the real one. The sight of the double blue tick next to his last message was a cold comfort. She had read his words, his attempt to bridge the gap between them, yet chose silence as her response.

This silent rebuke stung more than he cared to admit. The unspoken words between the ticks felt as heavy as the heated arguments they'd had. The realization that she chose not to respond, to leave his words hanging in the digital ether, was a reflection of the state of their relationship that was connected yet disconnected, close yet miles apart.

As the court date loomed just two days away, a thread of anxiety wove through Aditya's thoughts. There was an unsettling possibility that his next rendezvous with the NSD could inadvertently coincide with his court appearance. Yet, he made a conscious decision to sideline these worries. Instead, he found himself trapped in a mental game of speculation, pondering the nature of the assignment that awaited him. The NSD's awareness of his personal knots suggested to Aditya that any future communication would be timed with consideration. This sliver of understanding offered a modicum of comfort amidst the uncertainty that clouded his mind.

Days slipped by in a deceptive calm, the ticking clock marking time towards both his court appearance and the anticipated call that never came. The silence from the NSD was as perplexing as it was unnerving. Aditya found himself oscillating between moments of intense speculation about the assignment and the weight of the impending court date. It was a strange limbo, caught between the adrenaline-fuelled anticipation of serving his country and the dread of confronting the fragmented pieces of his personal life in the environment of a family court.

In the grim confines of the family court in South Delhi's Saket, the air was heavy with tension, the kind that precedes the storm. As the judge pronounced the conditions of the divorce with a cold, unforgiving precision, Aditya felt the walls of his world closing in. The decree stripped him not just of his assets but seemed to challenge the very essence of his identity as a father and a husband.

The mandate to see his daughter, Ameera, only once a week felt like a punishment far harsher than any assignment he had ever faced in the line of duty. The division of his income, the shared ownership of the apartment and the loss of his car felt like distant concerns compared to the visceral pain of being distanced from his child.

The courtroom, with its high ceilings and imposing decor, suddenly felt claustrophobic, as if every word from the judge was a brick added to the walls that imprisoned him. The surreal, alien-like buzz that overtook the judge's voice transported Aditya back to the battlefield, to moments when explosions rendered the world silent except for the ringing in his ears. This sound, a harbinger of chaos and destruction, now seemed to herald the collapse of his domestic life.

Renuka Sharma, his lawyer, leaned in, her voice a murmur of resistance against the unilateral verdict. 'We will challenge the order before the high court; it's too one-sided.' But her words were a distant echo in Aditya's turmoil. The court's decision, while legally binding, was emotionally shattering, severing ties that were once thought unbreakable.

As he made his way out of the courtroom, the echo of the bizarre, alien sound melded with the reality of his situation. Meera's glance, filled with a complex mix of emotions, momentarily caught his, before she diverted her gaze to draw the judge's attention to Aditya's departure. The judge's muttered, 'Arrogance …' felt like the final blow, not to his pride, but to his spirit.

Outside, the world continued unabated, indifferent to the upheaval within the courtroom. Aditya stepped into the daylight, the strange ringing in his ears a reminder of the explosions that once defined his life, and now, the silent implosion of his personal world. In this moment, Aditya stood at the precipice between his past and future, a man torn between the duty to his country and the love for his family, each demanding its own sacrifice.

4

The Silent Deal

December 2019.

In the frozen silence of Pauri Garhwal's Himalayas, the NSD's secluded farmhouse lay nestled amidst leafless apple orchards, a hidden retreat shielded from the prying eyes of the world. The air was sharp with cold, the peaks around it dusted in fresh snow and the tranquillity of the setting stood in stark contrast to the tense discussions that often unfolded within its walls.

The crisp mountain air carried the fragrance of ripening apples, mingling with the natural stillness, a fitting backdrop for a gathering of seasoned minds, veterans of espionage and covert operations. This was no ordinary farmhouse; it was a sanctuary for those who operated in the shadows, a place where plans were crafted far from the corridors of power.

A sleek, dark car rolled to a quiet stop at the farmhouse entrance. Inside sat Aditya, his eyes scanning the surroundings with the precision of someone always on guard. He casually cleared the fare to the Uber driver in cash before stepping out, lifting a well-worn green duffle bag made of canvas. It hung loosely on his shoulder, its weight familiar, a reminder of countless missions.

As he stood for a moment, Aditya took in the scene around him. No security guards in sight. The farmhouse appeared eerily quiet, almost too quiet for a place of such importance. The stillness unnerved him, but he didn't let it show. He glanced around once more, his senses heightened, before starting down the narrow track leading to the heart of the property.

With each step, the sound of his boots crunching softly against the gravel, Aditya could feel the weight of the upcoming meeting bearing down on him. This was not just a casual visit; it was a step deeper into the unknown, into a world where decisions were made in silence, with consequences that echoed far beyond these hills.

He scanned the area, searching for the NSD, but the place seemed deserted except for a lone security guard, bathing in the backyard from a country well, his shirt tossed over a nearby tree branch. A boy, possibly in his twenties, caught Aditya's eye next. Though dressed like a security guard, the deftness with which he brewed tea suggested he had more in common with a cook than a sentry.

As Aditya took in his surroundings, a figure caught his attention – the NSD, parking his rugged 4x4 Jeep in front of the farmhouse. The vehicle rumbled to a stop, and the NSD stepped out, casually hauling bags filled with vegetables, eggs, bread and chicken. Aditya moved to greet him, offering to help with the load.

The NSD, sizing him up with a quick glance, smiled but declined the offer. 'All good?'

'All good, sir,' Aditya replied, eyeing the bag. 'What's the occasion, sir?'

The NSD grinned, tossing the bag higher in his grip. 'How do I feed a hulk like you without going shopping?'

As if on cue, a house help appeared and took the bags from the NSD, who winked at Aditya. 'My wife isn't on this trip, so there's no one to question me in the kitchen. Let's cook up something and enjoy.'

'Sure, sir,' Aditya said, a hint of amusement in his tone.

The NSD gestured toward the surrounding hills. 'You should see the markets here. Everything's fresh, nothing like the soiled stuff we eat in Delhi.' He paused, his eyes twinkling mischievously. 'You want a beer?'

Aditya hesitated, unsure how to respond. But the NSD didn't wait for an answer. He simply chuckled and waved for Aditya to follow him inside, the invitation hanging in the cool mountain air.

'Go freshen up and come out to the lawn,' his host told him.

A little later, after stepping out of the shower and joining the NSD on the lawn, Aditya noticed someone unexpected. It was his boss, Ashok Awasthy, the chief of R&AW, seated comfortably beside the NSD. It took Aditya by surprise. Awasthy's presence was a rare sight, especially for someone like Aditya, who was seven rungs below in the strict hierarchy of the intelligence world. The gap between him and Awasthy was immense, let alone with the NSD, who sat even higher in the chain of command. The NSD indicated a chair between him and Awasthy. Aditya obediently sank down in it.

The only occasions Awasthy had ever interacted with Aditya were the annual addresses or formal ceremonies where agents like him were awarded medals for exemplary service. There had been that one time at Aditya's wedding party when Awasthy had made a brief appearance, but otherwise, his presence in Aditya's life was limited to news headlines and internal briefings.

Yet here he was now, sipping beer, casually seated between Awasthy and the NSD, the two most powerful figures in his world. It felt surreal, and Aditya couldn't help but feel the weight of the moment. Something big was definitely brewing. He sensed the air of gravity that hung between the two men, and the fact that they had called him here, to this secluded location, only heightened his awareness that what was to follow would be far from ordinary.

All three of them sat around the dining table, having just finished a hearty lunch. Aditya quietly complimented the NSD's culinary skills, offering subtle praise. The NSD chuckled, shaking his head. 'Most of it was the chef's doing, but hey, I don't mind taking credit when it's offered,' he quipped with a grin.

They continued with another round of beer, served by the NSD himself, who was clearly in no rush. Yet, despite the easy-going atmosphere, the sense of mystery lingered, hanging in the air like an unfinished thought. Aditya couldn't shake the feeling that this gathering was more than just casual camaraderie.

As the afternoon wore on, Awasthy excused himself for a brief siesta, retreating inside. Meanwhile, Aditya wandered through the orchard, his fingers brushing against the cool, dewy skins of apples, each fruit heavy with the promise of ripeness. He reached up to pick an apple and bit into its crisp, juicy flesh, savouring the moment of simplicity against the backdrop of something far more complex.

The peacefulness of the orchard was a stark contrast to the swirling thoughts in Aditya's mind, but the beauty of the place had its own quiet power, pulling him into a sense of calm before what he knew was going to be an important revelation. Something big was on the horizon. It was only a matter of time before the pieces fell into place.

As the afternoon waned into teatime, the aroma of frying aloo–dal pakoda mingled with the sweet scent of gujiya, creating the perfect setting for relaxed yet guarded conversations. The calm ambience, however, did little to quell the rising impatience gnawing at Aditya. It didn't take long for Awasthy to notice, and with a slight nod, he made it easier for his much junior colleague.

Turning to the NSD, Awasthy remarked, 'Maybe it's time you tell him what's expected.'

The NSD leaned back, his tone deliberate and measured. 'The time has come to bring to fruition our old homework on India's most wanted.' The simplicity of his words belied the portentousness they carried, instantly heightening the tension despite the barriers of rank and social status between them. It was clear that what followed would be of great consequence.

'India,' the NSD continued, his voice steady but intense, 'is besieged by threats, not just from forces within our borders but from those who have inflicted deep wounds and now find sanctuary abroad. These individuals are shielded by foreign powers, including Pakistan's ISI, and others who care little for our sovereignty or peace.'

He paused, letting the weight of his words settle in the silence. The only sound was the distant call of a bird, yet even that seemed muted under the sombre weight of what was being discussed.

'This mission,' the NSD said, locking eyes with Aditya, 'is about sending a resolute message to all terrorists and those who harbour them: that no matter where you are, no matter how long ago your crimes against India were committed, you are not safe. We will reach you. And we will teach you.'

The air crackled with anticipation. The NSD's words were not just a briefing; they were a declaration of intent, a shift in the very paradigm of how India would respond to its enemies.

He paused, then glanced at Awasthy. 'Anything you want to add?'

Awasthy, who had been listening intently, nodded. 'It's a clear signal that India's patience has limits. Our peace processes will not be held hostage by those who choose violence over dialogue.' His words, though few, echoed with finality. The mission at hand was about more than just retaliation – it was about redefining India's stance on security and justice.

Both the NSD and Aditya nod in agreement. And then the NSD spoke again directly to Aditya. 'In this mission, you will have no link with the government, and the government has no link with you. You're ghosts in this game.' He slightly pushed a glass of water on the table towards Aditya.

The NSD's gesture with the glass of water in such a moment was a means to ground Aditya and bring him back to the present from the whirlwind of thoughts and emotions that his proposal must have stirred within him. As Aditya sipped the water, the coolness of it seemed to offer a brief respite, a momentary pause that allowed him to collect his thoughts.

The NSD's tone was matter-of-fact, piercing the tense atmosphere in the room. 'As you might have already pieced together, Aditya,' he began, locking eyes with him, 'this situation, this meeting – it's of paramount importance.'

Aditya, feeling the gravity of the moment, simply nodded, his role in this conversation more of a listener than a participant.

Awasthy chimed in. 'Aditya, we're at a juncture where we need to ask you,' pausing for a brief moment and a glance at the NSD, 'are you prepared to embark on a mission? This isn't just any mission. It's one that carries significant risks and will undeniably alter the course of your life. You'll need to vanish, disappear from this country.'

The NSD cut in, adding weight to the R&AW chief's words, 'And once you're gone, there's no saying when, or even if, you'll return. It could be years.'

Aditya remained silent, the mention of the need to vanish igniting a fleeting image of Ameera, his two-year-old daughter, in his mind's eye.

Catching Aditya's sombre expression, the NSD pressed on, 'Of course, this mission ... it's not something you can discuss with anyone. Not that there's many you could share this with, right?'

Aditya's thoughts drifted to Meera, his ex-wife. The lies about his work, the secrets he had had to keep, all of which collectively had eroded their relationship beyond repair. Meera couldn't handle being constantly left out and alone. It's why she left, Aditya reflected silently, the pain of their divorce still fresh.

The only connection left now is Ameera, he muttered, more to himself than to the men in front of him, his voice tinged with regret.

The room fell into a contemplative silence, each man lost in his own thoughts, pondering the sacrifices demanded by duty and the invisible scars borne by those who serve in the shadows.

The silence that filled the room after the NSD's proposition was heavy, almost tangible. Aditya, caught in a whirlwind of thoughts, felt the weight of the moment press down on him. It was not just a decision about accepting a mission; it was about choosing a path that would irrevocably change his life and the lives of those he held dear.

The image of his daughter, Ameera, flashed again through his mind, a stark reminder of what he stood to lose. But what am I gaining? he wondered silently, the internal battle raging within him.

The NSD, observing Aditya's contemplation, broke the silence. 'I know it's a lot to take in, Aditya. But the importance of this mission cannot be overstated.'

Aditya nodded, his throat tight. 'And if I say yes, what then? I vanish into thin air? What about my daughter?'

Awasthy leaned forward, his expression solemn. 'It's the sacrifice we all make, in one way or another. Your daughter will be taken care of, you have my word. But yes, your life as you know it … it'll have to be left behind.'

Aditya let out a slow breath, the reality of the situation sinking in. 'I've been living in the shadows for so long, lying to everyone I care about. My marriage didn't survive it. And now, you're asking me to plunge even deeper into that darkness!'

'It's not just about going deeper, Aditya,' Aditya interjected, 'it's about what you're doing it for. You're protecting millions, saving lives. It's a noble cause, one that demands great sacrifice, yes, but also offers the chance to make a real difference.'

Aditya's gaze drifted, lost in thought. After a moment, he looked up, resolve hardening in his eyes. 'I took an oath to serve my country, no matter the personal cost. If this is where I'm needed most, then so be it. But,' he paused, his voice thickening, 'please, make sure my daughter, Ameera … make sure she knows her father loved her, that he didn't abandon her willingly.'

The room was quiet once more, the weight of Aditya's decision hanging in the air. The NSD reached across the table, offering a hand. 'She will know, Aditya. And one day, when this is all over, maybe the world will know the sacrifices you made for it.'

Aditya clasped the NSD's hand, a silent pact sealed between them. He was about to embark on a journey into the unknown, leaving behind everything familiar, driven by a sense of duty that transcended personal desire. It was a path of shadows and silence, but one that he chose willingly, for the sake of a nation and a daughter he hoped would understand his absence was a confirmation of his love.

The NSD, seeming to understand the turmoil within Aditya, offered a hand in parting. 'It's likely we won't meet again,' he said with a sombre sincerity, locking eyes with Aditya. 'So, let me wish you luck now. Good luck, no matter what path you choose.' The gesture, simple yet profound, underscored the magnitude of the task and the solitary journey that lay ahead for Aditya, regardless of his choice.

The weight of what had been said hung in the air, and Aditya, though still processing the enormity of the task ahead, knew that this was a moment of reckoning. Something irreversible had begun.

When Aditya had walked into his chief Ashok Awasthy's office in Delhi, promptly at noon the day following his crucial meeting with the NSD and Awasthy at the former's farm house in Garhwal, he was met with an unexpectedly nonchalant reception. His chief appeared cool, almost disinterested, as he glanced up from the clutter of papers and screens that dominated his desk.

'Yes?' he inquired, his tone betraying no hint of the weightiness of the situation.

'What next, sir?' Aditya prompted, standing firmly, his posture betraying none of the wild emotions churning within him.

The chief's response was a nod, distant and matter-of-fact, as if Aditya's query was the only logical follow-up to their previous, momentous discussion. This reaction, or lack thereof, didn't catch Aditya off guard. In the corridors of R&AW, overt reactions to assignments, no matter how unusual or dangerous, were rare. Yet, despite anticipating such a response, Aditya couldn't help but feel a touch of disappointment, a slight deflation amidst the rush of adrenaline.

'Wait a minute,' the chief finally said, breaking the brief silence that had settled between them. 'I want you to meet someone.'

Aditya was introduced to the crucial link for his mission not through a physical meeting but via a video call that connected him directly to London. The man on the other end was Altaf Raza, a Pakistani spice trader whose base of operations was in the very city Aditya was preparing to infiltrate. Altaf's image filled the screen, revealing a middle-aged man whose hair had prematurely greyed, with stooping shoulders that seemed to bear invisible burdens. Yet, his dark eyes sparkled with vivacity beneath heavy, bushy eyebrows, offering a glimpse into a complex personality.

Despite the initial strangeness of the situation, Altaf's manner was disarmingly warm. He was a sweet talker and the warmth with which he greeted Aditya felt as if it was borne out of a years-long acquaintance rather than a formal introduction. Although this easy familiarity did not stir feelings of kinship within Aditya, it did pave the way to a budding respect and liking for Altaf.

'You can call me uncle,' Altaf said, setting their newly formed connection with a familial undertone. 'You must have a lot of questions, and I may not have all the answers yet. But inshallah, that will be ready by the time you are here.'

Aditya responded with a respectful, 'Ji, Uncle,' acknowledging the role Altaf was to play in his life henceforth. This exchange, facilitated by the security in his chief's office, marked the beginning of Aditya's deep dive into his new identity and mission.

The chief laid out the premise of Aditya's undercover role with clarity. Aditya was to assume the identity of Altaf's nephew, integrating into his life and business in London as seamlessly as possible. This arrangement was not just for cover; it was to be Aditya's new reality, enabling him to operate within London with a legitimate front. The chief explained that the necessary documents and credentials for Aditya to function in this capacity were being arranged, involving coordination with the UK's Foreign Office to ensure everything was above board and without suspicion.

After a final exchange of pleasantries, filled with the warmth and familiarity of a newly formed uncle–nephew relationship, the video call with Altaf concluded. The brief interaction had set the stage for what was to come, embedding Aditya firmly within the narrative of being a part of the Pakistani expatriate community in London.

Turning back to the matter at hand, the chief's tone shifted to one of formality as he addressed Aditya directly.

'Anyway, before we talk about this,' he began, 'while the setup with Altaf is crucial, there are procedural aspects of the mission that need to be addressed first.' The word procedure hung in the air, a reminder of the bureaucratic and operational layers that underpinned even the most covert of operations.

This shift in focus was a twist back to the realities of espionage work, a domain where every detail mattered and where protocols, however mundane they might seem, were the backbone of operational success. Aditya understood this well; his training had instilled in him a respect for the process, knowing that in the world of intelligence, procedure was often what separated success from failure.

Aditya's initiation into his first major mission was marked not by a detailed briefing of tasks but by an amputation of his ties with the R&AW, summed up in a contract that explained a series of abandonments rather than responsibilities. This contract was an unambiguous declaration of the solitary path Aditya was about to tread, a path devoid of the usual safeguards provided by his employer.

The contract was a clear indication of the gravity and deniability of the mission Aditya was undertaking. By resigning from the R&AW, he was stepping into a realm where the usual lines of support and recognition from his country's intelligence apparatus would be non-existent. The document he was asked to sign starkly outlined the absence of support: no employment, protection, legal aid, acknowledgment of his work, consular assistance or medical help from the R&AW or any other establishment of the Indian government. In return, Aditya would relinquish any claim to assistance, hold the R&AW harmless for any consequences of his actions and maintain absolute secrecy about his relationship with the agency.

Each time the R&AW chief presented Aditya with a new document, he underlined the importance of understanding over formality. 'Do you understand what this says?' he would inquire, pushing the document towards Aditya. The emphasis on reading and understanding each clause before signing was a clear directive from the chief, ensuring Aditya was fully aware of the implications of his agreement. This process was not just about legalities; it was a solemn reminder of the isolation and risks inherent in the mission Aditya was willingly agreeing to undertake.

The chief's insistence on comprehension over mere acquiescence in signing the documents highlighted the seriousness with which the R&AW approached such covert operations. It was a safeguard for both parties, ensuring that Aditya was entering into this agreement with eyes wide open, fully cognizant of the weight of solitude and secrecy his mission entailed. This was a journey he would have to tackle without the usual safety nets, relying solely on his skills, wits and the preparation that had led him to this moment.

As Aditya signed on each document, a fleeting concern brushed his consciousness – the realization that he was venturing into this high-stakes mission without any leverage of his own. The thought of seeking legal counsel briefly crossed his mind, but the importance of his commitment, underscored by the prime minister's personal acknowledgement of his role in shaping a new India, quashed any lingering doubts. This was a mission about national service, a calling that demanded every bit of his allegiance and courage.

With the paperwork finalized, the chief provided Aditya with the practical tools for his mission. A contact number was handed over to him, belonging to an individual who would facilitate the acquisition of new travel documents. These documents were designed to be unremarkable, ensuring Aditya's movements across international borders would go unnoticed, free from the scrutiny that might compromise his mission.

In addition to this, Aditya was equipped with US $20,000 in cash, bonds worth a million euros, issued by a Swiss bank. These bonds, cashable at a select list of global banks, were a financial lifeline, ensuring that regardless of where his mission took him, he would have access to substantial resources. This financial preparation was complemented by the assurance that any additional needs would be met by his uncle in London, further weaving Altaf Raza into the fabric of his new identity and mission.

The chief's next assurance addressed a more personal concern. The promise that an amount equivalent to more than fifty percent of Aditya's salary would be regularly deposited in his ex-wife's account momentarily caught him off guard. The realization that the R&AW could easily access Meera's banking details was a stark reminder of the agency's reach and capabilities. While the notion was initially unsettling, it also provided a strange comfort that despite the severing of official ties, the organization was ensuring his familial responsibilities were not overlooked. The tools and promises handed to him by the chief were not just practical necessities; they were symbols of the trust and responsibility placed on his shoulders.

Aditya was about to cross into a world where the lines between personal sacrifice and national service blurred, armed with the knowledge that while he might be operating in the shadows, he was not entirely forsaken.

As the finality of the moment settled in, Aditya rose from his seat, the weight of the upcoming mission grounding his resolve. He approached his chief, the man who had overseen his transition from a known R&AW operative to a shadow figure about to embark on a mission of unparalleled importance. The handshake that followed was not merely a gesture of farewell but a symbolic severance of all official ties. The chief's next few words stressed the irrevocability of Aditya's decision: 'Once you have left my office, we don't know each other. Never met officially. But if you want to change your mind, you have to do it now before leaving this room. Do you follow, Aditya?'

Aditya's response, 'Loud and clear, sir,' was more than an affirmation; it was a declaration of his commitment, delivered with the precision and respect that had characterized his two years in the army and operative training. This exchange, brief yet profound, marked the culmination of his transformation. He was no longer just Aditya Singh, a R&AW operative; his identity, his connection to his past life and the agency that had moulded him, severed in all but spirit.

With a final nod, Aditya turned and left the chief's office, crossing the threshold into uncertainty. The door closed behind him, symbolically and literally, on his life as an official agent of India's premier spy agency. Ahead lay a path fraught with danger and shrouded in mystery, but Aditya stepped forward with a resolve forged in the knowledge that his actions, though unseen and unacknowledged, would be in service of his country.

∽

January 2020.

The NSD, accompanied by Ashok Awasthy, walked through the plush, softly lit corridor of a five-star hotel in Delhi. Their footsteps fell softly on the thick carpeting, which absorbed the sound as they made their way down the hall. After a few moments, they stopped in front of a door. The NSD knocked.

The door opened to reveal an elderly Sikh gentleman with a long, flowing beard – Ripudaman Singh Malik, once accused in the 1985 Air India Kanishka bombing. Behind him stood two other middle-aged Sikh men, all of them looking at the NSD with a mixture of gratitude and reverence. Malik gestured for the NSD to take a seat, his hands folded in respect.

Ripudaman Singh Malik was a prominent businessman and a leader in Canada's Sikh community. He gained notoriety for his alleged involvement in the 1985 Air India bombings, which claimed 329 lives, marking the deadliest act of aviation terrorism until 9/11. Malik and co-accused Ajaib Singh Bagri were arrested in 2000, but after a prolonged trial, both were acquitted. The court concluded that the Crown's case was weak, with key witnesses deemed unreliable. Although he was acquitted in 2005 due to lack of credible evidence, his name remained tied to the tragedy, raising controversies for years. Malik also faced numerous legal battles, including lawsuits for his business activities.

Born in Punjab, Malik emigrated to Canada and became a wealthy businessman, known for his role in Sikh education. He was instrumental in establishing the Khalsa Credit Union and Khalsa schools, championing Sikh cultural values. However, the Air India trial overshadowed his legacy.

'Thank you for coming, Shri Bhuvan Rawat Sa'ab. Let me take this opportunity to express my deep gratitude for removing my name from the blacklist and allowing me to visit India,' Malik began, his voice soft yet formal. 'On behalf of the entire Sikh community in Canada …' Before he could finish, the NSD cut in, his voice sharp, eyes locked on Malik as he settled into the corner of a sofa. Awasthy took a seat beside him, silent but watchful.

'Let's get straight to the point, Malik,' the NSD said, his tone cold and cutting through the formalities. 'The last thing I would've done is grant a visa to a man linked to a bombing that took hundreds of innocent lives. But I did because I'm hoping this is your chance to undo the past.'

The tension in the room thickened, and the weight of the NSD's words left Malik momentarily speechless, knowing the stakes had just been raised.

Malik's expression faltered briefly, a flicker of embarrassment crossing his face, though he quickly masked it with a small gesture of humility. 'It must have been God's will that I was acquitted by the court,' he said, his voice steady but laced with discomfort.

Before the NSD could respond, Ashok Awasthy leaned forward, his tone sharp as he cut in. 'Let's cut the technicalities, Malik. There's a new inquiry in the same case against you. So ...'

The NSD, not one to dance around sensitive subjects, leaned back slightly, his gaze steady on Malik. 'See, Malik, we've got a compulsion here. Your government isn't doing anything to check the rise of Khalistanis demanding Punjab as a separate state.'

Malik shifted in his seat but remained composed, though there was a certain sense of discomfort in his attitude. 'You must understand, sir,' he began, 'the Canadian government is not in my control. But I'm talking to the boys. They're young, impulsive, easily carried away. I'm heading to Amritsar to invite the leader of the Akal Takht to Canada. His presence there will strengthen my position. Give me some time, Rawat Sa'ab.'

The NSD, visibly impatient, cuts him off. 'Nothing will be achieved until this "plumber" of yours is dealt with, Malik.'

Malik couldn't suppress a faint smile at the reference. 'You mean Takkar?'

Awasthy's expression hardened. 'Yes, Gurdeep Singh Takkar.'

Malik sighed, rubbing his hands together as if contemplating his next words carefully. 'The problem is no one in Canada believes he's the terrorist India claims him to be.'

The silence that followed was thick with unspoken tension. Malik knew he was treading dangerous ground, but the forces at play were far larger than him; navigating these waters required tact, patience and, most importantly, time. But time was clearly something the NSD wasn't willing to grant easily.

The NSD turned to Awasthy, who calmly pulled out his phone, using it as a projector to present a dossier on Takkar. The room's focus shifted as the moving images appeared on the wall, revealing a web of connections that painted a vivid picture of Takkar's shadowy dealings. Clandestinely taken photographs flashed across the screen showing Takkar's visits to Pakistan, his covert collaborations with the ISI, and several images of him in Bangkok, where he was seen striking deals with Harvinder Singh Sandhu, better known as 'Rinda'.

Awasthy pressed pause on an image of Rinda, freezing the figure mid-action.

'You know this guy?' Awasthy asked, his voice carrying a quiet authority.

Malik glanced at the image and nodded slightly. 'Heard about him.'

'Rinda supplies arms, ammunition, explosives and funds to Takkar's Khalistan Tiger Force,' Awasthy continued, gazing intently at Malik.

Malik raised an eyebrow, though his tone remained neutral. 'Funding too? I haven't heard about that part. Where does he get it from? The ISI, maybe?'

Awasthy's face darkened. 'The ISI provides him protection in Pakistan, giving him a smooth base of operations. Rinda is heavily involved in the drug trade; he supplies heroin from Pakistan to cartels in Mexico and Colombia. A portion of the funds generated from those sales are funnelled directly to Takkar.'

The room fell silent again, the weight of the information hanging in the air. Malik's face betrayed a mix of surprise and calculation as he processed the revelations. This wasn't just about separatist movements anymore. This was a well-oiled machine with international reach, fuelled by a deadly combination of drugs, weapons and ideology.

Awasthy continued the presentation, projecting more images onto the wall. This time, they revealed Rinda's contacts within the cartels, gritty snapshots of meetings between his men and the underworld players in Bangkok. The next set of images showcased seized consignments of arms and drugs, intercepted at the US–Mexico border, linking the trade directly back to Rinda.

'We have definite intelligence that these shipments were sent by Rinda from Pakistan,' Awasthy said, his voice flat but firm.

The NSD's gaze shifted back to Malik. 'Malik, Takkar is the key.'

Malik, sensing the escalating tension, chose his words carefully. 'Look, any direct confrontation with him will bruise his ego. It's better if I persuade the smaller groups that support Takkar, convince them how waging a war against India will only lead to their decimation.'

The NSD's expression hardened. 'They must realize they're dealing with a different India now.'

Malik's body language shifted slightly as he drew the NSD's attention to his phone, pulling up a photograph of a Sikh man. He handed the phone to the NSD. 'This is Harinder Singh Dhillon.'

Awasthy and the NSD exchanged a look, one of recognition – they were already familiar with the name.

'He's an advocate by profession, but he's Takkar's main support. It's Dhillon who continually incites Takkar to defy any peace initiatives with India,' Malik explained, his tone serious.

The NSD glanced at the image again before handing the phone back to Malik. 'He's an American citizen. Dealing with Takkar through you is one thing, but Dhillon ... that's a different story. Let's focus on Takkar for now. If we can sway him, Dhillon's influence will naturally fade.'

With that, the NSD stood up, signalling the end of the meeting. The others followed his lead, rising from their seats. He extended his hand to Malik, who grasped it with both hands, nodding in gratitude.

'Peace by all means,' the NSD said firmly.

Malik and his men bowed their heads slightly, acknowledging the statement. As the NSD and Awasthy turned to leave, the atmosphere was heavy with the understanding that this meeting was not just a discussion, but the beginning of a chain of events that would have far-reaching repercussions. The decisions made in this room would ripple out, shaping the conflict in ways none of them could fully predict. But one thing was certain: the course of action they had set in motion would alter the future in profound ways.

5

Into the Disguise

February 2020.

Exactly a year after the Pulwama attack, Aditya stepped out of the clinic, the air outside felt different, charged with a sense of urgency that mirrored his own. The clinic, a place he had visited covertly in the past for various undercover operations, had today offered him a piece of advice that seemed almost ludicrous. The doctor suggested steroids to expedite the growth of facial hair. Yet, in the peculiar world of espionage in which Aditya operated, such eccentricities were often the linchpins of survival and identity disguise.

He paused momentarily, allowing the hustle of the city to wash over him, a stark contrast to the clinical sterility he had just left behind. The doctor's words echoed in his mind, a bizarre yet crucial recommendation for his next mission. With a new passport and identity on the line, the success of his upcoming operation hinged on his ability to transform his appearance within the next two weeks.

Pulling out his smartphone, Aditya scrolled through his contacts rapidly, his fingers stopping at a name that had never failed him. The call was made with an expectation of prompt action; the voice on the other end was an old asset based in London, someone who understood the stakes involved. 'I need the prescribed steroids within the next 24 hours,' Aditya said, his voice a mixture of command and urgency. There was no room for delay; the mission's success, and perhaps his own survival, depended on it.

As he disconnected the call, Aditya's gaze lingered on the city's life. People went about their daily routines, oblivious to the undercurrents of intrigue and danger that flowed just beneath the surface of their mundane realities. Aditya found himself at the precipice dividing these two worlds, about to embark on a journey that required him to vanish and re-emerge as someone entirely new.

The mission was shrouded in secrecy, its details known only to a select few, and now, it demanded of him not just a change in appearance but a complete immersion into a role that was yet to be fully revealed. As he merged with the crowd, his thoughts were a blend of anticipation and resolve. The operation was more than a test of his skills; it was a dive into the unknown, with the trust of the prime minister and the fate of untold lives resting on his shoulders. The transformation, both physical and metaphorical, was just beginning.

Over the next three weeks, Aditya submerged himself in an ocean of research, diving deep into the complexities of Pakistan. His apartment transformed into a makeshift study, littered with books, maps and notes that spanned the breadth and depth of Pakistan's rich tapestry. It wasn't just a refresher course; this was a mission to imbue himself with the essence of being Pakistani.

Every day, he dedicated hours to understanding the intricate layers of Pakistan's history, tracing its roots back to ancient civilizations and following the tumultuous journey to its present state. He absorbed the stories of its people, their struggles and triumphs, hoping to capture the spirit that pulsed through the nation's veins.

Culture and heritage became his next focus. Aditya explored the diverse cultural practices that painted a vivid picture of Pakistan's societal fabric. He studied traditional music, art forms and festivals, immersing himself in the rituals that defined the rhythm of Pakistani life. The goal was to grasp not just the facts but the feelings and sentiments attached to these cultural expressions.

Food habits required a more hands-on approach. Aditya ventured into the kitchen, experimenting with recipes that were staples in

Pakistani cuisine. He learned to distinguish between the subtle variations of spice and technique that differentiated regional dishes, understanding food as a language that communicated much about its people's geography and history.

The dialects of Pakistan demanded particular attention. Aditya practised tirelessly, familiarizing himself with the nuances of pronunciation, the cadences of speech and the colloquial expressions that would allow him to blend in seamlessly. It wasn't just about learning a language; it was about adopting a new way of speaking that reflected the identity of its speaker.

Finally, he studied the terrain and topography with the eye of a strategist, analysing maps and satellite images to understand the physical landscape of Pakistan. Knowing the lay of the land was crucial, from the bustling streets of Karachi to the rugged mountains of the north. This knowledge was his navigational guide, a way to move through the country with confidence and purpose.

Aditya's preparation took on a new dimension as he delved into the intricacies of typically Pakistani male habits, understanding the social fabric that wove men into the daily life and familial structures of the country. He studied the dynamics within families, noting the respect and roles accorded to women, mothers, fathers and siblings. Nothing was left to chance. Even his body had to reflect the identity he was assuming. On the advice of agency doctors, he underwent a circumcision, a procedure performed with precision and care, its healing managed so that it appeared to have been done in childhood. The transformation was complete, from the way he spoke and prayed to the marks his body carried, leaving no trace of the man he had once been.

His familiarity with Urdu and the political landscape of Pakistan provided a solid foundation, but to truly embody a Pakistani identity, he needed to absorb the subtleties that would allow him to tackle social situations faultlessly. The knowledge of Pakistan's terrain, especially the areas bordering India, PoK (Pakistan-occupied Kashmir) and Afghanistan, was strategic. Yet, to sound and appear genuinely Pakistani, he recognized the need to go beyond geopolitics and linguistics.

His persona of Hassan Raza needed a business. Spices became symbols of this deeper dive into authenticity. Aditya learned not just their names but their significance in Pakistani cuisine and culture. He explored how spices were more than just ingredients; they were a heritage passed down through generations, each blend telling a story of regions, traditions and family secrets. This exploration extended to dry fruits, integral to Pakistani hospitality and cuisine, understanding their varieties, uses and the cultural contexts in which they were shared and savoured.

Carpets, with their intricate designs and craftsmanship, were another area of focus. Aditya studied their patterns, learning to identify the different styles that represented various regions of Pakistan. He understood that carpets were not merely decorative items but pieces of art that carried the stories and skills of the artisans who created them. This knowledge was a sign of the deep respect for tradition and craftsmanship that was embedded in Pakistani culture.

These three weeks were a metamorphosis for Aditya, a process of shedding his own identity to clothe himself in another's. He wasn't just preparing for a mission; he was preparing to become someone else entirely, someone who could walk the streets of Pakistan not as a visitor, but as a native son.

With his facial hair now flourishing beyond his expectations, thanks to the timely arrival of steroids from London, Aditya examined his reflection with a sense of satisfaction. The transformation was striking; the well-groomed stubbly beard and moustache lent him a Pakistani look, an essential disguise for his mission. This physical change, coupled with his intensive study and practice, bolstered his confidence significantly.

Aditya spent countless hours in front of the mirror, fine-tuning his Pakistani accent. He mimicked conversations, practised common greetings and even rehearsed potential interactions, ensuring his accent bore the nuanced inflections and rhythm of a native speaker. This rigorous linguistic drill was more than mere practice; it was a ritual to embody the persona he was about to adopt fully.

Aditya's next move was critical, a step that would cement his transition from the known to the unknown. Acting on a contact given to him by his chief, he reached out to another trusted asset, this time with a request that carried the weight of his mission – the acquisition of a new passport. Not just any passport, but one that bore a new name, a new nationality: Hassan Raza who was born in Karachi, Pakistan. This document, purportedly issued by the government of Pakistan, was the key to unlocking his path forward, a tangible symbol of his transformation. The asset, an old hand with the R&AW, acted swiftly, ensuring that every detail on the passport, from the name to the personal particulars, was meticulously crafted to withstand scrutiny.

With the new Pakistani passport in hand, Aditya, now Hassan Raza, booked his ticket to London. This city was to be the first stop in his new life, a place where Hassan Raza, the widower and businessman dealing in spices and dry fruits, could exist unchallenged. The booking was made with precision, ensuring that his travel would not raise any red flags that could link back to Aditya Singh.

The night before his departure, Aditya stood before the mirror, studying the man reflected back at him. Hassan Raza stared back at him, a creation born out of necessity, but crafted with utmost care. The rigorous practice of his accent, the deep dive into the culture and customs of his adopted identity and now, the final piece of the puzzle, a new passport obtained through the chief's contact, all contributed to this moment of transformation.

Slipping out of India was a task handled with the same precision and care that had characterized every step of Aditya's preparation. The departure was unnoticed, a silent shadow moving through the night. Aditya Singh, with his ties to his past life as the son of Ramesh Singh, the former husband of Meera Desai and the father of Ameera Desai, had vanished. In his place, Hassan Raza, a Pakistani, made his way to the airport, blending in with the throngs of travellers, just another face in the crowd.

As the plane took off, Aditya felt the final strings that tied him to his former life loosen and drift away. He was entering a new phase of his mission, one that required him to embody Hassan Raza completely. London awaited, not just as a destination, but as the stage for the next act of his life. The city, with its vibrant mix of cultures and histories, was the perfect backdrop for Hassan Raza to emerge, a businessman with ties to the world of spices and dry fruits, yet a man with a mission that went far beyond the commerce of everyday life.

In the space of the past four weeks, more significant events had crowded into Aditya's life than in all his previous years combined. His life had changed from one moment to the next, though not entirely unbidden. After all, he had put himself in line for something like this by every one of his choices since his operative training in the Special Security Bureau (SSB). Still, from the moment the prime minister had wished him luck, Aditya felt totally out of control. It wasn't that he was frightened. He simply noted, with an almost clinical detachment, that he had finally done it. He had slipped overboard. He was in the water, and the tide was taking him out to sea. Like it or not, there wasn't a thing he could do. Swimming against the tide was clearly pointless.

As he flew away from his past, he revisited the final days leading up to this final break.

~

The timeframe for his departure to London had been tight, allowing for no more than two to three weeks of preparation. By the end of this period, Aditya anticipated being fully immersed in his role, engaging in discussions about spices and dry fruits with his new-found uncle, Altaf Raza. The necessity for a swift and effective transformation was clear; every aspect of his appearance and mannerisms needed to convincingly reflect his new identity.

Aditya's satisfaction with his new look resulted from the meticulous planning and execution of his transformation. Understanding the need for discretion and to avoid the inquisitive glances of neighbours who might question his sudden change in appearance, he had made a strategic move to Paharganj in central Delhi. This crowded neighbourhood, nestled in the heart of the capital, offered the perfect cover for someone seeking to blend in without drawing undue attention.

Paharganj, with its maze of narrow lanes lined with an eclectic mix of hotels, lodges, eateries and shops, catered to a diverse clientele.

The area's vibrancy was amplified by the presence of foreign tourists, backpackers and low-budget travellers, drawn by its reputation as a hub for international cuisine and affordable accommodation. This melting pot of cultures and nationalities provided Aditya with the anonymity he desired during this critical phase of his preparation.

However, Paharganj was not without its challenges. Reports of scams, drug-peddling and sexual assaults were a grim reminder of the neighbourhood's darker underbelly. Aditya was acutely aware of these concerns, yet his decision to stay here was driven by necessity. The imperfections of Paharganj, while regrettable, played into his need for a place where his sudden change in appearance and lifestyle would not spark curiosity or gossip. The bustling streets and the constant flow of people allowed him to move about unnoticed, just another face in the crowd.

Paharganj, with all its contradictions, served as the final staging ground for a dry run for Aditya's transformation from a R&AW operative to the undercover persona of Altaf Raza's nephew in London. His stay in Paharganj therefore was a crucial test of his ability to live convincingly under an assumed name and passport. By presenting himself as a Pakistani settled in London, he was effectively immersing himself in the role he would soon be playing on international soil. Living in his own country as a foreigner was a surreal experience for Aditya. It forced him to adopt the perspective of an outsider and cope with daily interactions through the lens of his assumed identity.

A week before his flight to London, Aditya made his way to see Ameera, his transformation for the mission rendering him less recognizable even to himself. The stubble on his face and the new hairstyle were necessary for his cover, yet they stood as barriers between him and his infant daughter, nearly three, who remembered her father with a different visage. As he entered the room where Ameera was playing, her initial reaction was one of curiosity, her small eyes squinting slightly as she tried to place this familiar stranger in the context of her limited world. The room, filled with the light laughter and chatter of a typical day, seemed to pause, waiting for the child's acceptance. When Aditya reached out to lift her from the walker, Ameera's reaction was not what he had hoped for. Instead of recognizing the loving embrace of her father, she pulled back, the confusion clear in her young eyes. This moment, meant to be a sweet reunion, turned into a poignant realization for Aditya; his physical transformation had alienated him from his own flesh and blood, leaving him a stranger in the eyes of his daughter.

Aditya felt a sharp sting in Meera's words, 'Don't bother the child more.' To him, Ameera was not just any child; she was his world, his daughter, a bond that went beyond the mere biological. Meera, perhaps sensing the depth of Aditya's hurt, tried to soften the blow with reason.

'Look, I am not blaming you, but you can see for yourself how she is responding,' she said, her voice carrying a mix of empathy and pragmatism.

Resigning himself to the reality of the situation, Aditya knew he had to approach this delicate moment with patience and understanding. He couldn't let his emotions overrule the need to make Ameera feel safe and loved, even if that meant keeping his distance for a while. He nodded quietly, acknowledging Meera's point, and took a seat nearby, not too close to intrude on Ameera's comfort but close enough to be within her sight.

Seeking a bridge to reconnect with his daughter, Aditya turned to his phone, scrolling through the gallery to find pictures of himself before the transformation. He selected a few where his features were clear and recognizable to Ameera, images that captured happier times, his face clean-shaven, his hair as she remembered. He held the screen towards her, his gesture a silent plea for her to see beyond the stranger before her and recognize the father who adored her.

He hoped that these visual memories would spark a recognition in Ameera, that the images of a happier, simpler time would remind her of the bond they shared. Ameera recognized her father in the photos instantly, tapping the screen excitedly and babbling, 'Pappa ... Pappa.' Each utterance of the word Pappa by Ameera, so familiar yet poignant, rattled him deeply. He had always cherished her recognition and calls, but now, faced with the looming uncertainty of their future encounters, the possibility that this might be one of their last interactions before his extended absence, was a silent spectre of the path he had chosen.

Hiding his turmoil was a skill Aditya had mastered over his years with the R&AW, but concealing the depth of his emotional struggle from Meera and Ameera was a challenge of a different sort. He knew that his family was an innocent party to the covert world he grappled with, and preserving their peace of mind meant swallowing his own fears and uncertainties. In an effort to appear normal before Ameera, Aditya busied himself with her toys, engaging in play with a forced cheerfulness that belied his internal strife.

And when Meera offered a cup of coffee, Aditya welcomed the opportunity, not so much for the desire for caffeine but for the additional time it gave him with his daughter. Every minute spent in Ameera's presence was precious, a fleeting treasure he was desperate to hold onto.

As the moment of departure arrived, unspoken emotions filled the air. Meera, guessing the gravity of the situation, asked Ameera to bid her father goodbye. Aditya found himself at a crossroads of emotion, contemplating whether to embrace his daughter one last time. The internal battle was brief but intense; he knew that prolonging the farewell would only serve to heighten the emotional toll of his departure. With a heavy heart, he chose to keep a semblance of distance, a decision that pained him more than any physical wound ever could.

In a final act of preparation, Aditya presented Meera with an old-style phone, a device stripped of all capabilities except to receive calls. This simple object was laden with profound significance, serving as a lifeline, a beacon of hope in the uncertain times that lay ahead. He explained its singular function: to be a receiver of calls, a potential harbinger of urgent news. The phone was a silent acknowledgment of the dangers his mission entailed. Meera's acceptance of the phone was a tacit understanding of the stakes. There was no need for words; the exchange spoke volumes about the seriousness of Aditya's assignment.

Meera, having been his partner through the vagaries of life and love, stood on the threshold of their shared past. Her soft farewell, 'Stay safe, Adi,' was more than a simple wish for his wellbeing; it was a reminder of the affection that once bound them together. The use of 'Adi', a name reserved for moments of tenderness and intimacy, revealed the layers of complexity in their relationship, a bond not entirely severed by the dissolution of their marriage.

Aditya's response, a plea that he not be erased from Ameera's heart, was a raw expression of his deepest fears. It was not just about his physical safety on the mission but about the preservation of his place in the lives of those he cherished most. Meera, caught off guard by Aditya's request, was momentarily stripped of her composure. The question that escaped her, 'Do you think I could ever do that?' was laden with pain and disbelief – a reminder of the bond that, though altered by circumstances, stayed alive.

As Aditya walked away from the building, the finality of the moment weighed heavily on him. The slow pace of his departure was not just a physical movement away from his former home but a symbolic distancing from a life he had once known. The conversation at the doorstep, brief yet profound, was a poignant reminder of the sacrifices demanded by his chosen path. It underscored the enduring human connections that persisted even in the face of duty's call, a reminder that, despite the bitterness of past conflicts, the underlying care and concern remained unextinguished, a flicker of hope in the shadow of parting.

In the quiet hum of the British Airways Boeing 787 Dreamliner, Aditya found a moment of tranquillity, dozing off in his window seat above the clouds. Stirred by the internal call to fulfil his spiritual duties, he glanced at his watch, recognizing the time for prayer. With a polite request, he excused himself past his fellow passenger, retrieved a bag from the overhead compartment, and made his way to the washroom.

The ritual washing was a quiet reflection, cleansing his face, hands up to the elbows, and feet, preparing him in body and spirit. He then unfurled a small carpet in the secluded space between the cabin crew area and the washroom, creating a makeshift sanctuary amidst the skies. As he offered namaz, the planes intercom gently broke the silence, announcing the descent towards Heathrow Airport in an hour's time, a reminder of the world awaiting below.

6

The Arrival of Hassan Raza

Aditya landed in London, August's warmth a stark contrast to the cold fear gripping him. London was at its best, but for Aditya, or 'Hassan Raza' as his passport claimed, the city's charm was overshadowed by the mission ahead. No friends or family waited for him; his only destination was his 'uncle' Altaf Raza's place in Redbridge.

Walking off the plane, his heart raced. This was his first time smuggling himself across borders under a false identity. What if immigration saw through his act? A single mistake, and he'd be caught, his career destroyed and his freedom gone.

As he moved towards passport control, every step felt like a gamble. Aditya knew too well the risks of being spotted by undercover agents. They were everywhere, watching for just the sort of slip he feared he might make. But he also knew he had no choice but to keep moving forward, relying on his training to blend in and pass through unnoticed. The next few minutes would determine everything.

Aditya quickly made his way from Gate C of Terminal 5 towards the main terminal, eyes on the lookout for passport control. He was acutely aware that among the crowd, hidden eyes were watching.

British intelligence and undercover airport police were scanning for anything out of place. He knew the danger of being profiled and stopped was real, but he also trusted his training. Aditya wasn't just any traveller; he was a spy, skilled in evasion and deception. The thought of being challenged, of having to use his wits to talk his way past suspicion, was a risk he was prepared to face. Every step he took was measured, blending in yet always ready to defend his false identity against anyone who might doubt him.

Aditya joined the line for foreign passport holders, relieved to see it moving quicker than he'd anticipated. Despite his efforts to appear relaxed, his nerves were frayed, his breaths shallow but controlled. Just a quarter-hour ago, as he filled out the immigration form, a moment of panic had almost undone him. Instinct nearly had him write his real name, a slip that could have spelled disaster. But he caught himself, aware that any sign of hesitation could attract unwanted attention. Observers, always on the lookout for the slightest inconsistency, preyed on such mistakes. Aditya was determined not to give them that satisfaction.

Aditya watched as the immigration officer, a middle-aged woman with a keen eye, scanned his face briefly before turning her attention to the pages of the Pakistani passport he had handed over. Her scrutiny was thorough, every page turned added weight to the silence between them.

Then, she looked up, her gaze piercing, 'You've got a multiple-entry UK visa, but I can't seem to find the stamp for your last exit,' she noted, her voice laced with a mix of curiosity and suspicion. A jolt of panic shot through Aditya. Could there have been a mistake, a crucial oversight by the asset back in India who had prepared this passport? His mind raced, but he kept his exterior calm.

With a steadiness he barely felt, Aditya replied, 'That's because this passport was recently issued. It's my first time visiting the UK with it.' His voice was smooth, betraying none of the alarm that had momentarily seized him. The officer's eyes narrowed slightly, 'I see. Do you have your old passport with you?' she asked, extending her hand expectantly.

Aditya felt the precarious balance of his disguise teeter on the brink. He didn't have an old passport, not one that would align with Hassan Raza's supposed history.

Aditya's mind raced as he realized the impossible position he was in; there was no old passport he could produce. Trying to maintain his composure, he admitted, 'I am not carrying it,' momentarily forgetting to maintain the Pakistani accent he had practiced so diligently. The slip was subtle, but to Aditya, it felt glaringly obvious. Quickly correcting himself, he added in a more carefully modulated tone, 'Is there a problem?'

The officer didn't respond immediately. Instead, she stood, casting a glance around the room as if seeking confirmation or support. At that moment, another officer approached, a silent sentinel who had been observing the exchange from the periphery. This second officer, with a swift efficiency, flipped through the passport once more, his eyes darting between the document and Aditya's carefully neutral expression.

Aditya felt as if he were under a microscope, every detail of his disguise scrutinized. Yet, despite the intense scrutiny, the officer found no fault. After a tense moment that felt like an eternity, he gave a slight nod, signalling Aditya could proceed.

With a curt gesture, he said, 'Everything seems in order. Welcome to the UK.'

Aditya barely suppressed a sigh of relief as he moved past the checkpoint, his heart still racing from the close call. The threat of discovery had loomed large, a stark reminder of the dangers his mission entailed. But for now, he was through, another obstacle dealt with in the shadowy world of espionage.

The close shave at passport control left Aditya with a profound sense of relief mingled with a sharpened awareness of the precariousness of his mission. It was a stark reminder that in the world of espionage, complacency could lead to catastrophe. Every move, every decision had to be meticulously planned and executed with the utmost caution. The unexpected had become his constant companion, and he had to be perpetually ready to face it head-on.

This incident had etched a crucial lesson in his mind: the margin for error was non-existent. Exposure was not just a failure; it was a potential death sentence. In the intricate dance of shadows he was engaged in, quitting was not merely undesirable. In fact, it was unthinkable.

Aditya Singh, the patriot, the spy, had ceased to exist in any official capacity. In the eyes of his homeland, he was now Hassan Raza, a fictional entity with no ties, no recourse to aid from either the Indian or Pakistani governments. He was a ghost, operating in the void between two identities, neither of which offered sanctuary or acknowledgement. The realization was chilling but clarifying. It underscored the isolation of his path, a solitary journey fraught with danger but necessary for the greater good. In this shadowy realm, Aditya's only allies were his wits, his training and his unwavering commitment to the mission at hand.

After securing his suitcase from the belt in Terminal 5, Aditya set his sights on the train station, his next waypoint on this clandestine odyssey. The digital board above the ticket counter confirmed his route: a journey through Stanford to Redbridge, promising to whisk him away in less than an hour's time. Decision made, he pressed on, ticket in hand, melting into the throngs of travellers, yet apart in purpose and the threat.

It was only as he headed towards the station that Aditya became acutely aware of the physical toll his mission had exacted. Beneath the layers of his nondescript attire, his skin was drenched in sweat, a reflection of the adrenaline that had surged through his veins mere moments ago. His mind, though, was yet to stop thinking what if he had been caught.

Yet, in this vulnerability, Aditya's resolve only crystallized further. Each heartbeat, a reminder of the sacrifice he had embraced for the sake of his country. He was more than just a man on a mission; he was a symbol of the silent warriors who fade into the backdrop of everyday life, their identities forsaken, their personal stories untold, all in the name of duty. In Aditya's relentless pursuit, despite the looming spectre of capture, readers find a hero not just to root for but to admire. His is a journey of courage, a lone figure against a backdrop of international intrigue, who carries the weight of his nation's security on his shoulders with unwavering determination.

~

Under the soft glow of the afternoon sun in Redbridge, East London, Altaf and Aditya were lounging on the balcony, the air still humming with the echoes of recent Eid celebrations. 'Terrorism,' Altaf began, his voice carrying weight, 'is a beast we're all fighting.' They were surrounded by the quiet of a post-lunch lull, with dishes from a lavish lamb biryani spread laid out before them, leftovers from the feast of Eid-ul-Adha (Bakrid), only three days go. Altaf, considering it the perfect meal to share with his 'nephew', had been pleased to offer it. What he didn't know was Aditya's restraint with red meat.

He politely declined a second serving, his actions in line with the controlled diet that kept him in peak physical form. Altaf couldn't help but jest about Aditya's James Bond-like attitude, suggesting he loosen up to better resemble the hearty meat-loving Pakistani he was supposed to be. 'Yes, with time,' Aditya agreed even as he sidestepped the sweet dishes that followed for a single scoop of vanilla ice cream. This simple exchange, set against the backdrop of a calm London suburb, painted a stark contrast to the complex, shadowed world of espionage that awaited beyond the safety of Altaf's home.

Listening to his host, it occurred to Aditya that even though Altaf had told him within the first five minutes of his arrival at his house what his mission was to be, he did not really understand it for about two more hours. He understood it in one sense, but in a deeper, more fundamental sense, he did not. When Altaf said, 'Your task is to destroy the terrorists who are wanted in India but enjoying safe havens outside India,' Aditya nodded in full agreement. It was about time. He was even a little relieved that the mission for which he had volunteered was not turning out to be a lonely spying assignment like it has always been. As for the word 'destroy', it was a natural term in espionage lingo used to mean a raid, the blowing up of an artillery installation, a supply depot, a communication centre or killing an entity through a surprise attack.

Altaf repeated his earlier thought with a bit more metaphor this time: 'Terrorism is a monster, but luckily it has only about a dozen heads. We should be able to chop them off, one by one.' Aditya, quick to point out a flaw in this strategy, countered, 'It will grow new ones.' Unfazed, Altaf smiled, showing off his fingernails as a visual aid, 'Depends on how you want to look at it. Don't we clip our fingernails even though they never stop growing? A terrorist is a fanatic. A top terrorist is a skilled and clever fanatic. They will always grow. But that doesn't mean they need not be clipped.' He stopped after speaking in a single breath, allowing his words to sink in.

Aditya's response was swift, acknowledging the depth of Altaf's analogy. 'You are talking to a convert. Carry on.' This exchange not only highlighted the daunting, Sisyphean task ahead but also consolidated Aditya's resolve. Despite the cyclical nature of their fight, the necessity of their mission remained unchanged. It was a battle of endurance and wit, one that required persistent effort, regardless of the inevitable resurgence of threats.

Altaf shifted the conversation from the philosophical to the practical with a sense of urgency. 'Anyway, we are not here to philosophize on terrorism. You're here for an operation,' he stated plainly to Aditya. The question, 'Like what?' escaped Aditya's lips, his curiosity piqued.

Altaf laid out the grim reality with a relentless pace. 'There's a host of terrorists, some Indians, some not, who've spilled innocent blood, shattered lives and demolished both homes and government structures without facing any consequences. They've slipped through the cracks, finding sanctuary across the globe. Be it in Bangladesh, Nepal, Pakistan, here in the UK, over in North America and even South America.

'They're scattered far and wide, shielded by those who once directed their violence towards India. Your country thinks now's the time to strike back. To eliminate them. To broadcast a clear message to both the emerging threats and their guardians: India will hunt them down, no matter where they hide, and end them.' Pausing, Altaf once again caught his breath after delivering this intense briefing in one go.

Aditya's gaze lingered on Altaf, trying to solve the complexities of the man before him. Trust wasn't the issue; after all, Altaf's role in this operation came stamped with the highest level of endorsement directly from the head of India's elite spy agency, the R&AW, and sanctioned by the prime minister himself. Yet, Aditya found himself wrestling with the moral and strategic implications of their mission. The targets were terrorists, yes, but ones who had fled India's grasp decades ago. Now, possibly in their 60s or 70s, these men were far removed from the violent acts they once perpetrated. The thought left Aditya questioning the ultimate value of their pursuit. Voicing his concern to Altaf, he noted, 'There is no peace at the end of this.'

Altaf's response was measured, his tone firm yet understanding of the dilemma shadowing Aditya's thoughts. 'Look Hassan,' he began, momentarily adopting Aditya's undercover identity to emphasize the seriousness of their conversation, 'My role here is to act as a service provider to you. If you're harbouring any doubts or questions, I'm here to address them. Or else, let's focus strictly on the operational aspects.'

They talked operations. The R&AW had given the matter much consideration, Altaf said, and decided that the best way to proceed was with a small, self-contained group. One that could survive on its own for months or even years. A team that would not depend on India for any support. A team that was composed of experts in various fields like weapons, explosives, logistics and documents.

'The idea,' Altaf continued, 'is to ensure that you don't have to rely on any of R&AW's usual resources. This way, you minimize the risk of exposure and enhance operational security. It's about keeping you safe while you're out there, as much as it is about maintaining operational integrity.'

Aditya understood that the essence of the strategy lay in creating a ghost team, virtually invisible and traceable only by the results of their actions. Agents often found themselves at greatest risk during those critical moments of contact with their command structures when receiving orders, collecting weaponry or acquiring necessary documents. It was these interactions that traditionally posed the highest risk of exposure.

However, by establishing a team capable of autonomous operation, forging their own documents, sourcing their own weapons and cultivating their own intelligence networks, they would significantly mitigate these risks. This team's operational blueprint was designed to ensure that its members would have no need to approach any of the traditional espionage touchpoints: embassies, resident agents or even the clandestine channels like dead-letter drops, which had been staples of spy craft for generations.

Moreover, the absence of conventional signals or dispatches through recognizable communication channels would render them nearly undetectable. This approach not only capitalized on the element of surprise but also reduced the likelihood of interception or compromise. In essence, Aditya, with Altaf's assistance, had to set up a team that could operate deep within enemy territory with no direct lines back to R&AW, making them a formidable force, a shadow team equipped to take on one of the agency's most sensitive and high-stakes missions.

Aditya understood that what Altaf was talking about was that it would be like a team of terrorists but with infinitely more strength. It was an operation that mirrored the modus operandi of the very targets they sought to eliminate, but with a key difference: their actions would be underpinned by a far greater purpose and backed by the full might of their training and resources. This team would not just mimic terrorist cells in operational tactics; it would potentially leverage the terrorists' own networks for logistical support, tapping into an existing ecosystem of safe houses, forged passports and explosives.

The brilliance of this strategy lay in its simplicity and audacity. By blending in completely with their surroundings, they could turn the terrorists' strengths into vulnerabilities. The fragmented nature of terrorist networks, with each cell often operating in isolation from the others, presented a unique opportunity. Their ignorance of each other's precise activities and members could allow Aditya's team to infiltrate these networks under the guise of fellow extremists.

As Altaf continued to outline the mission's details and complexities, Aditya felt a growing excitement, a sense of being on the cusp of something ground-breaking; something that he had never attempted in his entire spy career. This was the opportunity he had been waiting for, a chance to truly prove his capabilities and make a significant impact. The scale of the operation, its audacity and the strategic depth it required appealed to every fibre of his being as a field operative. This was not just another assignment; it was a mission that could define his career, set him apart as a master of his craft.

Yet, Aditya was careful to maintain an impassive exterior. Years of training and the ingrained lessons from countless psychological evaluations had taught him the value of emotional concealment. The agency prized operatives who could keep their cool under pressure, those who approached even the most thrilling prospects with a measured, analytical mind. They had no use for reckless enthusiasm or the pursuit of glory.

So, he listened, absorbed and planned, all behind a façade of contemplation, his face betraying none of the excitement that animated his thoughts. This stoicism was not just a professional mask but a strategic one, allowing him to fully absorb the gravity of the mission without the distraction of visible emotions. To Altaf, and to any who might observe them, Aditya appeared as the ideal operative: thoughtful, perhaps even burdened by the weight of what lay ahead, yet undeniably ready for the challenge.

The conversation took a more engaging turn after they reconvened from a brief interlude for afternoon tea. The air between them was charged with an undercurrent of anticipation as they delved deeper into the mission's logistics.

'This team,' Aditya ventured, breaking the silence, 'do I put it together?'

'Not exactly,' Altaf responded, his tone suggesting there was more to it. 'There is a list of six men. You can meet them and select. One … two … three. Whatever you need, up to you.'

'When can I meet them?' Aditya's question was straightforward, reflecting his eagerness to move forward.

Altaf's smile carried a hint of mystery. 'Sabar,' he replied in Urdu, emphasizing patience, 'everything in good time. They're … they're not in the country yet.'

Aditya felt a twinge of suspicion, his instincts suggesting there might be more to the story, but he pressed on. 'All right, what are they experts in? One guy is explosives?'

'Right,' confirmed Altaf, nodding.

'Another is documents?' Aditya prodded further, trying to piece together the composition of his potential team.

'Uh-hmm,' Altaf hummed his agreement.

'Then one or two for the job itself,' Aditya continued, his mind racing ahead to the operational details, noticing Altaf's confusion. 'Well … the hit, I mean. Push the button.'

'What do you mean, push the button?' Altaf's question was laced with genuine puzzlement.

Aditya, now the one puzzled, clarified, 'I mean a specialist in – you know, pulling the trigger. A guy trained to do the … the actual hit.'

Altaf's expression shifted to one of amazement, almost disbelief. 'A specialist in pulling a trigger?' he echoed slowly, as if weighing each word. 'You mean … you don't know how to pull a trigger? Four years in the army, you've never learned to pull a trigger?'

The question hung in the air, tinged with a mix of humour and incredulity. Aditya couldn't help but smile at the absurdity. 'Must you ask such a question?' he retorted playfully, acknowledging the rhetorical nature of Altaf's inquiry. 'But I am not the only one who would pull the trigger in an operation. There might be others as well.'

'Maybe, sometime it's you … all alone?' Altaf pressed, locking eyes with Aditya, searching for a deeper affirmation of his readiness.

'Maybe. It all depends on the nature of the operation.' Aditya's response was measured, revealing a readiness to embrace whatever the mission demanded, alone or not. Their exchange, filled with probing questions and veiled answers, only served to deepen the intrigue surrounding the mission, blending professional assessment with personal evaluation.

Aditya, grappling with a mix of confusion and curiosity, decided to confront the uncertainty head-on. It was a moment of vulnerability, perhaps even naivety, but the need to understand outweighed his reservations.

'Why me?' he asked, his voice carrying a blend of doubt and determination.

Altaf, momentarily caught off guard by the directness, responded with a hint of impatience, 'Why you what?'

'Why did you select me?' Aditya pressed, seeking clarity.

'I didn't. I am just a service provider,' Altaf clarified, his tone softening as he realized the depth of Aditya's inquiry. 'But if I may ask, what's wrong with you?'

'There's nothing wrong with me,' Aditya quickly retorted. He was confident of his abilities, his knowledge of Europe, his organizational skills and his determination to see things through. 'I know Europe, I'm a good organizer, I ... I think I can finish what I start. But why me? I've never done this kind of thing before.'

Altaf leaned in, adopting a more understanding attitude. 'Who has?' he asked, gently challenging Aditya's self-doubt.

'Yeah, that's true,' Aditya acknowledged, the realization dawning on him. The question wasn't about his past experiences or the lack thereof; it was about his unique qualities, his adaptability and perhaps even his readiness to confront the unprecedented. This exchange, though brief, was pivotal, offering Aditya a glimpse into the rationale behind his selection. It wasn't about having a specific background in such covert operations but about possessing the right combination of skills, mindset and potential for this unique challenge.

Aditya, driven by a blend of curiosity and a need for deeper understanding, posed a question that had been simmering within him. 'And who are you?' It was more than a query; it was a plea for transparency in a world cloaked in shadows.

Altaf's response came with a disarmingly sweet smile, as if to cushion the weight of his words. 'I am your uncle. I live here in

London. Trade in spices, dry fruits and carpets.' His attitude, relaxed and leaning back in his chair, carried an unspoken message, a gentle but firm boundary. The look in his eyes, meeting Aditya's, seemed to carry a silent warning, a hint of the limits of inquiry in their clandestine world.

Altaf, with his benign cover story, reminded Aditya of the layered realities they encountered where personal histories were obscured, and roles were multifaceted. Aditya, understanding the delicacy of their situation, recognized the boundary set by Altaf's smile and stance, and acknowledged the complexities of identity within the spy network.

~

The next chapter of Aditya's covert journey unfolded with a meticulous precision that spoke volumes for his training and the severity of his mission. He took a train to Geneva and made the city the backdrop for his next moves into a city synonymous with neutrality and discretion, ideal for the clandestine activities that lay ahead.

Upon arriving, Aditya effortlessly donned the role of an ordinary tourist or businessman, taking a room at the Hotel du Midi, which offered both comfort and anonymity. His actions in Geneva were calculated, moving with a purpose that was invisible to the casual observer. Driving across the iconic Pont du Mont Blanc, Aditya admired the serene beauty of Geneva, a stark contrast to the inner turmoil and complexity of his mission.

The Union de Banques Suisses was his destination, a place where wealth and secrecy intersected in the vaults and ledgers of Swiss banking. The building's old-fashioned façade belied the sophisticated financial operations within. Here, Aditya undertook a critical step in his mission's logistical preparation: the opening of bank accounts and the renting of a safe-deposit box. The transaction was smooth, a validation of the bank's professionalism and discretion. Yet, when the question of the money's origin arose – to check if it was drug money – a standard inquiry in the world of high-stakes banking, Aditya's response was both a deflection and a challenge, hinting at his Pakistani origin being a cause for racial profiling that often shadowed his assumed identity.

The bank's PR executive's apology, though polite, displayed the delicate balance of suspicion and respect that defined such interactions. Aditya, under the guise of 'Mr Hassan', overcame these challenges with the adeptness of a seasoned operative, ensuring his mission's financial foundation was securely in place without drawing undue attention to himself.

In the crisp, neutral air of Geneva, Aditya found himself at a critical juncture. With $50,000 discreetly tucked into his faux leather duffle bag, he moved through the city, a ghost among tourists, his mind a whirlwind of strategy and memories. The city's abundance of candy and chocolate stores served as bittersweet reminders of Ameera, weaving threads of personal longing into the fabric of his mission-oriented thoughts.

During his brief stay in Switzerland, Aditya remained in the guise of a tourist, all the while meticulously compiling a list of terrorists who had inflicted significant harm on India before vanishing into the shadows of international complicity. This task, though daunting, was sharpened by a message from Altaf, a directive that had originated from the heart of R&AW. The message was clear: Aditya was to initiate the first strike independently, armed with the intelligence and training he possessed. This first action, a litmus test of sorts, would be scrutinized for its precision, discretion and effectiveness in an age where anonymity was a myth, eroded by the pervasive gaze of surveillance technologies.

The weight of this directive did not escape Aditya. The understanding that every choice he made, from the selection of his target to the timing and location of the strike, would be under intense scrutiny, added layers of complexity to his task. Yet, within this web of expectations and surveillance, time was his ally. The open-ended nature of his mandate allowed him the freedom to plan meticulously, to act when the moment was ripe, not be rushed.

This autonomy, however, was a double-edged sword. The success of his mission hinged on his ability to negotiate the tightrope of operational security and the ever-present eyes of the world. It was a test not just of his tactical acumen, but of his ability to blend in, to make his strike felt without leaving a trace that led back to him or his handlers. As Aditya prepared to leave Geneva, the serene beauty of Switzerland belied the storm brewing within him, a storm of planning, anticipation and the looming spectre of the challenge he was about to face.

Aditya's meticulous preparation took him deep into the annals of history, scouring the internet and the dusty corners of London's libraries for newspapers and archives that could offer insights into his targets. The more he delved into his research, the clearer it became that his portrayal of a Pakistani needed to be beyond reproach. The stakes were high, and the margin for error was non-existent. His findings pointed him towards Pakistan as the nucleus of his mission, with names like Zahoor Mistry, Aijaz Ahmad, Ripudaman Singh, Syed Khalid Raza and Rasool Azhar emerging as key figures in the landscape of terrorism that had afflicted India. Azhar, known for his role in the Pulwama attack among others, was emblematic of the type of adversary Aditya was poised to confront. He was the same guy who enjoyed Chinese veto at the United Nations Security Council (UNSC) every time the organization attempted to declare him an 'international terrorist'.

The realization that Pakistan would be his starting point was not just a strategic decision but a necessary one. To infiltrate the ranks of those he sought to bring to justice, Aditya needed to embody the persona of a Pakistani so convincingly that no suspicion could be cast on his true identity or his intentions. This was a challenge that extended beyond mere physical appearance or linguistic fluency; it was about understanding and assimilating into the cultural nuances and the everyday realities of the people he aimed to blend in with. His study of Pakistan over two weeks before leaving India appeared to be a kindergarten course to be able to deal with the upcoming challenges.

While Altaf's support in London had been invaluable, Aditya recognized that relying on him within Pakistan's borders presented a different set of complexities. The dynamics of their collaboration would inevitably change in a landscape where Altaf's own allegiances and background could come under scrutiny. Acknowledging this shift, Aditya resolved to forge his own path, leveraging his interactions with the Pakistani community in the UK to build a network and perfect his cover.

His strategy was clear: to infiltrate, he needed to become indistinguishable from those he sought to observe and ultimately counter. This would require not just a deep understanding of their ideologies and movements but also an ability to work through their social structures as one of their own. Aditya's journey was morphing into one of dualities between his true self and the persona he needed to adopt, between allied and enemy territories and between the pursuit of justice and the risks of deep undercover work.

Aditya, now fully embodying the identity of Hassan Raza, began his delicate foray into the Pakistani community in London with a blend of caution and calculated boldness.

His approach was methodical, attending community events, frequenting places of social gathering and engaging in conversations that allowed him to gradually integrate without arousing suspicion. Aditya knew that trust within such close-knit communities was earned over time, through consistent interaction and the subtle demonstration of shared values and interests.

As the seasons changed, painting London by turn in the brilliant colours of autumn, the stark whites of winter, the tender greens of spring and the vibrant hues of summer, Aditya found himself transformed. The city, with its endless streets and hidden alleyways, became a treasure hunt, each discovery a jewel in Aditya's crown of experiences. From the quiet walks along the Thames, where the water whispered secrets of the past, to the bustling markets of Camden and the serene parks dotted across the city, every corner held a story, every face a friend not yet met.

Aditya walked on the tightrope with a precision that belied the clamour beneath the calm exterior. To begin with, he started attending cultural events and religious gatherings; each appearance deepened his cover. However, Aditya's first real test came unexpectedly during a community cricket match in a local park, a much loved affair among the diaspora.

As he stood at the crease, bat in hand, Aditya knew the eyes on him weren't just watching the game. A well-placed shot could win more than just the match; it could win trust. With the sun dipping low, casting long shadows on the field, Aditya's bat connected with the ball, sending it over the fence. The cheers that followed were more than applause for his skill.

As the match concluded and the players and spectators mingled, sharing their congratulations and recounting the highlights, Aditya found himself at the centre of attention. His success on the cricket field had afforded him a new level of camaraderie and respect within the community. Conversations flowed more freely, invitations were extended with genuine warmth, and Aditya, under the guise of Hassan, found doors opening to him that went beyond the boundaries of the cricket field.

But blending in was only part of the challenge. Aditya's nights were spent in series of conversations with Altaf, poring over maps and reports, planning his penetration of the diaspora in UK. The shop's basement became their war room, where whispered strategies filled the air, mingled with the scent of spices from above. In its privacy, Aditya's thoughts often drifted to the streets outside. He longed to explore, to find his place in this vast, vibrant city. And so, with the evening prayer as his compass, he stepped out, his steps echoing on the pavements of Waterloo Road, weaving through the crowds, a solitary figure with a heart full of hope.

~

In the sacred quietude of the mosque, as the day bled into dusk, Aditya discovered a profound sense of belonging. The act of prayer, a deeply personal communion with the divine, also served as a silent conversation with those around him. In this place, faith was the universal language, transcending the barriers of nationality, culture and individual experience. The exchange of nods, the warmth of shared smiles and the eventual blossoming of conversations in this holy space gently wove Hassan into the fabric of the community, transforming solitude into a budding sense of kinship.

Motivated by a genuine curiosity and a longing to connect with the essence of his undercover identity, Hassan ventured further into the heart of London's Pakistani community. The vibrant bazaars, with their lively haggling and array of colours, smells and sounds, transported him to the bustling streets of Lahore. The mosques, with their soothing calls to prayer, reminded him of a heritage both borrowed and deeply felt, a reflection of the intricate role he played.

At community gatherings, amidst the rich aromas of biryani and the resonant laughter of companionship, Hassan offered himself in service, friendship and empathy. He listened intently to stories that bridged generations, tales of struggle and triumph, of longing and belonging. Through these interactions, he became a conduit for shared histories and aspirations, a living embodiment of the power of empathy in forging connections.

Aditya's role as an undercover agent was imbued with a complexity that went beyond mere infiltration; it was a deep dive into the human experience, a lesson in the transformative power of understanding and compassion. In offering his hands in service, his heart in friendship and his ear in empathy, Aditya not only solidified his cover but also carved out a space within the community where his presence was valued and his contributions recognized.

On that particular evening, under the soft afterglow of sunset that bathed the mosque in the twilight hour, Hassan and his new friend Amir's steps fell into a harmonious rhythm as they exited the place of worship. Their conversation, initiated in the shared silence of prayer, unfolded with an ease that belied the briefness of their acquaintance. Amir, with the vibrant energy of youth, painted his experiences in London with a palette of hope tinged with the shadows of struggle. His stories, rich with aspirations and the inevitable challenges of a migrant's journey, resonated deeply with Hassan.

As they walked, their dialogue meandered through the realms of faith and the often harsh misconceptions that surrounded their beliefs. They spoke of the prejudice they faced, a cloud that distorted the essence of their truth, casting long shadows on their paths. Yet, in the face of such challenges, their spirits remained unbroken, buoyed by a resilient faith and the dreams that had carried them across seas and borders to these very streets of London.

Listening to Amir, Hassan felt a profound connection, a mirror reflecting his own silent contemplations and the invisible burdens of his dual identity. Here was a young man who sailed through the same turbulent waters of Islamophobia, yet did so with a quiet dignity and an unwavering commitment to his faith and ideals. This shared experience, discussed openly between them, bridged their worlds, drawing Hassan closer to the authentic essence of the community he sought to understand and protect.

Their conversation was a testament to the resilience of the human spirit, to the shared bonds of faith and hope that could transcend the barriers of background and circumstance. For Hassan, Amir's friendship offered not just insight into the personal narratives within the Pakistani diaspora, but also underscored the universality of their struggles and dreams.

Their steps led them to the banks of the Thames, the city lights dancing on the water, mirroring the stars above. It was here, in the openness of shared experiences, that Hassan spoke of his vision, of bridging the gap between the markets of Pakistan and the streets of London, of weaving the rich tapestry of his heritage into the modern fabric of his uncle's business. Amir's enthusiasm was a spark, igniting possibilities, the beginning of a friendship forged in the crucible of shared dreams.

The stakes were raised for Aditya when, at a fund-raising dinner, his cover was nearly blown. A misplaced comment about a Pakistani city he had claimed as home drew sharp looks from a group of volunteers. Thinking quickly, Aditya deflected with a laugh, blaming his mistake on the years spent abroad, his heart racing as he redirected the conversation back to safer waters.

Another test came unexpectedly. A late-night break-in at the shop turned into a confrontation with a burglar. Aditya's combat training kicked in, neutralizing the threat without revealing his true capabilities. The incident, explained away as an act of bravery by Altaf, served to solidify his standing in the community, but Aditya knew it was a close call. More so, when the local police repeatedly asked Aditya where he learned such combat skills.

As the days melted into weeks and months, Aditya, or Hassan as he was known within the community, unwittingly found himself the subject of a different kind of attention. His role had never been scripted to include the complexities of romance, yet the allure of his enigmatic presence did not go unnoticed among the women of the Pakistani community in London. His charm, coupled with a mysterious aura, marked him as distinct, setting the stage for an unforeseen chapter in his undercover saga.

Zara emerged as a figure of particular interest. Her fierce intelligence and outspoken nature made her stand out; she was a woman of conviction and curiosity. It was Hassan's reflective musings on cultural preservation that initially caught her attention, sparking debates that danced tantalizingly around the edges of their growing mutual attraction. Zara's fascination with Hassan was tinged with a hint of suspicion, his elusive nature challenging her to look closer, to question deeper. Yet, with each interaction, she found herself increasingly drawn to him, her initial curiosity blossoming into something more profound.

Their exchanges, rich with playful banter and intellectual sparring, became a highlight of the social gatherings they both attended. Zara, with a strategic flair, sought out Hassan, weaving him into her conversations, her words laced with an undercurrent of interest that went beyond mere social pleasantries. Her eyes sparkled with a fascination that was as much about cracking the mystery of Hassan's past as it was about understanding the man before her.

Zara's keen intelligence and the slight suspicion that shadowed her interest in Hassan posed a challenge, compelling Aditya to tackle their relationship with caution even as he was drawn into the warmth of her company. In this delicate dance of attraction and intrigue, the lines between the mission and personal connection began to blur, setting the stage for a narrative rich with the promise of romance, mystery and the ever-present thrill of the undercover world.

In the evolving montage of Hassan's life in London, another woman, Ayesha, represented a contrasting counterpoint to Zara's vibrant dynamism. Where Zara sparked debates with her fiery intelligence, Ayesha brought a sense of peace and introspection. Her quiet attitude and the depth of her faith struck a chord with Hassan, aligning closely with the persona he had crafted for himself. Ayesha's approach was gentle, yet her questions cut to the core, exploring spiritual realms and shared beliefs. Their conversations, rich with philosophical musings, hinted at a connection that transcended the physical, touching on the spiritual.

Aditya, ever the strategist, recognized an opportunity in Ayesha's interest. By adopting views that bordered on fanaticism in their discussions, he subtly reinforced his cover within the community, presenting himself as an ardent, if somewhat extreme, believer. This deliberate portrayal was a calculated move, designed to blend in more thoroughly with elements of the community where such fervour was not uncommon. It was a risky game, playing with perceptions and beliefs in this manner, but one that Aditya handled with careful consideration of the broader objectives of his mission.

As the seasons shifted, marking the passage of time with the fall of autumn leaves and the arrival of winter's chill, Hassan (Aditya) found himself navigating a complex emotional landscape. The women in his life, Zara with her challenging wit and Ayesha with her spiritual depth, represented divergent paths that offered both companionship and a deeper engagement with the community he was embedded in. Their influence extended beyond personal affection, suggesting potential partnerships that could further his undercover objectives, from expanding his uncle's business to fostering connections that bridged cultural divides.

Yet, amidst this interplay of personal and professional dynamics, Aditya remained acutely aware of the mission that had brought him to these shores. The relationships he had formed, while genuine in their moment, were entangled with the fabric of his undercover identity. His resolve, tested by the connections he had made, remained firm.

With each passing day, Aditya, as Hassan, wove himself deeper into the fabric of the community, his every move watched by unseen eyes, his every word measured for its impact. The line between the persona of Hassan and the reality of Aditya blurred, each encounter, each moment of risk, pushing him further into the shadows of a world where trust was both weapon and shield.

In the end, Aditya's time in London was a preparation for the ultimate mission. Each step, each risk taken, brought him closer to his goal. But as he stood once more in the quiet of the mosque, surrounded by the community he had fought so hard to blend into, Aditya couldn't help but wonder at the cost of his mission, the lines crossed in the name of duty. The final journey to Pakistan loomed ahead, a path fraught with danger, but Aditya Singh, known to the world as Hassan Raza, was ready. The game of espionage had no room for doubt, and Aditya was a player at the top of his game.

7

The Mission

January 2022.

In the beginning of the year, as the PIA flight from London to Karachi neared its destination, Aditya, under the guise of Hassan Raza, was following up on Pakistan's current news on the inflight entertainment system. The screen flickered with images of political unrest in public areas, riots, bomb blasts in religious places killing innocent lives and political debates across news channels, a window into the life of the nation he was about to step into.

The tensions between the country's prime minister and the Pakistan Army was rising by the day following the PM's attempt to appoint his own choice as the new intelligence (ISI) chief. While the Pak Army resisted the move, and the PM eventually backed down, the tensions continued amidst rumours of a counterattack by the Army. The opposition, led by a coalition of political parties, was out to bring down the government through a no-confidence motion. Aditya's focus was unbroken, absorbing every detail, every nuance of the society into which he needed to inconspicuously integrate himself.

It was the aircraft's gentle descent that finally pulled him away from the screen. As he removed his earplugs, the cabin's ambient noise rushed back in a mixture of chatter, the rustle of movement and the underlying hum of the engines.

His co-passenger, a middle-aged Pakistani man with a broad, engaging smile, seized the opportunity to strike up a conversation. 'First you slept like a baby, and then you were glued to that screen. We didn't get a chance to talk,' he remarked, a playful nudge in his tone before offering to shake hands, 'Myself, Pervez Rana.'

Aditya turned, offering a warm smile, an ambassador of his fabricated identity. 'I guess I was trying to catch up on what's happening back home. It's been a while since I've been back.'

The man chuckled, 'Well, you haven't missed much. Same old politics and rising problems. But tell me, what brings you back?'

Aditya's response was rehearsed yet sincere, 'Business, mainly. I've been living in London, helping my uncle's trade in spices, dry fruits. We're thinking of expanding our operations here.'

'Ah, a noble pursuit,' the man nodded appreciatively. 'Karachi is the heart of commerce. You'll find plenty of opportunities here. Just remember, it's a city that rewards those who deal with its odds with patience.'

'Thank you for the advice,' Aditya replied, his gratitude genuine even if his story was not. 'Well, my father used to say the same.'

As the wheels of the plane touched down on Pakistani soil, a mix of excitement and apprehension fluttered in Aditya's chest. This was the arena of his most challenging mission yet, a test of his years of training and preparation. With each step forward, he was walking deeper into a web of danger and deception, but Aditya Singh was ready. His alias, Hassan Raza, might be a fabrication, but his determination to succeed was as real as the ground beneath his feet. The game had indeed begun, and he was playing for keeps.

As Aditya stepped off the plane and into the crowded aerobridge, he felt the weight of his mission pressing down on him with every step towards passport control. The air hung oppressively with anticipation, a silent reminder that he was now in enemy territory. The casual chatters and laughs of returning families and businessmen did little to ease the tension knotting in his stomach.

Heading for the passport control, his heartbeat seemed to echo louder in his ears. The relative safety of the plane was behind him now; he was on Pakistani soil, a territory where the line between friend and foe was dangerously thin. The knowledge that Pakistani officials, some in uniform and others indistinguishable from the civilians around him, were scrutinizing arriving passengers added a layer of tension that clung to him like the humid air.

As he stood in the queue for immigration check, Aditya's gaze met that of an immigration officer, a man whose eyes seemed to miss nothing. The officer's gaze was sharp, piercing, as if he could peel back the layers of anyone who stood before him. Aditya's throat tightened, a silent battle raging within as he fought to maintain his façade.

When it was finally his turn, Aditya approached the booth with a practised ease, offering a polite 'As-salamu alaykum,' as he handed over his passport. The officer's scrutiny intensified, his fingers flipping through the pages with deliberate slowness. 'You've been away for quite some time,' the officer remarked, his tone neutral yet probing.

Aditya was expecting the question. 'Yes, I was exploring business opportunities in London,' he replied, striving to keep his voice even, 'but there's no place like home.'

The officer's gaze lingered on him; a moment stretched thin with tension. Then, unexpectedly, he leaned forward slightly, lowering his voice, 'Business, you say? Or got a second wife there?'

Aditya was certainly not expecting that. He laughed and said, 'Wish I had that luck, sir.' The officer studied him for a moment longer, the silence between them charged with unspoken questions. Then, as if satisfied, he stamped Aditya's passport and said, 'Better luck next time.' Aditya smiled and left wishing him, 'God bless.'

Aditya's hands were steady as he retrieved his large suitcase from the baggage carousel. The Pakistani branded luggage, a loan from Altaf, felt like a tangible link to his cover. He passed through the crowd of arrivals, blending in yet apart, his senses heightened to every detail around him. Outside the terminal, the cacophony of

Karachi's airport greeted him – a symphony of honks, shouts and the relentless hustle of the city.

Pulling out his phone, he opened the SIXT app. The address of Altaf's house in Gulshan-e-Iqbal was already bookmarked, a middle-class enclave that would serve as his base of operations. Despite the driver's acknowledgement of the destination through the app, the reconfirmation of the address was a ritual, a part of courtesy and caution that defined interactions here.

'Yes, Gulshan-e-Iqbal, near the university road,' Aditya confirmed, his accent meticulously neutral, betraying no hint of his years abroad.

As the taxi weaved through the noisy, bustling, ever-growing troubled Pakistani metropolis, Aditya found himself pressed against the window, eyes absorbing every detail of the city that was to be his home for the foreseeable future. The vibrant chaos of Karachi, with its blend of modernity and tradition, was overwhelming. Street vendors hawked their wares with loud calls, children played in narrow alleyways and the atmosphere was dense with the scent of street food and exhaust fumes. Aditya knew Karachi was Pakistan's largest city, and unarguably the most important; it was the original capital of the nation.

The driver, an elderly man with a friendly approach, glanced at him through the rearview mirror. 'You seem to be taking it all in, son. First time in Karachi?' he inquired, a note of curiosity in his scratchy voice.

Aditya offered a small smile, playing the part of a man returning to his roots. 'It's been a while since I've been back. Just visiting family and exploring some business opportunities,' he replied, keeping his story consistent.

The driver nodded; a common thread of conversation picked up. 'You lived outside Pakistan, then? The Gulf? Or farther west?'

'London,' Aditya answered simply, not offering more than necessary.

'Ah, London!' the old man exclaimed, his interest piqued. 'Must be a big change coming back here, then.'

Aditya chuckled, a sound he hoped conveyed ease and nostalgia. 'Indeed, but it's good to be back. How's the city been, especially with the political situation?'

The question seemed to open a floodgate, and the driver launched into a detailed commentary on the latest political developments, the economic challenges and the ever-present undercurrent of tension that gripped Pakistan ever since a cricketer was elected to be the prime minister. Aditya understood that the old man didn't like his prime minister. However, he listened, absorbing every word, every insight into the current state of affairs. It was information that might prove invaluable, a context to deal with the complex sociopolitical landscape of his mission.

The half-hour journey to Gulshan-e-Iqbal felt both long and fleeting, a blur of sights and sounds that steadied Aditya's resolve. When the taxi stopped before the address, a neat, modern bungalow that blended into the quiet respectability of the upper-middle-class neighbourhood, he felt a slow surge of anticipation. This was it, the beginning of his most dangerous game yet. Taking a breath, he adjusted his collar, and stepped out into the Karachi air.

He paid the driver, offering a polite nod of thanks and watched as the taxi disappeared into the traffic. Standing before Altaf's house, Aditya took a moment to steady himself. Every step, every interaction, had to be calculated. The risks were immense, but so were the stakes.

As he rang the doorbell, the reality of his situation settled around him like a cloak. Karachi was not just a backdrop for his mission; it was a living, breathing entity, a labyrinth of challenges and opportunities. And Aditya Singh, as Hassan Raza, was poised to test its depths, whatever it might take.

The door swung open to reveal the housekeeper, Usman Hamidi, a man with a warm, welcoming expression that immediately put Aditya at ease. His greeting was effusive, testifying to the renowned hospitality that Pakistanis prided themselves on. 'Welcome, sir!' Usman said, taking Aditya's large suitcase. 'It must have been a long journey, sir. What would you like to eat or drink?' he inquired, eager to attend to his guest's needs.

As he guided Aditya through the house, pointing out the various rooms and amenities, Aditya nodded along; the layout was familiar to him, not through personal experience but thanks to the video footage he had studied from Altaf's phone. Every corner, every piece of furniture was exactly as he had seen it in the digital walkthrough.

Seeking to maintain his cover story, Aditya waved off the housekeeper's attentiveness with a casual air. 'Please, don't bother yourself too much. I've been here many times before you started taking care of the house,' he lied smoothly, injecting a note of familiarity into his voice.

Usman's face fell slightly, embarrassment touching his features. It was a faux pas in a culture that valued hospitality and knowledge of one's guests above many things. 'My apologies, Janaab, for my ignorance,' he said, his tone sincere. 'Please, freshen up and let me know when you would like to eat. I am at your beck and call.'

Aditya offered a reassuring smile, appreciating the man's dedication and the immediate shift to rectify any discomfort. 'Thank you, that will be all for now. I'll let you know after I've settled in.'

As the housekeeper retreated to give him privacy, Aditya took a moment to absorb the reality of his surroundings. The house, though familiar from his preparations, was now a tangible part of his cover. Every interaction, even these seemingly mundane ones, played a role in cementing his identity as Hassan Raza.

When he came out of the bathroom after a shower, he noticed a welcome drink on his bedside table: a glass of iced Rooh Afzah, a rose sharbat very popular in Pakistan. Sipping the drink, Aditya allowed himself a brief moment of reflection. The weight of his mission, the complexity of his dual identity and the challenges ahead were stark against the backdrop of this well-kept house in Karachi. Yet, there was no room for doubt.

'Freshen up, Janaab, and let me know when you'd like to eat,' Usman's words echoed in his mind, a reminder of the role he needed to play. Aditya Singh, as Hassan Raza, was more than a guest in this house; he was a hunter disguised in the trappings of everyday life, ready to live in the perilous waters of his assignment with every tool at his disposal.

∽

The lunch spread before Aditya was a testament to the rich culinary traditions of Pakistan – lavish, flavourful and undeniably heavy. The goat meat biryani sat aromatic and inviting, its rice grains perfectly fluffy and infused with spices. Alongside it, the roti, made from white flour, was soft and warm, a perfect complement to the succulent grilled mutton and the deeply flavoured liver curry. The meal was rounded off with kulfi falooda, a sweet, creamy delight that was a refreshing end to the unexpected feast.

Aditya couldn't help but commend the housekeeper's efforts; the food was delicious, each bite a surge of traditional flavours. What he would like to avoid in future were the greasiness, and the richness of the meal that was far from his usual diet. The thought crossed his mind to discuss his dietary preferences with Usman, to perhaps steer future meals towards a lighter, less fat-laden direction. Yet, he hesitated, deciding against it for the moment. It was his first day, and he did not wish to start by imposing changes, especially when the hospitality offered to him was so heartfelt.

Besides, Aditya reasoned, a few days of indulging in the local cuisine wouldn't significantly impact his health. He was in good shape, and his body could handle the temporary adjustment. The additional fat from the day's heavy meal would be burned off on the streets, under the guise of a simple jog. But in reality, each stride would be a calculated move, blending in, gathering information and staying one step ahead in a game where the stakes were life and death.

Over the next week, Aditya's days were filled with the vibrant chaos of the city's streets, the cacophony of marketplaces and the myriads of scents that wafted from food stalls and spice vendors. This exploration was not just a mission requirement but also a means for Aditya to blend in, to become a familiar face in the neighbourhood and to understand the pulse of Karachi, a city as complex as it was beautiful.

He had arranged a meeting with a contact recommended by Altaf, a key supplier of dry fruits and spices that were exported to London. The man, a seasoned businessman with a keen sense for opportunities, was happy to learn Hassan's plans to expand the business in the UK. 'As you know, the demand for authentic Pakistani products in the UK is on the rise,' Hassan (Aditya) began, his voice confident. 'I'm planning to open more outlets across the UK. Our focus will be on dry fruits and spices, showcasing the richness of Pakistani cuisine.'

The supplier nodded; his interest piqued. 'Well, the more the merrier. The quality of Pakistani spices is unmatched. But the competition is very high. Expanding your outlets could tap into suppliers like us in Pakistan looking for new markets.'

Their conversation delved into the specifics, like potential supply chains, quality assurance and the logistical challenges of exporting goods from Karachi to London. For Aditya, this meeting was a delicate balancing act. Every word, every negotiation, had to reinforce his cover as a businessman keen on promoting Pakistani products abroad. The supplier, convinced of Hassan's sincerity and business acumen, agreed to a partnership. 'I believe this could be the beginning of a fruitful collaboration,' he said, extending his hand in agreement. As they shook hands, Aditya felt a twinge of satisfaction. This business venture, while a cover, provided him with the perfect guise to explore more sensitive areas and establish contacts that could unknowingly aid his mission.

In the days that followed, Hassan was seen engaging with various vendors, sampling products and discussing business in the bustling markets of Karachi. To any onlooker, he was a man passionate about his venture, eager to bridge the gap between Pakistani traditions and the Western market.

Aditya's next move was as bold as it was dangerous. His cover as Hassan Raza had so far been carefully maintained through his engagement in the dry fruits and spices trade. However, for the expansion of his business interests into carpets, he chose to venture into a more treacherous terrain – PoK, strictly referred to as 'Azad Kashmir' in Pakistan. A territory that once belonged to India but was snatched by Pakistan. This region, a subject of longstanding dispute between India and Pakistan, held a different significance for

Aditya beyond its geopolitical strife. He had traversed its rugged landscapes before, not as a businessman, but as an Indian covert operative executing missions with precision and stealth. The irony of his situation was not lost on him; he was about to enter the same territory from the opposite side, under a completely different guise.

Aditya had spent hours studying the carpet trade, familiarizing himself with the types of weaves and patterns, and the specific demands of the international market. He understood that to convincingly play the part, he needed to speak the language of the trade with as much fluency as he did his cover identity.

Middle of January 2022.

Aditya was travelling in a private taxi through the icy chill of PoK. The region's rugged beauty lay under a pale winter sun, its valleys dusted with snow and silence. Yet the serenity was deceptive; tension hung in the air like a thin mist, a constant reminder of the occupation and the conflict that continued to shape its existence. Aditya, as 'Hassan,' engaged with local artisans and traders, his keen eyes observing more than the quality of their craftsmanship.

As he approached the first major checkpoint, his heart rate accelerated, not out of fear but a heightened sense of alertness. The checkpoint was manned by a group of stern-faced security forces, their scrutiny palpable as they signalled his vehicle to stop. Aditya's preparations for this moment were about to be tested.

'Where are you headed?' one of the officers asked, peering into the vehicle with a mix of curiosity and suspicion.

'To the northern regions, for business,' Aditya replied, his voice steady. 'I deal in carpets, and I'm exploring new sources for my collection.'

The officer's gaze lingered on him, then moved to inspect the vehicle. Aditya handed over his identification and the fabricated documents that supported his cover story. The seconds stretched into what felt like hours as the officer examined the papers.

Going from Karachi to Azad Kashmir to buy carpets, Aditya had to answer the obvious question – why Azad Kashmir when Karachi or Lahore produced carpets in far larger numbers? But he was prepared to answer – he wanted to put Azad Kashmir's carpet makers on the world map when India kept issuing threats of 'recovering Azad Kashmir' from Pakistan. As a Pakistani, he considered it his duty to prove that these carpets were sought after by collectors and enthusiasts worldwide.

While the security officer bought his story, he still had more questions as he asked, 'You're aware of the situation in the areas you're heading to?'

'Of course,' Aditya responded with a confidence that belied his inner vigilance. 'But business must go on, and opportunities in those regions are too valuable to ignore.'

After a tense pause, the officer handed back the documents and signalled for him to proceed. 'Be careful,' he said, a warning that Aditya took to heart.

As he drove away from the checkpoint, a surge of relief washed over him, quickly replaced by a renewed focus. Each checkpoint was a hurdle overcome, each mile travelled a step deeper into enemy territory, and with every successful interaction, Aditya's confidence grew. He was becoming Hassan Raza, the carpet dealer, in every gesture and word, even as Aditya Singh, the covert operative, navigated through the underlying currents of his mission.

The response Hassan (Aditya) got from the dealers in Muzaffarabad, New Mirpur City and Rawalkot was overwhelming. Each conversation, while centred around carpets, was an opportunity for him to listen for undercurrents of dissent, to identify shifts in power and to detect any presence that might be of interest to Indian intelligence.

While planning to return to Karachi, Aditya's journey took an unexpected turn. The rugged terrain and the relentless demands of the road finally took their toll on his vehicle, which stuttered to a halt amidst the breathtaking landscape. Stranded, with the nearest town of Rawalkot a long way still, Aditya was forced to recalibrate his plans. The vehicle, stubborn in its refusal to start despite his attempts, left him with no choice but to seek shelter for the night.

The stay was an unplanned detour in his carefully planned mission, a night spent in a modest roadside inn that offered a glimpse into the lives of the people caught in the crossfire of geopolitics. It was a sobering experience, one that underscored the intricacies of the region he was crossing.

By morning, it was clear that the vehicle would not be fixed anytime soon. The mechanic, apologetic yet powerless against the scarcity of parts in such a remote area, suggested Aditya take a bus back to Karachi. Though far from ideal, Aditya accepted the situation with the adaptability that had become second nature to him. His mission, after all, was built on the ability to deal with uncertainties.

The bus journey back to Karachi was a far cry from the solitude of his vehicle. Packed with passengers, the bus was a microcosm of Pakistan itself – vibrant, diverse and teeming with stories. Aditya found himself amidst a cacophony of bantering, the air thick with the scent of body sweat, spices, flour, corn and marijuana smoke, and, of course, full of the warmth of humanity.

It was here, amidst the hum of the bus's engine and the chatter of its passengers, that Aditya met Khalid, a young man in his twenties, with a keen intellect and a thirst for knowledge that belied his years. Khalid, intrigued by the lone traveller who seemed out of place yet entirely at ease, struck up a conversation.

'You're not from around here, are you?' Khalid asked, his curiosity piqued by Aditya's accent, which, despite his efforts, carried traces of his time abroad.

'I've been living outside of Pakistan for a while,' Aditya replied, careful to weave his response within the fabric of his cover. 'But I'm here on business, exploring products for trade.'

The conversation flowed easily from there, with Khalid expressing his own aspirations and frustrations with the limitations imposed by his surroundings. He was a young man caught between the desire for progress and the chains of circumstance. Despite being a graduate, he had to work as a 'helper' in a motor garage in Karachi, let alone getting a chance to work as a driver.

Aditya, for his part, saw in Khalid not just a chance encounter but a potential asset. Here was a young, ambitious individual who could, with the right guidance, provide valuable insights into the local dynamics. Aditya's mission was to gather intelligence, and nurturing contacts was a vital part of that process. The bus journey became a conduit for a deeper understanding of the region's pulse, with Khalid unknowingly offering Aditya glimpses into the local sentiments and challenges.

Upon reaching the crowded bus terminus in Karachi, Aditya and Khalid disembarked into the sea of people that flowed in and out of the station. The journey had forged an unexpected connection between them, one that Aditya was keen to explore for its potential value to his mission. Khalid, with his local insights and evident ambition, represented an opportunity that Aditya couldn't ignore.

As they stood amidst the chaos, Aditya broached the subject that had been on his mind since their conversation on the bus. 'Khalid, I'm in need of a driver for some of my business endeavours here. Someone who knows the city well. Would you be interested?'

The offer seemed to light a spark in Khalid. His eyes widened with a mixture of surprise and excitement. After all, a job offer from this businessman was an unexpected turn of fortune. 'For sure, Janaab! I would be honoured. I can start right away. This ... this is a blessing,' he stammered, the excitement palpable in his voice.

Aditya observed Khalid's reaction casually, noting the eagerness and readiness to leap at the opportunity. It was a good sign, indicative of Khalid's desire to improve his circumstances, but Aditya was well aware of the need for caution. 'I appreciate your enthusiasm, Khalid. But let's not rush into things. I need to sort out a few details on my end first. If the need arises, I'll definitely get in touch. Consider this as me checking your interest for now,' Aditya explained, offering a reassuring smile.

Khalid's excitement simmered down to a hopeful anticipation. 'Of course, Janaab. I understand. Just the thought that you considered me is an honour. Please, take your time. I am here whenever you need me,' he looked for a pen. Aditya gave him one. Khalid scribbled a number on the back of the bus ticket and passed it on to Aditya. 'Don't tell them the purpose of your calling. Just say it is a call from a relative,' Khalid cautioned him.

As they parted ways, Aditya watched Khalid disappear into the crowd, a young man with dreams and aspirations that had momentarily intersected with his own covert objectives. The encounter had been serendipitous, providing Aditya with a local contact who could prove to be an asset in navigating Karachi's intricate landscape.

Back in the solitude of his temporary residence, Aditya contemplated the unfolding layers of his mission. Khalid, with his unguarded enthusiasm and local knowledge, was a reminder of the human element in espionage, a field where relationships could be both a tool and a test.

In the quiet hours of the night, when the bustling city of Karachi had finally surrendered to sleep, Aditya sat awake, his focus solid, and as the night stretched on, he found himself at a crucial juncture in his mission planning. That terrorists were hiding in Pakistan to avoid being caught by the Indian security agencies was an open secret. Being a R&AW operative who had worked on Pakistan earlier, Aditya knew much more. He was aware of terrorists like Zahoor Mistry, Harvinder Singh Sandhu, Syed Khalid Raza, Basheer Ahmed Peer, Paramjeet Singh Panwar – all of whom were given shelter by Pakistan.

Presuming they were alive and around, Aditya prepared a shortlist of candidates to begin the operation. The selection itself was not his to make. His task was to build a full plan and rank the options according to risk, access and deniability. Once his dossier reached Delhi, senior handlers would decide which name from his list would be executed and pass the order through Altaf. It was part of India's largest covert campaign, a war the state would never acknowledge. Operatives like him were assets, not allies. Trust would come only after execution. Until then, he was simply a weapon in the hands of the men who pulled the strings in Delhi.

Under the cover of night in Karachi, Aditya's thoughts drifted back to a crucial moment in history, the hijacking of Indian Airlines Flight IC-814 in 1999. This event, etched in the collective memory of his nation, was a stark reminder of the terror that JeM, led by Rasool Azhar, could unleash. Azhar's release from an Indian prison was the hijackers' demand, a demand that was met, setting a dangerous precedent.

This grim recollection led Aditya's thoughts to the more recent Pulwama attack, another brutal manifestation of JeM's terror under Azhar's guidance. The attack on Indian soil had not just claimed lives but had also stirred a national outcry for decisive action against those who harboured and supported such terrorists.

It was the Pulwama attack that had finally compelled the Indian prime minister to greenlight this mission, assigning the NSD the task of putting an end to the threat posed by these terrorists. Aditya, as one of R&AW's finest, found himself at the heart of this crucial mission, a silent warrior in a foreign land, tasked with delivering justice and safeguarding his country from further harm.

For a fleeting moment, Aditya felt as if fate itself was guiding his mission, a notion that seemed almost too coincidental to be mere chance. The links between past and present terror acts wove a complex web that now entangled him, a silent message from the annals of history urging him forward. Shaking off these philosophical thoughts, Aditya refocused on the task at hand, tapping into his well-honed ability to recall critical details about his adversaries.

He revisited the profiles of the hijackers involved in the IC-814 ordeal, a group that had succeeded in their demands, thereby emboldening the JeM network. Among them was Ibrahim Akhtar, hailing from Bahawalpur, not just Rasool Azhar's brother but also the father of Umar Farooq, the mastermind behind the Pulwama attack. This familial link underscored the generational depth of the terror network, a lineage of hatred and violence passed down and expanded upon.

Alongside Ibrahim were Shahid Akhtar Sayeed, Sunny Ahmed Qazi, Zahoor Mistry and Shakir. The realization that Shahid, Sunny and Zahoor had roots in Karachi, the very city that now served as Aditya's shadowy battlefield, lent an eerie proximity to the threat. These were not distant enemies plotted on a map; they were real, tangible and alarmingly close.

Aditya's mission in Karachi suddenly felt more personal. The city's happening streets and quiet alleys might well hide these architects of terror, individuals who had directly or indirectly wreaked havoc on countless lives. Knowing that some of the key players in this network were from Karachi added a layer of urgency to his mission. Aditya was not just hunting phantoms of the past; he was tracking down present dangers, with the hope of preventing future tragedies.

The night deepened around him, but Aditya's resolve only grew stronger. Armed with the knowledge of his enemies and the silent approval of fate, he prepared for the daunting task ahead. The streets of Karachi, with their unsuspecting calm, were about to become the stage for a silent hunt. A hunt that Aditya was determined to end with the predators caught in their own trap.

The most chilling episode of the IC-814 hijacking, which haunted every Indian deeply, was the ruthless murder of Rupin Katyal, a 25-year-old man returning with his wife from his honeymoon in Kathmandu. The brutality of his death, his throat slit by Zahoor Mistry, known disturbingly among his peers as 'doctor' for his macabre skill with a knife, was a stark reminder of the sheer inhumanity of these terrorists. Rupin was murdered in cold blood right in front of his wife, who was forcibly restrained by the other hijackers, a scene of horror that played out in the cramped space of the aircraft, leaving an indelible mark of terror on all who witnessed it.

Zahoor's warning to the other passengers, a sinister declaration made as Rupin bled out, underscored the hijackers' merciless resolve and their readiness to inflict further violence. This act of cruelty was not just an assault on an individual but a message of intimidation, meant to subdue and control through fear.

For Aditya, the memory of Rupin Katyal's fate was a grim reminder of the stakes involved in his mission. It reinforced the necessity of bringing individuals like Zahoor Mistry to justice, not just as an operative duty but as a moral imperative. The knowledge that Zahoor was potentially somewhere within Karachi, walking the same streets as Aditya, lent a visceral urgency to his task. The shadows of the city seemed to whisper of the lurking dangers, but Aditya was undeterred; he was ready to ensure that the tragic fate of Rupin Katyal and the suffering of his wife would not be in vain.

Aditya found his thoughts becoming increasingly turbulent. Seeking refuge from the storm inside his mind, he turned to yoga, a practice that had always offered him solace in times of turmoil. The disciplined movements and focused breathing helped to clear the fog of emotions, allowing him to find a moment of peace amidst the chaos.

As he moved through the poses, the tension in his body began to dissipate, and his thoughts gradually untangled. Yoga, with its blend of physical discipline and mental focus, was his sanctuary, a place where the war within could be stilled, if only for a while. Finally, the calm it brought coaxed him into a deep, restorative sleep, a rare escape from the constant vigilance his mission demanded.

The next morning, refreshed by a few hours of sleep and seated in the modest kitchen of his safe house, Aditya sipped ginger tea prepared by Usman, the housekeeper whose culinary skills had become a small comfort in his undercover life. The warmth of the tea, coupled with the clarity brought on by last night's meditation, allowed Aditya to focus on the task ahead.

It was in that moment of quiet reflection, warmed by the sharpness of ginger and the calm that followed his yoga, that Aditya accepted what had come from Delhi. Zahoor Mistry, the man whose cruelty aboard IC-814 had shadowed him for years, was to be his first target. The instruction had reached him through Altaf in London, and Aditya took it without hesitation. This was not revenge. It was a calculated beginning, a move against the terror that had scarred his country for far too long.

Aditya understood the challenges that lay ahead. Tracking down Zahoor in a crowd of 15 million people in a city like Karachi, where every shadow could be an ally or an enemy, would require all of his skill, patience and cunning. But he was ready. The decision set a clear path forward, and with the calm determination that had settled over him, Aditya was prepared to begin his hunt.

8

Revenge Is a Dish Best Served Cold

February 2022.

The mission transcended mere orders; it was Aditya's personal crusade for justice. Each step he took was shadowed by the looming spectre of danger, yet the haunting memory of Rupin Katyal and the myriad souls tormented by Zahoor's cruelty steeled his determination. Dawn unfurled over Karachi, revealing the city's veiled threats and silent narratives. Amid this awakening, Aditya moved, a phantom avenger threading through the alleys, his heart set on rectifying the scars etched by history.

In London, shrouded in secrecy, Aditya had made a connection through the dark web – a Russian who provided him with something invaluable for his mission: untraceable SIM cards. These cards, now tucked away in his gear, were his lifeline, each one a beacon in the murky waters of espionage he dealt with. With the dawn of his confrontation nearing, the time had come to activate them. Alongside, he had packed spare phones, each destined for a single use before being destroyed. This was his fail-safe, a meticulous strategy to erase any digital footprints that might lead back to him. The precision of his plan left no room for error; every move was calculated to keep the shadow of suspicion from his trail.

Aditya discreetly activated one of the SIM cards and reached out to a trusted informer in Delhi, seeking a bridge to Karachi's underbelly. The answer to his call was a name wrapped in notoriety: Colonel Ghulam Mohiuddin Cheema, a shadow in the retired ranks of the army, now the mastermind behind the city's 'Velvet Underground' events. This wasn't just any gathering spot but a nexus for the elite and the notorious, where drugs, women and secrets changed hands under the guise of revelry. Cheema was a legend, his connections spanning the upper echelons of Pakistan's military, intelligence and even the criminal underworld. While the parties he threw were lucrative, it was his trade in information that truly enriched him, making him a formidable player in a dangerous game of double allegiances.

Under the cover of another new dawn, Aditya carefully unwrapped a fresh SIM card, a potential key to unlocking his next move. He dialled the number of his 'uncle' Altaf in London, a man whose knowledge of Karachi's underground could prove invaluable. Altaf, familiar with the shadowy figure of Colonel Cheema and his infamous gatherings, knew the significance of Aditya's request. With a promise as cryptic as it was reassuring, Altaf simply replied, 'Consider it done.'

The wait was a test of patience and nerve. Within a tense 24 hours, the landline at Altaf's residence in Gulshan-e-Iqbal crackled to life, a voice on the other end cutting through the silence with news that set Aditya's heart racing. An invitation had been secured; Colonel Cheema was expecting Hassan Raza at the next Velvet Underground event. This call was not just a message; it was the opening of a door into a world where every shadow could be friend or foe, and every face masked a deeper story.

In the heart of a sprawling metropolis, home to 15 million souls and notorious for its fractious political landscape, gang skirmishes and violent territorial disputes, a luxury hotel hosted an event that stood in stark contrast to the city's usual headlines. The clock had just swept past midnight, signalling the start of a private gathering cloaked in exclusivity and opulence.

The venue, covered in the soft, intricate light of chandeliers, buzzed with the energy of select guests shedding the limitations of their day-to-day lives. The air vibrated with the pulsating rhythms of electro-funk, courtesy of Daft Punk, masterfully curated by a young DJ whose tanned skin and bold tattoos mirrored the audacity of the night. The bar, a focal point of activity, was a flurry of motion as guests looked for the bartender's attention, eager to sip on crafted cocktails and let the music wash over them.

Amidst a scene of decadent abandon, men in sharp suits and ties stood out, their conversations punctuated by the glow of their cigarettes, a visual sign of their attempt to blend leisure with the remnants of formality. Meanwhile, the dance floor was a swirl of movement, with women in slinky dresses moving with a grace and confidence that asked for attention, their forms silhouetted against the flickering lights, personifying the essence of the party's unspoken promise: a night of escape, however fleeting, from the chaos that lay beyond the hotel's fortified walls.

As the rhythm of the party ebbed and flowed around him, Aditya found himself drawn into a conversation that peeled back another layer of this hidden world. 'This is a private affair,' the host, Colonel Cheema said with a sense of pride, his hands holding a Cuban cigar and Johnny Walker Blue Label in an exquisitely cut French whiskey glass. 'We steer clear of social media, Facebook … It's all word-of-mouth among friends.'

A woman, her movements a dance to the music's pulse, leaned closer, her voice a blend of defiance and longing. 'Without pubs, this is our sanctuary,' she confessed, revealing the void that these gatherings filled in their lives. As the night wore on, she turned to Aditya with an invitation, her eyes sparkling with the promise of continued adventure. 'The night doesn't end here. We're heading to the beach; will you join us?'

Aditya's mind raced. The allure was tempting, but the stakes were high. The mastermind of this underground party was no ordinary host but an ex-army tactician with a mind trained in deception and strategy. Aditya couldn't afford to forget his true identity, that of an Indian spy on foreign soil, where every friendly gesture could mask a trap. The connection with Altaf provided little reassurance; in the grand chessboard of espionage, pawns could easily be sacrificed.

Feigning concern for domestic harmony, Aditya demurred, 'My wife ... she wouldn't take kindly to my late return.' It was a cautious retreat, a move to maintain his cover and handle the intricate dance of trust and suspicion. In a world where every decision could lead to discovery or disaster, Aditya chose the path of caution, aware that in the shadows of espionage, not every hand extended in friendship is free of ulterior motives.

In the dimly lit secretive ambience of the hotel bar, now a private sanctuary for the remnants of the night's elite, Aditya found an unexpected ally in Cheema. The room they had occupied earlier was no longer available, leading them towards the seclusion of the bar, where conversations flowed as freely as the drinks. Amidst the clink of glasses and the murmur of late-night confessions, Aditya wove a delicate façade of feeling high and emotional, in a strategic display of vulnerability.

Cheema, with a tactician's eye, watched Hassan with a mix of curiosity and calculation. There was an unspoken understanding in the air as Cheema sought to uncover the true purpose behind Hassan's persona. The interruption by the waiter with the bill, a mundane conclusion to an evening of fun was met with Cheema's contempt, a silent reminder of his stature in this hidden world. Nobody dared to place a bill until he had asked.

Aditya's response to the situation, however, was anything but ordinary. In a move that blurred the lines between pretense and reality, he fumbled with a wad of US dollars, the 100-dollar notes fluttering to the floor like leaves in a sudden gust. The display was ostentatious, perhaps too much so, leaving Cheema to ponder the true nature of this man who seemed to oscillate between control and abandon. As they both stooped to gather the scattered notes, Cheema's respect for Aditya deepened, not just for the wealth he seemingly commanded but for the enigma he presented, that of a puzzle Cheema was now eager to solve.

As the night drew to a close, the lines of their alliance were drawn, not in trust, but in the unspoken promise of mutual benefit amidst the clandestine chessboard of espionage and duplicity.

Aditya steered the conversation towards the heart of his mission with a casual mention of 'Ibrahim Zahoor Mistry'. The name seemed to spark a flicker of amusement in Cheema, his smile tinged with mischief, as if recognizing the weight of the name within the intricate web of Karachi's underworld. Aditya, perceptive to the subtle cues, chose not to dwell on Cheema's reaction, pushing forward with his fabricated narrative of personal vendetta.

He crafted a tale of betrayal, painting Mistry as the villain who had wronged his family, specifically targeting his brother-in-law in a fraudulent business scheme. Cheema, sensing the emotional charge behind the story, offered Aditya the figurative rope to weave his narrative further, eager to see how deep the rabbit hole of deceit and revenge went.

Aditya, seizing the opportunity, let his guard down or so it appeared. His accusations against Mistry became more pointed, his story imbued with the fervour of a man wronged, seeking not just retribution but a path to reclaim what was lost.

Cheema, ever the strategist, was not easily swayed by tales of betrayal and loss. His instincts honed from years within the military and the murky world of information trade, whispered of deeper currents beneath the surface of Hassan's story. With a discerning eye, he probed further, challenging the authenticity of Aditya's vendetta against Mistry. 'Are you truly laying all cards on the table?' he asked with scepticism.

Aditya, understanding the delicacy of the moment, peeled back another layer of his cooked-up narrative, introducing a more personal story. 'You're right,' he admitted, his voice carrying the weight of untold agony. 'It was, to be honest, my sister who bore the brunt of Mistry's cruelty.' He wove a tale of deceit that cut closer to the bone, a promise of marriage, a future dangled before his sister's eyes like a mirage, only to be cruelly snatched away. Mistry's withdrawal, shrouded in mystery, left his sister teetering on the edge of despair, contemplating the unthinkable. Aditya's story, whether fact or fabrication, was delivered with a convincing blend of sorrow and rage, painting him as a brother driven to the brink by the suffering of his kin.

As the night drew to its inevitable close, Cheema, with a glance at his watch, subtly reminded Aditya of the price of their extended stay and conversation. Aditya, unfazed by the implication, responded with the ease of a man for whom money was no object. The casual act of slipping a stack of hundred-dollar bills into Cheema's jacket pocket in a gesture of gratitude and a down payment on future alliances.

Standing up, Aditya swayed slightly, his performance of inebriation not yet over, as he requested Cheema to call him a taxi. Cheema, ever the pragmatist, leaned in close, his voice low with a hint of amusement at the oversight. 'Hassan,' he cautioned, 'you can't pay your way through Karachi with American dollars.' It was a gentle prod towards practicality, a reminder of the nuances of blending in, even in something as mundane as currency.

Aditya's reaction was swift, a laugh that cut through the quiet of the bar, rich with the irony of the situation. Handing over the remaining dollars, he played his part to the hilt, the loud, boisterous laugh a cover for the strategic exchange taking place under the guise of drunken folly. 'Enough to get me rupees?' he joked, his laughter masking the calculated depth of his ploy.

This exchange, layered with subtext, was more than a simple transaction; it was a dance of wits and wills between two men each playing their part in a much larger game. For Aditya, it was another step in weaving his persona of Hassan into the fabric of Karachi's underworld, a means to an end in his quest. For Cheema, the generous display of wealth was proof of Hassan's potential as a lucrative ally, further entangling their fates in the shadowy world they inhabited.

As Aditya made his way toward the hotel's grand lobby, his steps measured and purposeful, the night's transaction hung in the air between him and Cheema like a silent pact. Outside, the promise of anonymity awaited in the form of waiting taxis, their engines idling softly in the quiet of the early hours, ready to whisk him away from this chapter of his mission.

Cheema watched him go, both admiring and intrigued. There was a glimmer of respect, perhaps even a hint of camaraderie, in his gaze as he called out, 'See you soon, Hassan bhai.' The words, though casual, carried the weight of an unspoken agreement, a recognition of the roles each would play in the unfolding drama that lay ahead.

As the taxi pulled away, blending into the web of Karachi's restless streets, the night's events settled into the backdrop of Aditya's mind, pieces of a larger puzzle he was determined to solve. The road ahead was fraught with risk, but for a spy deep in enemy territory, risk was a familiar companion, and every encounter, a step closer to the heart of the maze.

Two days after their late-night encounter, Cheema's message arrived like a beacon, cutting through the uncertainty that had begun to cloud Aditya's mission. The message was brief and a nudge in the right direction. 'Zahid Akhund' and 'Crescent Furniture' in Akhtar Colony were the keys Cheema offered. To anyone else, it might have seemed like a simple lead, but to Aditya, whose life was woven with threads of subterfuge and deduction, it was a revelation. His understood that Zahid Akhund and Zahoor Ibrahim Mistry were one and the same.

February 2022.

Akhtar Colony, a neighbourhood nestled in the eastern part of Karachi, became his new focus. Its proximity, a mere 19 kilometres from his temporary base, meant that the pieces of the puzzle Cheema had handed him were now aligning.

Navigating the streets of Karachi to reach Akhtar Colony was a task that required little effort. A 30-minute drive was all it would take to cover the distance between him and his target, yet the journey was laden with the weight of anticipation and the silent tension of what lay ahead.

In the cool embrace of mid-February, Karachi's weather remained a mild companion to those navigating its bustling streets. Dressed in an olive-green Pathani suit, his attire blended tradition with a hint of military precision, the brown jacket adding a layer of nondescript authority. His branded sneakers whispered of affluence, a stark contrast to the otherwise down-to-earth ensemble, while the dark Ray-Ban goggles shielded his eyes.

Aditya's beard, neatly trimmed, was a silent representation of his personal ethos, a deliberate choice that distanced him from the rugged, untamed aesthetic often associated with the Taliban. This carefully curated appearance was not just a matter of personal pride but a calculated element of his cover, designed to project a specific image to those who might notice him.

The journey to Crescent Furniture was a study in caution and strategy. Aditya had committed to memory the intricacies of routes that crisscrossed the neighbourhood of Akhtar Colony, a mental map that allowed him to navigate with the ease of a local. Yet, his movements were anything but predictable. He changed his course repeatedly; a serpentine path designed to confuse and shake off any potential followers. This was not mere paranoia but the ingrained habit of a man who knew the stakes of the game he played.

Aditya's arrival at Crescent Furniture, after a deliberately prolonged journey, was a moment charged with a complex mix of emotions. The façade of the furniture shop, rather than its opulence or the quality of goods it housed, sparked a visceral reaction within him. There was no awe at the craftsmanship or the luxury items that adorned the showroom; instead, a deep-seated anger coursed through him, a palpable sense of injustice at the sight before him.

This was not just any business owner thriving in the heart of Karachi. This was Zahid Akhund, previously known as Zahoor Ibrahim Mistry, a man whose hands were stained with the blood of innocents, a figure whose past was a mosaic of terror and violence. The wealth that seemed to flow through the premises of Crescent Furniture was a stark, infuriating contrast to the memories Aditya carried of the victims, of Rupin Katyal and the countless others whose lives were forever altered by Mistry's actions.

The source of this wealth was immaterial to Aditya, whether it was the patronage of the ISI or the funds of JeM, the terror group to which Mistry was inextricably linked. What mattered was the glaring reality that a man responsible for heinous acts of terror was now masquerading as a successful businessman, shielded by the veneer of respectability that wealth and power often provide.

As Aditya engaged the workers in conversation, feigning interest in the luxury items that filled the space, his guise as a potential buyer was convincing. Yet, beneath the surface, his true intent simmered in a keen, unwavering focus on the man he had come to confront.

When Zahid Akhund, the proprietor known to the world as a legitimate businessman but to Aditya as Zahoor Mistry, the terrorist, made his appearance, the air seemed to shift. Mistry's physical transformation over the years, for instance his overweight frame, the conspicuous baldness contrasting with a thick beard, did little to mask the essence of the man Aditya recognized as the hijacker of the IC-814 and killer of many. Despite the changes time had wrought upon his appearance, the underlying coldness, the demeanour of a man capable of ruthless violence, was unmistakable.

Aditya's observation was swift, his years of training and experience allowing him to pierce through the disguise of normalcy that Mistry had adopted. Aditya maintained his composure, his smile a mask that hid the turmoil and resolve churning within.

His words to Mistry were measured as he spoke of the unaffordability of the goods; Crescent Furniture was beyond his reach, contrary to the belief that led him there. Aditya's mention of divine will and his polite request for permission to leave were not just the concluding remarks of a disappointed customer but a calculated retreat, a step back to reassess and plan his next move. This encounter, brief as it was, served a dual purpose: confirming Mistry's identity and maintaining Aditya's cover, setting the stage for the next phase of his mission.

Zahoor's interest was piqued by Aditya's style of approach, an openness prompting him to seek the name of this customer who stood out from the rest. Aditya's response, 'Hassan Raza,' was delivered with ease. Zahoor's request to Aditya to stay a bit longer was a move laden with hospitality yet underscored by an undercurrent of strategy. The offer of a chair and the initial suggestion of sharbat, quickly revised to tea in light of the winter which was still not over, came from the hospitality that marked Pakistani culture. Aditya's acceptance, coupled with a sheepish smile and an apology came from strategy. He got more time to spend with his target.

Over cups of tea, the atmosphere between Aditya and Zahoor subtly shifted, giving way to a more relaxed conversation as they traversed the length and breadth of the shop. Zahoor, with the pride of an owner, showcased his collection, pointing out the craftsmanship and variety that Crescent Furniture boasted. He made an offer to Aditya – he would tailor a selection that fit both Hassan's needs and budget.

Aditya's request to take pictures seemed innocuous, a potential buyer capturing images for consideration, yet it was a carefully calculated move. Each snapshot was not just of the furniture but of the layout, the exits, the security features, every detail that could serve as intelligence for his mission. And then the pretext of using the washroom, guided by one of Zahoor's men to the backyard, offered Aditya a valuable glimpse into the shop's back-end operations and layout.

~

Upon his return, Aditya's expressions of gratitude, coupled with the promise of a forthcoming list and a hopeful return, were laced with deeper implications. His polite departure, peppered with the respectful 'inshallah' and a deference to Zahoor's ability to accommodate his future needs, was the closing act of a meticulously performed play of deception.

As he retraced his steps back to Gulshan, employing the same cautious, convoluted route to avoid detection or tailing, Aditya's mind was racing with the information gathered during his visit. This reconnaissance, disguised as a shopping trip, was a crucial step in laying the groundwork for what was to come.

In espionage, deciding on a plan means looking closely at the targets' living conditions, their security and how much they're protected by the authorities. The operative – in this case Aditya – also sizes up each target's physical shape and quickness, figuring out if they could fight back or overpower him if they came face to face.

Additionally, the layout of where these people lived was key in Aditya's planning. He looked at how easy or hard it was to get into these places, if there were any CCTV cameras watching and how everything was arranged. Places with a lot of cameras or tough landscapes made the mission trickier, raising the chances of getting caught or failing.

Walking into and out of the furniture shop, Aditya saw no security measures. It seemed Zahoor had become a forgotten detail, even to ordinary Indians, allowing him to live with little protection. Inside the shop, there was a CCTV camera, but none outside; Aditya didn't spot any. There were no guards around either. He noticed a Honda City parked outside, possibly Zahoor's. He made sure to remember its license plate.

Aditya delved into the details of his surroundings and potential operational paths. By scrutinizing the layout around Crescent Furniture, he identified multiple escape routes, a crucial aspect of his plan that ensured flexibility and safety post-operation. Streets No. 4 and 5 provided alternative avenues for a getaway, allowing him to adapt to unforeseen circumstances or threats that could emerge after the strike.

Next morning, Aditya sent a discreet message, via landline, requesting Khalid to contact Hassan in Gulshan.

The confirmation regarding the ownership of the Honda City parked outside Crescent Furniture added another layer to Aditya's understanding of Zahoor's alias and operational security. Discovering that the vehicle was registered under the name Zahid Akhund, listed as a businessman, validated Aditya's suspicions about the identity Zahoor had assumed to blend into his surroundings and live under the radar, possibly with ISI's protection.

Khalid's arrival, coinciding with Aditya's return from his evening jog, stirred not only curiosity but also a hint of unease in Usman. His concern was whether Khalid was brought in as a potential replacement. Aditya, ever observant, didn't miss the undercurrents of tension betrayed by Usman's body language. With a reassuring attitude, he addressed Usman's unspoken worries, advising him to focus on his responsibilities and assuring him of his irreplaceable value in their current setup.

Aditya inquired about the timeframe required for Khalid to acquire a motorcycle in decent shape; not a brand-new one, but rather a used vehicle. Khalid responded, 'It could take one to two days through a second-hand dealer, but merely 30 minutes if I go to Chor Bazaar.' Aditya recommended Khalid went for the second option and provided Khalid enough cash for the purchase. Khalid was taken aback by such an unexpected gesture. He gazed at his new employer, filled with astonishment. Aditya urged him to depart immediately to ensure he wouldn't miss out on the day's best deal at Chor Bazaar.

He next tasked Khalid with another assignment.

In the shadowed streets of Akhtar Colony, Khalid moved with a purpose, his eyes scanning every corner, every face. Tasked with mapping the security landscape around Crescent Furniture, his movements were discreet, his observations sharp. The deal was simple: observe, report and ask no questions. The reward for his silence was going to be handsome, a golden rule in Aditya's playbook.

Aditya, operating under the alias Hassan, knew the stakes. Khalid, for all his usefulness, was a pawn in a much larger game. A game where loose ends were tied up, one way or another. Trust was a luxury, and Aditya spared no expense to ensure loyalty. Yet, the shadow of doubt lingered – Khalid's ignorance was his shield, but also his Achilles' heel.

As Khalid returned, his report in hand, the wheels were set in motion. The absence of guards, the scant surveillance, each detail a piece in Aditya's meticulous plan. In the world of espionage, knowledge was power, silence was currency and betrayal was met with swift retribution.

Aditya's mind was clear, his resolve unwavering. If Khalid ever crossed the line, became a threat, Aditya knew what had to be done. Years in the shadows had taught him well – the mission above all, no matter the cost.

Khalid's news cleared the decks for Aditya: Zahoor Mistry, a ghost from the past, living with barely a shadow of security. Just two CCTV cameras stood between Aditya and his quarry, their electronic eyes easily blinded.

'Want them gone?' Khalid's words were a spark to Aditya's resolve.

'What's the risk?' Aditya asked, the wheels turning.

'Leave it to me. I've got people,' Khalid assured, a hint of pride in his voice.

Money exchanged hands, no names, no trails. In the cloak of night, the cameras vanished, a silent proof of Aditya's reach and Khalid's street savvy. The path to Zahoor was now clear, the stage set for a confrontation years in the making. Aditya's pulse quickened at the thought. The game was on, and he was closer than ever to the endgame.

Aditya was at a critical moment, needing to finalize a date that would align with their intricate plans. Meanwhile, Khalid, eagerly anticipating a sizeable reward from Aditya, was preparing for his journey home for Shab-e-Meraj, a night of deep spiritual significance commemorating Prophet Muhammad's (SAW or 'peace be upon Him') ascension through the heavens. Celebrated on the last day of February, it was an occasion marked by devout worship and collective prayers in significant religious locales.

Khalid's aspirations to return to his hometown of Rawalkot on 27 February were thwarted by Aditya's sudden cancellation of his leave, plunging him into a state of dejection. This year, the stakes were higher for Khalid. The windfall he had received was beyond anything he had ever imagined. He had envisioned returning home, laden with gifts and surprises from Karachi, transforming the ordinary into the extraordinary for his family and friends.

'Janaab, my family, they're waiting for me. I've never ... we've never had a chance like this before,' Khalid said, his voice tinged with a mix of hope and disappointment, reflecting his humble background and the rarity of such opportunities.

Aditya, understanding the delicate balance of emotions at play, reassured him, 'I know this means a lot to you, Khalid. And I assure you, we'll make it work. Think of this as an investment in our future. Your family will have many more celebrations like this, I promise.'

Despite the reassurance, Khalid couldn't help but feel a twinge of suspicion about the lavish expenditure on him. His concerns were not just about the money but also about the underlying intentions.

'Janaab, it's a lot of money … I know you are very generous, but why?' Khalid ventured cautiously, acutely aware of his own socio-economic standing in comparison to Hassan's. So, he added, 'Pardon my tongue sir … but we are very poor people … we know nobody in case we're in trouble or … questioned.'

Aditya met his gaze, a reassuring smile playing on his lips. 'Let's just say, your skills are indispensable to me right now. This isn't about the date or money; it's about trust. Can I trust you, Khalid?'

Khalid weighed his options, the money in his hand a tangible proof of Aditya's need for his services. Finally, he nodded, the suspicion in his eyes dimming. 'You can, Janaab. You have my word.' After a pause, Aditya again said, this time with dash of warning, 'Khalid, trust is the currency we trade in. I see the value you bring. So, this money is just my way of acknowledging that. This is just the beginning.'

As Khalid pocketed the money, Aditya knew he had once again addressed the tricky waters of trust and suspicion. Khalid's loyalty, for now, was secured, his curiosity satisfied by the promise of wealth and a carefully woven narrative of mutual reliance. The path was clear for what needed to be done, with Khalid unwittingly playing his part in a larger scheme he barely understood. Aditya bid him with 'Shabba khair' and gave with two new tasks: Khalid was to follow Zahid Akhund when he got back home from his shop, note the distance and time he took.

After Khalid left, a thought occurred to Aditya, leading him to reach out to Zahoor directly. However, Zahoor himself wasn't available to take the call. Instead, his assistant picked up, informing Aditya that due to the observance of Shab-e-Meraj on the twenty-eighth, the shop would remain closed, suggesting they meet on the first of March instead. The assistant explained that after the night's celebrations, Zahoor would likely arrive later than usual, recommending Hassan plan his visit for some time after lunch to ensure Zahoor's presence.

Aditya, seizing the opportunity to nail down specifics, pressed for a more definite time. He explained that he would be travelling a considerable distance to make the meeting and intended to bring a substantial amount of cash for the transaction. The prospect of waiting indefinitely, without a clear sense of Zahoor's arrival, was less than ideal under these circumstances. In the background, Zahoor's voice sounded faintly, offering a direct instruction to his assistant. 'Tell him I'll be there by 2.30 p.m.' This piece of information was exactly what Aditya needed, allowing him to strategize his approach with more confidence, knowing when exactly his target would be at the shop.

The morning after Shab-e-Meraj, under a clear Tuesday sky, Zahoor stepped into his Honda City. Dressed in a sky-blue Pathani suit paired with light brown loafers, he felt the comfortable familiarity of his neighbourhood in Defence Housing Authority (DHA), Phase V, part of the Clifton Cantonment. That day, like any other day, he was heading to his shop in Akhtar Colony, expecting the usual 15-minute drive. The weather was on his side – clear skies with a gentle breeze that made the drive more than pleasant. As he steered the familiar streets, Zahoor felt he had little to worry about. His life, predictable and peaceful under the protection of ISI, gave him no cause for concern.

But today was different, and danger lurked in the shadows of normalcy. Unknown to Zahoor, as he smoothly passed the bustling market of DHA Phase V, a pair of watchful eyes fixed on him. Two men, blending into the morning crowd, had taken a keen interest in him. With stealth and determination, they started following him. Zahoor, absorbed in the comfort of his routine, didn't notice the silent threat that had started to tail him. The city of Karachi, with its blend of the mundane and the hidden, was about to show Zahoor a side he had never expected.

Khalid was a natural when it came to handling vehicles, and his skills were on full display as he manoeuvred the newly acquired motorcycle through the streets of Karachi, maintaining just the right distance behind Zahoor's car. Aditya, sitting behind him, occasionally leaned forward to whisper instructions, ensuring they kept their target in sight without drawing attention.

'Keep this pace, Khalid. We don't want to spook him,' Aditya murmured, his voice muffled by the scarf wrapped around his face, a makeshift barrier against the city's pollution and the unseasonably cool breeze.

Khalid nodded slightly; his focus unwavering. The helmet hid any expression, but his grip on the handlebars was steady and confident.

Both men were dressed in nondescript bikers' jackets, the kind that were sold on Karachi's pavements, and blended perfectly with the city's bustling motorcycle crowd. Aditya had insisted on this, knowing well the art of blending in. 'We're just two more bikers in the city,' he had said when they set out, the scarf around his face and dark shades over his eyes completing the disguise.

Aditya glanced at Khalid's footwear, noting the floater sandals. It was an unusual choice for a biker, but Khalid seemed to prefer it. With a chuckle, Aditya had copied him, slipping into a similar pair before they embarked on their mission.

Their attire was meticulously chosen to avoid drawing any undue attention. In a city teeming with people, the key was to remain invisible, and today, they were just two more faces in the crowd, shadowing their unsuspecting quarry with a blend of caution and precision.

The motorcycle's registration plate bore a number that didn't exist in any official record, a fake, sourced from Chor Bazaar. Hidden within their jackets, they also carried a second set of plates, a contingency plan whispered between them in hushed tones.

'If anyone catches on to the first number, we switch to the second. No trails,' Aditya instructed quietly, his eyes scanning their surroundings for any sign of suspicion. Khalid, with a nod, patted the inner pocket of his jacket where the spare plates and a screwdriver were safely tucked away. 'Got it. Always one step ahead,' he replied, his voice barely audible over the hum of the city around them.

Khalid might not have grasped the full extent of Hassan's plans, but he was swept up in the thrill of it all, feeling like he was the protagonist in his own adventure. For once, he was doing something that felt significant. Deep down, he recognized that not everything they were doing was by the book. Yet, the concept of 'righteousness' seemed abstract, almost alien to him, considering his experiences back in Rawalkot, at the auto garage, and even within his own family.

Throughout his life, Khalid had been familiar with deprivation, his rights overlooked, his dues never fully given. But with Hassan, the equation changed. Hassan didn't just pay him well – he offered him respect and recognition, treasures Khalid had never known.

'Why does this feel different, Janaab? Why do I feel like I'm finally doing something that matters?' Khalid once asked, his voice tinged with a mix of curiosity and doubt, as they prepared for another day's reconnaissance. Aditya's response was measured, carrying a weight that seemed to acknowledge Khalid's internal turmoil. 'Because, my friend, for the first time, you're not just surviving; you're living. You're making a mark; however invisible it might seem.'

That conversation stuck with Khalid, haunting him with its simplicity and truth. It was a stark reminder of his life's stark contrasts between what he had always accepted and what he was now experiencing. Despite the questionable nature of their activities, Khalid felt a sense of belonging and purpose he hadn't found elsewhere. For him, this adventure, under Hassan's guidance, was a leap towards something greater, a chance to redefine his understanding of right and wrong, of respect and recognition.

Zahoor signalled a left turn off Street No. 5 in Akhtar Colony, making his way towards Street No. 3 where his shop, Crescent Furniture, awaited. It was a routine manoeuvre, one he had made countless times before, but today, it marked a critical juncture in a carefully monitored pursuit.

From a distance, Aditya, with his sharp, observant gaze, noted the gradual deceleration of Zahoor's Honda City. 'He's slowing down, Khalid. The shop's just ahead, about 200 yards,' he whispered urgently. 'Now's our chance. Close in on him before he reaches the shop. We need to speak with him outside.'

Khalid nodded, a silent signal of understanding, and expertly reduced the distance between them and the Honda City, ensuring they remained inconspicuous. Aditya's voice, low and steady, carried a final piece of instruction, 'Keep the engine running, and just give it a gentle rev now and then. We can't afford to draw attention or seem like we're waiting.'

As Khalid manoeuvred the motorcycle closer, the hum of the motorcycle's engine, subtly revving under Khalid's controlled touch, was like a heartbeat, marking time as they prepared to make their move.

Unaware of the pursuit, Zahoor shifted his car into neutral, coming to a gentle stop in front of Crescent Furniture. At that moment, Khalid manoeuvred the motorcycle beside the passenger side of Zahoor's car, positioning Aditya perfectly to initiate contact. With a simple gesture, Aditya signalled Zahoor, who, puzzled but cooperative, rolled down his window to address the stranger, assuming the riders were looking for an address.

Zahoor stepped out, intending to fetch someone from his shop who could assist. However, Aditya's next move cut through the ordinary morning air with the precision of a knife. Stepping closer, he directly addressed Zahoor, uttering his full name Zahoor Ibrahim Mistry, with a chilling familiarity.

Zahoor, taken aback by the mention of his name and the stark, unexpected confrontation, faltered for a moment. His life in Karachi, under the protective gaze of the ISI, had been uneventful until now. The surprise in his eyes was evident as he tried to grasp the situation, his voice barely a whisper, 'What are you talking about?'

Aditya, revealing his true intent, took a decisive action that changed everything in a heartbeat. He took a gun out and shot Zahoor in his belly and chest twice. The quiet of the street was shattered, and Zahoor found himself caught in a maelstrom of confusion and fear, his dying thoughts scrambled as he tried to comprehend the turn of events. Zahoor was collapsing on the ground, Aditya shot him thrice, the last two precisely in the head.

As quickly as it had begun, the confrontation ended. Aditya, with a swift move back to the motorcycle, signalled Khalid. The urgency in his voice was palpable. 'Go, now!'

Without a second's hesitation, Khalid accelerated, leaving the scene behind in a blur of motion and dust. Their next destination was going to Chor Bazaar to dispose of the motorcycle where no questions were asked; only money and goods changed hands. He knew the motorcycle would be dismantled within minutes of its disposal. That was how Chor Bazaar functioned.

Slowly, the quiet of Street No. 3 was broken by the gathering crowd, drawn to the shocking sight in front of Crescent Furniture. Employees of Zahoor, alongside bystanders, rushed forward in a desperate attempt to help, but it was too late. The man who had been a respected figure in the furniture business, known to people in the area as Zahid Akhund, lay still, bleeding. Just as Zahoor, had left the young Rupin Katyal to a tragic fate aboard the hijacked aircraft, he too lay motionless, having succumbed to his injuries.

The parallel was stark and somber, a reminder of the cycle of violence that had claimed so many innocent lives. Zahoor's motionless form, now at the centre of a rapidly growing crowd, served as a grim witness to the long shadows cast by acts of terror, shadows that, even after two decades, had finally reached one of their own.

9

The Match Is Far from Over

March 2022.

Pakistan and the city of Karachi in particular were alive with whispers and rumours following the dramatic shooting of Zahoor Mistry. GEO TV led the media frenzy, broadcasting CCTV footage that had captured the harrowing incident outside Crescent Furniture in Akhtar Colony. The footage, raw and unflinching, became the talk of the town, leaving the authorities in a precarious position. Officially, no one was willing to comment, a silence borne out of a reluctance to reveal the victim's true identity. Zahid Akhund was a cover, a façade that had hidden Zahoor Ibrahim Mistry's real identity, a man with a dark legacy tied to the hijacking of IC-814 and his connections to JeM.

In the aftermath, Aditya, who had meticulously planned every aspect of his mission under the guise of Hassan Raza, found himself facing an unexpected complication. The realization that merely stealing two of the CCTV cameras near Zahoor's shop by Khalid's men hadn't been enough struck him with force. The oversight was glaring; more cameras had captured the event, leaving a trail he hadn't anticipated.

Sitting in the low light of his safe house, Aditya mulled over the possibilities. Had Khalid's handlers botched the operation, or worse, had they intentionally misled him, leaving evidence that could expose everything? The thought was a splinter in his mind, a reminder of the delicate balance of trust and deceit in the shadowy world of espionage.

He watched the CCTV footage broadcast on GEO again and again, and felt it would be very difficult to recognize the riders and lead to him. The motorcycle was already disposed of, the clothes they wore destroyed and the fake registration plates dissolved in acid in the backyard of his safe house.

Aditya knew the stakes were higher than ever. The CCTV footage out in the public domain not only threatened to expose his carefully constructed cover but also hinted at the intricate network of surveillance that had eluded his planning. The mission had taken an unexpected turn, and now, Aditya needed to handle this new challenge with the same cunning and resolve that had brought him to Karachi.

As the news rippled through Pakistan, the identity of the victim broadcast by GEO TV was carefully framed as a 'businessman', avoiding any direct mention of his dark past or affiliations with JeM. Despite the careful wording, the city's undercurrents swirled with speculation and whispered truths. The name Zahoor Mistry was on everyone's lips, accompanied by murmurs of his notorious history. Yet, amidst this storm of rumours, the official narrative remained conspicuously sanitized, a deliberate omission that only fuelled more speculation.

The Karachi police, meanwhile, maintained a strategic silence on the deeper implications of the incident. Their statement, framing the brutal shooting as a result of 'business rivalry', seemed almost too convenient, a veneer of normalcy over a situation that was anything but. The detail about the five empty shells recovered at the scene was the only concrete piece of evidence they disclosed, a clue that spoke volumes yet revealed little about the true nature of the crime.

The corridors of power in Islamabad hummed with urgent deliberations. The government issued discreet advisories to the media, a concerted effort to decouple Zahid Akhund from Zahoor Mistry, the latter a name tied to shadows and secrets too volatile to be dragged into the light. The directive was clear: maintain the façade, preserve the narrative. Yet, despite these efforts, the truth had a way of asserting itself, seeping through the cracks of the orchestrated silence.

The media frenzy in India had reached fever pitch. Every journalist was relentless in their pursuit of the gritty details surrounding the audacious assassination of the Pakistani hijacker tied to the infamous IC-814. It wasn't just news – it was vindication, a deeply satisfying development for a country that had long sought closure over one of its darkest episodes. Television panels lit up with analysts dissecting the operation, while print and digital outlets splashed bold headlines speculating on the covert genius behind the strike. The jubilant tone mirrored the celebratory mood of the prime minister's loyal supporters, who were quick to hail the decision as a testament to his uncompromising leadership. For them, this wasn't just about retribution; it was about reclaiming India's pride on the global stage. Among whispers of 'what next?' the name that floated most frequently in studios and living rooms alike was Dawood Ibrahim. For decades, the man synonymous with India's underworld had eluded justice, shielded by Pakistan's high-security apparatus. Now, the collective imagination of a nation wondered if the long arm of Indian resolve was preparing to stretch even further into enemy territory.

The NSD received quiet congratulations from a select group of insiders, those few privy to the covert machinations that had put India on the offensive. With characteristic humility, he deflected the praise, insisting that if credit was to be given at all, it belonged to the government's leadership. He refrained from naming anyone explicitly, though it was clear his words pointed toward the prime minister. After the formalities, the NSD picked up the phone and called the leader, briefing him on his upcoming meeting with his Japanese counterpart in Tokyo. As the conversation wound down, the NSD casually inquired if the prime minister had managed to glance through the morning's news. The prime minister, in his usual composed manner, mentioned he had gone through the key bullet points of domestic and global developments that had been presented to him. 'But nothing too significant,' he added, dismissively.

Sensing the gap, the NSD decided to bring up the headline that had the nation buzzing. He asked if the prime minister had read about the assassination of one of the hijackers of IC-814 in Karachi. The prime minister's response was calm yet revealing. '*Woh toh kal raat ko hi patah chal gaya tha. Jo bhi ho, aapke liye toh* divine justice *hua hoga* [We'd heard about it last night iteself. Whatever it might be, for you it must have been divine justice],' he remarked casually, referring to the NSD's direct involvement as one of the negotiators during the infamous hijacking. The NSD smiled faintly, recognizing the prime minister's uncanny knack for staying ahead of the curve, always gathering information in his unique way. He ended the call, quietly reflecting on the weight of those words, the layers of understanding shared between them.

After ending the call with the prime minister, the NSD reached out to his counterpart in Dubai, recommending that they curb any further publicity surrounding the Karachi incident. The Dubai counterpart assured him that measures were already in place, which explained why Pakistani security officials remained tight-lipped. He also promised to continue monitoring the situation to ensure that India's name stayed uninvolved. Lightening the tone of the conversation, the UAE NSA suggested that the Indian NSD manage the exuberant Indian media, which was in a celebratory frenzy, a situation over which the latter admitted he had no control.

Later, the NSD convened an online meeting with his team, instructing them to ensure that no information related to the Karachi incident was leaked to the media. He emphasized the importance of letting the Indian media rely solely on Pakistani sources for updates, confident that this would help the buzz around the incident subside naturally.

The funeral for Zahoor Mistry, though shrouded in a veneer of discretion, became a focal point of interest. Among the mourners was Ibrahim Akhtar, brother of Rasool Azhar and a prominent figure in JeM, lending a silent but potent acknowledgement of the deceased's true identity and significance. This gathering, observed from a distance by hidden eyes, was a confirmation of the complex web of loyalties and allegiances that defined the shadowy world Zahoor had inhabited.

While Pakistan's official stance was one of calculated silence, the narrative across the border in India took on a starkly different tone. Indian media, seizing upon the incident with fervour, peeled away the layers of Zahoor Mistry's assumed identity, revealing the contours of a past marred by acts of terrorism. The contrast between the two countries' approaches to the story could not have been more pronounced. In India, the shooting was not just a news item but a vindication, a moment to underscore the long-standing accusations against Pakistan for harbouring terrorists, as indicated by countless celebratory posts on the social media.

Post the operation, Aditya, aware of the psychological toll the day's events had taken on Khalid, insisted they lie low together in Gulshan for the next 24 hours. The operation had escalated beyond Khalid's expectations, transforming what he thought was an adventure into a killing in broad daylight. He saw himself as an accomplice in the murder. Aditya, under his alias Hassan, watched Khalid closely, gauging the tumult of emotions that played across the young man's face. Khalid, who had been enthusiastic about his role in their covert activities, was now grappling with the magnitude of their actions. The revelation that they had ended a life, even that of a notorious terrorist, weighed heavily on him.

Throughout the night, Khalid lay awake, his mind racing with thoughts he couldn't silence. The news reports, which peeled away the alias Zahid Akhund to reveal the true identity of Zahoor Mistry, shocked him to his core. The man he had helped track down was not just any businessman but a feared terrorist, responsible for countless innocent lives lost. This realization brought a storm of questions to Khalid's mind, questions about morality, justice and his own unwitting role in the events that had unfolded. Yet, the fear of confronting Hassan, the man he had trusted, kept him silent. Khalid was torn between the respect he had for Hassan and the horror of what they had done.

Aditya, observing Khalid's struggle, knew the importance of managing the situation delicately. He understood that Khalid's silence was not just out of fear but also a deep-seated conflict about the nature of their mission. Aditya had stepped into this murky world with his eyes open, aware of the sacrifices and moral compromises it entailed. For Khalid, however, the journey from being a mere participant to an accomplice in a high-stakes operation was a jarring transition. Knowing his limitations, Khalid left it to the Almighty to decide his fate.

Aditya chose to break the silence with a carefully crafted narrative. As Hassan, he spun a tale of international intrigue and nationalistic fervour, placing their recent actions within a larger story of geopolitical manoeuveing. He spoke of the Financial Action Task Force (FATF), an international body that, he claimed, was being wielded as a weapon by Pakistan's adversaries, mainly India, along with some Western nations, to undermine the country's standing on the global stage.

Hassan painted a vivid picture of the consequences of these international pressures: prestigious banks turning their backs on Pakistan, citing concerns over terror financing. This, he argued, was at the root of the financial hardships plaguing ordinary Pakistanis like Khalid. The narrative was compelling, casting India as the antagonist in a struggle that had forced Pakistan into a corner, compelling it to disavow and eliminate those whom India had unjustly accused of terrorism.

By framing their mission as part of a directive from Islamabad to address these international accusations and cleanse the country of terrorists, Hassan aimed to realign Khalid's shaken beliefs. He portrayed himself as a patriot, driven by an unwavering love and loyalty to Pakistan, engaged in a clandestine battle for his country's honour and future.

Khalid listened; the seeds of doubt sown by the revelation of Zahoor Mistry's true identity beginning to find new soil. Hassan's words offered a lens through which the world's complexities were simplified into a narrative of 'us' versus 'them', of loyalty against betrayal. This perspective, whether entirely genuine or a façade for deeper, unspoken motives, provided Khalid with a semblance of justification, a way to reconcile his actions with a greater cause. Aditya's manipulation was a masterstroke of psychological reassurance, designed to anchor Khalid's loyalty and silence his doubts.

Khalid couldn't claim to fully understand or even believe all that Hassan had explained to him, but the narrative offered a semblance of relief, a narrative that made the chaotic world around him seem slightly less daunting. It was at this juncture, sensing Khalid's gradual shift towards acceptance, that Aditya introduced the idea of a visit back home. 'A trip to see your family might do you some good,' he suggested, a notion that instantly brightened Khalid's mood, planting a seed of hope amidst his turmoil.

Yet, this sliver of joy was quickly tempered by the revelation that Hassan planned to accompany him. This unexpected decision underlined Hassan's cautious approach; it was a clear sign that, despite the growing bond between them, Hassan was not ready to fully trust Khalid's loyalty without oversight.

Khalid accepted Hassan's decision to accompany him to Rawalkot. Understanding he had little say in the matter did not dampen his spirits entirely, especially when Aditya booked their flights to Islamabad, marking Khalid's first-ever experience on a plane. The thrill of flying, of soaring above the clouds, was a novel excitement for him, a silver lining in the cloud of his complex relationship with Hassan.

Despite his reservations about Hassan's presence in what was meant to be a personal journey, Khalid couldn't ignore the security that came with it. His life had become a balancing act between his own desires and the demands of the mission, with Hassan playing a pivotal role in navigating this new reality. The trip, therefore, symbolized more than just a visit home; it was a reminder of their intertwined fates. Khalid was becoming increasingly aware of their mutual dependence: he needed Hassan's guidance and protection, while Hassan relied on Khalid's cooperation and trust.

~

Middle of March 2022.

For Aditya, the journey served a dual purpose. Beyond the immediate goal of maintaining his cover and ensuring Khalid's alignment with the mission, it was also a strategic move to reinforce his control. By setting foot in Khalid's hometown, Aditya subtly communicated a powerful message: he knew where to find those Khalid cared about most. This unspoken threat, veiled beneath the guise of camaraderie and concern, was a clear signal to Khalid of the stakes involved. It was a reminder that, despite any semblance of normalcy their visit might offer, the underlying dynamics of power and surveillance were ever-present.

Also, the journey to Rawalkot with Khalid was not just a mission of emotional reassurance or a mere tactical manoeuvre; it was also a carefully laid plan for an escape route, should the need arise. The porous border between Pakistan and India, a line that had seen countless tales of conflict and escape, was a path Aditya was prepared to tread if circumstances demanded.

His official entry into Pakistan was proof of his expertise in navigating the sinister realms of international espionage. Yet, Aditya was equally prepared to abandon official channels if his mission required it. The route from Rawalkot to Srinagar was etched in his mind, not just as a map, but as a living, breathing landscape he had committed to memory. The terrain and topography were not mere geographical features but allies in his potential journey back to safety. His connections, cultivated with care in both private circles and official capacities, were his lifeline, a network that could be activated with a single, coded message.

Aditya's mission had been executed with precision, a display to his skills and dedication. The elimination of Zahoor Mistry, a task assigned by New Delhi, was a significant strike against a target that had long been in the sights of Indian intelligence. Having accomplished this with exemplary success, Aditya now found himself in a liminal space, waiting for the next directive from his superiors.

As Aditya contemplated his position, the landscape of Rawalkot offering a backdrop to his thoughts, he was reminded of the dual nature of his existence – between the overt and the covert, the official and the clandestine, the past and the future. The wait for the next order was not just a pause in action but a preparation for the next chapter in a life dedicated to serving his country from the shadows.

The brief sojourn in Rawalkot offered Aditya and Khalid a respite from the undercurrents of their mission, immersing them in the serene beauty of its landscapes. For Khalid, it was a return to his roots, a momentary escape into the simplicity of life before returning to the complexities of his entanglement with Hassan. For Aditya, the days spent in the picturesque surroundings of Rawalkot were a strategic pause, a necessary blending into the backdrop of Khalid's life to cement their bond and to reassure Khalid's family of his good intentions.

Khalid's parents, in their gracious hospitality, saw Hassan as a guardian angel in their son's life, unaware of the deeper undercurrents of their relationship. Their request for him to extend his stay was born out of gratitude and the traditional hospitality that characterized their community.

Upon their return to Karachi, Aditya swiftly transitioned back into the role of Hassan, guiding Khalid on the next steps with the precision of a seasoned operative. He instructed Khalid to return to his daily life, emphasizing the importance of maintaining a low profile by resuming work at the garage and avoiding any financial extravagance that might raise suspicions. Khalid, now deeply ingrained in the complexities of Hassan's world, understood the importance of these instructions. His recent experiences had not only enriched him financially but had also given him a glimpse into the world of espionage, marked by Hassan's meticulous planning and execution. The trust between them had solidified, with Khalid assuring Hassan of his loyalty and discretion, a loyalty forged through shared secrets and the realization of the stakes involved.

Khalid's commitment to his family, demonstrated by his decision to use all his money to free his family's land from mortgage, was an endorsement of his values, further proving his reliability to Hassan. This act of responsibility highlighted Khalid's grounded nature, making him an even more valuable ally in Hassan's eyes.

The return to Gulshan brought with it an unexpected development that even Aditya, with all his years of espionage and intelligence work, hadn't foreseen. Usman passed a name card to Aditya and said a man from the army had come looking for him, waited for him, had tea and departed. He, however had not left any specific message for Aditya. The name card belonged to Colonel Ghulam Mohiuddin Cheema.

Aditya understood the gravity of the situation. The information that had once been a mere piece of the puzzle in Aditya's mission, the contact details of Zahoor Mistry, had originated from Colonel Cheema himself. However, the outcome of this exchange, the assassination of a notorious figure like Mistry, had taken even Cheema by surprise. For Aditya, this visit was an unexpected challenge, a curveball that his years of training and experience had not fully prepared him to face.

As Aditya pondered over Colonel Cheema's motivations and contemplated his next move, the chessboard of espionage on which they were all players became even more convoluted. Each piece was moving according to a strategy that was revealing itself in real time, with alliances, betrayals and the ever-present shadow of danger shaping the course of events. The message, or lack thereof, left by Colonel Cheema was a puzzle piece in a game that was far from over, signalling the beginning of a new chapter in Aditya's mission, one that promised to test his skills and resolve to their limits.

Aditya was set to meet Colonel Cheema, who was now eagerly anticipating their encounter. Cheema, having previously divulged Zahoor Mistry's whereabouts to Hassan, was oblivious to his guest's real mission. He believed Hassan was simply looking to collect intelligence on a terrorist under the protection of the ISI, a matter he thought tied to Pakistan's precarious standing with the FATF, which had placed the country on its grey list. And since their meeting was facilitated by fellow Pakistani Altaf Raza, one of Cheema's long-standing contacts, he had no reason to doubt Hassan's motives.

Cheema was aware of other terrorists who were also enjoying the support of the Pakistan Army. However, the idea that Hassan, under the guise of seeking information, would actually eliminate Zahoor, had never crossed his mind. If Cheema had any inkling of Hassan's true intentions, he would have demanded a much higher price for the valuable information he provided.

Realizing the missed opportunity, Cheema saw a chance to capitalize on what he had come to know about Hassan's actions. Rather than resorting to blackmail, which could be dangerously unpredictable given the uncertainty of Hassan's possible ties with the Pakistan government, Cheema decided on a safer route. Money had always been his primary motivator, and he knew he had more information that could be valuable to Hassan. With that in mind, he considered offering intelligence on other protected terrorists, assuming Hassan might be interested in continuing his mission.

Cheema already knew that Hassan had been staying at Altaf's house in Gulshan. Deciding to seize the opportunity, Cheema attempted a visit for a direct conversation. However, upon arrival, he discovered Hassan was away. Undeterred, Cheema left his name card with the caretaker Usman, a move that soon proved fruitful when Hassan reached out to him. In response, Cheema invited him to his beach house for lunch.

For Aditya, the stakes in meeting Cheema were high, given Cheema's awareness of his involvement in Zahoor's death. Yet, Aditya calculated the risk as manageable, banking on Altaf's influential connections to protect him. He trusted that any direct threat from Cheema would be mitigated by Altaf's ability to mobilize support within Islamabad's power circles. As Cheema believed Hassan would not turn up and had slipped through his fingers, he was taken by surprise by his arrival. Greeting Hassan with a robust laugh, Cheema welcomed him, masking the underlying tension of their encounter.

The initial conversation flowed casually, drifting through topics like the weather, local cuisine and the current political upheaval in Pakistan, a thinly veiled dance around the tension simmering beneath. Then, slicing through the pleasantries, Cheema veered towards his true interest.

'How long do you plan to stay here?' he inquired; his gaze sharp.

Aditya, maintaining his guise as Hassan, kept his expression unreadable. 'Depends on the progress of my business,' he responded evenly.

'You mean your business of spices and dry fruits?' Cheema's voice carried a hint of sarcasm, his smile slightly mocking as he observed Aditya.

'And carpets,' Aditya added without a hint of emotion, his face a mask of neutrality.

Around them, the room was filled with the rich aroma of Cheema's Havana cigar, the smoke swirling lazily in the air. Cheema, ever the host in his own domain, indulged in a sip of JW Blue Label, the whiskey's amber liquid catching the light in his expensive glass. Aditya, on the other hand, had opted for a stark contrast with his simple black coffee. Despite the apparent safety net provided by Altaf's influence, Aditya was acutely aware of the boundaries of his trust in Cheema. The luxury surrounding them couldn't mask the underlying game of cat and mouse they were engaged in.

Cheema leaned back, letting out a stream of smoke before making a pointed observation. 'I gather you got your last supply at a very low price. Must have made a good profit, no?' The air hung heavy with the unspoken implications of his words.

Aditya, under the guise of Hassan, didn't miss a beat. His response was careful, designed to work through the treacherous alleys of their conversation. 'In Karachi, what's cheap and what's expensive can be a matter of perspective,' he said smoothly. 'I rely on my instincts when it comes to business, hoping they lead me to profit.'

Their exchange continued in this veiled manner, a delicate dance of words where each tried to uncover more from the other without revealing too much. It became a game of patience and wit, with Cheema attempting to peel away the layers of Hassan's façade, and Aditya deflecting with consummate ease.

After a while, Cheema recognized the toughness in Hassan. He was not the type to give in easily to indirect pressures. Acknowledging this silently to himself, Cheema decided it was time to shift gears, to be more forthright with his intentions.

'Let's cut to the chase,' Cheema finally said, setting his cigar aside as he fixed his gaze on Aditya. 'We both know there's more to your stay here than just trading in spices, dry fruits and carpets.' Aditya replied with caution, 'Yeah, you are right. Maybe some mangoes?'

Cheema laughed first but then sensing an opportunity to delve deeper, ventured thoughtfully, 'If you're looking for more … mangoes, I might be able to help.' His eyes searched Aditya's face for any sign of interest or desperation.

Aditya, however, remained as inscrutable as ever. 'That would depend on what's needed back in London, I will check with London,' he replied smoothly, deflecting the offer with a reference to his fictitious uncle's business. 'Demand fluctuates, and so does our need for … certain types of goods.' Thinking they were talking in riddles for too long, Cheema came down to the point when he said, 'Information is power, Hassan bhai. You can continue to benefit from my library.'

With this, Aditya subtly shifted the balance of their conversation, putting Cheema in a position where he had to tread carefully. Aditya, for his part, was careful not to express any direct interest in other terrorists protected by the Pakistani state. He was well aware of the major players, thanks to his briefing, but his hands were tied; the decision on who to pursue next wasn't his to make. That directive would come from New Delhi, relayed through Altaf, keeping him one step removed from direct involvement and maintaining his cover.

∽

As the midday sun climbed higher, lunch was served in Cheema's beachfront retreat, an array of dishes laid out that would tempt even the most discerning palate. The table boasted of pilaf made from aromatic Basmati rice, rich beef nihari, succulent lamb chops served dry, creamy yellow lentils, freshly baked tandoori rotis, an assortment of salads and, for a sweet finish, ice cream of an international brand.

Aditya, with a strategy in mind, leaned heavily into the beef preparation, pairing it generously with the tandoori rotis, and later indulged in several scoops of ice cream. This choice was not merely dictated by appetite, but by a calculated attempt to blend in, to seem undiscriminating and natural in his preferences. Choosing beef over lamb, he hoped, would subtly reinforce his cover as Hassan, making him seem more at home in his assumed identity. While not typically averse to beef, it wasn't his usual fare, making this meal an exercise in blending in as much as it was a culinary experience.

However, despite the sumptuous meal and the opulence surrounding him, Aditya found himself slightly at odds with one element of the setting: the pungent smell of ozone wafting in from the sea. The luxurious beach house offered an uninterrupted view of the vast, rolling ocean, a sight so captivating that the house must be designed so it could be seen from every corner of the residence, he surmised. Yet, for Aditya, the beauty of the seascape was marred by the reminder that his mission, and indeed his life, hung in a delicate balance. Every moment in Cheema's company was a step on a tightrope, where even the natural choice between lamb and beef felt laden with consequence.

Lunch concluded with the dishes cleared away, leaving the two men amidst the lingering scent of spices and the ocean's pungent embrace. It was then that Colonel Cheema steered their conversation towards the delicate subject of Pakistan's financial tribulations and the 'unjust decision by the FATF to keep the country chained to its grey list'.

Aditya, quickly grasping the direction Cheema was taking, decided to engage with a tactical counter. 'Considering the FATF's decisions are influenced by the Western world, and India's involvement is no secret, isn't it also true that ignoring the ongoing issues of money laundering and terror financing won't make them disappear?' His question was a carefully placed mine in the conversational battlefield.

Cheema, sensing the shift in Aditya's approach, responded with a nuanced acknowledgement, 'Certainly not. And that's precisely why the government's silence on the recent incident in Akhtar Colony, the furniture shop owner's demise, was a calculated decision.' His words hinted at a deeper understanding and an implicit acknowledgement of the complex interplay of international pressure and domestic policies.

In this mental game of chess, where roles of spy and informant blurred, Aditya remained an inscrutable fortress, his reactions guarded as he sipped his second black coffee, contemplating Cheema's next move.

Unfazed, Cheema continued to weave his narrative, the smoke from his freshly lit cigar curling into the air like a signal of the nuanced conversation unfolding. 'Despite the FATF keeping Pakistan on its grey list, urging us to rectify the remaining shortcomings in our financial system, there has been progress. Take, for instance, Hafiz Saeed's recent sentencing to 33 years in jail this April. It's a significant move,' Cheema noted, his tone carrying a hint of pride mixed with a challenge. 'Moreover, the FATF has acknowledged our efforts, confirming that Pakistan has addressed all 34 action items it required. They're now planning an on-site visit to assess the long-term effectiveness and sustainability of our measures against money laundering and terrorism financing.'

With a strategic pause, Cheema let the information hang in the air, watching Aditya closely. He was testing how far this talk of progress could be stretched before Hassan revealed what he really thought of Pakistan's sincerity. The move was calculated, meant to guide the discussion towards actions that served Cheema's hidden purpose.

Aditya, weighing his words carefully, ventured into the discussion on the FATF's perspective, 'Perhaps the FATF views Hafiz Saeed's imprisonment … kind of … superficial?'

Cheema, quick to seize upon Aditya's comment, probed further, 'So, do you think the FATF's lack of trust in Pakistan is justified?'

Aditya, seasoned in handling such sharp inquiries, maintained his diplomatic front. 'Colonel, it's not about our personal views. Ultimately, it's the FATF's perceptions that carry weight.'

Undeterred, Cheema pressed, 'Yet you didn't answer my question.'

After a moment's pause, Aditya decided to tread slightly into the terrain Cheema was guiding them towards. 'Is it possible the FATF harbours doubts about the coherence between the Pakistan army and the Prime Minister's Office?'

Cheema, seizing the narrative, dismissed it with visible frustration, 'That's nothing but a narrative spun by India for the Western world, and they've all too readily danced to India's tune.'

Cheema's retort, spontaneous and charged, belied a quicksilver mind that was already piecing together the cryptic mosaic of Hassan's responses. It dawned on him that Hassan's subtle emphasis might not be coincidental; it hinted at a deeper allegiance or concern for the PMO over the military's influence. This nuanced preference suggested Hassan might be involved in operations aimed at bolstering the prime minister's public image, possibly by challenging the narrative that the PM was bowing to military pressure, especially regarding the FATF directives.

This epiphany sharpened Cheema's suspicions about the real motive behind Zahoor's assassination – was it a strategic move to polish the prime minister's image in a game of shadows and light?

Eager to explore this avenue further, Cheema ventured into another topic, hoping to uncover more or perhaps redirect Hassan's focus. 'Speaking of cross-border nuisances, there's an Indian drug lord currently in Lahore,' Cheema began, his tone hinting he was intrigued. 'Interestingly, his name surfaced in connection with the assassination of the renowned Punjabi singer, Ranjeet Moose Wala. It seems the web of crime and politics is more tangled than we thought.'

Cheema's insinuation about the Indian drug lord served as a clear signal to Aditya that fresh intelligence was on the table. Yet, the deliberate emphasis on 'Indian' heightened his alertness, reminding him of the precarious nature of his undercover mission. He gave a slow nod, masking his caution behind a faint smile. 'Lahore seems to attract all kinds these days,' he said lightly, setting his cup aside. 'We can pick this up later.' His tone was courteous and detached, just enough to acknowledge the remark without inviting more. Then, glancing at his watch, he rose from his seat, bringing the meeting to a natural close.

'They are the worst sort,' remarked Aditya lightly. 'Enemies of both our country and their own.'

Recognizing the moment as an opportunity to gracefully exit without arousing suspicion, Aditya decided it was time to take his leave. He stood, offering Cheema a polite nod. 'Thank you for the exceptional lunch, Colonel. I must say, the beef was truly unparalleled. It's a flavour I doubt I'll find anywhere in London,' he remarked with a smile that skirted the perfect line between gratitude and diplomacy.

As they stood up, Cheema extended his hand to Aditya, offering a firm handshake that seemed to seal more than just a farewell. 'Don't hesitate to get in touch in the future,' Cheema said with a hint of earnestness.

'The pleasure is entirely mine, Colonel. I liked talking to you. I got to learn new things,' Aditya replied thoughtfully.

'You're always welcome to reach out to me, Hassan.' Then, as if an afterthought but clearly a calculated one, he added, 'By the way, I came across another interesting piece of information. That Indian drug lord I mentioned? It appears he might have been involved in a terror attack in Mohali, Punjab – he's known as Rinda.'

The notorious name and the repeated invocation of 'India' and 'Indians' did not escape Aditya's notice. It was clear Cheema was deliberately threading these references into their dialogue, perhaps to gauge Aditya's reactions or loyalties. Choosing his words with the utmost care, Aditya responded with a casual shrug, feigning a nonchalance he did not feel.

'India has always been overly anxious about terror attacks. They're quick to see a terrorist in every shadow. Thank goodness the individual you're talking about is Indian; otherwise, they'd probably find a way to pin it on Pakistan as well,' he remarked, aiming to mirror Cheema's sentiment without committing to any stance.

Cheema nodded, a sign of approval at Aditya's diplomatic manoeuvring. There was a moment of shared understanding, a recognition of Aditya's – or rather, Hassan's – grasp of the delicate interplay of geopolitics, even as both men remained caught up in their respective roles within the larger game at play.

With a nod and a polite 'God willing, our paths will cross again,' Aditya stepped away, his words hanging in the balmy air between them. Cheema echoed the sentiment, 'God willing,' his voice carrying a genuine warmth as he watched Aditya's figure retreat into the distance.

Aditya stepped out of Cheema's beach house and into the uncertain chess game that lay beyond. His mind was already turning over the day's conversation, weighing his next moves in the intricate dance of espionage.

The app taxi carrying Aditya soon blended into the traffic, disappearing from sight, leaving Cheema alone with his thoughts. Without hesitation, he pulled out his cell phone, the weight of his next move apparent in his actions. As he dialled a familiar number, the anticipation of the conversation to come was palpable.

'As-salamu alaykum, Janaab,' came the greeting from the other end, the voice steady and expectant.

Cheema, his gaze still fixed on the vanishing point of Hassan's departure, responded with a customary, 'Wa alaykumu s-salam,' before his voice took on a decisive edge. 'Note down a name. Hawaii, America, San Francisco, San Francisco, America, Norway … Russia, America, Zebra, America …' His words were cryptic, yet they carried the weight of significance, hinting at Cheema wanted to inquire about Hassan Raza and whom he was working for, before he made his next move.

10

From Rookie to Predator

April 2022.

A satellite phone arrived for Aditya at Gulshan, its origins a mystery. He was not meant to hear from anyone, neither Delhi nor Altaf. Yet the sight of the device stirred unease. Could it be Colonel Cheema, or Altaf somehow reaching out through a line that was never meant to exist? Having carried out an assassination in Pakistan, Aditya had learned to expect the unexpected. The silence since Zahoor's fall five days ago weighed on him. No message from Altaf, his handler. No word from Delhi. He knew both sides were bound by silence, yet part of him could not stop questioning what that silence truly meant.

That New Delhi would choose silence did not surprise him as distance was their ally in this high-stakes game. But Altaf's absence? That was a void too vast to ignore, a silence that spoke louder than words, hinting at unspoken dangers or perhaps a betrayal deep within the web of espionage that had ensnared him.

Before a creeping sense of unease could fully take hold, the new satellite phone buzzed to life, breaking the silence. Aditya eyed the screen – caller ID stubbornly blank. Hesitation gripped him; was this a trap? The local authorities, perhaps? Opting for caution, he let it ring unanswered. The silence returned, thick and expectant.

Then, Usman's cell phone shattered the quiet. 'It's Altaf Sa'ab,' Usman announced after a brief exchange, eyeing Aditya, 'He's asking for you.' Before Aditya could respond, the line went dead.

'They cut off,' Usman said, puzzled.

Aditya's mind raced. Altaf's message was clear: pick up the next call. Ten minutes crawled by before the satellite phone demanded attention once more. This time, Aditya answered.

'Hassan? It's Altaf. We need to talk,' came the voice, veiled in urgency but unmistakably familiar.

Aditya let out a breath he hadn't realized he'd been holding. 'I'm listening,' he replied, stepping further into the shadows of intrigue that surrounded him.

Altaf's voice, devoid of emotion yet carrying an undercurrent of approval, broke through the static. 'Hassan, your work in Karachi has met my expectations. It might be time for you to return to London. We'll plan our next steps together here.'

Aditya absorbed the directive. The suggestion of leaving Karachi behind, the city that had been his shadowed playground and battlefield, sparked a flicker of anticipation.

'When's the earliest I can fly out?' Aditya inquired, the pragmatist in him surfacing.

'Book the next flight to London. But remember, don't reach out to anyone before you leave. And the satellite phone? Leave it with Usman. It'll be taken care of.'

Aditya nodded to himself, a plan forming. He turned to Usman, 'Looks like Uncle wants me back in London.'

Usman, understanding the situation, simply nodded. As Aditya began to pack, a mix of relief and tension filled the air. The game was changing, moving to a new stage and Aditya was once again at its centre, navigating the shadows.

He made no attempt to reach out to either Khalid or Cheema. The less they knew, the safer his exit would be. What puzzled him was the silence from the authorities. After all, CCTV footage should have placed him near the scene by now. Yet, there had been no search, no questions, no tightening of the net. Whether it was luck, timing or something deeper at play, Aditya couldn't tell.

He made a choice that mirrored the essence of his life in espionage: indirect, always veiling his true intentions. Shunning the straightforward path, he booked two separate flights. Karachi to Lahore with PIA, economy class to blend in and then Lahore to London aboard an Etihad business class flight, befitting his cover as a businessman from London. This labyrinthine approach wasn't just a habit; it reflected his existence, a life lived in the shadows, revelling in the complexity of each deceptive turn.

His journey from Karachi felt like navigating another layer of the intricate maze he'd come to love. Each move was calculated, with the awareness that a misstep could shatter the design of his clandestine work. Lahore was going to be just a brief pause, a deceptive manoeuvre in the grand scheme of his mission. Aditya understood the stakes; in this world of espionage, straightforward paths were often the most perilous.

Upon touchdown in Lahore, Aditya's movements were as precise as the hands of a clock. The shuttle to the international terminal was just another cog in his well-oiled routine. Checking into Hotel Alma Iqbal, he was a ghost passing through, invisible to those who might seek to trace his steps. The hotel room, a temporary refuge, offered a brief respite from the constant vigilance his life demanded.

A shower washed away the grime of travel but not the weight of his profession. Freshly clothed, he nourished his body with a meal as light as his sleep would be and then surrendered to the fleeting solace of a power nap.

Awakened by the digital chime of his alarm, evening had already cloaked the city. He peered out, finding the horizon bleeding crimson into the twilight, a canvas of divine artistry. The call to prayer, the Azaan, filled the air, its call a sacred melody echoing from the mosques and through his television screen, a reminder of the world's beauty and complexity beyond the shadows in which he dwelled. In this moment of tranquility, Aditya found an odd sense of belonging, a peace amidst the storm of his clandestine existence.

Maybe it was the serenity of the Azaan; it nudged Aditya's thoughts towards a part of his life draped in what-ifs and might-have-beens. The image of his little daughter, Ameera, surfaced in his mind, her smile a bittersweet reminder of the life he had left behind. It had been a little over two years since he last saw her, her presence now a ghostly comfort in his solitude. Their conversations, few and far between during his brief stays in London, were always shadowed by the unsaid.

His divorced wife Meera's frustration with his veiled existence had reached its breaking point. She refused to let their daughter grow up tangled in the web of his mysteries, fearing she would inherit a legacy of doubt, unable to discern her father's truth from his necessary lies. Meera's stance was unwavering, a line drawn in the sand. She demanded a normalcy he couldn't provide, a transparency antithetical to the essence of his being. In her eyes, he had become an enigma, a phantom father figure cloaked in ambiguity, his true self obscured by the roles he played.

Aditya understood her fears, her desire to protect their daughter from the complexities of his life. Yet, this understanding did little to bridge the chasm that his profession had carved between them. As he sat in his darkening hotel room, the emotional distance felt as vast as the physical one that separated them.

The directives from New Delhi were clear and non-negotiable. Direct contact with his family was a line that couldn't be crossed, a luxury too fraught with risk for the government to condone. Yet, they offered him a meagre consolation – a digital glimpse into the life he was barred from, through videos sent sporadically, showcasing the overt activities of his family. These brief windows into their world were both a solace and a torment, reminding him of all he had sacrificed for the greater good.

Aditya's heart ached with questions that had no answers. What narrative had Meera woven about him for their daughter? Was he a memory, a story of a father lost too soon? Or had Meera chosen the finality of death to explain his absence? A hero fallen in battle, rather than a father who simply vanished? To a small child concepts like 'missing' or 'divorced' were abstract, perhaps too innocuous for the harsh truths of their reality. Yet, the idea of being remembered as missing, a question mark in his own daughter's life, seemed far worse to Aditya.

He found himself grappling with the notion that perhaps it was better for his daughter to believe he had died a hero's death, rather than grow up shadowed by the uncertainty of his existence. This internal debate, the weighing of truths against the welfare of his child, was a battle as fierce as any he had fought in the field. The very thought of his daughter living a life overshadowed by his choices, by the necessary lies and secrets of his profession, was a burden he bore heavily, a silent sorrow that echoed in the depths of his being.

~

As Aditya approached the passport control in Lahore, a familiar sense of anticipation tightened in his chest, mirroring the feeling he had experienced upon his clandestine entry into Pakistan through Karachi. Yet, this time, a veneer of confidence cloaked him, a silent armour forged from the success of his recent mission. He had manoeuvred through the shadows, executed an assassination with surgical precision, and all without leaving a trace that could lead back to him or his handlers.

Standing in the queue for the immigration check, Aditya played the part of just another traveller. Inside, however, he meticulously replayed every step he would take, every answer he might need to give. 'This too shall pass,' he reassured himself, the internal mantra of a man who had made the extraordinary act of vanishing into thin air seem ordinary. Each moment he inched closer to the counter was a step closer to leaving behind the labyrinth of Karachi, the ghosts of his actions there, and moving towards a new chapter that awaited him in London.

As he handed over his documents, his mind was alert, ready for any sign that the persona he presented might be scrutinized. But he was prepared, as always to face any untoward situation.

Clearing immigration turned out to be smoother than Aditya had anticipated. His paperwork was impeccable, a flawless façade that belied his true identity. Nonetheless, the life of an international spy left no room for complacency. Every step he took was measured; every interaction weighed for potential risk. As the immigration officer returned his Pakistani passport, now adorned with a fresh exit stamp, a ripple of relief passed through Aditya, though he allowed no hint of it to show.

His mind, however, remained on high alert, scanning the crowd for any sign that he might be under surveillance. In this line of work, the absence of trouble was no guarantee of safety; it merely meant that if danger lurked, it had yet to reveal itself.

With his official clearance out of the way, Aditya moved towards the shopping arcade, blending in with the throng of travellers. Here, he purchased a new hand trolley, a mundane act, yet part of his carefully constructed normalcy. Each move was calculated, even in the choice of his luggage, designed to deflect attention rather than attract it.

His next destination was the Business Class lounge, a sanctuary for those in transit. Aditya negotiated the terminal with practised ease, his demeanour that of any other business traveller seeking a moment of respite before their flight.

Aditya commenced his wait in the lounge with a modest meal, choosing pita bread paired with hummus, complemented by two bananas, and a bottle of kiwi juice, a selection that was nourishing yet light, in keeping with his need to remain alert. His visit to the washroom was strategic, utilizing the private space to meticulously repack his belongings, including the day's acquisitions, into the newly purchased hand trolley. Each movement was deliberate, his actions matching those of countless other travellers.

Returning to the lounge, Aditya sought out a quiet corner sofa, a spot where he could catch a moment of rest, his body and mind always half-awake to the possibilities around him. However, the call for Salat-e-Isha over the lounge's paging system prompted a change in his plans. Setting aside his immediate desire for rest, he joined others in one corner of the lounge for prayer.

Here, in the act of prayer, Aditya found a semblance of peace, a brief respite from the constant vigilance that defined his existence. It was a rare instance where he could blend in not just as a strategy, but as a participant in a collective expression of faith, momentarily setting aside the isolating burdens of his clandestine role.

The prayer had just concluded, and the serene silence that followed was abruptly broken by the gentleman next to Aditya, who turned to him with a question that sent a shockwave of panic through Aditya's core. 'Brother, how come you didn't perform wudu before prayer?' he inquired, his tone casual yet carrying an undertone of curiosity that felt like an accusation to Aditya.

For a split second, Aditya felt as though the ground beneath him had shifted. The question was a direct hit to his cover, exposing a crack he hadn't anticipated. The ritual cleansing of wudu was basic, an essential preparation for prayer, and his failure to perform it was a stark oversight for someone trying to blend in as a devout Muslim.

Steam seemed to pour from his ears as he scrambled for a response. Gathering his wits, he managed to reply with a carefully controlled edge of irritation, 'You might have not seen me coming from the washroom.' His voice carried a mix of defensiveness and upset, a natural reaction for someone accused of skipping a sacred ritual.

But as soon as the words left his mouth, Aditya realized his blunder. Wudu had its designated areas, especially in a place as well-equipped as a business lounge. His attempt at an explanation could easily raise more red flags, spotlighting his ignorance or flouting of a fundamental practice.

The tension in the moment was palpable. Aditya, while maintaining an outward appearance of slight annoyance, was internally recalibrating, ready to face this unexpected challenge. The interaction was a stark reminder of the thin ice he was skating on, posing as someone he was not.

The stranger's reaction to Aditya's discomfort was one of understanding, his smile an attempt to ease the tension. 'Don't take offense, brother,' he said, his tone gentle, aiming to clarify rather than confront, 'but a washroom isn't quite the place for wudu.'

Aditya, quick on his feet and unwilling to back down, crafted his response with a mix of pragmatism and humility. 'I'm aware,' he retorted, 'but the crowd at the wudu area made it clear I wouldn't have made it to prayer in time.' He paused, then added, 'I'll be more careful next time.' It was a calculated admission, one that sought to balance respect for the ritual with the practicality of his situation.

This concession seemed to satisfy the stranger, who nodded and said, 'Never mind.' Aditya, relieved, acknowledged the understanding with a bow of his head and swiftly moved to claim a solitary corner sofa. As he tried to settle in for a brief rest, his mind was anything but quiet. The interaction had left a lingering trace of unease, a stark reminder of the constant vigilance required to maintain his cover. Each moment, each encounter, was a test of his adaptability, his ability to think on his feet.

Even as he later walked through the vast expanses of Heathrow's Terminal 5, the incident shadowed his thoughts. The potential consequences of his slip-up, had the conversation taken a different turn, weighed heavily on him. It was a sobering reminder of the precarious nature of his existence, where a single misstep could expose months, even years, of careful planning. The memory of this encounter, a seemingly minor hiccup in the grand scheme of his mission, accompanied him on his train ride to Redbridge via Stanford, a silent companion amidst the throngs of oblivious travellers around him.

Aditya's gaze lingered on the shifting landscape beyond the tube's window, the urban sprawl of London gradually giving way to the more serene vistas of Redbridge. As the train carved its way through the city, he couldn't help but reflect on the stark contrasts between his life's turmoil and the steady rhythm of the world outside.

March in London was a herald of spring, the chill of winter loosening its grip to reveal the first hints of renewal. The city, caught in the delicate balance of cold snaps and the warming embrace of longer days, was slowly awakening. Amidst this backdrop of gradual change, Aditya found his thoughts drifting back to Ameera, a constant presence in his heart despite the physical and emotional distances that separated them.

Compelled by a surge of longing, he retrieved his phone, navigating through layers of security to access a hidden email account. There, nestled among the scant personal treasures he allowed himself, was a video attachment, a window into a past life. The clip, simple yet profoundly moving, featured Ameera on a swing, her expressions oscillating between delight and apprehension. Meera's hands, visible in the frame, provided gentle encouragement, a tangible connection to what he had left behind.

The sight of the Guess wristwatch on Meera's wrist struck a deep chord within Aditya. That he had chosen it for her, and that it still adorned her wrist after everything – divorce, distance and the silent agreements to protect their daughter from the complexities of his life – spoke volumes. It was a silent reminder of a past filled with love, a reminder of connections that, despite the passage of time and the unfolding of their shared life, remained unbroken.

In that moment, the weight of his choices, the sacrifices made in the name of duty, and the personal cost of his profession settled heavily upon him. Yet, seeing Meera still wearing the wristwatch, a token of their once shared life, offered a sliver of solace, a sign that perhaps not all was lost in the shadowy dance of his existence.

Upon returning to the familiar confines of his London safe house in Redbridge, Aditya wasted no time in shedding the remnants of his journey. A quick shower to wash away the travel, a crisp apple from the refrigerator for sustenance and a change into fresh clothes – he was ready to confront the next chapter of his clandestine life.

The short trip to his 'uncle' Altaf's shop in Waltham Forest was uneventful, a small mercy in the life of someone for whom every moment could spell danger. As he greeted Altaf Raza with a respectful 'adaab', the semblance of familial bonds wrapped around their professional relationship like a veil. Altaf's response was typical, his demeanour unreadable, yet his words carried the weight of approval. 'You didn't leave any room for complaint, and did a remarkable job,' he said, an acknowledgement that, in their line of work, was as close to praise as one could get.

The invitation to walk was unexpected, a deviation from their usual terse exchanges. 'You must be tired,' Altaf said, eyeing him for a moment. Aditya smiled. 'Me and feeling tired? Not in this life,

Uncle. Let's go,' he replied with a laugh, a brief flicker of levity in the dense fog of their covert operations.

As they stepped out into the cool London air, Aditya braced himself for what was to come. These walks were rarely just walks, but rather moving meetings where plans were forged and fates decided. Yet, as he matched his pace with Altaf's, Aditya felt a surge of readiness. Whatever the challenge, whatever the mission, he was prepared to face it head-on, with the unwavering resolve that had become his hallmark.

~

In the crisp atmosphere of March, Altaf Raza and his nephew Hassan Raza wandered through the Waltham Forest area of London, deeply engrossed in a secretive conversation. The ambiance around them was a gentle reminder of winter's departure, with the chill in the air beginning to relent to the subtle warmth of the approaching spring. Early blooms and budding trees added a soft touch of colour to the urban landscape, creating a serene backdrop for their discreet dialogue.

As they meandered through the streets and green spaces, they blended perfectly into the vibrant tapestry of the area, known for its rich cultural diversity and lively community life. The surrounding environment hummed with the quiet activity of a weekday; local cafes emitted the comforting aromas of coffee and tea, mingling with the fresh scent of spring. But they chose to walk and talk.

Small bookshops, galleries and vintage stores dotted their path, offering distractions that allowed them to pause and look around, thus avoiding any suspicion from passersby. The quiet corners of parks and the less crowded pathways of the forest area became their preferred routes, where their low voices could mingle with the rustling of leaves and the distant hum of city life.

As they threaded through the secluded pathways, Altaf's voice took on a graver tone, the list of names he recited a litany of shadows, each casting vast webs across the geopolitical landscape. These were not mere individuals but nodes in a network spread across Pakistan, Afghanistan and Canada, all linked by the tendrils of terrorism stretching into Punjab and Kashmir. Their unified goal was sinister; to sow discord, destabilize the peace that India had fought hard to maintain and tarnish the image of the prime minister's governance.

When Altaf uttered the name Harvinder Singh Sandhu alias Rinda, along with the names known in the world of crime and terrorism, a chill coursed through Aditya. Goosebumps raised on his skin, not just from the name itself but from the realization of its significance. That this same name had spilled from Colonel Cheema's lips only added layers to the enigma.

Aditya's mind raced as Altaf's words sank in. The mention of Rinda, a name tied to both Altaf and Colonel Cheema, seeded a kernel of doubt in Aditya's thoughts. He couldn't help but suspect the possibility of a deeper, perhaps undisclosed, alignment between Altaf and Cheema regarding Rinda. Was he merely a pawn in a larger strategy, one orchestrated to play out personal vendettas or settle hidden scores under the guise of national interest? It could be coincidence, Aditya mused silently as they walked. Rinda's name on New Delhi's list for Altaf, and Cheema mentioning Rinda while proffering information to sell. It seems Cheema has more names, terrorists under official protection in Pakistan, valuable to India. This succinct thought offered a straightforward explanation, minimizing the web of potential conspiracies without dismissing the complexities of espionage.

After a moment of contemplative silence, Aditya broached the delicate subject. 'How come, Uncle, you have the same name that Cheema mentioned in Karachi?' The question landed like a spark on dry tinder, Altaf's reaction immediate and charged with offence. 'Are you suspecting me of colluding with Cheema?' he shot back, the question sharp, loaded.

Aditya, though taken aback, was not unprepared. 'No. I'm only seeking clarity,' he responded, striving to maintain a neutral tone amidst the rising tension. Altaf's reply was brisk, a blend of warning and reprimand. 'Alright, if that was the case. Or else, mind your intelligence.'

The air between them thickened, the remainder of their walk subdued, marked by an unspoken discomfort. The conversation, once fluid and engaged, dwindled to a trickle, until Altaf called a taxi to return to his shop. The absence of an invitation for Aditya to join was a silent yet eloquent expression of Altaf's displeasure.

Watching Altaf depart, Aditya was left to ponder the rift his question had created. He understood the sting his inquiry had delivered, the delicate balance of trust and suspicion they dealt with daily now momentarily upset. Resolving to address the matter upon their next meeting, Aditya recognized the need for careful diplomacy. His field of work was as much about managing relationships as it was about intelligence and counterintelligence.

Lingering in the aftermath of Altaf's abrupt departure, Aditya let the significance of their mission settle over him. The names Altaf had mentioned were Gurdeep Singh Takkar, Paramjit Singh Panjwar, Syed Khaled Raza and Basheer Ahmed Peer that echoed in his mind, each carrying the weight of history and consequence. In an afterthought, he added one more name to the list, Harvinder Singh Sandhu, better known as Rinda.

With the weight of the task ahead pressing upon him, Aditya made the decision to return to Redbridge, to the solitude and security of his safe house. However, as he covered the streets of London, an impulse diverted his path. Stopping at an Indian store, he immersed himself in the familiar sights and scents of home, selecting items with a sense of purpose. The act of shopping, so mundane, offered a momentary respite from the complexities of his existence. Then, at another shop, he purchased goat meat, an addition that spoke of a desire for normalcy, perhaps a plan to cook a meal that connected him to memories of a simpler life.

Returning to his sanctuary in Redbridge, Altaf's home, Aditya stepped into the kitchen and made yakhni biryani with the ingredients he had picked up on the way back. It was not just about preparing a meal; it was an attempt to bridge the distance that had formed between him and Altaf, a gesture of reconciliation without words. The aroma that soon filled the house was rich and warm, a quiet olive branch offered through food.

Altaf's surprise on discovering biryani for dinner was obvious, and it deepened when he tasted it. The flavour made him look up in astonishment. 'Hussain, kis hotel se mangwaya hai yeh?' he asked, half-joking, half-impressed. Hussain smiled and pointed towards Aditya.

'Yeh sab unhone banaya hai, Janaab,' he said.

Altaf turned to Aditya, disbelief giving way to curiosity. 'Tumne?'

Aditya nodded, standing a little awkwardly. 'Ha, Chachaa. Socha aapko yaad aayegi apni mulk ki biryani.'

Altaf studied him for a moment, then asked softly, 'Aur yeh meherbani kis khushi mein?'

Aditya set his plate down and rose. Folding his hands in front of him, he said, 'Chachaa, mujhse badi zyaadti ho gayee. Mujhe maaf kar dein.'

For a heartbeat, Altaf said nothing. Then he got up, came around the table and pulled Aditya into a tight embrace.

'Bas, beta,' he murmured. 'Dil ka saaf insaan galti bhi saaf dil se maanta hai.'

They sat down again, the earlier distance between them gone.

By choosing to say sorry through the universal language of food, Aditya bridged the gap created by suspicion and hurt. The gesture was simple but deep, a reminder that even in their world of secrecy and shadow, there was still room for loyalty, affection and forgiveness.

~

June 2022.

Aditya found himself back at the drawing board, armed with the five names Altaf had given him at the instructions of Aditya's superiors in New Delhi. Each name came with a brief note detailing their activities. He spent the next few days in gathering intelligence on them. He made calls to some of his assets, informers and a former contact who was doing time in London's Belmarsh Prison. The following was what Aditya came up with

1. GURDEEP SINGH TAKKAR, residing in Canada. Served as the chief of the Khalistan Tiger Force (KTF). Takkar relocated to Canada in 1997, utilizing a counterfeit passport. Despite his

refugee claim being denied, he married a woman who attempted to sponsor him for immigration, but this effort was also rejected.

In 2020, India officially declared Takkar as a designated terrorist due to his active involvement in recruiting and training individuals for the banned terrorist group, KTF. Additionally, he was affiliated with the separatist organization Sikhs for Justice (SFJ), which conducted a Khalistan referendum in September 2021.

India has repeatedly expressed concerns regarding Takkar's terrorist affiliations over the years. In 2018, then Punjab Chief Minister Captain Amarinder Singh provided a list of wanted individuals to the Canadian government, requesting Takkar's extradition to India.

Takkar is wanted in multiple cases, including the 2007 explosion in Ludhiana, Punjab, which resulted in six fatalities and forty-two injuries.

In 2010, the Punjab Police filed a case against Takkar for his alleged involvement in a bombing near a temple in Patiala. UK-based Paramjit Singh Pamma, another wanted terrorist, was among the primary suspects in the case.

In 2015, Takkar faced charges related to targeting Hindu leaders, and in 2016, he was accused of funding Mandeep Dhaliwal and conspiring to assassinate Hindu leaders. Look Out Circulars (LOC) and Red Corner Notices (RCNs) were issued against him in 2015 and 2016, respectively.

The National Investigation Agency (NIA) initiated an investigation into Takkar's role in the killings of RSS leaders in Punjab in 2018.

In 2022, the NIA offered a reward of Rs 10 lakh (1 million) for information leading to Takkar's arrest, following allegations of his involvement in a conspiracy to assassinate a Hindu priest in Jalandhar, Punjab.

2. PARAMJIT SINGH PANJWAR, residing in Pakistan. Joined the Khalistan Commando Force (KCF). Wanted for numerous heinous crimes.

He is accused of murdering Maj. Gen. B.N. Kumar (retd), former chairman of the Bhakra Beas Management Board (BBMB), in Chandigarh in 1988.

Panjwar is wanted for the tragic killing of nineteen students at Thapar Engineering College in Patiala in 1989.

He is also wanted for the abduction and murder of Rajan Bains, the son of SSP Batala, IPS Govind Ram, in 1989.

Panjwar faces charges in India for orchestrating a bomb blast that claimed ten lives in Sector 34 of Chandigarh in 1999, along with several other cases involving murder and kidnapping during the peak of militancy in Punjab in the mid-1980s.

He fled to Germany and later relocated to Pakistan in 1990, where he currently resides in Lahore under the protection of Pakistan's ISI.

India designated him as a terrorist under the Unlawful Activities Prevention Act (UAPA) in July 2020.

Panjwar is reportedly involved in the smuggling of arms and drugs via drones from Pakistan into Punjab, India.

3. SYED KHALID RAZA, residing in Pakistan. A former commander of the Pakistan-based terrorist organization Al Badr, played a significant role in orchestrating violent attacks in Jammu and Kashmir during the 1990s. Additionally, he has ties with the Jamaat-e-Islami (JeI) and its Talba wing in Pakistan.

   The Pakistan-based Al Badr terrorist outfit, designated as a Foreign Terrorist Organization by the United States, was established in June 1998 with the aim of bolstering the 'Kashmiri freedom struggle' and achieving the 'liberation' of the Indian state of Jammu and Kashmir to merge it with Pakistan. It emerged as one of several terrorist factions affiliated with the Jamaat-e-Islami and often collaborated closely with the notorious Hizb-ul-Mujahideen (HM).

   Al Badr's roots can be traced back to 1971 when Pakistan-sponsored Islamic militants carried out atrocities against the Bengali-speaking population in East Pakistan (now Bangladesh).

Subsequently, Al Badr became affiliated with Hizb-i-Islami, an Islamic terrorist organization based in Afghanistan and led by Gulbuddin Hekmatyar. It made its first appearance in Kashmir in 1990, launching a jihad against India under the HM banner. With support from Pakistan's ISI, HM was established in 1990 as the armed wing of JeI. However, in 1998, Al Badr diverged from HM due to ideological differences and emerged as an independent separatist entity.

Employing violence to advance its objectives, the terrorist organization targeted government officials, security forces and civilians, causing disruption and chaos through weapons supplied by Pakistan and other terrorist entities. Alongside Lashkar-e-Taiba (LeT) and JeM, Al Badr was among the few groups to integrate suicide (fidayeen) attacks into its operational strategy. It propagated its agenda through the Urdu journal *Al Badr*, established in Pakistan in 1999.

Syed Khalid Raza, a former commander of Al Badr, resides in Karachi under the protection of the Pakistan Army.

4. BASHEER AHMED PEER, residing in Pakistan. Served as a commander of the HM terrorist organization and was primarily tasked with overseeing the recruitment and infiltration of armed militants into Jammu and Kashmir.

   He was officially designated as a terrorist by the Indian government in October 2021 due to his involvement in facilitating the infiltration of militants and providing logistical support for terrorist activities in Jammu and Kashmir.

   As the 'launching chief' of the HM in Pakistan, Peer plays a crucial role in the recruitment and deployment of infiltrators, as well as the smuggling of arms and ammunition into the Kashmir valley.

   He resides in Rawalpindi, Pakistan, under the protection of the ISI since 2005.

   Following his designation as one of the most wanted terrorists by India under the UAPA, properties owned by Peer in Kashmir were seized by the local administration.

Aditya jotted down a few quick notes on a piece of paper. His handwriting was sharp, purposeful. At the top, he scribbled: Operation 'Shadow War' – a codename that carried weight. Below it, the words 'To be executed on Assembly Line Model' appeared, underlined twice.

The 'Assembly Line' was a methodical approach, a way of breaking down an action into precise, sequential steps, each completed independently but in perfect sync with the others. Aditya envisioned the operation functioning much like a factory conveyor belt – every phase detached, yet essential to the whole.

He drew a straight line and divided it into seven clear segments, labeling each meticulously:

A: Initiation
B: Logistics & Cash Support
C: Arms Procurement
D: Criminal Recruitment
E: Surveillance & Reconnaissance
F: Execution
G: Support & Back-up

Each segment was a cog in the machine, but Aditya understood something critical – the number of segments might change depending on the mission. What mattered was that each part functioned independently, without knowledge of the others. 'A' wouldn't know 'B', and 'B' wouldn't know 'A' or 'C'. It was a foolproof design, with firewalls between steps. No leaks, no weak points.

Aditya paused, tapping the pencil against the paper. This kind of compartmentalization – what did it mean for the operation as a whole? It meant precision, secrecy and, above all, protection. If one part fell, the others would remain intact, insulated from the fallout. 'Shadow War' would run like a machine, flawless and untraceable.

His years of training and the countless operations, including the ones where he had failed, had all drilled one key lesson into Aditya: this method was bulletproof. A breach in one segment would be just that a breach, nothing more. The rest of the operation would remain airtight, untouched and untraceable. The compartmentalized structure ensured that no single misstep could expose the entire mission or expose its covert nature.

In other words, if anyone got caught, no one else would be compromised. Each operative only knew their own piece of the puzzle, never the whole. This level of anonymity allowed the concerned government to distance itself completely: no names, no links, no accountability, whether the person was alive or dead. The operation's integrity would remain intact, while the system shielded those in the shadows.

The soft hiss of the electric kettle broke his trance. Aditya blinked, momentarily pulled from his thoughts, and made himself a cup of tea. The warmth of the cup in his hands was familiar, grounding him. But for some strange reason, he couldn't refocus. His mind kept drifting back to Ameera.

It was almost three years since he last saw her. She had turned four. Of course, Meera, his ex-wife had the decency to send a picture of Ameera's birthday celebration just three months ago. She looked so innocent, blowing out the candles on her cake. But between them stood a ghost. A ghost that lived between her, Meera and their mutual contact, Altaf. Meera believed that ghost was Aditya, and she wasn't wrong. But for her safety and Ameera's, she could never be allowed direct access to him. It was a hard truth, one he had to accept.

Even for someone like Aditya, a seasoned and deadly spy who had compromised everything else, family was the one thing that remained off-limits. Untouchable. Protected at all costs.

He sighed deeply, staring into the light brown liquid in his cup. The silence pressed down on him as he wondered if he would ever see them again. If Ameera would ever know who he truly was.

Aditya tried to shake off the memories, forcing his focus back to the task at hand. But the unease lingered, gnawing at him. He felt restless, unable to work, so he decided to step out for a walk, hoping the fresh air would clear his head. He wandered aimlessly for a while, but the heaviness in his mind refused to lift.

Taking a break seemed inevitable, but what kind of break? The options swirled in his mind – should he go to a bar and drown himself in alcohol? Visit a brothel for a night of wild, meaningless sex? Maybe take drugs to numb the mental chaos? The thoughts circled him like shadows, but none felt right. He was lost, unsure how to quiet the storm raging inside.

In the end, he chose something simpler. He found a relatively quiet spot along the Thames, far from the bustling crowds. Sitting on the banks, he let his mind drift back to the memories of Meera and Ameera – the only treasure he had left that truly mattered. He thought of their shared moments, the brief flashes of happiness and for the first time that day, he felt something close to peace.

The tension eased from his body, and without realizing it, Aditya fell asleep on a bench, cradled by the cool breeze and the gentle lull of the river. It wasn't until the raucous cries of gulls jolted him awake that he realized how much time had passed. But for the first time in hours, his mind felt clear, at least for the moment.

11

The Puppeteer's Agenda

Beginning 2023.

The inmate sitting across from Aditya, separated by a glass partition, in Belmarsh Prison, was in his early thirties. He had the unmistakable look of a short-haired Sikh, with trimmed beard, semi crew-cut hair, sharp eyebrows and a fair complexion, the last even paler due to his time away from the outside world. His name was Sukhvinder Singh Chahal, though everyone called him Sukkhi. He was lean, almost gaunt, the result of two years behind bars. Before his conviction for rioting during a violent mob protest, he had served at a Sikh gurudwara on Merton Road, southwest of London. In just a week's time, he would be free.

Aditya and Sukkhi spoke with the ease of two men who knew each other well, their conversation carrying the weight of unspoken history.

'Counting down the days to freedom?' Aditya asked, his voice calm but edged with curiosity.

'Yeah,' Sukkhi replied, the relief evident in his tone. 'Just a matter of one more week.'

'How's prison life been treating you?' Aditya inquired, leaning in slightly.

Sukkhi let out a chuckle, his smile thin. 'You should try it sometime. Quite the experience.'

Aditya's eyes softened. 'I owe you, Sukkhi. For your sacrifice.'

Sukkhi's face took on a look of quiet resignation. 'As long as the end goal is achieved, I'm good with it.'

'That's all that matters,' Aditya said, standing to leave. 'I'll see you soon.'

'See you soon,' Sukkhi echoed.

Pausing before turning away, Aditya asked, 'Where's your passport?'

'In the magistrate's custody. I'll get it back after my release,' Sukkhi replied.

Aditya nodded, gave him a final glance and headed towards the exit, the conversation lingering between them like an unfinished sentence.

The house in Redbridge was filled with the rich, intoxicating aroma of yakhni biryani. As Aditya entered, the scent caught him off guard. Who else could have made it? He was certain only he knew how to prepare this particular dish. Could it be that someone was simply reheating the leftovers from the meal he'd cooked? Intrigued, Aditya made his way to the kitchen.

There, standing by the stove, was Altaf, quietly plucking mint leaves from a pot – the kind of mint Aditya had only ever seen used in Karachi. He paused behind his 'uncle', inhaling deeply, savouring the familiar yet different scent. Altaf, sensing his presence, turned slowly, a faint smirk playing on his lips, as if to silently say: *You may have thought your yakhni was good, but wait until you taste mine*. He didn't say a word, but the challenge was clear.

Aditya felt a wave of humility. There was so much to learn in life, he realized lessons that extended beyond the kitchen, beyond his cynicism. Altaf scooped a spoonful of the steaming biryani, holding it just inches from Aditya's mouth.

'Close your eyes and taste it,' Altaf instructed, his voice calm, assured.

Without a word, Aditya complied, his eyes shutting as he opened his mouth. The moment the food hit his tongue, he was lost in the layers of flavour, savoring each second. He held the bite in his mouth, reluctant to swallow, as if doing so would end the experience. It was more than just food – it was an offering, a moment of trust.

Altaf placed a gentle hand on his shoulder, tapping lightly. 'Now, open your eyes and bring the pot to the table,' he said, his tone soft yet commanding.

As Aditya obeyed, carrying the pot of biryani, he felt something solidify in his mind. Altaf, this man he called 'uncle', couldn't possibly betray him. The biryani had done more than fill his senses; it had built a bridge of unspoken loyalty between them.

As they ate the biryani, Altaf casually inquired about Sukkhi, who was set to be released from prison in a week's time. Aditya didn't hold back. He explained that Sukkhi had once been a terrorist in Punjab before surrendering to R&AW and becoming an asset just over four years ago. Aditya had been working on the intricate links between Punjab militants operating in India and their counterparts based in Canada and the US. His plan was to plant Sukkhi among the British-based militants before sending him to Canada. It would provide the perfect cover on the surface, the British militant groups would appear to be the ones sending Sukkhi to Canada, making his arrival seem natural, seamless. The transition into the militant networks in the West would go unquestioned.

Post the 2019 elections, neutralizing the militants demanding a separate state for Punjab in India had escalated to a top priority for R&AW. Altaf, always calculating, asked what Sukkhi's strengths were.

'He's a sharpshooter,' Aditya said between bites, 'and he knows his way around sniper rifles.'

Aditya's plan was clear; once Sukkhi was out of prison, he would be dispatched to Canada without delay. The timing had to be perfect, and the stakes couldn't be higher.

After finishing the biryani, Aditya stood up and made his way to the wash basin, meticulously scrubbing his hands clean. The aroma of the spices still lingered in the air, but the cool water against his skin grounded him, bringing him back to the moment. Once done, he returned to Altaf and casually asked, 'Did you go through the accounts I submitted earlier? The expenses are all detailed.'

Altaf nodded, his expression unreadable. 'I already did. I've communicated to Delhi that more funds should be sent.'

Aditya relaxed slightly, but before he could speak, Altaf continued, his tone shifting. 'However, there's a new development. The money won't be coming from Delhi ... or from India at all.'

Aditya's brow furrowed. 'What? Wouldn't that compromise the mission?' His mind raced with possibilities. Perhaps India's missions abroad would now fund the operation? That seemed plausible, but still risky.

Altaf's response was calm, almost nonchalant. He met Aditya's gaze and spoke a single word: 'Dubai.'

The word hung in the air between them, heavy with implications. Aditya asked, 'Why Dubai?'

Altaf responded with a simple shrug, 'No idea.' The game had just taken on a new dimension, and the stakes were rising faster than they had anticipated.

What neither Aditya nor Altaf knew was that the success of their operation relied on alliances woven far beyond the immediate battlefield. The ruling families of the UAE and Saudi Arabia played pivotal roles in ensuring the mission's success. Their involvement wasn't just a matter of convenience; it was born out of necessity, a shared threat that extended beyond India's borders and reached into the heart of the Middle East. The terrorists India sought to eliminate were the same ones sheltering under the protection of Pakistan and threatening the fragile stability of the Gulf.

For the UAE royal 'Al Rashid al Rayan (ARR)' and the Saudi royals, these terrorist groups posed a direct challenge to their regimes, threatening their national security and their increasingly delicate geopolitical balancing acts. Their softened diplomatic stance toward Israel had already made them targets of these extremists, emboldened by hostile nations, such as Pakistan, Turkey, Malaysia, Syria and Iran among others, backing their cause. It was this existential threat that motivated both the UAE and Saudi Arabia to back India's covert operations, knowing fully well that any blow struck against these terrorists served to protect their own lives.

But for ARR, there was another reason for his quiet support that was a personal debt to India's NSD. Years earlier, when Princess Habiba had defied her father and fled the kingdom, it was an Indian Coast Guard operation that had intercepted her along with her physical trainer on the high seas near Goa. Despite her protests, the princess had been returned to her father, and a quiet understanding was forged. ARR knew he would be called upon one day, and when the NSD reached out for help to fund the operation, he was ready to oblige. Not that India had any shortage of funds, but the NSD didn't want even a nickel used in the operation to be linked to India.

Dubai's role in the mission was crucial but discreet. The UAE had agreed to provide the financial muscle, funnelling funds through its well-established banking systems, ensuring India's covert operations were fuelled without leaving a trace. Safe houses in both countries were ready to open their doors, giving Indian operatives the ability to prepare and stage their mission in anonymity. Their governments issued travel documents, allowing the movement of mercenaries and agents under the radar, while their control over local media ensured that no unwanted attention would disrupt the delicate operation.

Most critical of all, however, was the intelligence UAE and Saudi Arabia agreed to share. With deep-rooted networks inside Pakistan's government and military, the Gulf nations were ready to offer invaluable insights into the target's movements, potential security threats and the political landscape, which could impact the mission's outcome. This intelligence could be the linchpin to allow Aditya or his team to move with precision, their steps guided by the whispered secrets of powerful allies.

Two days later, Altaf led Aditya to an inconspicuous building in the heart of the city, its sign reading International Bank of Commerce. The exterior gave no indication of the secrets it held within. Aditya, always sharp-eyed, couldn't help but notice the security guards stationed discreetly near the entrance, their gazes scanning the surroundings with trained thoroughness.

As they stepped inside, Altaf reached into his coat pocket and fished out a small, silver key, its edges worn but still gleaming under the fluorescent lights. He handed it to the bank official, who nodded knowingly before guiding them down a narrow corridor. The walls of the bank seemed to close in as they approached the locker room, each step reverberating through the silence, the sound amplifying the tension in the air.

In the cool, brightly lit room, Altaf inserted the key into a steel locker and turned it with a soft click. The locker door swung open to reveal several steel boxes neatly arranged inside. Altaf pulled one out, setting it on the table with a deliberate thud. He opened the box to reveal neatly stacked wads of crisp currency, dollars and pounds, shimmering in the cold light like forbidden treasure.

Aditya's eyes widened for a moment, unable to mask his surprise. The sheer amount was staggering. Altaf broke the silence, his voice low but firm. 'Four million – two in dollars, two in pounds. In case you need more, let me know. But only after submitting the accounts.'

Aditya raised an eyebrow, his lips curling into a slight smirk. 'Secret service funds are neither accountable nor audited, Uncle.'

Altaf had anticipated this response. His expression remained steady, as if he had heard it a hundred times before. 'That's only for public consumption, son. Every single penny is internally audited.' His tone carried the weight of experience, an subtle reminder that even in the shadowy world of espionage, nothing was left unchecked.

Aditya nodded, a silent acknowledgement of the unspoken rules of their game. He didn't have a bag with him, an oversight that became glaringly obvious as he began stuffing the bills into his jacket and trouser pockets. The bulging stacks of cash made his movements awkward, but there was no time to dwell on it.

'You should've brought a bag, knowing we were coming to a bank,' Altaf chided, his voice light but carrying an undertone of practicality.

Aditya shrugged, offering a playful grin. 'I didn't realize I'd be leaving with a fortune.'

But beneath the surface, both men knew the stakes were higher than mere currency. The money wasn't just cash; it was fuel for the dangerous world Aditya was about to reenter, a world where every dollar and pound could mean the difference between life and death.

May 2023.

Aditya stood in front of a stark wall, the weight of the moment heavy on his shoulders. Before him hung a long list of India's most wanted, their names etched into the fabric of the country's security apparatus. Each name represented a labyrinth of networks, attacks and bloody history. Altaf, acting on orders from Delhi, had recently added even more names to the list. Now, the rogue's gallery stared back at Aditya like ghosts haunting the corridors of power.

The names were written in bold, black letters, each one a reminder of the men who had wreaked havoc across borders. He scanned the list, the tension in the room palpable:

1. SHAHID LATIF – mastermind behind the Pathankot attack. His name alone evoked nightmare memories of the violent siege.
2. PARAMJIT SINGH PANJWAR – leader of the KCF, fuelling the separatist fire that refused to die.
3. SYED KHALID RAZA – a Hizbul commander responsible for supplying terrorists to Kashmir, his network deeply entrenched.
4. HAFEEZ SALMAN BHUTTAVI – Hafeez Sayed's deputy, one of the architects behind the devastating 26/11 Mumbai attacks.
5. HARVINDER SINGH SANDHU alias RINDA – another name that sent chills down the spine, his operations spreading across India's borders.
6. DAWOOD MALIK – closely tied to Rasool Azhar, the man behind nearly every JeM attack on Indian soil.
7. BASHIR AHMED PEER – Hizbul commander, a key supplier of militants and weapons in Kashmir.
8. SYED NOOR – smuggled terrorists, explosives and arms into Kashmir, his fingerprints on countless deadly incidents.
9. HUSSAIN ARAIN – a top leader of LeT, orchestrating several attacks with chilling precision.
10. AIJAZ AHMED – a Kashmiri terrorist linked with ISIS, representing a fusion of dangerous ideologies.

11. ZIAUR RAHMAN – an LeT operative who trained youths from across India in terror camps inside Pakistan.

Aditya studied each name, each face. The list was more than just names. It was a blueprint of threats, a catalogue of enemies who needed to be neutralized. He felt Altaf's presence behind him, a silent acknowledgement of the burden they both shared.

'Delhi wants swift action,' Altaf said quietly, his voice slicing through the tension. 'These men have been operating with impunity for too long.'

Aditya didn't reply. He knew the stakes. Every one of these names represented a potential war, a clash of intelligence and a race against time. His eyes lingered on one name in particular, Shahid Latif. The Pathankot attack had left scars, both personal and professional.

Turning away from the list, Aditya clenched his fists. The battle ahead wasn't just about eliminating threats; it was about preventing the next attack before it became another mark on the wall.

Altaf sat back, arms crossed, waiting for Aditya's feedback on the list. Delhi needed answers, and they needed them fast. Aditya, with his usual calm precision, began classifying the names into different categories.

'Three of them – Syed Khalid Raza, Hussain Arain and Ziaur Rahman – are in Karachi, under ISI's protection,' Aditya said, his tone clipped, all business.

Altaf nodded, unsurprised. 'And Bhuttavi?'

Aditya's eyes narrowed slightly. 'He's locked up in Muridke – at least that's what they want us to believe. It's a front. They're keeping him there to protect him from a strike.'

Altaf leaned in, a mischievous glint in his eye. 'No sweat, just enter the jail and screw him,' he said, grinning.

Aditya raised an eyebrow, bemused. 'Sorry, Uncle. I thought you had better taste?'

Altaf winked, his grin widening. 'You bet.'

Shaking his head with a smirk, Aditya continued. 'Bashir Ahmed Peer is hiding in Rawalpindi, and Paramjit Singh Panjwar is in Lahore, both under the ISI's protection.'

Altaf scoffed. 'Obvious. Who else would be keeping them safe?'

Aditya glanced back at the list, his voice dropping slightly. 'Shahid Latif is in Sialkot, Dawood Malik in North Waziristan, Syed Noor in Khyber Pakhtunkhwa, and Aijaz Ahmed … he's in Afghanistan.'

Altaf leaned back again, tapping his fingers on the table, his eyes scanning the list as if sizing up each name for a hit. 'That's quite the collection of bed bugs you've got there.'

Aditya couldn't help but chuckle at Altaf's casual quip. But beneath the banter, both men knew the truth: this list represented a population of threats, each one protected by layers of geography, politics and powerful connections. Striking at any of them would take more than just intelligence. It would require precise planning and a ruthless execution.

The weight of what lay ahead settled over the room. Aditya, ever methodical, knew the next steps were critical. Altaf, with his half-joking bravado, understood that the game they were playing was deadlier than ever.

Aditya leaned against the wall, his eyes scanning the list again. 'I'm trying to figure out how to go after them. It's no longer a solo job … this is about multiple hits within one country.' His voice had the edge of someone who knew the complexity of the task ahead.

Altaf, who had been quietly observing, interjected, his tone cautious but firm. 'Besides, the establishment in Pakistan is on high alert after what happened in Karachi. They're not going to be as complacent.'

Aditya nodded in agreement, his brow furrowing. 'Yeah, protection around these guys would be tighter now … I'll need to set up multiple hit squads.'

Altaf gave the list another glance, his mind working through the potential moves. 'Three of them are in Karachi,' he pointed out. 'But going after all three? That's risky. Pick just one.'

He paused, then added with a hint of doubt, 'But are you sure about going back to Karachi so soon?'

Aditya smirked, a glint of calculated determination in his eyes. 'I doubt they're expecting a repeat in the same city. That's exactly why

I want to strike there again … catch them off guard. I will pick one from Karachi, and then hit targets in different cities. Spread it out.'

Aditya's finger traced the names on the list as he spoke. 'Syed Khalid Raza in Karachi … Bashir Ahmed Peer in Rawalpindi … and Paramjit Singh Panjwar in Lahore.' His selection was deliberate, each name carrying a specific weight, a history of violence that needed to be ended.

That was not all. Aditya's voice had gained a new burr of compressed excitement, his pointing finger held the faintest tremor, and his eyes glittered with a new light that disturbed Altaf as he watched him.

Altaf said nothing for a moment, the gravity of the situation sinking in. He knew that Aditya had already set himself on a path from which there was no return. Unlike Aditya, Altaf wasn't a spy. He was an informer, an asset, a handler, a middleman. He'd never picked up a gun, never gone after anyone. But he had a sharp sense for reading people, and his instincts told him something undeniable: Aditya had become dangerous. Not just to others, but to himself. The thrill of the hunt had started to consume him.

For the powers controlling these missions, Aditya's transformation was a gift, a skilled operative who was becoming more effective, more ruthless. But Altaf knew that for Aditya, this path was destructive. He had already lost so much in his personal life. The thought of more loss, more tragedy, weighed heavily on Altaf's mind. He didn't want to see his 'nephew' whirl further into the abyss.

Aditya interrupted the silence with a flash of excitement. 'I'm getting closer now. Let me pinpoint their exact locations, study their daily routines, and figure out the security around them.'

Altaf made one final observation, his voice quiet but pointed. 'Don't reuse any of your assets from the last operation. Switch it up.'

Without missing a beat, Aditya nodded in agreement. 'Absolutely. No repeats.'

The exchange left an unspoken tension in the air, the weight of the mission pressing down on both men. Aditya was on the brink of something lethal, and Altaf, despite his calm exterior, could see the storm building inside the younger man.

Altaf quietly observed Aditya, noticing how deeply immersed he was in the mission. It struck him how far gone this man, now known to the world as Hassan Raza, was. He was treading a perilous path where danger lurked at every turn, and Altaf knew that if something went wrong, no one would mourn his loss. Aditya had made himself dispensable. Perhaps, when the end came, there would be no more than a cheque – compensation delivered to his ex-wife, the only person Aditya had ever nominated, even after their divorce. The cold finality of it all gnawed at Altaf.

Aditya was blind to the larger forces at play. He didn't know that the mission he had been entrusted with wasn't just about neutralizing enemies of the state. It was not just India's biggest ever covert war. No, it had an ulterior motive, one that was far more political than military, far removed from national security. This operation was part of a broader, more cynical game. If Aditya succeeded, the results would be paraded in front of the electorate, much like how the Balakot strike had bolstered support in the last election. It wasn't about protecting the nation. It was about securing votes.

Altaf's thoughts swirled with a mix of concern and guilt. He wasn't a spy like Aditya. He didn't face the same risks, the same life-or-death stakes. But he knew what was at stake for Aditya, even if the man himself remained oblivious. And that knowledge weighed heavily on him.

As Aditya continued planning, seemingly indifferent to his own fate, Altaf couldn't shake the feeling that this mission was leading Aditya into a trap, one where, even if he completed the job, he would be little more than a pawn in a larger, darker game.

12

Thorn with a Thorn

May 2023.

Aditya was preparing Sukkhi for the next strike, sizing him up with a scrutinizing gaze. The freshly released prisoner had proven his skills as a sharpshooter, but Aditya needed to know if he could handle something more intricate. Something beyond the standard close-range motorcycle hit. That method, while effective, was predictable. Sukkhi had mastered it, but the stakes were rising, and with it, the complexity of the mission.

This time, Aditya had been considering a different approach. An assassination modelled on the principles of an 'assembly line'. It was a tactic not commonly used, a carefully orchestrated, multi-step process where each participant played a vital role. Unlike the usual straightforward hit, this method required total understanding and precise coordination.

In espionage an 'assembly line' assassination is a deliberately compartmentalised operation in which the mission is broken into a string of simple, discrete tasks. Each agent is given one role and nothing more. That separation is deliberate: it limits who can describe the plan if caught, it fragments the chain of evidence and maintains plausible deniability for those who ordered the strike. Intelligence agencies often use this method so that the action appears, to any external observer, as several small, unrelated events rather than a single connected conspiracy.

Think of it laid out from A to H. Position A picks up the target and moves him; B stages a traffic hold; C monitors the route and signals the moment it's safe; D creates a diversion; E disables cameras and trackers; F in plain clothes carries out the strike; G removes or conceals evidence; H disperses the team and provides the alibi. No one knows the full script. Each man operates with just his piece of the plan. The fewer the overlaps, the smaller the risk that a single arrest or interrogation can expose the entire operation.

Aditya knew that for Sukkhi to succeed, a crash course on this unconventional technique was essential. He couldn't afford any missteps, not with what was coming. There was no room for error. Sukkhi had to be more than just a skilled gunman now. He had to understand the method, the rhythm and the seamless execution it demanded.

The lesson, Aditya thought, would begin immediately.

In the middle of his lesson, Aditya shifted gears, easing into a narrative, his voice calm but filled with intent, as if directing Sukkhi through the scene of a suspenseful film.

'Imagine somewhere in Dubai,' he began, his tone calm, pulling Sukkhi into the world he was creating. He started describing the scene:

> A car rolls to a stop, its windows tinted, shielding the exchange happening inside. An Arab man, seated behind the wheel, hands a thick envelope to a man in the passenger seat, Jaggi. The recipient, Jaggi, doesn't speak. He simply takes the envelope and slips it into a small bag at his feet. The Arab man then hands him a piece of paper with a single telephone number scribbled on it.
>
> The car pulls away, and after a few moments, it comes to a halt. Jaggi steps out, the Dubai heat clinging to his skin as he walks toward a public telephone. He dials the number with methodical precision.
>
> 'I got the stuff,' Jaggi says, his voice low, barely above a whisper.
>
> A voice crackles at the other end. 'Look for Crown Mobile Store.'

Jaggi pulls out his phone, searches for Crown Mobile Store on the map, and heads in that direction. As he approaches, blending into the flow of pedestrians, a passerby moves close, whispering into his ear as they walk past.

'Skip four shops from your destination and wait.'

Without hesitation, Jaggi follows the instructions, stopping four shops away and waiting. He keeps his eyes ahead, every muscle in his body tuned to his surroundings. Moments later, a salesman appears, tapping him lightly on the shoulder.

'My boss wants to see you.'

Jaggi doesn't speak, just nods and follows the man into a nearby shop. Inside, the atmosphere is sterile, the air thick with unspoken tension. The shop owner sits behind a desk, his face impassive, offering no words, no greeting. It's a silent transaction.

Jaggi understands the drill. He hands over the bag without a word.

The salesman breaks the silence. 'How much is inside?'

Jaggi shrugs, his expression neutral. 'I don't know.'

The owner opens the bag with deliberate slowness, revealing wads of crisp, new American dollars stacked neatly inside. Without so much as a glance at Jaggi, the owner examines the contents, then nods to the salesman.

The salesman gestures for Jaggi to leave.

The scene plays out like clockwork, each participant playing their role without a single wasted word. It's an assembly line of covert transactions, seamless and silent.

Jaggi, having completed his silent exchange, steps out of the shop and makes a quick call from his cell phone. His tone is brief, almost curt.

'It's done,' he says to Aditya, then immediately hangs up.

Without breaking stride, Jaggi heads to a nearby public toilet. Inside the stall, he pulls out the SIM card from his phone, snaps it between his fingers, and drops it into the toilet. With a quick flush, the evidence is gone. Once he exits, he heads toward a public dustbin and casually tosses the now-useless phone into the trash, blending seamlessly back into the busy streets of Dubai.

Sukkhi, still sitting across from Aditya, was listening intently, completely absorbed in the story. His wide-eyed expression made it clear he was both intrigued and rattled by the precise, cold efficiency of the operation.

Aditya, sensing the moment, stood up and returned to the whiteboard. He grabbed the marker and calmly ticked off the third segment.

'"C" – arms procurement.' He spoke the words with a sense of finality. 'Now that the funds are ready, we approach the next step: arms procurement.'

He turned back to Sukkhi. 'I want you to visualize everything I've told you so far. Now, follow the trail from where we left off.'

Sukkhi nodded, still processing the layers of the story as Aditya resumed his narration.

'The shop owner in Dubai wires 3.7 million dirhams to an 'importer' of 'grapes' in Afghanistan,' Aditya continued, his tone measured, drawing Sukkhi back into the web of their covert operation.

Each word added to the meticulous plan, the larger game takes shape, step by calculated step.

> Far away in the bustling market area of Kandahar City, a modest office stands in the middle of the commercial chaos, its signboard reading 'Afghan Red Grapes'. Inside, a middle-aged Afghan man sits behind a worn wooden desk, meticulously making entries in a thick ledger book. His movements are steady, practised. Among the entries is one that stands out: 71,413,330 Afghani wired from Dubai. He doesn't flinch as he notes the figure. This is routine.
>
> After finishing the entry, he picks up an old rotary phone, dials a number, and begins speaking in a cryptic, coded language, his tone even and deliberate.
>
> Somewhere in a dilapidated building nestled in the rugged terrain of Afghanistan, a Taliban soldier listens intently, a scribbled note in front of him. He decodes the message with swift precision, jotting down the following:
>
> Beretta M9 / 2
> Glock 19 / 2
> Galil Sniper / 1

The soldier eyes the note, then burns it, the ashes crumbling into the cold, unforgiving dirt.

Back in the room, Aditya turned to Sukkhi, watching for his reaction. 'Just to recheck,' Aditya said, his tone focused. 'None of these segments so far has any clue about the other. The person at A, who initiated the operation, doesn't know who B is, that's Jaggi. The Arab who provided the cash is C, and Jaggi has no idea who he's receiving the money from or who he's delivering it to, the shop owner, who's D in this chain. Each link moves in isolation, without knowing what the next or previous one is doing.'

Sukkhi absorbed the information, starting to see the intricacy of the plan in which each piece was isolated, unaware of the others, just as Aditya had planned.

Sukkhi, his curiosity piqued, asked, 'And I presume the shop owner doesn't know Jaggi?'

Aditya nodded. 'That's right.'

Sukkhi's mind raced as he tried to piece together the complexity of the operation. 'But the shop owner knows the exporter of grapes to the UAE … that trading company called …' He paused, trying to recall the name.

'Afghan Red Grapes?' Aditya prompted.

'Yes, that's it,' Sukkhi replied.

Aditya shook his head. 'No … he doesn't. Because Afghan Red Grapes is a shell company. It undertakes hawala operations for the Taliban and launders their drug money.'

Sukkhi leaned in. 'Shell company?'

Aditya explained, his tone patient but firm. 'A shell company is an inactive company. It's used as a vehicle for various financial manoeuvres or kept dormant for future use in some other capacity. It exists on paper but doesn't conduct any actual business.'

The realization dawned on Sukkhi. Every layer of this operation was designed for one purpose: concealment. The more he understood, the more he saw how deep the game went. Each player, each segment, was kept in the dark about the other, forming a chain of isolated moves in a deadly assembly line.

Aditya turned to a projector, flicking through a series of satellite images. The screen displayed trucks crossing the Torkham border, entering Pakistan from Afghanistan. He pointed to the images. 'These are goods trucks carrying coal briquettes from Badakhshan in central Afghanistan.'

Sukkhi studied the images, trying to connect the dots.

'But here's where it gets interesting,' Aditya continued, his voice lowering slightly. 'The coal briquettes are real, but hidden inside them are weapons procured from the Taliban.'

Sukkhi leaned forward, intrigued.

'One of our assets, someone embedded with the Balochistan rebels, receives the delivery,' Aditya explained. 'Once they've secured the consignment, they extract the weapons and prepare for the next move.'

A glint sparked in Sukkhi's eyes as the pieces of the puzzle began to fall into place. For the first time, he could sense his potential role in the operation. 'Meaning … he'll deliver it to me?'

Aditya met his gaze, a subtle smile playing on his lips. 'That's what my plan is.'

The weight of the words hung in the air. Sukkhi knew now that this wasn't just an abstract lesson. It was his initiation into the heart of the operation. The stakes were real, and he was about to be pulled in deeper.

Aditya rearranged the video footages on his laptop, lining up two clips side by side. He motioned for Sukkhi to watch closely.

'Here's what we're dealing with,' Aditya said, pulling up the first clip. 'Video 1' played, showing a prison in Karachi. The grainy footage focused on the entrance of the prison as an inmate was being released.

Aditya then switched to 'Video 2', which showed four East European backpackers hanging around a busy street, seemingly tourists. Three were men, one was a woman, all in their early thirties, blending effortlessly with the crowd. Their casual movements masked a hidden agenda.

Aditya turned to Sukkhi, pointing to the screen. 'This is segment 'D', which is criminal recruitment. We have two sets of manpower at our disposal.'

He paused Video 1 at the moment the inmate stepped out of the prison, his face partially obscured by shadows. 'This guy was recently released,' Aditya explained. 'Now, watch closely.'

Switching back to Video 2, Aditya resumed the footage of the four tourists. 'This,' he said, 'is segment 'E', which is surveillance and reconnaissance. The tourists aren't just sightseeing.'

He unpaused the video, letting the scene play out as the tourists moved through the crowded streets, seemingly aimless but always watching, always tracking.

Sukkhi leaned forward, absorbed in the shifting footage, as Aditya dropped the final piece of information. 'What you're looking at in Video 1, the prison footage – that was captured by this team of East Europeans. They've been shadowing the release for days, unnoticed.'

Aditya's words sank in. The web of the operation was tightening, and Sukkhi could now see the full scope of it, each piece connected in ways that weren't immediately obvious.

The focus shifted back to Video 1. A drone shot captured the recently released prisoner, wandering aimlessly around the streets outside the Karachi prison. The camera tracked his movements as he loitered for a while, blending into the chaotic rhythm of the city. Eventually, a figure in an auto-rickshaw approached, and the prisoner climbed in, disappearing into the throng of traffic.

Sukkhi, intrigued, glanced at Aditya. 'Who were those phirangi tourists in the other video? Did you know them?'

Aditya shook his head, offering a slight smile. 'The footage was placeholder material for now, just to mark the stages. The real players will come soon. There will be mercenaries from a country Indian intelligence hasn't worked with before.'

Sukkhi raised an eyebrow, his curiosity growing.

Aditya continued, his tone deliberate. 'These mercenaries will be armed by the Baloch rebels, just like you will be. They're going to set the stage for the final hit, laying the groundwork for the striker to score. The target will be under surveillance from all angles – far and near.'

He paused, letting the gravity of the situation sink in. 'The farthest will be the operative we call the "standoff weapon".' His eyes narrowed as he emphasized the term. 'That's the one who monitors the target from a distance, waiting for the right moment.'

Sukkhi's mind raced. He could sense the layers of complexity in the operation, the methodical way each piece was being arranged. He wasn't just a participant anymore – he was part of a larger game, one that was about to unfold with deadly precision.

Aditya shifted the footage, drawing Sukkhi's attention to an image of a lone operative positioned at a high vantage point, a sniper rifle in hand. The figure blended into the surroundings, poised, waiting for the moment to strike.

Sukkhi's eyes narrowed as he studied the shot. 'Will that sniper be me?' he asked.

Aditya shrugged, his tone measured. 'Could be,' he said. 'But there will be backups.' He clicked to the next image; this time showing two young foreigners inside a van, their expressions focused, weapons lying ready at their sides.

'These guys are the backups,' Aditya explained. 'In case the striker fails, they'll step in.'

Sukkhi, his eyes sharp with determination, responded, 'I won't fail.'

Aditya glanced at him, a hint of a smile on his face. He appreciated the confidence, but in this line of work, nothing was guaranteed. 'Good,' he replied. 'I like that attitude.'

Still, Sukkhi's mind kept working through the possible scenarios. 'What if I get intercepted?' he asked, the edge in his voice betraying a flicker of concern.

Aditya's expression remained calm, controlled. 'Then these backup operatives will be ready. They'll come to your rescue.'

The words hung in the air, and Sukkhi understood every angle had been covered, every scenario planned for. But deep down, he knew that once he was out there, it would be just him and the target, with everything riding on that one critical shot.

Aditya continued, his voice steady as he laid out the next phase of the plan. 'While you, the striker, are on your way to execute the target, the backup team of four will be controlling everything behind the scenes to facilitate the hit.'

Sukkhi listened, the weight of the operation becoming clearer with each word.

'Now,' Aditya said, leaning in slightly, 'imagine this: you're on your way, expecting to meet the target at a particular location. But the target, who's in a vehicle, gets stuck in traffic. What do you do?'

Sukkhi stared back, momentarily drawing a blank.

Aditya smiled knowingly. 'In that situation,' he explained, 'those tourists you saw earlier, who also happen to be expert hackers, will manipulate the traffic lights to ease congestion. They'll deactivate CCTV cameras in the area to ensure you aren't captured at the time of execution.'

Sukkhi blinked, stunned. This was beyond anything he could have imagined. He was being drawn into a world that felt almost surreal, a place where technology, espionage and assassination converged seamlessly.

Aditya, noticing Sukkhi's disbelief, stood up and made his way to the kitchen. Moments later, he returned with two cups of tea, setting one down in front of Sukkhi. The steam swirled between them as Aditya took a sip, watching Sukkhi scratch his head, trying to digest it all.

Finally, Sukkhi spoke, still reeling from the revelations. 'You didn't tell me about the last segment of the assembly line – "G".'

Aditya laughed, appreciating the growing hunger for information in his apprentice. He leaned back, a glint of amusement in his eyes. 'I have to admit, I didn't expect you to be so eager,' he said, the warmth in his voice betraying a sense of pride. 'You're catching on faster than I thought.'

After the tea break, Aditya leaned forward, his tone growing more serious as he prepared to explain the final piece of the puzzle. 'The last segment, "G". Support and backup, is all about denial,' he began. 'Once the hit is executed, our job is to ensure no trail leads back to us.'

Sukkhi listened, but his mind drifted, grappling with the irony of it all. He, a former terrorist, was now working for the state, his actions suddenly justified and protected under the guise of national security. And Aditya, an officer of the law, a spy by profession, was orchestrating these hits with the same cold precision as any militant. The lines between law enforcement and terrorism blurred with every step. In this game of shadows, Aditya was slowly transforming into something unrecognizable, someone who was more of a terrorist than Sukkhi had ever been.

But Sukkhi dared not voice these thoughts. Not now, not when the opportunity was within his grasp. For him, it was all commerce – a transaction to secure the future of his family back in Punjab. The moral questions he might have once entertained had been drowned out by the imperatives of survival.

Aditya's voice broke through his thoughts. 'In this game, the killing is just one part. The real art is in making sure no one ever knows who was really behind it.'

Sukkhi nodded, the truth settling in. Aditya continued, 'The concerned parties will inform the media that the killing was the result of an internal feud … gangs, terror outfits in Pakistan. Maybe even the ISI. Let them point fingers at each other while we disappear.'

Sukkhi understood now: in this world, justification was nothing more than currency, traded and manipulated by those in power. For him, it was simply a means to an end, to keep his family going. The rules didn't matter. Only the outcome mattered.

~

Middle of May 2023.

An Indian diplomat, seasoned both in diplomacy and covert intelligence, meticulously drafted a confidential report. His words were sharp, precise and heavy with the weight of his findings. The rising tide of Khalistani movements, carefully orchestrated from the soil of Canada and the UK, had gained alarming momentum. This was no ordinary rebellion. It was a well-oiled machine fuelled by foreign sympathizers. As he sealed the report and marked it for the PMO, he knew this document wasn't just an update; it was a ticking bomb waiting to go off in the highest corridors of power.

URGENT CONFIDENTIAL REPORT

To: The Joint Secretary, PMO, New Delhi

From: [REDACTED], First Secretary, Indian Mission, [REDACTED]

Date: May 2023

Subject: Escalating Khalistani Extremism in the UK and Canada – A Dire Threat to National Security

Classification: Top Secret

Summary

The situation concerning Khalistani extremists based in the UK and Canada has reached a critical juncture, and if immediate action is not taken, the repercussions for India could be catastrophic. Over the last few years, pro-Khalistan elements have amplified their activities, vandalizing Indian missions abroad, and desecrating national symbols with little to no punitive action from local authorities. These extremists have projected India in a negative light on the international stage, exploiting Western political environments that are driven by the Sikh vote bank, especially in Canada and the UK.

Unabated Extremism and Vandalism: Recent attacks on Indian missions in London, Vancouver and Toronto by pro-Khalistan mobs demonstrate a boldness that was previously unseen. They have openly defied the law, raising Khalistani flags and vandalizing mission premises. The lack of substantial action by the respective governments has emboldened these extremists, painting India as weak in the international sphere. This should be seen as not only an affront to our sovereignty but also as a well-planned campaign of disinformation to stoke separatist fires in Punjab.

Pakistan–China Nexus: Intelligence reports indicate a dangerous alliance forming between Khalistani groups in the West and vested interests from Pakistan and China. Arms, ammunition and funding are being smuggled into the West, with certain groups receiving training and support in Pakistan and, in some instances, at the behest of Chinese intelligence. This raises the possibility of targeted attacks against Indian interests, both domestically and abroad, as these extremists are increasingly militarized. The involvement of China is particularly concerning, given the geopolitical context and Beijing's desire to destabilize India indirectly.

Political Complicity and Sikh Vote Bank: Canada and the UK have turned a blind eye to these extremist activities due to their domestic political interests. Both countries have sizeable Sikh populations, who represent critical voting blocs. In Canada, the administration has notably softened its stance on Khalistani separatists to avoid alienating these voters, a pattern mirrored by UK politicians. These governments have repeatedly overlooked evidence of Khalistani groups' involvement in terror funding, arms smuggling and even narcotics operations, all to maintain political goodwill within their Sikh communities.

Arms and Explosives Supply Chains: The supply of arms, explosives and manpower from Pakistan to the UK- and Canada-based Khalistanis is growing, especially since 2021. There is credible intelligence pointing to sophisticated logistical operations that funnel resources into separatist networks, all under the radar of local law enforcement. Explosives intercepted at Heathrow Airport last year, and arms recovered from a warehouse in Surrey, Canada, reveal a growing sophistication in the supply chain intended to fuel a resurgence of violence in Punjab. These findings, though critical, were ignored by local governments, downplayed as isolated incidents rather than being recognized as part of a broader strategy.

Potential for Domestic Unrest in India: The ongoing radicalization efforts in the UK and Canada are likely to ignite fresh separatist sentiments in Punjab. The propaganda disseminated through social media and diaspora channels has already begun sowing seeds of discontent among younger generations in Punjab. We risk witnessing the rebirth of an insurgency similar to the violent movement of the 1980s. If the Khalistani referendums being organized by groups like SFJ gain further traction, Punjab could become the epicentre of a renewed separatist struggle with international backing.

Urgent action: It is imperative that the Government of India elevate this matter diplomatically and strategically with the highest urgency. The potential for coordinated attacks or separatist movements cannot be overstated. Given the direct involvement of external forces like Pakistan and China, the Khalistan issue has evolved from a diaspora problem into a multi-front challenge threatening India's sovereignty and security.

The window for pre-emptive action is rapidly closing. If our missions continue to face unchecked violence, and if the arms and propaganda networks are not dismantled, we will be confronting not only a diplomatic crisis but also an escalation of violence within India. Measures to diplomatically pressure Canada and the UK must be coupled with intelligence operations to neutralize these networks before the situation escalates out of control. Therefore, the following is recommended:

Escalate Diplomatic Pressure: Immediate high-level talks with both the UK and Canadian governments, demanding stronger action against pro-Khalistan extremists operating with impunity.

Targeted Covert Operations: R&AW must consider covert operations to dismantle the supply chains of arms and ammunition being funnelled to these groups through Pakistan and other intermediaries.

Global Narrative Shift: India must proactively shift the global narrative by engaging with Western media and human rights organizations, exposing the nexus between these extremist groups and terrorism. This should be paired with efforts to delegitimize Khalistani demands through public diplomacy.

Heightened Surveillance and Pre-emptive Strikes: Surveillance of key Khalistani figures abroad must be enhanced, and actionable intelligence should be used to prevent violent attacks on Indian missions and domestic soil.

Conclusion:
Khalistani extremism has entered a new phase of organized violence, one that threatens not only the stability of Punjab but also the international standing of India. The continued inaction by the UK and Canadian governments, due to their electoral considerations, has allowed these networks to flourish unchecked. We must act swiftly and decisively to eliminate this threat before it metastasizes further.

[REDACTED]
First Secretary
Indian Mission, [REDACTED]

The report landed like a stone in still waters, creating ripples of concern across the highest echelons of power. It was rare, unprecedented even for such intelligence to be directly addressed to the PMO. This breach of protocol set off alarm bells, forcing an urgent meeting. The PMO summoned the NSD, the chief of R&AW and the foreign secretary in swift succession. As they gathered, a quiet tension simmered in the room. The foreign secretary, ever sharp and calculating, quickly pieced together the puzzle. This wasn't just a routine briefing. It was a carefully orchestrated move by the PMO, a way to tighten the reins on the NSD and R&AW, putting them under pressure to act decisively. The stakes had been raised, and the game was now far more complex than it appeared.

The foreign secretary cleared his throat, trying to steer the conversation towards his ministry's efforts. 'Sir,' he began, addressing the prime minister, 'we have conveyed to the respective countries that India expects more than just verbal assurances. We want to see concrete action taken against the perpetrators.'

The prime minister, with his gaze steady and unflinching, responded, 'Make it clear to them that India hopes they will act decisively ... prosecute those involved, not just offer promises.'

Without missing a beat, the prime minister turned his attention to the NSD. 'What's the status from your side?'

The NSD, ever measured in his response, nodded. 'Sir, as always, whenever there's a potential threat to the security of our missions abroad, we immediately raise the issue with the local governments. This time will be no exception.'

The prime minister shifted his stance slightly, his voice growing firmer. 'This issue of the Khalistanis ... it needs to be prioritized.'

He then locked eyes with the NSD. 'Let's stop being soft. Time for a change in approach.'

The NSD, catching the undertone, gave a curt nod, understanding the prime minister's directive clearly. Meanwhile, Ashok Awasthy, the head of R&AW, spoke up, his tone carefully neutral. 'Sir, we've been working through Ripudaman Singh Malik. He's been negotiating with some of the militant factions. Malik's also openly praised the steps you've taken for the Sikh community.'

The prime minister's expression remained impassive. 'Yes, I know. He wrote to me as well. But I'm more interested in results, not just compliments. Do something concrete so that they praise you all – and keep me out of it.'

Awasthy, reading between the lines, nodded. 'Understood, sir. May I suggest that we hold off any hard action against the militants for now, at least until we see if Malik fails to deliver?'

The prime minister turned back to the NSD, his eyes seeking a second opinion. 'What do you think?'

The NSD, contemplative for a moment, agreed. 'Yes, Malik is crucial ... at least for now. Let's give him some room to work.'

Shortly after the meeting at the PMO adjourned, the NSD and Ashok Awasthy retreated to the NSD's office, setting up a secure video call with Ripudaman Singh Malik. Malik's face appeared on the screen, his expression a mixture of resolve and weariness. Awasthy knew the NSD's mere presence could be intimidating, so he took the lead as always and positioned himself to handle most of the conversation, with the NSD lurking quietly in the background.

Ashok Awasthy's tone was firm but not without a hint of urgency. 'Malik, you've got to set a deadline for Takkar. Get him on the table for a dialogue. Convince him that India means business … or else, we'll stop negotiating with someone like him altogether. He knows what comes after that.'

Malik responded with measured humility, his frustration barely concealed. 'Sir, I'm working on this daily. But he's stubborn. He refuses to speak with me directly … he only sends his underlings. Worse, he's turning the Sikh community against me, branding me a traitor.'

Awasthy leaned forward, cutting through Malik's explanation. 'Malik, I don't need to hear your difficulties. India's situation is becoming hostile by the day.'

Malik, with a hint of desperation, interjected, 'Sir, Khalistanis are Sikhs, but not all Sikhs are Khalistanis.'

The NSD, who had remained silent until now, finally spoke, his voice calm but steely. 'Then talk to the Sikh diaspora, Malik. Build a narrative that Takkar is nothing more than a criminal hiding behind the guise of Khalistan. He's running a cartel … that of guns, drugs, human trafficking. Use that to undermine him.'

Malik nodded, though there was hesitation in his eyes. 'I understand your point, sir, but …'

Before he could finish, Awasthy cut in sharply. 'You've got all the intel from us, Malik. Information is power. Use it against him … unless, of course, you're afraid of doing so.'

Malik's tone sharpened as he straightened in his seat. 'Afraid, and *me*? No way, Awasthy Sa'ab. The newsletter of my organization is going to carry a major article on Takkar, backed by the information you've given me. Let them call me a traitor – I don't care. I'll do it for India.'

Both the NSD and Awasthy exchanged a brief glance, trying to gauge Malik's sudden burst of enthusiasm. Was it genuine patriotism, or just an act to keep New Delhi satisfied? The air hung heavy with uncertainty, each man weighing the risks.

13

The Tipping Point

May 2023.

At the end of the month, the laptop screen flickered to life in front of Aditya, revealing a labyrinth of routes and financial transactions. A web of ghost accounts in Dubai was ready to move the money, while weapons would be smuggled from Iran, crossing the rugged Baluchistan border. Aditya sat back for a moment, quietly recapping his plan in his mind, fine-tuning every detail. The scenario he had presented to Sukkhi earlier – involving the Taliban and Afghan routes – had been entirely fictional, a cover story crafted to protect the real source and prevent any accidental leaks. Only Aditya knew the true pipeline, and he intended to keep it that way.

His strategy was to enlist Iranian traders, who smuggled fuel into Pakistan, to transport the arms. The route was long and fraught with risks, but it was the least likely to attract attention. Unlike the notorious gun runners who operated in the area and were relentlessly monitored by the DEA and CIA, this network moved under the radar, making it the safer bet.

But a new obstacle had emerged – UAE's tightened restrictions on money transfers to Iran. Aditya would need to reroute the funds through Hong Kong before they could reach Iran. He knew the

Iranian traders had bank accounts in the British Virgin Islands (BVI) through Hong Kong, where confidentiality, flexibility and minimal oversight made it the ideal location for discreet transactions. The BVI accounts were a gateway to move the money smoothly, avoiding the increasing scrutiny in the region.

As he mulled over the logistics, Aditya paused to take a sip of his now lukewarm tea, the cup leaving a faint ring on one of the strategic maps scattered across the table. The silence in the room was broken only by the occasional clink of the spoon against the fine bone china and the soft tapping of his fingers on the laptop keys.

Since using his old assets for this operation in Pakistan was out of the question, Aditya had to find new allies who could handle the job. He picked up his internet phone and dialled a secure number, his voice calm and measured as he spoke. The conversation was brief, but the message was clear – they would need multiple strikers for several coordinated hits across Pakistan.

However, recruiting that many operatives from within Pakistan itself posed a significant risk. Aditya had already carried out an extrajudicial killing there, and stirring the pot further could expose him. The delicate balance between finding fresh talent and avoiding detection weighed heavily on his mind.

Aditya needed three strikers, for now calling them Alpha, Bravo and Charlie. Alpha would blend in with the oil traders moving across the Sistan border from Iran into Pakistan. Bravo would take a more conventional route, flying into Islamabad under the cover of a textile merchant. Both men would be sourced from mercenary groups in Iran, the same groups often employed by oil smugglers.

Their roles were designed to complement each other. If one failed to hit the target, the other would act as a standoff weapon, striking from a distance. However, there was a significant challenge: neither of them could carry weapons while travelling. They'd have to rely on securing arms once inside Pakistan.

The room was quiet for a while. Aditya rubbed his temples, feeling the dull ache building from hours of staring at the screens. His contact on the other end of the line remained silent, waiting for him to resume the conversation. When he finally spoke again, they discussed the recruitment of Charlie. Aditya had someone in mind – Sukkhi. He trusted Sukkhi for this role, but he chose not to mention the name to his contact just yet.

The contact, however, had an intriguing suggestion: Charlic could be recruited from within Pakistan itself. There was no shortage of drug addicts in the region, desperate for supplies and willing to do anything in exchange for their next fix. It was a tempting idea, one that could simplify certain logistical challenges.

Aditya found the idea intriguing, but his contact wasn't finished. There was more on the table – the Iranian mercenaries and Charlie would serve distinct roles. While Charlie would be the primary striker, the mercenaries would act as the standoff weapons, ready to engage from a distance if things went wrong. Aditya liked the structure of the plan, the layers of redundancy it provided.

Yet, despite the promising setup, a nagging feeling lingered. He leaned forward and said, 'I don't know why, but something about this feels too good to be true.'

When Altaf knocked on the door, Aditya was immersed in a sea of maps and images of weapons. He was on the phone, just starting a call with an arms supplier in Iran, using an 'anonymous proxy' to ensure the conversation couldn't be traced. He didn't respond to the knocking, so Altaf remained outside.

Aditya kept his tone casual but direct. 'Arsalan? Everything good?'

'Everything's good,' Arsalan replied in a clipped tone.

'I need the usual stuff,' Aditya said, cutting to the chase.

'What exactly?' Arsalan asked, his voice calm.

'White powder, six kilos; sugarcane, three kilos,' Aditya replied, using their code. 'Quality has to match Pakistan's standards.'

'Drop point?' Arsalan inquired.

'Keep it ready. I'll give you the details later,' Aditya said, keeping things vague for now.

'Two hundred thousand,' Arsalan stated flatly.

'I'll wire it from Hong Kong,' Aditya confirmed. 'It's a BVI account, but I operate through Hong Kong.'

Altaf stood outside, straining to catch the muffled conversation through the door. Inside, Aditya's voice was calm, almost too calm, as he discussed weapons and codes over the phone. But Aditya wasn't fooled. He had sensed the presence beyond the door long before the knock. Without breaking his rhythm, he ended the call and moved swiftly, opening the door just in time to catch Altaf mid-lean.

'Guns, drugs and thugs,' Altaf quipped, trying to play it cool, though a hint of unease flickered in his eyes.

Aditya's gaze sharpened, his expression unreadable. He responded to Altaf's unspoken question: 'White powder? That's 9mm pistols. Sugarcane? Sniper rifles. 'Pakistan standard' is just the spec for weapons used by their army.' He paused, then added with a knowing smirk, 'Oh, and Altaf ...when my door isn't bolted, there's no need to lurk outside like a spy. Come in, join the party.'

His words were light, but there was an unmistakable edge to them, leaving Altaf unsure whether to smile or feel the tension tightening around them both.

Altaf's face tightened, his irritation clear. The sarcastic tone in Aditya's voice didn't sit well with him. 'There's nothing to enjoy about what you're up to,' Altaf snapped, stepping into the room with more frustration than intent. 'I'm here to get an update to send back to Delhi. That's all.'

Aditya knew he'd struck a nerve. Altaf didn't like being caught eavesdropping, even if his excuse was official. Despite that, eavesdropping always left a bad taste. Trying to ease the tension, Aditya threw in a lighthearted jab about listening at doors.

But the joke fell flat. Altaf, still visibly irritated, crossed his arms and pressed, 'When's your progress report going to be ready?'

Aditya leaned back in his chair, the playfulness draining from his face. 'I won't know until my homework's done,' he replied, his voice measured but losing its warmth.

Altaf wasn't having it. 'Delhi won't buy that. They need a deadline.'

Now it was Aditya's turn to bristle. His voice dropped, quiet but edged with frustration. 'You'll have to wait for that. A deadline isn't 'langar food' at a gurdwara available on demand, round the clock.'

He paused, staring Altaf down. 'I'm working on it, and a realistic deadline is it will be ready in a couple of days.'

The air between them thickened with tension, as Altaf reluctantly accepted the answer, though not without a hint of discontent.

Altaf's eyes swept the room, taking in the coded messages, charts, drawings and maps strewn across the table. He frowned. 'Isn't this risky? Leaving all this out in the open? If an outsider gets wind of it, the whole mission could blow up.'

Aditya paused, fixing Altaf with an unreadable gaze before responding in a calm, almost nonchalant tone. 'I destroy all my work material every day. Sometimes even twice, depending on how much piles up.'

Altaf's curiosity was piqued, but he kept his questions to himself. He wanted to ask where and how Aditya disposed of everything but chose to remain silent, aware that Aditya's methods were likely as meticulous as the rest of his operation.

Sensing Altaf's lingering doubt, Aditya gestured to the room. 'Go ahead, check for yourself. See if there's a single trace of anything important left behind.'

Altaf's gaze shifted toward Aditya's laptop and iPad, but before he could ask, Aditya gave a confident smile. 'Those? They're password-protected. No one can crack them without my cooperation.'

The assurance in his voice left little room for doubt, and the weight of his words hung in the air, reminding Altaf of the calculated precision that defined every move Aditya made.

Altaf gave a curt nod, a hint of appreciation flashing in his eyes before he turned and left the room. As the door closed behind him, Aditya called out, his voice laced with playful sarcasm, 'Interested in one more joke about eavesdropping?'

But the room had already returned to its quiet solitude. Altaf was gone, leaving only the faint echo of Aditya's words hanging in the air. With a smirk, Aditya shook his head, amused at the fleeting moment of levity that no one but he seemed to appreciate.

Aditya's eyes were locked on a photograph of Bashir Ahmad Peer, the notorious commander of the HM. The intensity in Aditya's gaze spoke volumes as he studied the face of the man who had evaded justice for far too long. With a quiet exhale, Aditya shifted his attention to the satellite images on his laptop. The screen displayed a narrow street in Rawalpindi, the focus zeroed in on a modest but bustling spot – Kamaal Gazi Biryani Centre.

This was where Bashir Ahmad Peer spent most of his evenings, unwinding before returning to his perfume shop in Raja Bazar. Aditya's mind raced, piecing together the information. The familiar thrill of a plan forming began to stir within him.

Something clicked. Without wasting a moment, he stood up, descending quickly to the ground floor of the house. He found Altaf and, without any explanation, pulled him back upstairs.

Once they were inside the room again, Aditya's eyes gleamed with focus as he began to lay out his plan, the urgency unmistakable. This was it. The next move in a dangerous game.

Aditya worked swiftly, his digital pencil gliding across the iPad screen as he sketched out the plan with precision. The detailed strokes formed the layout of the Kamaal Gazi Biryani Centre and the surrounding streets. His movements were deliberate, almost choreographic, as if he were mapping out a deadly performance.

Aditya pointed to the screen, using a digital pencil to illustrate his plan. 'There will be two strikers,' he explained, his voice calm but intense. 'Striker-1 will be inside, blending in with the customers, eating biryani. Striker-2 will be outside, just close enough, waiting on a motorcycle with the engine running. Striker-1 shoots target and walks out. Then, Striker-2 swoops in, picks up Striker-1 on the pillion, and they disappear.'

Altaf, watching the plan unfold on the screen, frowned. 'And how do you plan on knowing exactly when the target shows up at the biryani shop? Someone tailing him?'

Aditya swiped to the next set of images on his iPad, showing an aerial view of Raja Bazar. 'We'll know,' he said. 'The shopkeeper's boy is one of ours now. He'll send a signal when Peer arrives.' He zoomed in on the tangle of narrow streets. 'This is Raja Bazar. It's a chaos zone. Look at the congestion. There's no easy way out. His shop is right in the middle of it all, and making an escape from here would be a nightmare.'

Altaf's brow furrowed as he studied the images. The complexity of the area, the sheer density of the streets and the tight spaces made it clear that an escape would be anything but straightforward. It was a challenge that required flawless timing and coordination, or the whole operation could get exposed in seconds.

Altaf's gaze lingered on the images before he turned to Aditya, his expression more serious now. 'How well do you know these strikers?' he asked, the underlying question clear: How reliable were they?

Aditya didn't hesitate. 'They're proxy mercenaries from Iran,' he replied. 'Breakaway hitmen from groups like the Fatemiyoun and Zainabiyoun. They've been doing this kind of work for years.'

Altaf remained thoughtful, absorbing the information without an immediate reaction. His silence said more than words – that he wasn't entirely convinced.

Sensing the hesitation, Aditya shifted gears. 'I have another option,' he added, bringing a different layer to the plan. 'Runaways from drug deaddiction centres. Offer them cash and drugs, and they'll do whatever's asked.'

Altaf frowned. 'What's the guarantee they'll even know how to handle a gun?'

Aditya leaned back, a calm certainty in his voice. 'They won't need to be experts. They'll shoot from close range, point-blank. The standoff guns will be handled by the Iranians. And don't forget, Sukkhi is going to be my main striker. He'll make sure the job's done cleanly.'

Altaf's face tightened, the full import of the plan sinking in. The mix of mercenaries, desperate addicts and a skilled striker made the operation both risky and unpredictable, but Aditya spoke with a confidence that left little room for doubt.

Altaf, still absorbing the details, spoke thoughtfully. 'It would be better if, God forbid, a local gets caught pulling the trigger rather than a foreigner. Less heat that way.'

He paused, his brow furrowed as another thought struck him. 'Are you following the same modus operandi as last time?'

Aditya shook his head, his voice calm but firm. 'No. Trying to get too sophisticated or clever with the execution would only raise red flags. The moment it looks like an outsider's hand is involved, the whole thing could blow up. Simplicity works … it blends into the chaos. That's the style we need here.'

Altaf considered his words, realizing the importance of not overcomplicating the plan. Aditya's approach was to camouflage the operation within the local fabric, avoiding any signs of foreign precision that might draw unwanted attention.

Aditya pulled up the details for his next target – Syed Khalid Raza, a figure who resided in Karachi. Karachi was already a city marked by Aditya's touch, a place where he had struck once before. But this time, his plan involved a more intricate manoeuvre.

He turned to Altaf, his voice steady. 'For Raza, we'll use the Sindhudesh Revolutionary Army (SRA). India has funded them from time to time. They're fiercely anti-Pakistan, and right now, they're desperate.'

Aditya's fingers tapped lightly on the table as he outlined the situation. The SRA was low on both cash and ammunition, their resources dwindling to dangerous levels. It made them the perfect ally for his plan but only on his terms.

'Tell Delhi,' Aditya continued, 'that no further aid should come from R&AW to the SRA. Let the group turn to me for their needs. I'll give them the cash and the arms … but in exchange, I want Khalid's head.'

The room grew heavier with the weight of the decision, Aditya's strategy weaving together both leverage and violence. Altaf silently nodded, understanding the cold calculation behind every word.

Aditya's plan for Syed Khalid Raza was as meticulous as it was lethal. He outlined the strategy with precision, his eyes focused on the map of Karachi's Gulistan-e-Jauhar, where Khalid took his daily evening walks outside his bungalow.

He pointed to the screen again, laying out an alternative plan. 'Instead of focusing on long-range sniping, this approach will rely on misdirection and close combat.' His voice was steady, calculated. 'We'll have two teams: one will be positioned in a parked car near Khalid's location. Their job is simple – create chaos.'

He zoomed in on a section of the map, circling the area. 'A small, controlled blast will go off beside the route,' he said. 'Not to kill, only to create panic and force him to seek shelter.'

Aditya tapped the screen, indicating likely places Khalid would fall back to: the narrow recessed doorway of a shop, the canvas awning of a street stall, a row of parked vehicles, or the dark mouth of an alley. All of them offered quick, instinctive cover in a bazaar like this.

'That is where our second team will be,' he continued. 'They will be working openly carrying tools, manning a scaffold, sweeping the pavement ... just the kind of presence you expect in a market. Their positions cover the likely exits and the main pockets of cover so that when Khalid moves into shelter the confusion funnels him into a limited space. The action will be fast and controlled. One precise shot, nothing theatrical, then the team melts back into the crowd.'

Altaf listened carefully, nodding slowly as Aditya concluded. 'The key here is to make it look like Khalid got caught in the chaos. The media and investigators will focus on the explosion, while we quietly slip away. The fewer loose ends, the better.'

The complexity of the operation, the layers of deception, were designed to derail any investigation, leaving Khalid's death shrouded in mystery and confusion, with suspicion turned back on Pakistan itself.

Aditya's plan didn't stop at the execution. There was another layer, one that involved media manipulation and turning the narrative against Pakistan.

'And once Khalid is dead,' Aditya continued, his voice measured but brimming with calculated intent, 'New Delhi can flood the media with a carefully crafted story. We'll make it look like Pakistan's own ISI took out Khalid, an INTERPOL-designated terrorist, to meet the FATF stipulations.'

He glanced at Altaf, his eyes sharp. 'It's perfect. Pakistan will be forced into a defensive position. The world will believe they eliminated Khalid to prove their commitment to fighting terrorism and satisfying the Financial Action Task Force.'

The brilliance of the plan was not just in the execution but in the aftermath, a web of misinformation and strategic leaks designed to humiliate Pakistan on the global stage, making it seem like they were cleaning house out of necessity, not ethical principles.

~

Towards the end of May 2023.

New Delhi was pleased with the progress of Aditya's mission. The NSD was in constant coordination with his counterpart in Dubai, quietly facilitating critical elements of the operation. Fresh travel documents for Sukkhi were being arranged, wire transfers were routed through secure bank accounts and, unknown to Aditya, a soft surveillance was in place to track his movements.

It wasn't unusual. Monitoring agents was a standard practice in the intelligence world, ensuring that no one went rogue or considered defection. Gulf intelligence agencies were discreetly keeping tabs on Aditya, just as they would any other operative.

Aditya, however, was blissfully unaware of the scrutiny. Not that it would have mattered. As a seasoned spy, he knew such measures were routine, and he trusted his instincts above all else. He'd always operated on gut feeling, and this time was no different.

Even if someone had tipped him off, Aditya, in his characteristic style, would have shrugged it off with a dismissive 'Fuck it.'

But everything shifted with one piece of news from Canada. Ripudaman Singh Malik had been killed.

The report arrived swiftly at R&AW Headquarters in New Delhi, the details stark and undeniable. It was a blow that shook the intelligence community, and the reaction was immediate. New Delhi was furious. Malik's assassination had the potential to upset delicate geopolitical balances, and the timing couldn't have been worse.

> Subject: Urgent Report on Ripudaman Singh Malik's Assassination and its Implications
>
> To: HQ, New Delhi
>
> From: [REDACTED], Canadian Desk, Cabinet Secretariat
>
> Date: [REDACTED]

Classification: Top Secret

The assassination of Ripudaman Singh Malik on 15 July 2022, is a flashpoint in the escalating power struggle within Canada's Sikh community. Malik's murder in Surrey, British Columbia, has far-reaching implications for our efforts to build bridges with pro-Khalistan groups abroad.

Malik, acquitted of involvement in the 1985 Air India bombing, became a vocal pro-India voice following his 2019 trip to India, during which he met Sikh religious leaders and secured permission to print the Sri Guru Granth Sahib (SGGS). This angered radical Sikh factions led by Gurdeep Singh Takkar and Moninder Boyle, both closely tied to the Khalistan movement and reportedly supported by Pakistan's ISI.

These factions orchestrated a campaign to discredit Malik, labelling him a 'traitor' to the Sikh cause. Pamphlets, public speeches and accusations of 'beadbi' (desecration) over the printing of the SGGS further isolated him within the community. Intelligence suggests that Malik's murder was a carefully planned operation, executed by hired hitmen Tanner Fox and Jose Lopez, likely under the directives of Takkar and Boyle, backed by pro-separatist forces. The two radicals' campaign against Malik culminated in the fatal shooting, followed by the burning of the vehicle used in the assassination.

Canadian authorities arrested Fox and Lopez, but the deeper conspiracy remains under covers, likely due to political sensitivities in the Canadian government, which has long been cautious with pro-Khalistan elements to secure Sikh votes.

It is crucial to note that Malik's assassination occurred amid increasing tensions within the Khalistani groups. Takkar's involvement in Malik's killing cannot be ruled out, as both he and Boyle stood to gain by eliminating Malik – a figure who had begun to embrace pro-India sentiments and publicly supported the prime minister's outreach to the Sikh community. This killing sends a strong, dangerous message to other Sikh voices abroad who have warmed to India's cause.

Malik's assassination is a major blow to our efforts in diplomatically engaging the Sikh diaspora in Canada. It emboldens the more radical, pro-Khalistan factions and signals that any pro-India sentiment within the Sikh community will be met with deadly consequences. Malik's transformation from a supporter of Khalistan to a government ally marked him for death, and this serves as a chilling precedent for those who might follow in his footsteps.

The involvement of Pakistan's ISI in stoking this conflict, both in the assassination and in fostering separatist sentiment, is highly probable and needs further investigation. This event has the potential to derail the fragile peace efforts between the Sikh diaspora and India's government. The name of one gangster turned terrorist, Harvinder Singh Sandhi aka Rinda, is being linked to Malik's death, although the RCMP's homicide division has been tight lipped about it.

End of report.
[REDACTED]
Intelligence Officer, Canadian Desk, Cabinet Secretariat

The assassination of Malik sent the NSD into a fury. For years, the agency had worked to plant a credible, trustworthy voice within the Khalistani network in the West, someone who could gradually soften the hardliners and steer the movement away from violence. Ripudaman Singh Malik had become that man. His transformation from a former suspect to a respected community leader had been carefully nurtured by the NSD, a slow and delicate operation that was finally beginning to yield results. His growing acceptance among influential Khalistanis had opened a covert channel of communication that Delhi desperately needed. By eliminating him,

Takkar and his backers had destroyed years of patient infiltration and shattered the fragile bridge the NSD had built to reach into the diaspora. Malik's death wasn't just a loss. It was a calculated strike to cripple India's covert network abroad.

The NSD's mind was already working ahead, seeing the implications clearly. Central to his strategy was neutralizing the lifeblood of Gurdeep Singh Takkar's KTF, an operation that now had to be fast-tracked. And the first step? Taking down one of the most formidable and elusive figures on their radar, Harvinder Singh Sandhu, better known as Rinda.

Rinda was no ordinary target. His deep connections within the militant ecosystem made him a critical player, and his elimination was now a priority. The stakes were rising, and the mission had evolved far beyond what Aditya had initially set out to do.

At the NSD's command, R&AW produced a comprehensive report on Harvinder Singh Sandhu, better known as Rinda. The dossier traced his evolution from a feared gangster and drug lord to a high-profile terrorist, now the backbone of Takkar's KTF.

Rinda's expertise in recruiting hitmen and his mastery in financing terrorist operations through the lucrative narcotics trade had made him indispensable to the KTF's machinery. His operations spanned the infamous Golden Crescent, where the poppy fields of Pakistan, Afghanistan and Iran provided a steady stream of funds for terrorism.

But Rinda's reach extended far beyond South Asia. His intricate web of connections fuelled both terrorism and drug addiction across the globe, with tentacles stretching into the streets of Western nations, including Canada, where he was instrumental in expanding the KTF's influence.

Rinda wasn't just a kingpin; he was a shadowy figure whose networks fed a deadly combination of terrorism and narcotics, a linchpin in a global menace that New Delhi could no longer afford to ignore.

The NSD sat across from the prime minister, the air between them thick with the implications of what had just unfolded. The prime minister listened intently as the NSD laid out the situation.

'The focus is shifting, sir,' the NSD began, his voice measured. 'From Pakistan, POK and Afghanistan – we're now looking squarely at Canada.'

The prime minister raised an eyebrow, but said nothing, allowing the NSD to continue.

'This won't be like our past operations,' the NSD pressed on. 'If we want to conduct covert actions on Canadian soil or for that matter, in the US or the UK ... we need more than just operational precision. We'll need ... leverage.'

The prime minister leaned back slightly. 'Leverage with whom, exactly?'

'The president of the United States,' the NSD said, the words hanging in the air. 'If we're going to pull this off, we need the Americans to look the other way or, better yet, subtly endorse it. That kind of silence can only come from the top.'

The prime minister exhaled, tapping his fingers lightly on the table. 'And you think he'll just agree to that? Canada is their ally.'

The NSD nodded. 'True, but the president also understands the bigger picture. There's a common enemy here ... terror networks operating on Western soil. If we position this as a mutual interest, a threat that endangers them as much as us, we can make him see reason.'

The prime minister studied him, eyes sharp. 'And you think my personal intervention is needed?'

'Absolutely, sir. It's a delicate balance. We're not asking for a favour – we're offering to eliminate a threat. But it has to come from you, directly. The president needs to know this is in the best interest of the US too. If he gives the nod, we have the green light for anything we need to do – without interference.'

The prime minister leaned forward, his gaze steady. 'If I do this, there's no turning back.'

The NSD smiled faintly. 'There never was, sir.'

After securing the trust of South Block, which housed the PMO, the NSD wasted no time. He called an emergency meeting with R&AW chief Awasthy, the director of the Intelligence Bureau

(DIB) and the foreign secretary. The room was charged with urgency as they gathered around the table, faces stern, aware of the stakes.

The NSD took the floor. 'Let's not mince words here. If India is to act against the Khalistani extremist leaders operating from Canada, the UK and the US, what are our options? Or do we wait – rely on those governments to act on our behalf?'

Awasthy leaned forward, his expression serious. 'Waiting for them to act is a gamble, and a slow one at that. These extremists are entrenched in those countries, protected by the legal systems. If we leave it to them, we'll be waiting forever.'

The foreign secretary nodded in agreement. 'Diplomacy has its limits. These governments have their own priorities, and while they might sympathize with our concerns, their actions are bogged down in red tape. We cannot afford to wait for their wheels to turn.'

The NSD glanced around the room. 'So, what do we do?'

Awasthy's voice was steady. 'We take matters into our own hands. Covert operations – targeted strikes, if necessary.'

The foreign secretary added, 'We've done this before. It's risky, yes, but the alternative is watching these leaders continue to destabilize our country from afar. We can't allow them to operate freely under the guise of political asylum.'

The room was silent for a moment, the weight of the decision hanging in the air. The NSD broke the silence. 'So, we're all in agreement?'

There was no hesitation. Everyone at the table spoke in unison: 'Let's go for it.'

The NSD nodded, the decision made. The path forward was clear – India would act. No more waiting. This time the foreign secretary and DIB were privy to the discussion, which added a layer of official validation to a programme already underway. It would only need a little tweaking and speeding up.

The DIB, heading an organization traditionally tasked with domestic intelligence, had recently expanded its reach to limited operations overseas. He felt the time had come for India to demonstrate that it could act independently on the global stage, no longer reliant on the backing of superpowers. As he spoke, his voice carried a sense of pride and determination.

'New India,' he said, repeatedly emphasizing the phrase. 'The world must recognize that this is a different India … self-reliant, politically ready to step into foreign territory when necessary. We can no longer sit idle while threats are nurtured abroad, waiting for others to take action. This is not the India of old. This is New India.'

His tone, however, took on an unusual edge, more like a publicist than a seasoned intelligence officer. The room couldn't help but notice it. The DIB's emphasis on India's growing boldness felt almost like a press release, a declaration meant for headlines rather than the secrecy that typically shrouded his profession.

The NSD, listening from the side lines, couldn't help but raise an eyebrow. For an intelligence officer whose foundation was supposed to be discretion, the DIB's grandstanding seemed almost out of place. But in a time of high stakes, perhaps this new public confidence was part of the evolving strategy, whether the world was ready to acknowledge it or not.

The foreign secretary leaned forward, his voice rising with conviction as he spoke from the heart. 'India has a right to reply,' he said firmly. 'When terrorists flee to Pakistan, and instead of handing them over, Pakistan shelters them, arms them and enables them to continue waging war against our sovereignty, what other choice do we have? What option is left but for India to enter Pakistan and eliminate the threat ourselves?'

His words hung heavy in the room, the reality of the situation undeniable. 'India has always sought peaceful relations with its neighbours – with every country, for that matter. But when someone repeatedly shows us their angry eyes … when they step onto Indian soil and promote terrorism – we cannot continue to turn the other cheek. We cannot spare them any longer.'

He paused, his gaze moving around the table before he added, 'And yes, I agree with the DIB. The world must take note … this is a New India. We won't hesitate to defend ourselves, even if it means crossing borders. The message has to be clear: India will no longer tolerate threats, no matter where they come from.'

The foreign secretary's words were passionate, reflecting the shifting stance of a nation no longer content to wait for justice, but willing to seek it wherever necessary.

The NSD leaned forward, his eyes sharp. 'And what if India has to act against a terrorist in Canada, the US or the UK?' His question was direct, cutting to the heart of the matter.

The foreign secretary didn't blink. His response was swift and unwavering. 'India would treat those countries no differently than Pakistan,' he said, his tone steady and resolute. 'Such firm and decisive action wouldn't be aimed at the countries themselves, but to send a clear message to the terrorists: "You are not safe anywhere."'

He let the weight of his words sink in before continuing. 'India will find them. Hunt them. No matter where they hide. The message must be loud and clear ... terrorism has no sanctuary. And no country, no border, will shield them from the consequences of their actions.'

The room fell into a heavy silence, the foreign secretary's declaration echoing the shift in India's stance. This was a New India, one that would no longer wait for others to act. The hunt was on, and the world would be watching.

The narrative in New Delhi had taken a sharp turn, one that now focused heavily on Rinda's involvement in the assassination of a popular Punjabi rapper and singer. The brutal act had not only shocked the entire subcontinent but also led to a cascade of events, with Rinda fleeing India and eventually being tied to the killing of Ripudaman Singh Malik. With over 40 cases pending against him and an INTERPOL red alert limiting his movements, Rinda had found a safe haven in Lahore, Pakistan, under the protective shield of the ISI and the Pakistan Army.

But the NSD was undeterred. The enormity of the task, penetrating the layers of protection around a figure as elusive and dangerous as Rinda, didn't faze him. His vast network of informants, operatives and covert allies across the region was already in motion – in particular, his special man already handpicked and put in place.

Turning to Awasthy, the NSD spoke with steely determination. 'Tell Altaf to focus on Aditya. He's going to face new challenges in breaking through the protective bubble around Rinda. The rest on his target list can wait.'

The decision was final. Aditya's mission had just become infinitely more dangerous. But the NSD knew that Rinda, with his intricate web of connections and sanctuary in Lahore, had to be neutralized, no matter the cost.

The wheels were in motion. New Delhi was prepared for what lay ahead.

14

The Unthinkable Pact

June 2023.

At the beginning of the month, the prime minister of India leaned forward in his khadi-upholstered chair, a symbol of his commitment to tradition and simplicity. The secure line connected, bringing the faint hum of international communication into the quiet of his office. This was not just another conversation; it was a strategic manoeuvre. Through the influence of the American president, he intended to manage the delicate situation with Canada indirectly, yet decisively.

Direct engagement with the Canadian prime minister were fraught with complications. The political landscape of Canada, shaped in part by Sikh organizations that held considerable sway over votes and election funding, meant any misstep could have far-reaching consequences. India had gathered credible intelligence, suggesting that Malik's withdrawal from the Khalistani cause had not gone unnoticed. Some within the more radical factions of the Sikh separatist movement were enraged by his defection, and Indian intelligence had pieced together a chilling narrative. His murder, it seemed, was not a simple act of violence but the result of deep-seated feuds within Canada's Sikh community.

The prime minister's thoughts turned toward Gurdeep Singh Takkar, a name that had surfaced repeatedly in the intelligence briefings. Some accused him and his allies of orchestrating the killing. The situation was delicate. One wrong move, and it could escalate into a diplomatic nightmare.

He sighed, staring at the blinking light on the secure phone. The Americans would understand the stakes, he thought. They had a way of exerting the kind of pressure that wouldn't require overt involvement from India. The Canadian prime minister, mindful of his political alliances, would likely prefer an indirect nudge rather than a full-blown confrontation.

He leaned back slightly, letting the soft texture of the khadi remind him of the values he represented.

'We can't afford to push too hard,' he murmured, almost to himself. 'But with the Americans in the picture, the message will be clear enough.'

The room was quiet, save for the occasional rustle of papers on his desk. His thoughts were already a few steps ahead. This wasn't just about managing a single incident; it was about preventing an internal Canadian issue from spilling over into something far more complicated on the world stage. The stakes were higher than they seemed on the surface.

Malik's murder had shaken the Sikh diaspora, and the reverberations were being felt across continents. What started as a feud within the community was now threatening to become an international concern. The prime minister knew the Americans were the key to controlling the narrative without making any direct waves in Canada.

The secure line connected, and after a brief pause the president's face appeared on the screen. The Indian prime minister straightened in his chair, his expression composed but intent.

'Mr President,' he began, exchanging a few words of courtesy before steering the conversation to what mattered. 'I need your quiet support on an issue that concerns both our nations.'

He didn't waste time. 'The men we're dealing with Takkar and Dhillon who are by no means idealists or freedom fighters. They're profiteers hiding behind the language of revolution.'

The president listened, his brow furrowed.

'To understand them,' the prime minister continued, 'think of the Revolutionary Armed Forces of Colombia, or the Liberation Army of Tecala. They fooled the world once… spoke of justice, of the poor but their leaders thrived on kidnapping, drugs, and arms trafficking. Takkar is no different, only his partners are more dangerous: Pakistan's ISI and the cartels of Mexico and Colombia.'

He paused, letting the weight of that comparison settle. 'All I ask,' he said quietly, 'is your discretion and your understanding. We'll handle this our way. But your silent support could make all the difference.'

The prime minister's voice sharpened as he touched on a matter that had caused particular outrage in New Delhi. The Indian government had been appalled when Canada chose to ignore the RCN issued by INTERPOL against Takkar. That single decision revealed the deep complexities of Canada's political manoeuvring.

Just as he made this point, the American president leaned back in his chair, a slight smirk playing on his lips. 'The Canadian government believes that guy is just a plumber who spends most of his time in religious work,' he said cryptically, his tone hinting at the political naivety or perhaps wilful ignorance of their northern ally.

The prime minister's fingers tapped rhythmically on his desk, his thoughts racing. Canada had chosen to turn a blind eye, but the truth was far more sinister than the image of a humble tradesman with spiritual leanings. The real question was, how much longer could the façade last before the weight of reality forced Canada to confront the darker forces within its borders?

The Indian prime minister, appreciating the American president's cryptic remark, decided to delve deeper into the web of conspiracy surrounding Ripudaman Singh Malik's assassination. He carefully outlined the key players in the plot, beginning with Gurdeep Singh Takkar and the US-based advocate Harinder Singh Dhillon.

Dhillon, who had already been declared a designated terrorist by India's Ministry of Home Affairs, was at the heart of the conspiracy.

The prime minister's tone grew more deliberate as he laid out the scenario, connecting the dots with precision. Dhillon had been working relentlessly to further his vision of an independent Punjab, and in his mind, Malik stood in the way. Once a prominent supporter of the Khalistani movement, Malik's shift toward cooperation with India had branded him, in Dhillon's eyes, as a traitor and an 'Indian stooge'. Dhillon had skillfully manipulated Takkar into believing that Malik's continued influence was a direct threat to their cause, and that his removal was necessary to clear the path for their separatist agenda.

As the prime minister recounted the events, it was clear that Malik's assassination was not just an act of violence but a calculated move to silence opposition within the separatist ranks. Both Dhillon and Takkar had seen Malik's change of heart as an unforgivable betrayal, one that had to be punished. The prime minister's voice carried the weight of the geopolitical implications, reminding the American president that these weren't isolated incidents – they were part of a larger, dangerous game being played on multiple fronts.

The prime minister continued, stressing that all this information had been shared with the American CIA by the Indian government on multiple occasions. His tone became more pointed as he explained that these details were not new, but part of a long-standing effort to keep international intelligence agencies informed about the growing threats.

He then shifted to the tensions that had flared between Ripudaman Singh Malik and certain factions within the Sikh community, which had further strained the situation. One particularly sensitive issue was the *jathedar* of the Akal Takht, the highest religious authority in Sikhism, who had planned a visit to British Columbia in late June 2022, just three weeks before Malik's assassination. However, the visit was abruptly cancelled due to internal disputes surrounding Malik's involvement in printing unauthorized copies of the Sri Guru Granth Sahib, the Sikh holy scripture.

The prime minister emphasized how this dispute had worsened the already fragile relationship between Malik and those who saw him as a threat to their cause. The controversy over the unauthorized printing had made Malik a target not just politically, but within the religious community as well, compounding the reasons for his eventual assassination. The cancellation of the jathedar's visit was a clear signal that Malik's role in the Sikh diaspora was increasingly contentious and dangerous.

With this context, the prime minister made it evident that Malik's death was the result of a perfect storm of political, religious and personal grievances, all skilfully exploited by figures like Dhillon and Takkar to eliminate their opposition.

The prime minister moved swiftly to denounce the allegations made by the Royal Canadian Mounted Police (RCMP) that India had orchestrated Malik's assassination. He firmly told the American president that the claim was baseless. In fact, Malik had been working as a mediator between the West-based Khalistani extremists and the Indian government. His role as a bridge between the two made it absurd to suggest that India would have any interest in his death.

The prime minister's voice held a tone of measured indignation as he explained that Malik had been attempting to negotiate a peaceful resolution, smoothing tensions rather than inflaming them. His efforts had been viewed positively by New Delhi, making the idea of Indian involvement in his assassination even more implausible.

He also pointed out that Malik's own family, who had been the closest witnesses to the events surrounding his life and death, had never publicly accused the Indian government. They believed that Malik had reconciled with India, and they saw no reason to suspect that the government would turn against him. This, the prime minister emphasized, was a key detail that the international community and especially Canada needed to recognize.

For India, Malik's death was a setback, not a victory. His role as a mediator had been invaluable, and his loss had only added to the complexity of an already tense situation.

The American president, having patiently listened to the Indian prime minister's detailed briefing for over ten minutes, offered his assurance of full cooperation. His tone was supportive, but as the conversation shifted, the president became more direct. He made it clear that while his government was open to collaboration, they would not tolerate any action on American soil unless it was backed by irrefutable proof.

'I'll have an exclusive talk with my spy chief,' the president added, 'and I'll get back to you soon.'

However, he was quick to remind the Indian prime minister of the realities of political leadership. As a fellow politician, the American president noted, the Indian prime minister must understand that if any action taken by India displeased the American people or was seen as a breach of sovereignty, the president would have no choice but to stand with his own government, even if it meant publicly denouncing India. He emphasized that such a stance, should it be necessary, must not be misinterpreted as a deterioration of Indo–American relations on other fronts.

The Indian prime minister nodded thoughtfully, understanding the diplomatic nuance in the president's words. Beneath the cautious phrasing and conditional assurances, there was an unmistakable approval, an unspoken nod to India's plans for covert actions. The message was clear: as long as India remained discreet and provided proof, the American administration would not interfere. The Indian prime minister, with his years of political experience, sensed the opening he needed to move forward.

The successful outcome of the conversation between the American president and the Indian prime minister was quickly relayed to the NSD. The green light for retaliatory strikes against Gurdeep Singh Takkar in Canada and Harinder Singh Dhillon in America seemed almost within reach. But as the NSD sat with the R&AW chief Ashok Awasthy, reviewing the implications of direct action, he chose a different path. One far more subtle and strategic.

In a hushed conversation, the NSD laid out his vision. Rather than rushing into targeted operations, he proposed a game of disinformation. The Khalistani extremists operating from foreign soil had long thrived on the clarity of their cause and the certainty of their mission. The NSD's plan was to muddy those waters, to introduce doubt, confusion and paranoia into their ranks.

'We hit them with shadows, not bullets,' the NSD said, his voice calm but resolute. He knew the power of disinformation could be just as effective, if not more so, than direct action. By feeding carefully curated false intelligence, they could fracture the trust between these extremists and their networks, leaving them vulnerable from within.

Ashok Awasthy nodded in agreement, recognizing the brilliance of the strategy. Direct action might make martyrs of men like Takkar and Dhillon, but disinformation could isolate them, turning their allies into adversaries and sowing chaos without a single shot fired. This approach, the NSD believed, would weaken the Khalistani cause more effectively in the long run, while keeping India's hands clean on the international stage.

It was time to play a far more dangerous game, one where trust would be the first casualty.

Following the assassination of Ripudaman Singh Malik, both the CIA and the RCMP promptly alerted the Khalistan lobbies in the United States and Canada. They warned them that leaders like Gurdeep Singh Takkar and Harinder Singh Dhillon were under imminent threat from interests believed to be close to the Indian establishment. This warning came at a time when intelligence agencies had compelling reasons to suspect Takkar's involvement in Malik's murder.

The logic was simple: Malik had been working as a mediator between the Indian government and the Khalistani groups in the West. His assassination, therefore, would be seen as an act of sabotage against the very idea of reconciliation, a move that would hardly sit well with New Delhi. If Malik was attempting to bridge the divide, killing him only deepened the fracture, something that would understandably provoke the Indian government.

As tensions mounted, security around Takkar was ramped up, not just by his own supporters but by the Canadian authorities as well. The heightened surveillance was a clear indication that both his allies and the Canadian government took the threats seriously. The air around him grew tense as eyes from all sides kept a close watch, aware that any misstep could escalate the already fragile situation. Takkar, now a marked man, lived under the dual scrutiny of those protecting him and those potentially plotting his downfall.

The R&AW carefully weighed its options and concluded that no action should be taken that would arouse suspicion within the Takkar group. Let them continue believing that India wouldn't dare touch Takkar on foreign soil. The disinformation campaign had to be subtle, maintaining the illusion that India's reach was confined to familiar battlegrounds – Pakistan, PoK and Afghanistan. For now, Takkar and his associates could remain in the shadows, unaware of what might come next.

At the same time, the focus was clear: India's most pressing interest remained in destabilizing threats in Pakistan. Resuming operations there was the logical next step. While the eyes of Takkar's group remained fixed on the possibility of retribution on North American soil, India's real intentions were taking shape elsewhere.

Aditya Singh, often referred to in intelligence circles as India's own James Bond, had already made his mark in Karachi with the elimination of Zahoor Mistry, a high-profile target with deep ties to anti-India activities. Mistry's demise had been a key victory in India's ongoing operations across the border, and Aditya was now primed for his next mission. His targets were set, and R&AW was ready to unleash him once again, this time with even greater precision and stealth.

For India, the game was far from over. As tensions mounted in North America, the real action was shifting back to familiar territory, where Aditya Singh was poised to strike again, moving through the murky underworld of Karachi with lethal intent.

The challenge was not simply eliminating the list of terrorists sheltered in Pakistan. Now it was in balancing those operations while simultaneously laying the groundwork for a future strike against Takkar. India had already conducted extensive planning and reconnaissance across Pakistan, pinpointing key targets in Karachi, Rawalpindi and Muridke. The strikes were imminent, but the Takkar operation presented an entirely different level of complexity.

Targeting Takkar was a long game. It would require months of careful planning, intelligence gathering and, most critically, the subtle manipulation of people close to him. Turning a few of his loyalists to India's side was essential, but it would take time and delicate manoeuvring. Moreover, understanding the security setup around Takkar, and possibly coordinating with certain local agencies, was key to assessing the feasibility of an assassination. Unlike the terrorists in Pakistan, Takkar was a protected public figure and any move against him had to be flawless.

The difficulty, however, lay in the fact that Aditya Singh, India's top operative, was already deeply embedded in operations within Pakistan. His focus was currently locked on the high-value targets in Karachi and Rawalpindi, leaving little room to devote his expertise to the Takkar mission. With Aditya tied up in Pakistani operations, the question remained: How would India execute a plan of this magnitude against Takkar without its best man on the job?

It became clear that timing and resource allocation would be crucial. For now, Pakistan remained the priority, but the groundwork for Takkar would need to be laid in parallel, ensuring that when the time came, every detail was in place and India could strike without hesitation.

Awasthy, ever the strategist, proposed a backup plan: sending someone to Canada to assess the situation on the ground. The NSD, however, wasn't initially convinced about introducing a second operative into such a sensitive mission. Adding another player would complicate things, and trust was always a critical factor. But Awasthy pressed on, suggesting a R&AW operative who was already embedded in California. She had spent over a decade in America, forging solid connections within the CIA, and her familiarity with the intelligence community in the West was an advantage Aditya simply didn't have.

'She's better suited to deal with the CIA than Aditya,' Awasthy argued, knowing that Aditya's experience and network in the West were limited compared to this operative's deep roots in the American system.

The NSD, after careful consideration, reluctantly agreed but laid down one strict condition: she would not be told the ultimate purpose of her surveillance around Takkar. Awasthy, understanding the need for discretion, gave his assurance. 'No way,' he said firmly. The operative would work with limited information, focusing only on the immediate tasks.

The NSD suggested that her first priority should be investigating Takkar's affairs; his movements, his contacts and any vulnerabilities that could be exploited later. The decision on Dhillon would come later. Awasthy nodded in agreement, knowing the scope of the mission was expanding, but each step had to be calculated.

The operative in question was Mridula Swamy, a seasoned spy with over fifteen years of experience in R&AW. A graduate of IIT Madras, Mridula had carved out a unique position for herself in the intelligence community. A spinster by choice, she had successfully maintained a low profile in the American social fabric, blending in seamlessly. Known to those around her as a devout Christian actively involved in church activities, Mridula had the perfect cover. But beneath her amiable exterior, she was both brave and a ruthless killer, precisely the type of operative needed for this mission. Her ability to navigate through American society while keeping her true nature hidden made her a valuable asset for the task ahead.

With Mridula in play, the groundwork for the Takkar operation was finally beginning to take shape. She would observe, gather intelligence and remain in the shadows, waiting for the moment when her mission would become clear.

Awasthy knew the importance of coordinating the next steps and wanted to schedule a meeting with Altaf for further alignment with Aditya. However, the NSD had a different strategy in mind. While Mridula focused on gathering intelligence around Takkar, Aditya's task, operating from the shadows, would be to dismantle Takkar's support system. The NSD suggested starting with one of the most crucial figures, Harvinder Singh Sandhu, known as Rinda, a man who had transformed from a feared gangster into a high-profile terrorist. Rinda's operations had made him a cornerstone in Takkar's network, and taking him out would be a critical blow.

Living comfortably under the ISI's protection in Pakistan, Rinda had become a formidable and elusive figure. His influence stretched far, making him not only a logistical powerhouse but also a source of inspiration for many within Takkar's circle. Removing him from the equation would be no small feat, but his absence would weaken Takkar significantly, turning him into a fish out of water. Without Rinda, Takkar would lose a key pillar that held up much of his operations.

The NSD's advice was clear: while Mridula played her careful, undercover role in America, Aditya's expertise would be used to strike at the heart of Takkar's infrastructure. If Rinda could be neutralized, Takkar's carefully constructed empire would start to crumble. And in that chaos, India could finally close in on its long-elusive target.

Awasthy nodded, recognizing the brilliance of the dual approach. While one operative worked on Takkar's personal circle, the other would destroy his operational foundations. The game was far from over, but India was now playing from a position of strength.

Mridula Swamy possessed a statuesque grace that seemed almost effortless, her well-proportioned hourglass figure naturally commanding attention. Her balanced shoulders, defined waist and elegant posture gave her an air of sophistication that went beyond mere appearance. Thanks to her stylish mother's influence, Mridula had developed an impeccable sense of dressing that complemented both her body type and her dark skin tone. Whether in traditional Indian attire or modern cuts, she always looked timeless, her look exuding a quiet aura of class that left a lasting impression.

In photographs, her silhouette was striking, each angle creating a perfect image of poised beauty. During a fashion photography session at the Indian Institute of Technology (IIT), Mridula had surprised everyone, crafting looks that were not just visually stunning but captured an effortless elegance. She could have easily become a model, her ability to merge tradition with modernity making her a rare find in that world.

But what the modelling world lost, the world of intellect and power gained. Mridula had grown up in opulence, her father leaving behind a considerable fortune, while her mother inherited a sprawling estate from Mridula's grandfather. Yet, despite her privilege, Mridula's mind was her sharpest asset. Instead of fashion runways, she walked the hallowed halls of IIT, excelling in ways that would later lead her into a world where beauty was an asset, but intellect and influence were the ultimate currency, a world of shadows and secrets, where danger lurked behind every door.

In fact, Mridula wanted to become a doctor in her childhood, inspired by her father, who passed away when she was still young. His early death left a void, and though she was raised by her mother, a lecturer of higher mathematics in Madras, the dream of following in her father's footsteps gradually faded. Under her mother's influence, the idea of studying medicine slowly drifted away. Her mother, a staunch academic, subtly guided her towards a different future, one rooted in education and intellectualism. Her mother's own depth of understanding, not only in mathematics but in subjects like history and English literature, shaped Mridula's academic path. By the time she reached college age, the idea of becoming a professor seemed less like a personal calling and more like a natural progression influenced by her upbringing.

She attended IIT in Guindy, Madras, and graduated with a degree in computer science, a choice that suited her analytical mind. Many of her peers urged her to follow the typical route of pursuing an MBA at the Indian Institute of Management (IIM), but Mridula, much like her mother, was drawn to academia. Teaching seemed like the logical next step, especially with the weight of her mother's career hanging over her decisions.

Mridula enrolled in a PhD programme with the aim of teaching at one of the IITs, a career path she pursued with dedication, if not passion. She was greatly encouraged by Dr Prashant Aiyar, her former professor in the computer programming lab and, later, her lover. Their relationship, however, was complicated by the fact that Prashant was already married. Despite his personal circumstances, Prashant remained a strong advocate for Mridula's academic pursuits.

Yet, the looming reality that they had no future together, due to his inability to obtain a divorce, cast a shadow over their relationship. While her mother's influence pushed her toward academia, it was Prashant's support that sustained her through the complexities of life and love.

While Mridula's mother never approved of her relationship with Prashant, knowing it was a dead end due to his marriage, Mridula took a more casual approach. She loved Prashant, but her primary focus was still on becoming a teacher at the IITs. However, everything changed during her PhD when an unexpected encounter altered the course of her life.

While on a tour of Europe with her mother, she unexpectedly ran into one of her former professors, Dr Arvind Ranganathan, in Brussels. It was a pleasant surprise, and Mridula was delighted to meet someone from her academic community in such an unexpected place. Neither saw any harm in hanging around together, exploring the cities that coincided with both their itineraries.

During this time, Mridula discovered a side of Dr Arvind Ranganathan she had never seen before. It was his vast understanding of international relations and geopolitics. His grasp of world affairs was nothing short of a revelation. Mridula found herself drawn in, fascinated by ideas that had rarely figured in her conversations with her mother or in her own world of disciplined scholarship. Her mother, a scientist by training, had little interest in politics, and discussions at home were always confined to academia and research. Watching her mother now engage with Dr Ranganathan on matters of global significance was a new and thrilling experience. She had never witnessed such lively exchange between her parents either; her father had passed away before she was old enough to see such dynamics unfold. It felt as if a new world had opened before her. A world that was filled with perspectives she had never imagined.

Mridula was young and impressionable when Arvind entered her life. His presence, both charismatic and intellectually sharp, made a deep impact on her. Under his mentorship, she began to regret her decision to study computer science instead of fields like political science or international relations, areas that now fascinated her deeply. Arvind, ever perceptive, noticed this internal conflict and offered her a lifeline that there was still time to pivot. He assured her that her technical skills could be invaluable in serving the nation, perhaps in ways she hadn't yet considered.

He planted the idea that her future didn't have to be confined to academia, teaching at IITs or other prestigious educational institutions. Instead, she could leverage her academic background to serve the country in more dynamic ways. The notion of joining the government, particularly in a role that involved strategy and international affairs, began to take root in her mind.

What Mridula didn't know at the time was that Dr Arvind Ranganathan's own role extended far beyond the classroom. His teaching position at IIT was more of a front. In reality, he was an analyst working for R&AW, India's external intelligence agency. His assignment in the university allowed him to keep tabs on the brightest students, those who excelled in various fields, tracking who was headed abroad after graduation. It was a subtle recruitment strategy as Arvind quietly identified which students had the potential to be tapped for intelligence work, either from within India or from strategic positions overseas.

Under Arvind's subtle guidance, Mridula's world began to expand, and her dreams of serving the nation shifted from the theoretical to the tangible. The idea of intelligence work had a pull she could not resist, and soon, her path was set in a direction she hadn't anticipated but felt strangely drawn to.

Upon returning from her Europe tour, it was clear that something had shifted in Mridula's life. She began spending significantly more time with Arvind than anyone else, their conversations evolving from academic discussions to something far more intriguing. While she didn't neglect her research, her focus seemed to widen, as she and Arvind delved into how her academic work could be used for the greater good of the nation. She spoke of its potential applications with a newfound passion, and Arvind was more than willing to guide her, offering her glimpses into career possibilities beyond the world of academia.

What Mridula didn't realize, however, was that Arvind had a quiet, deliberate motive behind his mentorship. While he encouraged her intellectual curiosity, he was subtly steering her towards the world of secret service, gently nudging her to consider a career with R&AW. The idea wasn't presented outright, but rather woven into their discussions, as he made her see how her skills and knowledge could be leveraged in a field she had never imagined for herself, though he did not yet specify what field.

Her growing interest in this new, entirely different world did not go unnoticed by those closest to her. Her mother, a woman of academia and traditional values, was alarmed. She couldn't understand Mridula's sudden fascination with politics, strategy and international affairs. The idea of her daughter leaving the safety of teaching for a shadowy, unknown world troubled her deeply.

Two opposing reactions from the people she most trusted– one filled with concern, the other with encouragement – left Mridula at a crossroads, torn between her loyalty to her mother's academic values and the pull of an entirely different path she had never envisioned for herself.

Mridula's mother, though concerned about her daughter's sudden interest in intelligence and politics, couldn't help but see the silver lining. To her, this new preoccupation under Dr Arvind's guidance was a welcome distraction from Prashant, as that was a relationship she had never approved of. Prashant, being married and unable to offer Mridula a stable future, was, in her eyes, an obstacle to her daughter's happiness and security. The mother quietly saw this shift as a good change, hoping that Mridula's new career ambitions would pull her away from the man who could never give her the life she deserved.

Prashant, on the other hand, saw the situation very differently. To him, Mridula's burgeoning interest in exploring new career options, especially when she was still far from completing her PhD, was troubling. He saw it as a premature leap into uncharted territory, one that could derail the path she had already chosen for herself. After all, she had dedicated herself to earning a PhD, a necessary qualification if she wanted to pursue her original plan of teaching at IIT.

Prashant couldn't understand why Mridula was suddenly so eager to abandon that track for something so uncertain and, in his view, distracting. He questioned why she would even entertain the idea of changing course when she was so close to completing her research. To him, this newfound interest felt like a dangerous distraction, one that could pull her away from the stability and predictability of academia, something he believed she needed now more than ever. He felt the pull of this world of international affairs was something Mridula could ill afford at this stage in her life.

Mridula took offense at Prashant's voiced concerns, interpreting his words as thinly veiled jealousy. To her, it seemed like he was uncomfortable with her newfound ambition and the fact that she was being guided by someone else, Dr Ranganathan. This accusation stung Prashant deeply. He was fully aware that his inability to offer her a conventional future, a life of marriage, children and stability was a sore point in their relationship. But that didn't mean he didn't want the best for her.

But now, seeing her drawn into a world he believed she wasn't fully prepared for, Prashant grew uneasy. What troubled him most was Arvind's sudden, intense interest in Mridula's career, which seemed to go beyond mere mentorship. To Prashant, it felt like there was something more, something hidden beneath the surface. Unable to shake this feeling, he took a drastic step: he voiced his concerns to Dr Nageswara Reddy, the director of IIT Madras and an eminent scientist in his own right.

Dr Reddy, though respectful of Prashant's concerns, brushed off the warnings as an overreaction. He didn't see the issue with Dr Ranganathan's involvement, chalking it up to professional interest. But Mridula's interpretation of the situation remained unchanged. She saw it as jealousy on Prashant's part. In her eyes, Prashant couldn't stand the fact that someone else, particularly Arvind, was now guiding her career, and his reaction was a way to keep her under his influence.

This difference in the interpretation of Prashant's motives only deepened the divide between them. While he worried for her future, she saw only a man struggling with his own insecurities, unable to accept the growing influence of another figure in her life.

Arvind, having carefully observed the potential in Mridula, decided it was time to take a calculated risk. One evening, during one of their usual discussions, he confessed his true intentions to her: he believed she had tremendous promise in serving the country, not as an academic, but as a spy. His admission landed like a bombshell in Mridula's otherwise controlled and orderly world. The revelation shook her to the core, as it was something she had never imagined for herself. What impressed her the most was Arvind's honesty.

Up until that moment, she had outright dismissed Prashant's suspicions that Arvind harboured hidden motives in steering her career down this unexpected path. She had seen Prashant's concerns as nothing more than jealousy, rooted in his discomfort with her growing closeness to Arvind. But now, hearing the truth from Arvind himself, her reaction was quite different. Instead of fear or betrayal, she felt an undeniable thrill. A life as a spy, working in the shadows, serving her country in ways she had never envisioned, not even in her wildest dreams, excited her deeply.

In hindsight, Prashant hadn't been entirely wrong in his suspicions. It wasn't just intellectual admiration that had drawn Mridula to Arvind. She had developed an undeniable crush on him, an infatuation that she hadn't fully acknowledged even to herself. It wasn't a betrayal of her love for Prashant, but rather a fascination with Arvind's charisma, his magnetic personality and the aura of power he carried. It had subtly influenced her, making her more open to the possibilities he dangled before her.

Arvind, for his part, had expertly read the situation. He knew how to mould young, impressionable minds, and Mridula was no exception. He had used his charm and intellect not just to guide her academically, but to steer her towards a future in the intelligence world. There was no denying it. Arvind was a recruiter for R&AW. And while his methods might have blurred the lines of personal and professional ethics, his goal was clear: to recruit promising minds like Mridula, who could serve the country in ways most people couldn't even fathom. He had taken a risk, but it was one that paid off.

By this time, Arvind's influence had taken full hold, and Mridula was a convert. Her mind was made up, and she was no longer willing to entertain objections, not even from her mother. The academic future her mother had envisioned for her was now a distant memory. Mridula made the bold decision to abandon her PhD and prepare for the Civil Services Examination, determined to enter public life. It was a gruelling path, but she threw herself into it with single-minded focus. A year later, her name appeared among the top ranks of successful candidates. She was selected for the Indian Administrative Service (IAS) and called to the Lal Bahadur Shastri National Academy of Administration in Mussoorie, the cradle of India's future civil servants.

But Mridula chose the Indian Police Service (IPS), signalling a complete 360-degree shift in her life. The girl who once dreamed of becoming a professor was now preparing to serve the country in a far more dangerous, covert capacity. Her transformation was complete, and she was fully immersed in the world Dr Arvind Ranganathan had opened up to her.

Her mother, though heartbroken at first, eventually had no choice but to accept her daughter's decision. Mridula's resolve was unshakable, and as her only child, her mother could do little but watch as she pursued a life, not of teaching in lecture halls, but of shadowy operations and high-stakes intelligence work. The academic career was left behind, and in its place, Mridula embraced a future filled with uncertainty, danger and the weight of serving her country in ways that few could understand.

15

Gurdeep Singh Takkar

June 2023.

Clad in a simple churidar–kurta, her head modestly covered with a dupatta, Mridula blended effortlessly into the crowd gathered for the Sunday mass langar at the Guru Nanak Gurdwara in Surrey, British Columbia, Canada. The attire was a far cry from her usual fieldwork gear, but she knew appearances mattered in this place. Any hint of being an outsider would draw eyes she couldn't afford. Her face bore almost no makeup, and her hair, carefully gathered in a neat bun atop her head, mirrored the traditional style of Sikh women, offering her the perfect cloak of anonymity.

She ate quietly, taking in the atmosphere as the community around her chatted and exchanged smiles. She interacted sparingly, barely lifting her eyes from her plate. For Mridula, the silence wasn't just about blending in; it was about observing. The gurdwara was more than a place of worship – it was a hub for Khalistani activists and sympathizers, and her mission hinged on understanding who was who.

After finishing her meal, she washed her hands with deliberate calm and made her way to the donation counter, where support for the Khalistani cause was openly solicited. The booth was run by a group of men, their demeanour cautious, their eyes scanning every face that approached. Mridula's movements were steady, measured. She pulled out a crisp 100-dollar bill and handed it over, watching as the man behind the counter glanced at her for a moment before accepting the money.

Without hesitation, she gave her name as Satwant Kaur Gill, a resident of Richmond Hill, New York, a fabricated identity, carefully crafted to hold up under surface-level scrutiny. The man at the counter scribbled the details without question, and with a brief nod, she walked away.

It was a small interaction, but an important one. Each step, each action, added another layer to the trust she was slowly building within this close-knit community. Her presence here, carefully concealed beneath layers of cultural familiarity, was all part of the larger plan. She needed access. Access to conversations and to confidences, and blending in were the key.

The gurdwara was packed, mostly with young faces. It wasn't just because it was a Sunday when they had gathered to hear Gurdeep Singh Takkar, the leader of the KTF. The air buzzed with excitement as Takkar's fiery words echoed through the hall, calling for a separate Sikh state in India. His speech ignited the crowd, especially the young, whose eyes burned with fervour.

As Mridula quietly observed, her attention split between the charged atmosphere and the people around her. Takkar's impassioned words filled the space, but her focus remained sharp, as for her this was a place for studying behaviour, not for being swayed.

Takkar was declaiming:

> The Indian government has tried every trick in its book, labelling me and countless other Sikh freedom fighters as 'terrorists', spreading false propaganda, and trying to suppress our voices. But let me tell you this – no force on earth can stop the march of the Khalsa. No label, no Red Notice, no amount of Indian state violence will break our spirit or our resolve to demand Khalistan, a free and sovereign Sikh homeland.

The Indian state has oppressed our people for decades. From the dark days of 1984 when they massacred our brothers and sisters, to today, where they use every arm of the government to silence those who speak up for Sikh rights, their strategy has always been the same ... intimidate, suppress and divide. But they cannot divide us. They cannot break us.

India calls us 'terrorists' yet it is the Indian state that continues to terrorize our community, using its police and army to crack down on innocent Sikhs, trying to paint our struggle for justice and freedom as an act of violence. But we are not terrorists. We are freedom fighters. We fight for our rights, our dignity and our sovereignty. And if the Indian government thinks that by calling us names they can stop this movement, they are gravely mistaken.

Our movement is not just a cry for help; it is a demand for justice. A justice that has long been denied to us. And while we are committed to the path of peaceful struggle, let me be clear ... if India continues to push our people, if they continue to trample on our rights, they are forcing us down a path that they will regret. No Sikh will ever bow down to tyranny.

I stand before you today, not just as a leader but as a servant of the Sikh community. I urge the Indian government ... do not make the mistake of underestimating the strength and unity of the Khalsa. We want peace. We want justice. We want Khalistan, a place where Sikhs can live without fear, without persecution and without oppression. But if you push us, if you compel us to take up arms to defend our honour, the world will see who the real terrorists are.

We are prepared to fight politically, legally and diplomatically ... but do not force us to take the final step. We do not desire violence, but we will not shy away from defending our people if necessary. The time is coming, and

> no amount of Indian propaganda, threats or violence can change the destiny of Khalistan.
>
> Let us stand united in this fight for freedom, and let the Indian government know … we will not stop. Not until Khalistan is a reality. The Sikh nation has risen before, and it will rise again.

Mridula needed no special ability or intelligence to interpret his speech as anti-India and that of a seditionist. The response from the crowd was ecstatic, especially the youngsters. They saw a 'true leader' in Takkar.

After the speech, Mridula slid through the crowd, her presence unnoticed, like a shadow moving between eager faces. She casually struck up conversations with some of the younger members of the congregation, to understand how deep their dream for Khalistan ran. Was it real, or just another fantasy born of youthful rebellion?

The responses were a mixed bag. Some were startling in their passion, men who spoke of Khalistan with a conviction so fierce it seemed carved into their souls. They saw a true leader in Takkar. They talked of revolution, of standing up to a government they felt had wronged them for generations. These were the ones ready to die for a cause, any cause, as long as it made them feel alive.

But others, a quieter minority, surprised her with their hesitation. A few admitted that the idea of Khalistan felt outdated, a relic of another time. They had built lives here, in Canada. Comfortable lives. 'Why ruin it all?' one man whispered, his voice barely audible over the din. He glanced around, as though even speaking the thought out loud might brand him a traitor.

Violence was a line they wouldn't cross. For some, the price of revolution was too high, the scars of the past still too fresh. But for others, the fire for Khalistan was already burning, whether they knew it or not.

~

Mridula's entry into Canada from the US had been as quiet as a whisper. A new name, slight changes to her face and a fresh passport that traced no roots to her true identity. She avoided the obvious routes, such as busy terminals like Vancouver International or Toronto Pearson. Instead, she slipped into the country through a smaller, less monitored crossing, away from the eyes of immigration and customs.

For someone like Mridula, invisibility wasn't just a necessity – it was her art. Her presence here had to be an absence. She couldn't afford the luxury of mistakes. Every move, every action, had to be clean, precise. She knew well that the most dangerous missions weren't the ones where bullets flew, but where silence prevailed.

Her primary task was already in motion. Before she'd even set foot on Canadian soil, her network had been quietly gathering intelligence. Now, on the ground, it was her job to connect the dots. Takkar's movements weren't a secret; not entirely. His appearances at the gurdwara, his public speeches, even the gatherings he held with his closest circle, were all public knowledge, hidden in plain sight. But it wasn't enough to know where he would be. She needed to understand the rhythm of his life, the timing of his every step.

Every morning, as the city of Surrey came to life, Mridula was already working in the shadows. Public sources were her initial map, the schedules of gurdwara events, the sociopolitical rallies where he made his presence known, even the times he stopped for tea at a local stall and held short meetings. She began creating a timeline of his routine, noting every small detail, every point where his guard might lower.

In her initial stakeout, Mridula spent hours, sometimes days observing from a distance, always blending into the crowd, a faceless presence among the devout. The gurdwara in Surrey was her main point of focus. It was Takkar's sanctuary, the place where he felt most untouchable. But to Mridula, no place was ever truly safe.

She would slip in and out of the crowd, unnoticed, a shadow among shadows. Every visit had a purpose. From different angles, she memorized the layout, taking note of entry and exit points. There were the obvious ones such as the front gates, guarded during public events, and the more discreet paths used by staff and volunteers.

The gurdwara wasn't the only location. Takkar's influence reached into the local businesses, into the fabric of Surrey itself. Wherever he went, Mridula followed, never close enough to be noticed but always near enough to observe. With every move, she painted a clearer picture of his life, his habits, his routine and the moments when he was most vulnerable.

Next came her network. It was time to tap into her old sources. Mridula still had assets buried deep within the Khalistani networks across Canada. The men and women she had cultivated years ago. Some had gone so far undercover that extracting them now would jeopardise their lives and years of work. Others lived in plain sight, blending into gurdwara committees, transport businesses and cultural organisations, quietly feeding back fragments of intelligence when it was safe to do so. Together, they formed the invisible web she had once spun and now needed to awaken again.

One of her oldest assets was Satnam Singh Dhingra, a man whose loyalties were bought not by ideology but by necessity. He ran a small confectionary shop in Surrey, a quaint front that masked his past. A casual meeting at his shop, cloaked under false pretences. She pretended to merely need information on the ground – a delicate balance had to be maintained, reviving old connections without setting off any alarm bells.

As they sat in the back of his shop, the faint smell of sugar and flour mixing with the tension in the air, she studied his reactions. His eyes flickered with uncertainty at first, but the mention of an unrelated mission, something small and far from the Khalistani cause, seemed to ease his nerves.

Then she gently steered the conversation towards matters closer home.

'This isn't about Takkar,' she said, her voice smooth, neutral. 'But I do need information about the pulse on the ground here. I need to know if things are shifting … under the surface.'

Dhingra hesitated for a moment, but the lure of money or perhaps survival was enough. 'Things are tense, but people are starting to question. There's talk of infighting, even among the loyalists. You know how it goes. No one trusts anyone fully.' It was what Mridula had hoped to hear. Takkar's stronghold wasn't as impenetrable as it appeared from the outside. Fissures were forming, and through those cracks, Mridula would find her way in.

As she instructed Dhingra to keep his eyes open, her voice remained measured, betraying none of the pressure she felt. 'Watch him closely. Watch them all,' she said. 'Subtle shifts, changes in behaviour, mood swings. Especially since things have grown more radical. People change when they feel the ground shifting beneath them.'

Takkar's vulnerabilities were the real prize. Did he have any weaknesses hidden from the public? Secret vices, private moments of indulgence or unguarded behaviour either at home or at the gurdwara? Information like that was more valuable than gold in operations like this.

But she couldn't share everything with Dhingra. He didn't need to know the full extent of her plan, at least not yet. The lower-level guards, staff members and foot soldiers around Takkar could be manipulated. It was just a matter of identifying the right person: someone desperate, someone tired of living under Takkar's thumb. Once she had that person, she could offer money and security, or even use leverage against something they held dear. But she couldn't reveal this part to Dhingra. Trusting too much too soon could unravel everything.

'I'll check in again in a week,' Mridula said quietly, as the conversation wound down. She slipped a roll of $2,000 into Dhingra's hand, the bills wrapped tightly in a rubber band, a silent assurance of their ongoing relationship. 'Be careful. We'll need more soon.'

As she walked out of the shop, a large, gaily-coloured bag of candies and cookies held ostentatiously in her hand to explain the long visit to any watchers, her Uber was already waiting, the engine idling quietly. She slid into the back seat, her mind already racing ahead. Dhingra would deliver, and she would be one step closer to finding Takkar's weak link.

Back in California, Mridula sat down and prepared a report on Takkar. It was necessary in espionage practices. Basically, a step in building up a case to back a spy's future mission. The organization needs to know about a target before he is attacked. She swiftly sent the dossier to her chief, Ashok Awasthy, who passed it on to the NSD in New Delhi.

Gurdeep Singh Takkar

Gurdeep Singh Takkar arrived in Canada under a false identity. Known by the alias Ravi Sharma, Takkar initially presented himself as a humble plumber but has later emerged as one of the most wanted Khalistani terrorists by Indian authorities.

Takkar, the chief of the KTF, had been on India's radar for nearly a decade due to his involvement in pro-Khalistan activities and his close ties with Harinder Singh Dhillon, a leader of SFJ. Like many Khalistani separatists, Takkar has found sanctuary in Canada, where he operates with relative impunity.

Takkar's bid for asylum did not immediately succeed. His case remained unresolved for four years, during which time he married a Canadian citizen to strengthen his claims. Despite the dubious nature of his background, he finally received Canadian citizenship in 2001. Around this time, Takkar began associating with the Babbar Khalsa International (BKI), using his links with Jagtar Singh Tara, the former chief of the KTF. BKI, once led by Sukhdev Singh Babbar, a feared Khalistani terrorist, had been responsible for numerous acts of violence before Babbar was gunned down by Punjab Police in 1992.

Takkar's deep connections within the Khalistani network became even more apparent in 2014, when he travelled to Thailand to assist Tara, who had been arrested there for his involvement in the assassination of former Punjab Chief Minister Beant Singh. Takkar had provided financial aid to Tara, attempting to coordinate his escape from Thailand with the help of Pakistan's ISI. Although the escape plan failed and Tara was eventually extradited to India in 2015,

Takkar's close ties with international terror networks were confirmed.

That same year, Takkar was detained by Thai authorities while travelling from Lahore to Vancouver via Bangkok. This incident, coupled with intelligence reports linking him to the establishment of a terror training camp in Mission City, British Columbia, placed him squarely in the crosshairs of Indian security agencies. The camp, as detailed in a 2016 report, had trained operatives to carry out attacks in Punjab, prompting Indian authorities to seek Takkar's extradition.

Takkar's influence extended far beyond mere advocacy. He trained militants in the camp, including Mandeep Singh Dhaliwal, in handling AK-47s and sniper rifles. He played a central role in Mandeep's indoctrination, offering him ideological guidance and financial backing. In the wake of the Pathankot terror attack in 2016, Indian intelligence agencies issued alerts to the Canadian government about the threat posed by pro-Khalistan terrorists like Takkar. Despite these warnings, no decisive action was taken against him. Reports indicate that Takkar, along with Mandeep Singh, frequently travels to Pakistan to receive arms training from the ISI. Photographic evidence even places them brandishing AK-47s outside the Nankana Sahib Gurdwara in Pakistan.

In 2016, sensing the increasing scrutiny from Indian authorities, Takkar wrote a letter to Prime Minister Justin Trudeau, dismissing the allegations against him as 'fabricated' and 'politically motivated'. He framed himself as a peaceful activist fighting for Sikh self-determination and human rights, specifically advocating for a referendum to create an independent Khalistan in Punjab. Takkar's claims of being a peaceful nationalist, however, are contradicted by ongoing intelligence reports linking him to violent separatist activities.

> Since 2020, Takkar has been officially designated as a terrorist under the UAPA, with charges related to financing and training Khalistani operatives. His name is tied to at least four NIA cases involving Sikh radicalism, including a plot to assassinate Kamaldeep Sharma, a Hindu priest from a temple in Phillaur, Jalandhar. The NIA has placed a ₹10 lakh bounty on Takkar's head in 2022, underscoring the high level of threat he poses to Indian national security.
>
> Working closely with Arshdeep Singh Dala, another Canada-based terrorist, Takkar has orchestrated a larger conspiracy aimed at assassinating Hindu religious figures to instil fear and promote communal disharmony. This operation mirrors similar Khalistani strategies, where separatists routinely deface Hindu temples in both Canada and Australia, using violence and vandalism as a means to spread their message.

The dossier on Takkar prepared by Mridula presented a harrowing account of how Khalistan terror networks have flourished on Canadian soil, radicalizing individuals and training them for acts of terrorism within India. Her report went on to lay bare the connections between local extremists and prominent Khalistani figures and organizations abroad, detailing the systematic manipulation of vulnerable communities to fuel separatist violence.

Among the radicalized individuals was Mandeep Singh Dhaliwal, a native of Chakk Kalan, Ludhiana. After emigrating to Surrey, British Columbia, in 2012, what began as a hopeful immigrant's story quickly devolved into one of radicalization, driven by the Khalistan movement. The dossier meticulously tracked Dhaliwal's transformation, highlighting how ordinary individuals can be pulled into violent extremist agendas.

> Upon settling in Surrey, Mandeep Singh began frequenting the Guru Nanak Gurdwara, where he was exposed to anti-India rhetoric delivered by radical Khalistani ideologues. Coupled with glorifying literature about slain militants

from Punjab's past, Mandeep's sense of grievance grew, and he developed a clear ambition: vengeance for the Sikh youths killed during the militancy era.

His path to militancy escalated in July 2015, when he connected with Gajinder Singh, the head of Dal Khalsa, through Facebook. Gajinder introduced him to Gurdeep Singh Takkar, the leader of the Khalistan Tiger Force (KTF). Takkar, a designated terrorist, played a central role in Mandeep's indoctrination, offering him ideological guidance and financial backing. This relationship gained geopolitical significance after Takkar's assassination, which led to accusations against Indian operatives by the Canadian government, sparking a diplomatic row.

In December 2015, Takkar organized formal arms training for Mandeep and three others in Mission Hill, British Columbia. They were trained in AK-47 rifles and sniper weaponry, with the explicit goal of preparing them for terrorist operations in India. Mandeep was sent to India in February 2016, with orders to assassinate prominent figures such as Mohammad Azhar Alam, a former Punjab Police officer, and Baba Mann Singh, a spiritual leader. However, Indian authorities arrested him upon his arrival on 24 May 2016, foiling the plot. Despite securing bail in January 2017, his case remains unresolved.

Mridula's dossier also examined the activities of Moninder Singh Bual, based in Vancouver, and Parvkar Singh Dulai of Surrey, both deeply embedded in the Khalistani network. Bual's family ties to Avtar Singh Narwal, a notorious terrorist linked to BKI, and his association with Takkar, placed him at the heart of terrorist activities. In January 2015, Bual facilitated Takkar's trip to Thailand to assist Jagtar Singh Tara, a Khalistani figure involved in the assassination of Punjab CM Beant Singh. Bual's 2014 meeting with UK national Jagtar Singh Johal further solidified his role in the Khalistan movement, as they discussed plans to glorify militants like Sukha and Jinda through media, promoting the Khalistan cause.

> Parvkar Singh Dulai, a well-known activist with the banned International Sikh Youth Federation (ISYF), owned a Punjabi TV channel in Surrey that he used to propagate extremist narratives. In November 2015, Dulai travelled to Pakistan, meeting with Babbar Khalsa's Wadhawa Singh and Pakistan's ISI officials to strengthen anti-India efforts. His ties to Jaggi Johal and other extremists reveal his deep involvement in international networks fuelling terrorism in India.
>
> By 2017, Dulai's role in Khalistani militancy intensified when he allegedly supplied weapons to an ISYF/BKI module within India, backed by Lakhbir Singh Rode in Pakistan. His involvement in plotting an attack on Sumedh Singh Saini, the former DGP of Punjab, underscores the operational reach of his network. In May 2018, Canadian authorities added Dulai and Bhagat Singh Brar to the no-fly list, marking a crucial step in curbing their terrorist activities. This designation highlighted the growing concerns around Dulai's influence in furthering Khalistani militancy through his connections in Canada, Pakistan and India.

The response from New Delhi was immediate. New Delhi took the information seriously, instructing Mridula to push forward and make progress with her mission. The stakes had just been raised, and time was running out.

~

Second week of 2023. Aditya's task was nothing short of impossible as he arrived in Lahore under a new alias – *Aftab Qureshi*, a Karachi-born export agent dealing in dry fruits and leather goods. The name and documents were fresh, the identity watertight on paper, yet he knew that on any enemy soil, no cover was ever completely safe. After Zahoor Mistry's assassination in Karachi, the ISI and local police had torn through the city's underworld, probing every rumour, every whisper. Aditya could never be sure how much they had uncovered about the man behind that hit. In the world of espionage, exposure rarely came as a bullet; it came as a quiet watchfulness. The enemy might spot you, track you, even let you move just to study your pattern before deciding how to strike. That knowledge stayed with him like a shadow. One wrong step and he would be dead, or worse, caught alive. Yet here he was again, back in the lion's den, with another name on his list: Rinda.

Rinda was no ordinary target. The man had become a linchpin in the global terror network, supplying heroin from the Golden Crescent to Colombian cartels and financing Khalistani extremists under Gurdeep Singh Takkar's command in Canada. Eliminating Rinda wasn't just about taking down a criminal; it was about crippling the infrastructure that fed into larger terror cells abroad. But doing this in Pakistan, where the ISI watched every corner, was a gamble that could cost Aditya his life.

But Aditya had come prepared. The dossier on Rinda was his blueprint. It detailed not only Rinda's crimes but also his indulgences, his vices. The man was addicted to heroin, living in a bubble of excess and violence. He wasn't a terrorist by ideology; he was a mercenary, driven by greed and self-interest. Drugs, prostitutes, weapons and money – that was Rinda's world, and it was the world Aditya would infiltrate.

Rinda's compound in Lahore was a fortress. Guards armed with semi-automatic rifles patrolled every corner, and security cameras scanned every angle. The ISI didn't trust him entirely, but they needed him, which was why they had provided such a heavy security detail. Breaking through this protection was nearly impossible.

Aditya knew that brute force would be suicide; he needed to think like Rinda, live in his world and become a trusted figure in his life. Disguises and false identities had been Aditya's specialty during his covert missions, but this required more than just a fake name. He had to penetrate Rinda's circle without raising an ounce of suspicion.

Rinda's life was one of excess. He indulged in heroin, wild parties and the company of thugs and prostitutes. His addiction to a life of indulgence had always been his greatest weakness. Rinda didn't see himself as a terrorist, just a businessman who would do anything for the right price. Aditya understood that mindset well. It was a crack in Rinda's armour, the same crack that would be his undoing.

Aditya found his way into the outskirts of Lahore under a new identity. He had posed as a mid-level operator with connections to drug syndicates – a role that aligned perfectly with the types of people Rinda kept close. Word spread fast in Rinda's world when someone was dealing in Afghan heroin. Aditya had set up a controlled web, leaking his presence and capabilities to the right people. Within days, the invitation arrived.

His first meeting with Rinda was at one of his notorious parties. The kind of event where women and drugs were served as casually as drinks. The walls of the mansion were bathed in neon lights that cast eerie shadows, and the air was thick with smoke from Afghan heroin, ganja and cigarettes. Every laugh felt forced, every conversation filled with deceit. Rinda sat at the heart of it all, lolling in a luxurious chair like a king surveying his debauched court.

The man was heavily built, his face weathered from years of excess. His eyes, however, were sharp, constantly scanning the room for threats or opportunities. When he saw Aditya, he didn't smile. There was no warmth in Rinda's gaze, only suspicion.

'You're the one who is looking for the pure stuff?' Rinda asked, his voice low but with an edge that suggested this wasn't a question but a test.

Aditya took a moment before answering, his body language calm. He knew Rinda's type. They didn't respond to eagerness. 'I don't buy from just anyone,' Aditya replied coolly, lighting a cigarette and meeting Rinda's gaze head-on. 'If you're asking, then you already know I pay the best.'

Rinda's eyes flickered, a mix of interest and mistrust. He leaned back, pulling deeply from his drug laced Shisha, exhaling slowly as if sizing Aditya up. The room around them buzzed with activity, but it felt like a dangerous game of chess between the two men.

'You think you're untouchable, don't you?' Rinda asked, his lips curling into a half-smirk.

Aditya didn't blink. 'I don't think … I know.' It was a line borrowed from one of his favourite Amitabh Bachchan films.

The cryptic exchange ended with Rinda letting out a short, gruff laugh. It wasn't approval, but it wasn't a dismissal either. He motioned for Aditya to sit. The invitation had been extended not just to the seat, but to the inner circle.

Aditya spent the next few weeks meticulously cultivating Rinda's trust. He never overplayed his hand, always letting Rinda lead, always making the man feel in control. They drank together, snorted lines of coke, shared women, the rituals of men who lived in shadows. Rinda began to talk more, his guard lowering bit by bit.

But Rinda's world was always on edge. The ISI was watching him just as much as they were protecting him. Every conversation, every deal was laced with suspicion. Even in the most private moments, Rinda's paranoia seeped through. He would stare at Aditya with those piercing eyes, as if waiting for him to make a mistake.

'You've been around too long,' Rinda said one night after a particularly wild party. 'Men like you don't stick unless they want something more.'

Aditya leaned back, letting a cloud of smoke escape his lips. He had expected this moment. 'I'm not here to make friends, boss,' he said, voice steady. 'I'm here because you and I can both make more money than you've ever dreamed of.'

Rinda raised an eyebrow. 'More than I've dreamed of? You think you can offer me more than I already have?'

Aditya's eyes darkened. 'You've got your supply lines to Mexico and Colombia. I'm not questioning that. But what you don't have is stability … no protection. You're too dependent on middlemen who can turn with the wind. I'm talking about cutting out the weak links, tightening your network, and expanding into Europe and Southeast Asia. You'll control not just the flow, but the safety of every shipment at both ends, supply and demand.'

Rinda's smile was predatory. 'And what's in it for you?'

'Power. Same thing that drives you,' Aditya replied with a shrug. 'We both know that money is just the means to an end.'

That was the moment. Aditya had planted the seed. Rinda wanted more, and he began to see Aditya not as a threat but as a tool, a key to unlocking bigger things.

But beneath that surface trust, Aditya never forgot who he was dealing with. Every interaction had the potential to blow his cover, and the ISI's presence around Rinda was suffocating. Every day felt like walking a tightrope, where one misstep would send him plummeting.

As Aditya spent more time with Rinda, he started feeding into the man's addictions. He noticed how Rinda's drug habits had become a crutch, something that dulled his sharp instincts. He began to increase Rinda's concoctions, small doses of heroin that were stronger than what Rinda was used to. Just enough to keep him hooked. Just enough to keep him wanting more.

And then came the night when Aditya knew it was time. Rinda was deep in his addictions, his mind clouded by power, paranoia and a strange emptiness. The party raged around him, the air thick with smoke and music, yet none of it seemed to reach him. The drugs no longer gave him pleasure; they only dulled his body and slowed his reflexes. That hollow craving, the need without satisfaction was exactly what Aditya had been waiting for.

They were in Rinda's inner sanctum, a room where no one entered without his permission. His henchmen stayed outside, guarding the corridors, never allowed into this space where he indulged his vices. Aditya sat beside him, syringe in hand. The heroin was ready, stronger than anything Rinda had taken before. The man didn't even flinch as Aditya slid the needle into his forearm. He leaned back, eyes half-closed, a faint sigh escaping his lips as the drug began to take hold.

But Aditya had gone beyond the limit. The dose was lethal.

For a moment, Rinda didn't notice. He simply sat there, basking in the euphoria. But slowly, his breathing grew shallow, his eyes unfocused. He tried to speak, but his lips barely moved. Panic flickered across his face as he realized something was wrong.

'W-what did you ...' Rinda gasped, struggling to speak. Once he was sure Rinda was not going to make it, Aditya took another dose of the drug so that he too appeared in a state of overdose and no one suspected him of any foul play. He took a calculated risk that could have cost him his life. He was not into drugs, even a regular dose of heroin could have been fatal for him.

Aditya was not much in position to respond. But he managed to watch as the drug took over. Rinda's body began to convulse, his fingers twitching uncontrollably. The room around them erupted into chaos as Rinda collapsed, but by then, it was already too late.

The ISI guards rushed Rinda to a hospital, but the damage was done. The doctors declared him dead on arrival, another victim of his own excess.

Aditya slipped away into the night, unseen amidst the confusion. He had done it. He had entered Rinda's world, gained his trust and killed him without anyone suspecting the truth. But he knew the danger wasn't over. The ISI would soon come hunting, and they wouldn't stop until they realized one more ghost from R&AW came and scored.

But for now, he had succeeded. Rinda was dead, and with him, a significant arm of the terror network had been severed. Takkar's operations in Canada would soon feel the impact, their supply of arms and drugs cut off at the source.

But Aditya knew this was just the beginning. The war was far from over. He still had a long list of India's most wanted.

The news of Rinda's death spread like wildfire across the ISI and Lahore Police. There was no doubt in their minds that India's hand had been involved, but publicly admitting that would open a Pandora's box of embarrassment. It would mirror the Zahoor Mistry incident, where India's R&AW had covertly eliminated a wanted terrorist under Pakistan's very nose. To acknowledge that Rinda, another high-profile asset sheltered by the ISI, had met the same fate would be a blow Pakistan could not afford.

So the Pakistan government stayed tight-lipped.

The Pakistani media, however, smelled blood. Press conferences were flooded with demands for answers. Some journalists questioned the very basis of Rinda's presence in Pakistan, asking why a hardened criminal with such a long record of terrorism and narcotics smuggling had been given sanctuary since 2020. The Indian media, by contrast, screamed Rinda's life story across their airwaves. Crime, terror, heroin smuggling, all of it was broadcast, leaving Pakistan with no plausible response. The walls were closing in on the ISI, and they couldn't afford to let the local media fan the flames any further.

In a desperate attempt to control the narrative, the Pakistani government quietly asked the press to lie low, promising answers but delivering none. Behind closed doors, the situation was imploding. The ISI scrambled to salvage their reputation.

Meanwhile, R&AW in India seized the moment. Disinformation became their weapon, and they wielded it masterfully. Indian intelligence planted stories across various channels, reaching out to splinter groups like Jaspreet Singh Jassi's gang. Soon, the underworld was abuzz with rumours that Davinder Bambiha's men had orchestrated Rinda's death. No specifics were given, no details of the assassination, no clarity on the method; but that suited R&AW perfectly. The ambiguity added fuel to the fire.

Fake social media accounts began churning out alternative theories, some even suggesting that the ISI had orchestrated Rinda's death. The whispers grew louder: Rinda had fallen out with the ISI over money, fed up with how much protection was costing him. Others claimed that he had been planning to escape to Canada, perhaps to join his contacts in Takkar's terror network, and the ISI, suspecting betrayal, had eliminated him before he could act.

Aditya smirked as he read the reports flooding his phone. The media frenzy, the rumours, the chaos, all of it were exactly what he had envisioned. For a brief moment, the memory of Rinda's last gasping breath flickered in his mind. But there was no time for remorse or guilt. His mission was far from over, and the list of names he needed to cross off was long.

Rinda was just the beginning for New Delhi's 'Mission Takkar'.

16

Hits One after Another

June 2023.

In the third week of the month, Sukkhi had arrived in Pakistan ahead of Aditya. Travelling from London aboard a merchant ship, he assumed the identity of Amin Latif, a 34-year-old British national of Pakistani origin. His new passport supported the cover, showing him as a man who had settled in London years ago, working odd jobs and crewing on cargo vessels for a living. The position of Ordinary Seaman (OS) on the ship fit perfectly with that modest, carefully fabricated life.

Once in Lahore, Sukkhi took refuge in a shelter home on Khayaban-e-Jinnah Road. With Aditya also stationed in Lahore, the priority was clear: debrief with him before setting out for the targets. Syed Khalid Raza was based in Karachi, while Bashir Ahmed Peer resided in Rawalpindi. The stage was set, and Sukkhi knew that this briefing would dictate the course of his next deadly moves.

Sukkhi's reason for staying at the shelter was simple; he had no job, no income and no savings. While he searched for work, the shelter provided him a temporary haven. The NGO that managed the facility in Lahore had branches in Rawalpindi and Karachi, which suited Sukkhi's plans perfectly. He approached the management, requesting permission to stay at the Rawalpindi branch during a visit. His excuse? He needed to pay his respects at his mother's grave, which he claimed was in Rawalpindi. The management, swayed by his story, granted the request.

Aditya had already shared his reconnaissance and research on Bashir Ahmed and Syed Khalid Raza with Sukkhi. In both Rawalpindi and Karachi, Sukkhi spent days tracking their movements, studying their routines and gathering crucial intelligence. Though he remained in contact with Aditya, occasionally meeting him in person, Sukkhi had no idea what Aditya was up to in Lahore. He didn't even know if Rinda, the elusive target behind Aditya's extended stay in the city, actually lived in Lahore.

Following Aditya's precise instructions, Sukkhi discreetly received the arms from a Baloch asset in the shadows of Rawalpindi's underbelly. Earlier, Iranian mercenaries had crossed the hostile terrain of Balochistan with oil smugglers, sneaking into Pakistan under the cover of night. The Baloch asset, a man well-versed in the art of moving unseen, had secured the weapons and guided them through the labyrinthine routes into the city. As Sukkhi laid the weapons out before him, two sleek Beretta 9mms, two Glock 19s with the unmistakable heft of reliability, and the cold, deadly precision of the Galil Sniper SA, he felt the weight of what was to come. Under the dim light of the safehouse, the cold steel gleamed ominously. With each weapon accounted for, Sukkhi swiftly composed a coded message to Aditya, confirming the arms were in his possession, the signal sent with all the weight of an irreversible step forward.

Soon after, Aditya arrived in Rawalpindi. In the dim confines of their safe house, they met with the three Iranian mercenaries to finalize the plan. The roles were clear: Sukkhi would be Striker-1, Aditya, Striker-2. The mercenaries, hardened and precise, would serve as the 'stand-off weapon'. Armed with the Galil sniper rifle, they would track the target from nearly a kilometre away, remaining out of sight but always in range. Their task was to shadow the target's every move – home, work or wherever he went – while staying under the watchful radar of Sukkhi and Aditya. As the final details were discussed, the room hummed with a tension that signalled the impending strike. Each man knew his role; now, it was a matter of executing it with lethal precision.

Fourth week of June 2023.

It was a Monday evening, around 7.30 p.m. The streets near Rawalpindi's congested Fawar Chowk were bustling, but Bashir's perfume shop in Raja Bazar was unusually quiet. Early in the week always meant slower business. Bashir Ahmed Peer, the medium-built HM commander, stood behind the counter. His long, unkempt hair, parted in the middle, framed a weathered face that bore the scars of battles fought and storms weathered. He was a man hardened by survival, but tonight, all Bashir Ahmad craved was a plate of biryani.

A native of Kashmir's Kupwara district, Bashir had been living in Pakistan for over fifteen years, under the protective shield of the ISI. Since that time, the country had become his home, and its food, his comfort. Though he came from the rich wazwan culinary tradition of Kashmir, the bold flavours of Pakistani cuisine had cast a different spell on him, a charm he couldn't resist since the day he arrived. So, it had become a ritual that after a weekend of home-cooked meals, Bashir needed the familiar spices to awaken his taste buds. He couldn't resist. With a nod to his partner, Mohammed Lala, Bashir slipped out of the shop, the craving leading him towards his next meal as the night inched closer to danger.

But the popular Kamaal Ghazi Biryani Centre was as packed as ever, its smoky air richly redolent with the scent of grilled meat and spices. The crowd swarmed the narrow lanes, customers spilling out onto the street, but Mian Ghazi, the owner, spotted Bashir immediately. A man like Bashir didn't go unnoticed. Knowing his regular customer all too well, Ghazi pulled a chair seemingly out of thin air, placing it right beside his counter, his command post from which he watched over the bustling restaurant, managing the chaos like a seasoned general.

Without missing a beat, Bashir settled into his spot, nodding at Ghazi as he ordered his usual – a platter of barra kebab with a side of the rich, fragrant Bombay biryani. The clatter of utensils and sizzling of kebabs surrounded him, but Bashir's mind was already focused on the familiar meal, his senses sharpening for what was to come, oblivious to the shadow of danger creeping ever closer.

As Bashir waited, the air filled with the aroma of grilling kebabs and slow-cooked rice. The crowd inside the Kamaal Ghazi Biryani Centre ebbed and flowed like an unstoppable tide, but within the chaos, Bashir remained unmoved, his eyes scanning the familiar surroundings. Mian Ghazi, ever attentive, barked orders at his men.

Sukkhi wasn't far from where Bashir had settled. Sitting just a few tables away, he blended seamlessly into the crowd, his presence barely registering amid the busy din of the restaurant. With the subtlety of a shadow, Sukkhi quietly inched his chair closer to Bashir, his movements precise and deliberate, careful not to draw even the slightest glance in his direction. The distance between them closed with every quiet shift of his seat, positioning him perfectly within reach, while the hum of the restaurant masked his intent.

In an afterthought, Bashir glanced at Mian Ghazi. 'Is the Bombay biryani on the menu tonight?' he asked, aware that the biryani offering changed daily. Mian Ghazi, ever the gracious host, smiled and bowed slightly. 'For you, Mian Bashir, we always have a plate of Bombay biryani, no matter the day.' Bashir gave a nod of humble acknowledgement, feeling a rare sense of obligation in return. Ghazi, in his usual booming voice, turned toward the bustling kitchen. 'Mian Bashir is here! Bring out his Bombay biryani … make it perfect!' The call rang through the restaurant, commanding attention, but Bashir remained composed, his eyes flickering with a hint of satisfaction.

Meanwhile, a waiter arrived with Sukkhi's order which was a plate of regular chicken biryani. But Sukkhi reacted sharply, standing up and insisting he had ordered Bombay biryani. His voice was firm, yet controlled, just enough to make people glance in his direction. The waiter, caught off guard, shook his head in disagreement. 'You ordered chicken biryani, sir,' the waiter asserted, but Sukkhi held his ground, his voice lowering to a tense growl. 'I said Bombay biryani, and that's what I expected.'

The atmosphere in the restaurant subtly shifted as the disagreement escalated. The waiter, trying to keep his composure, explained that Bombay biryani wasn't served on Mondays, only on Wednesdays, Fridays and Saturdays. But Sukkhi wasn't backing down. What had begun as a simple clarification now turned into a heated argument, the tension thickening with each passing moment. Their voices grew louder, sharp enough to cut through the general chatter, drawing the attention of nearby tables.

Soon, Sukkhi's anger became unmistakable, and the situation started to go out of control. The waiter, overwhelmed, could barely respond as Sukkhi's agitation grew. The scene was escalating fast enough that Mian Ghazi himself had to step in, his presence commanding calm but failing to defuse the rising tension. All the while, Sukkhi's mobile phone lay face down on the table, quietly connected to Aditya, who was listening intently at the other end, hearing every word, every rising voice, as the storm brewed inside the restaurant.

Ghazi, trying to keep the situation under control, approached Sukkhi with a forced calmness. 'Please,' he said, lowering his voice, 'don't create a scene. You're disturbing the atmosphere.' He even offered a compromise, suggesting that he'd be happy to serve the Bombay biryani on its regular day, even free of charge, if Sukkhi would just stop the ruckus. But instead of calming him down, this offer only stoked the fire in Sukkhi's eyes. His expression darkened, and he leaned in, his voice cold. 'Mind your own business, old man.'

The tension reached a boiling point. Suddenly, there was a commotion. Bashir, having watched the scene unfold, stood up from his seat. Holding his untouched plate of Bombay biryani, he calmly approached Sukkhi and offered it to him, his voice steady but firm. 'Here, take it,' he said, 'and let everyone enjoy their evening.'

But instead of gratitude, Sukkhi's response was laced with venom. 'Don't pretend to be magnanimous,' he sneered, his voice cutting through the room like a blade. Ghazi, watching the interaction, felt a flash of anger surge through him. How dare this man insult one of his VIP customers like Bashir without provocation? The tension snapped, and before anyone could react, Sukkhi and Ghazi jostled with each other, the argument escalating into a physical confrontation.

Bashir tried to step in, his hands raised to separate the two, but in an instant, everything changed. In one fluid motion, Sukkhi reached into his jacket, pulled out his gun, and fired. The sound of the gunshot echoed through the crowded restaurant, deafening in its suddenness. Bashir staggered back, clutching his abdomen, the shock on his face matching the horror in the room.

Time seemed to freeze as the crowd erupted into panic, scattering in every direction, chairs tipping over, dishes crashing to the floor. Ghazi stood frozen in shock, speechless, as Bashir collapsed to the ground, his blood quickly pooling beneath him. But Sukkhi wasn't done. Coldly, he approached the motionless Bashir and fired two more shots into his body, each one hitting with brutal finality. Bashir lay still, lifeless, as silence fell over the room, the once-bustling restaurant now a scene of blood and fear.

Before anyone could even react, Sukkhi was already on the move. The moment the last shot rang out, he slipped through the chaos like a shadow, vanishing into the night. Outside, Aditya had heard the gunshots and was already in position, waiting at the entrance of the Biryani Centre, eyes sharp and alert. As Sukkhi burst through the door, he wasted no time. In one smooth motion, he leapt onto the pillion seat of Aditya's bike. With a roar of the engine, they sped off into the darkened streets, disappearing like ghosts in the wind, leaving nothing but confusion and fear in their wake.

While the chaos erupted inside the Kamaal Ghazi Biryani Centre, one of the Iranian mercenaries kept his rifle trained on the restaurant's entrance, his finger hovering over the trigger. His task was clear, if the target somehow managed to flee, he would strike with precision. Meanwhile, the other two mercenaries operated from inside a van parked nearby, working with cool efficiency. Their mission: to deactivate the surrounding CCTV cameras, ensuring that neither Aditya nor Sukkhi would be captured on any footage. Aditya had already taken precautions, his face fully covered as he waited outside. Sukkhi, however, couldn't afford to enter the restaurant with his face hidden, posing as a regular customer. But the moment he leapt onto the back of Aditya's motorcycle, he swiftly pulled a mask over his face, vanishing into anonymity as they roared away into the night, leaving no trace but the terror they had sparked.

Target number two on Aditya's hit list was eliminated. But many more still remained to be executed, each one a ticking bomb. Today's incident, however, would raise eyebrows and heighten suspicion. The killing could easily be linked to the assassination of Zahoor Mistry in Karachi, which had unfolded almost exactly a year earlier. The parallels were undeniable, the same precision, the same audacious escape. The modus operandi was strikingly similar, and Aditya knew it wouldn't be long before the dots were connected.

Aditya brought the motorcycle to a halt at a nondescript location, blending into the shadows of the deserted street. Moments later, the mercenaries pulled up in their van, their headlights dimmed to avoid drawing attention. The van's rear doors swung open, and Aditya and Sukkhi quickly stepped inside, bringing the motorcycle with them. Once inside, Aditya wasted no time. With practised precision, he set to work on transforming Sukkhi's appearance.

In the dim light of the van, Sukkhi's beard was shaved clean, his long hair chopped short, and his eyebrows carefully trimmed. Aditya handed him coloured contact lenses, and as Sukkhi slipped them into his eyes, his entire face seemed to change. By the time Aditya was done, Sukkhi was unrecognizable, a man with a completely different look.

The plan was seamless. They dropped Aditya off in a quiet, upscale neighbourhood, where he would blend into the evening calm. Meanwhile, the mercenaries carried on with Sukkhi and the motorcycle, driving towards an isolated spot where the bike would be destroyed, ensuring no trace remained of the night's events.

That night, Aditya finally allowed himself a brief moment of relief as the message from Sukkhi came through. The mercenaries had successfully moved him to a safe house, hidden away from prying eyes. The plan had gone off without a hitch. Before the first light of dawn touched the Rawalpindi skyline, they would be gone, vanishing into the shadows, leaving no trace of their presence. Aditya exhaled deeply, knowing that, for now, one more mission was complete but the road ahead was still long, and far more dangerous.

~

Two days later, Syed Khalid Raza undertook walks after his evening meal, in the lane outside his bungalow in Gulistan-e-Jauhar, a prominent neighbourhood in Karachi East. The neighbourhood is distinguished by a myriad of apartment blocks, contributing to its dynamic urban landscape. Syed Khalid lived in a bungalow provided to him by the ISI, as guarding a person in an apartment is more difficult than in a bungalow.

Exactly a week had passed since Aditya and Sukkhi had eliminated their second target, Bashir Ahmed, in Rawalpindi. The clock was ticking, and the pressure was mounting as the Pakistani media buzzed with the news of Bashir's assassination.

In an interview with the daily *Dawn*, one of Bashir's associates, speaking on the condition of anonymity, claimed that Bashir 'had no conflict with anyone'.

'He had been receiving threats from across the border, where his father and brother were killed by Indian forces during the ongoing resistance,' the associate added.

Uzair Ghazali, a prominent activist based in Muzaffarabad and head of an organization for Kashmiri migrants, pointed the finger squarely at India's intelligence agency, R&AW, for orchestrating the killing.

'India is systematically silencing every voice that dares to demand self-determination and freedom for Jammu and Kashmir, using both its military and hired mercenaries,' Ghazali asserted.

Bashir was the third high-profile figure connected to the Kashmir independence movement to be gunned down in recent months. Local police described the killing as a 'targeted attack'. Without directly naming India, Syed Salahuddin, supreme commander of HM, accused 'the enemy's mercenaries' of carrying out the hit on Bashir.

Senior officials from two separate Pakistani intelligence agencies had expressed strong suspicions of India's involvement in as many as twenty targeted killings since 2020 before the international media. They referenced key evidence from previously undisclosed investigations into several instances of killings. The materials, which include witness testimonies, arrest records, financial transactions, WhatsApp conversations and passports, were said to provide detailed insight into operations allegedly carried out by Indian spies to eliminate targets on Pakistani soil.

Aditya understood that the plan for Syed Khalid needed a completely different approach, both in execution and strategy. The idea of using an explosive device to create chaos now seemed too risky. Aditya suspected that the media coverage of previous assassinations had prompted local security agencies to ramp up their presence, especially in areas where terrorists were sheltered under ISI protection. The heightened vigilance meant that any explosive could easily draw unwanted attention, complicating the operation.

To make matters worse, both the drug addicts with criminal records Aditya had hired for the shootout disappeared. With US $5,000 each in hand and substantial quantities of drugs to back their addiction, neither saw the need to complete the job for the balance payment. Their life was made. Aditya had to make some quick phone calls – one of whom was Salahuddin Rashid.

The sun was setting over Karachi, casting long shadows across the streets of Gulistan-e-Jauhar. It was the same city where Aditya had executed his first target a year ago. And once again, it was a Monday, exactly a week after the Rawalpindi assassination when Syed Khalid, a creature of habit, stepped out of his bungalow for his usual evening walk. Unaware of the danger lurking, he had no idea that, just like Bashir the previous Monday, his time was running out.

A Suzuki passenger van idled quietly a block away, inconspicuous among the other vehicles. Inside, Aditya monitored everything through the drone camera, its silent rotors keeping it airborne, invisible against the darkening sky. Sukkhi, carrying a 9mm Beretta, sat next to him. The feed from the drone gave them a bird's-eye view of Khalid's path, the corners of the streets, and most importantly, their two teams of killers. Aditya wore a Bluetooth device in his ear, his voice calm as he relayed commands in real time.

'Rashid, get ready. He's approaching the corner,' Aditya murmured, eyes locked on the screen as he tracked Khalid's movement. The

Taliban fighters on the motorcycle, Rashid and Pasha, received the command, silently moving into position, their hands steady on the handlebars, prepared to act on Aditya's signal.

From a distant vantage point, one of the Iranian mercenaries lay prone, nestled on a rooftop about half a kilometre away. The Barrett M82 sniper rifle rested in position, its scope trained on Khalid's path. The mercenary's breath was steady, his trigger finger ready, waiting for the precise moment. He, too, was listening to Aditya's commands through a Bluetooth earpiece.

Inside the van, Aditya glanced at Sukkhi. 'He's moving as expected.'

'Copy that,' Aditya said into the mic, keeping his voice measured. 'Rashid, proceed. Make it look good, but no engagement.'

As Khalid rounded the corner, the motorcycle riders moved in, not too fast, not too slow, just enough to catch the eye of any witnesses. They made a show of aiming at Khalid, pointing their weapons menacingly but never pulling the trigger. The goal was simple: cause panic, create confusion.

Khalid, startled and realizing he was being targeted, broke into a run. The motorcycle riders kept up the illusion, tracking him just enough to make it appear that they were responsible for the hit.

'Hold position,' Aditya's voice was calm as he watched Khalid rush toward the narrow alleyway between two buildings. 'Let him take cover.'

From the rooftop, the Iranian mercenary adjusted his aim, locking onto Khalid as he ducked into the alley, completely unaware that he had just entered the kill zone.

'Wait for it …' Aditya's voice crackled over the mercenary's earpiece. 'Take the shot.'

The sniper fired, the deep, reverberating crack of the Barrett M82 slicing through the night. The .50 calibre round crossed the half-kilometre distance in a heartbeat, striking Khalid squarely in the chest. The force of the impact slammed him against the alley wall, his body crumpling to the ground.

'Target down,' Aditya confirmed, watching Khalid fall on the live drone feed.

'Rashid, Pasha … disengage,' Aditya commanded through Bluetooth. The motorcycle riders made a sharp turn and sped away, leaving behind a chaotic scene but no solid leads.

As the van pulled away from the area, Aditya leaned back, allowing himself a moment of satisfaction. The plan had gone off without a hitch. Eyewitnesses would swear the shooters on the motorcycle were the assassins, but the truth was far more complex.

Aditya's strategy was different this time. The weapon used was a Barrett M82, a .50 calibre sniper rifle, known for its power and range. The idea was to mislead the investigation. Eyewitnesses would have claimed that they saw the motorcycle shooters pull the trigger, but when they examined the body, the post-mortem would reveal a .50 calibre round.

Similarly, the ballistic report will show that the bullet was fired from a Barrett M82, a weapon commonly used by Pakistan Army commandos. It would confuse the entire investigation, sending them down a rabbit hole of their own making.

The motorcycle riders may have appeared to be the attackers, but the real shot had come from the rooftop, a clean, distant kill. The Pakistani authorities would be left chasing shadows, trying to piece together a puzzle designed to mislead them from the start.

That night, Aditya and Sukkhi sat in a small food joint in Karachi, the burden of their mission momentarily lifted. Syed Khalid was out of the picture, but one more target remained. Paramjit Singh Panjwar.

For Sukkhi, this brief respite was a rare moment of indulgence, something he wouldn't have dreamed of just a few years ago. The delicious spread before them, Karachi's finest biryani and chapli kebabs were a reminder of how far he had come. As a terrorist he could have been rotting in a morgue somewhere in Punjab long ago. But Aditya had pulled him from that and given him a new life. Everything he had now, freedom, security, money to clear his family's debts, was because of Aditya. To Sukkhi, Aditya wasn't just a superior; he was a god.

Sukkhi spoke with reverence, his words soft, almost deferential, as he reluctantly raised his glass to Aditya's. The alcohol eased his nerves, but the ever-present fear of being recognized in enemy territory kept him alert. He smiled nervously, making the occasional light-hearted comment, but always keeping a watchful eye on Aditya, as though seeking his approval for every joke, every remark.

For Aditya, the mission was never far from his mind. He sipped his drink calmly, his focus unbroken. He had been through this before, the temporary calm before the storm of the next mission. Sukkhi, however, wore his gratitude like a second skin. Every glance at Aditya was filled with quiet indebtedness.

They finished a bottle of whiskey and their meal, the lingering flavours of Karachi's rich cuisine offering a fleeting sense of comfort. Sukkhi, though feeling high from alcohol, looked at Aditya with awe as they stood up to leave, his shoulders slightly hunched in deference. He would follow Aditya anywhere, even into the fire of Lahore's heavily guarded streets.

As they stepped into the night, Aditya gave a brief nod, signalling it was time to move forward. Sukkhi, ever loyal, fell into step beside him, knowing that whatever came next, he would follow without question.

Beginning July 2023.

With each successful mission, Aditya's confidence surged. The list of enemies taken down was growing, and with every target eliminated, the sense of invincibility crept in. But this time it was different. The thought of returning to Lahore brought a dark cloud over his thoughts. It was the same city where he had already executed Rinda, one of the most feared men among the gangsters as well as in the drug cartels.

Aditya knew that the ISI and Rinda's men would be hunting for him. His face, his movements, everything about his time with Rinda would be etched in the memory of Lahore's underworld. The CCTV cameras must have caught him in all the places he had frequented – the smoky dens of Rinda's parties, the shady business deals that cemented his cover, the nights of binge drinking that blended into mornings spent in the shadows of Lahore's brothels and private hotels.

Panjwar was a prime target – easily the biggest on Aditya's list so far. The man had slipped into Pakistan in the 1990s, finding sanctuary under the protection of the Pakistani deep state. As the chief of the KCF, Panjwar's outfit had orchestrated some of the most brutal attacks on Indian soil, including the assassination of General Arun Vaidya, the Army chief during Operation Blue Star. His presence in Pakistan was no secret. Twelve years ago, in March 2011, India had handed over a list of fifty most wanted fugitives sheltered in Pakistan during bilateral home secretary-level talks. Panjwar's name was among the most notorious.

The irony wasn't lost on Aditya. There was a time when the name Panjwar commanded respect in Sukkhi's eyes, a symbol of rebellion and power. In fact, Sukkhi had once idolized the KCF. Now, though Sukkhi remained loyal to Aditya, his admiration for the KCF lingered beneath the surface. It created a conflict that gnawed at Aditya's thoughts. Could Sukkhi be trusted for this mission?

As Aditya prepared for what was easily one of the most dangerous assassinations of his career, he questioned whether keeping Sukkhi by his side was a risk he could afford. Repeating a striker in sensitive assassination missions was generally frowned upon in the world of espionage. Using the same operative over and over came with its risks as familiarity bred vulnerability. Was it time to cut Sukkhi loose, or was his debt to Aditya enough to guarantee his loyalty?

Aditya knew that taking down Panjwar would be more than just a personal victory. It would be a landmark strike for Indian intelligence, a message that no terrorist was untouchable, not even on Pakistani soil. But somewhere beneath the professional duty was a pulse of something personal, a fierce need to finish what he had started. He wanted this kill not only for his country but for himself.

He also knew he was crossing a line. This wasn't sanctioned. Definitely not in the way his previous missions had been. By planning to hit Panjwar without waiting for Delhi's formal clearance, Aditya was breaking protocol, stepping into the grey zone where orders blurred into instinct. He told himself it was necessity, not defiance.

But deep down he knew the truth: this was his mission, his way. Precision was vital, secrecy absolute. He would trust no one, not even Sukkhi. For this one, Aditya was going dark.

One man, one target. That was the only way to ensure no trails were left behind.

Lahore was a territory where he had eliminated Rinda, a major drug player, by posing as a dealer. The kill had been clean, an overdose, leaving no trace. The operation not only took out Rinda but also gave Aditya valuable connections in Lahore's drug underworld.

Aditya reached out to an old contact, one who had helped him infiltrate Rinda's camp. The man was a mid-level drug runner, still operating in Lahore's underbelly, and he had recently widened his dealings to accommodate Panjwar's growing interest in the narcotics trade. It didn't take long for Aditya, under his old cover as a dealer, to reconnect with this man. Aditya's cover story was simple: he had returned to Lahore to expand his operations, looking for new clients and Panjwar's name was at the top of the list.

The contact quickly arranged a meeting, knowing Panjwar's inner circle, though tight, wasn't impenetrable. Panjwar needed new suppliers, making him open to new players in the drug world. Aditya used his old alias, still recognized in the Lahore drug circuit, and slowly integrated himself into Panjwar's operations. The initial meetings were all business, with Panjwar's men being cautious, but the rising demand for drugs made them willing to accept a new supplier. Aditya stayed in the background, observing Panjwar's routines and weaknesses. Over time, Aditya gathered crucial intelligence, noting that Panjwar, though ruthless, lacked the experience of Rinda. His greed made him reckless, expanding too fast and trusting too many. This was the vulnerability Aditya planned to exploit.

Aditya's infiltration into Panjwar's world had gone smoother than expected. Over the weeks, he had earned Panjwar's trust, leveraging his drug connections to secure a spot within the Khalistani leader's inner circle. They shared several meetings, and slowly, Panjwar began to lower his guard. Their bond culminated in a late-night drinking session at Panjwar's house.

Panjwar lived alone in his bachelor pad in Lahore. His family had settled in Germany, far away from the dangers of his militant life, and the Pakistani government had refused them visas to visit. The isolation took its toll on Panjwar, and after several rounds of drinks, he began to open up.

As they drank, Panjwar's frustrations spilled out. 'I gave everything to this fight,' he slurred, waving his glass around. 'And what do I get? I can't even see my family … no visa, no visits. The ISI protects me, but I'm their prisoner.' Aditya listened quietly, nodding along, keeping his own feelings carefully masked behind his composed façade. The tandoori food on the table remained untouched, the smell of charred spices hanging in the air as Panjwar ranted on, his voice thick with alcohol.

After a while, Panjwar slumped onto the sofa, muttering incoherently before falling into a drunken sleep. Aditya remained awake, his eyes quietly watching the man who would soon be his target. The weight of the mission pressed against his chest, but he showed no sign of it. When Panjwar finally stirred, getting up to use the bathroom, Aditya feigned sleep, one eye barely open, his breathing controlled. This was Aditya's best chance to kill Panjwar but he didn't carry his gun. It was hidden somewhere outside for a reason. This was just another step in the long game.

The next morning, Panjwar went for his usual walk. It was routine and no one would suspect otherwise. Aditya, having stayed the night, took his leave soon after, walking calmly to the point where he had parked his motorcycle. Hidden beneath the seat were his disguise and weapon. He changed quickly, transforming from Panjwar's trusted associate into a nameless assailant, ready to complete his mission.

As Panjwar walked his usual route inside the Sunflower Society, the motorcycle roared to life. But as Aditya approached the area, he realized he couldn't take the bike inside – the main iron gate was closed, with only a small side entrance left open. He had to abandon the motorcycle and proceed on foot, a delay he hadn't accounted for. Cursing his oversight, Aditya knew his time was running out and hurried forward. Now, in disguise, he entered the society's premises and quietly approached Panjwar from behind, gun in hand. Everything seemed to be going according to plan – until, at the last moment, Sukkhi appeared. Somehow, he had gotten tangled up in the operation, following Aditya without warning.

The attack happened in a flash. Aditya shot Panjwar in the head, dropping him instantly. But Panjwar's bodyguard, quicker than expected, fired back, and Sukkhi took the hit on his abdomen. Blood gushed from the wound, Sukkhi's face a mask of pain as they sped away from the scene.

The shootout raised an alarm. Security guards and morning walkers started gathering around the scene of crime. Windows and doors opened from different directions. Aditya flashed a Lahore Police ID and rushed Sukkhi out. Sukkhi in his semi-conscious state understood the seriousness of the situation. He tried to feign being a junior staff in the special task force of Lahore Police. Someone helped them get an ambulance.

Even as Aditya rushed Sukkhi to a hospital, the sirens wailed through Lahore's streets, Sukkhi's breathing was shallow, his body shaking from blood loss, but he clung to life. The hospital was only minutes away, but Aditya's mind raced with a new dilemma.

If Sukkhi survived, he would be taken by the Pakistani police, interrogated and tortured, and inevitably, Aditya's cover would be blown. There was no room for loose ends. The thought gnawed at him as they sped toward the hospital. He had already given Sukkhi a second life once, but now that life posed a deadly risk to the mission.

As the ambulance reached the edge of the hospital's entrance, Aditya made his decision. He leaned over Sukkhi, his hand brushing the oxygen support that was keeping his former comrade alive. Sukkhi's eyes fluttered open, barely aware of what was happening, his mouth trying to form words.

There was no time for sentiment.

With a calm, deliberate motion, Aditya disconnected the oxygen support. The interior of the ambulance fell into a deathly silence as Sukkhi's breathing slowed, his body convulsing weakly before going still. Aditya sat there, watching him die, his mind cold, his heart steady.

As the Bolan ambulance rolled to a halt at the hospital gates, Aditya slipped out through the side door, a feature common to these vans and melted into the commotion outside. Attendants shouted, stretchers clattered, and no one noticed a man in a blood-stained shirt disappear into the crowd. Within moments, he was gone, swallowed by the restless night of Lahore.

~

Before the mission, Aditya and Sukkhi had gone their separate ways, with Aditya intending to carry out the Panjwar assassination solo. Sukkhi, however, had remained in Lahore, as he could not leave without Aditya's help. Though they hadn't discussed Panjwar's details openly, Sukkhi, loyal to Aditya to the point of obsession, had his own suspicions. He knew something big was coming, and his instincts told him that Panjwar was the next target.

Aditya had been careful not to share too much, but Sukkhi had learned over time to read between the lines. During a casual conversation with one of their old contacts in the drug world, a small detail slipped out, a reference to the disguised Aditya's meetings with Panjwar's men. The contact didn't know the full extent of Aditya's plan but was aware of some kind of operation involving Panjwar. Sukkhi pieced it together.

Feeling indebted to Aditya and desperate to prove his loyalty, Sukkhi tracked Aditya's movements, tailing him through the city without being detected. His intuition led him to Panjwar's house the night Aditya visited for drinks. From a distance, Sukkhi kept watch, trying to figure out Aditya's next move.

When Aditya made his way to the spot where his motorcycle was parked, Sukkhi knew it was time. He anticipated the hit would happen soon. He wasn't invited, but he couldn't stay away. At the last moment, as Aditya prepared to strike, Sukkhi showed up.

Aditya was momentarily startled but didn't protest. Sukkhi's silent arrival at the critical moment was an intrusion, but in Sukkhi's mind, he was protecting Aditya, ensuring that his 'god' wouldn't carry out this dangerous mission alone. It wasn't part of the plan, but Sukkhi had always had a habit of showing up where he wasn't expected.

As Aditya went on with the shot, Sukkhi's presence weighed heavily on Aditya. He hadn't planned for this. But now that Sukkhi was involved, the weight of Sukkhi's devotion became a liability. When Panjwar's bodyguard fired back, Sukkhi took the hit, in a clear proof of his unwavering loyalty, but also a reminder of the cost of trusting someone who might still be too entangled in the past.

Aditya had made a clean break and now he waited, alone, to watch for the fallout of these last killings.

The killing of Panjwar had immediately raised suspicions, especially with Pakistan's intelligence agencies, ISI, MI and the CTD, who quickly cordoned off the area. The fact that they kept the media at bay only deepened the mystery. Panjwar's ties to these agencies and his protected status made the situation delicate, suggesting a desire to prevent sensitive information from leaking.

Pakistani investigators claimed they had warned Panjwar that his life was in danger about a month before his assassination. This warning came amid increasing threats to Khalistani activists residing in Pakistan. A police official stated that it was too early to determine the motive behind Panjwar's killing, and that investigators were pursuing all possible leads. He declined to comment on reports suggesting that one of the assailants had been injured during the crossfire. Panjwar's body was transferred to the city morgue for an autopsy, and police were working to obtain CCTV footage from the crime scene to gather more details about the suspects involved in the assassination.

Sukkhi's end was as tragic as it was unceremonious. After his death in the crossfire, the Lahore Police and ISI made sure his body vanished without a trace, quietly dumping it in a desolate landfill. In the chaos and secrecy surrounding the assassination of Panjwar, Sukkhi became a forgotten casualty. His body, abandoned and exposed to the elements, was left for scavengers to devour. No grave, no last rites. Only silence and decay. In death, Sukkhi became another nameless victim of the shadowy world of espionage, his tragic end buried under the weight of forgotten loyalties and discarded lives.

None of this found mention in Pakistan's major media outlets. His death, like his life, was shrouded in silence, erased from public record by the very forces that led him to his downfall. At the same time, Panjwar's cremation was likely arranged in an unmarked place, a quiet conclusion to his once-feared presence. The ISI handlers, those who protected him for years, would see to it that he disappeared without fanfare, ensuring no martyrdom followed his death.

It was no secret that the Khalistan operation had long been overseen by a powerful figure – an army colonel within the ISI directorate who pulled the strings behind the scenes. Panjwar was part of this larger game, but in the end, Aditya's mission brought an era to a close. With Panjwar gone, the legacy of his terror was extinguished, and a clear message was sent: no one, not even those most protected, could escape justice forever.

Aditya had always known the weight of his actions, but after Sukkhi's death, the burden felt different – heavier, more personal. The cold, calculated decisions that defined his work now left him feeling hollow. Killing Sukkhi wasn't just another mission; it was a betrayal of someone who trusted him completely. The guilt gnawed at him, dragging him into a darkness he couldn't escape. Depression set in, shadowing his every move.

In the second week of July 2023, unable to cope, Aditya made a clandestine trip back to India without informing the intelligence agencies or his superiors. This wasn't a mission. It was something personal. Moving through one of the covert routes used by smugglers along the border, he crossed into Punjab under the radar. His first stop was Sukkhi's village in Tarn Taran. Sukkhi's parents still lived in the simple, weathered home where he had grown up. Aditya watched them from afar, torn over whether to tell them the truth about their son's death. In the end, he couldn't bring himself to break their hearts. He handed them a bundle of money, muttering only that it was for their future, then slipped away into the fog of Punjab's rural landscape before they could ask him any questions. The truth of Sukkhi's fate would die with him.

From Tarn Taran, Aditya travelled to Delhi, a city brimming with memories of the life he'd left behind. His daughter, Ameera, was the light that had once anchored him in a chaotic world. The bitter custody battle had ended with Meera, his estranged wife, being granted custody, leaving him adrift. He had gone to Delhi with the idea of seeing Ameera, even hoping foolishly for some kind of reconciliation with Meera, despite the finality of their divorce. At least, she hadn't moved to Mumbai like she had threatened. There seemed to be some hope.

But reality hit him harder than he had ever anticipated. When Aditya arrived at Meera's house, it wasn't his daughter he saw. There was another man in Meera's life. From not too far, he saw them together getting into a car. Their body language clearly showed their relationship. Aditya understood it was a family that no longer included him. It wasn't the formal legal separation that broke him, not the courtroom battle over Ameera's custody; it was seeing Meera settled, happy, with someone else. The love he had once held onto, however strained and broken, was now gone – replaced by a life that no longer had space for him.

Aditya stood there for what felt like an eternity, watching the car Meera boarded along with her new man disappearing. He then looked up to see that the windows and doors of his previous house were all shut. His heart sank lower than it ever had during his missions. This was a pain no mission or enemy could have inflicted – the feeling of being replaced.

He turned away, leaving without a word. The door to that life was now closed forever.

Desperation had next driven Aditya to Ameera's school. He wanted to see his daughter face to face. But his arrival was met with cold bureaucracy. The school authorities refused him entry, pointing out that his name was nowhere in their records. Ameera's father, in their eyes, didn't exist. The realization hit him hard, his connection to her had been severed on paper, too.

Only Meera could help him now. She was the one with access, the one whose name appeared everywhere connected to Ameera. But the last thing Aditya wanted was to face Meera, not after seeing her with another man. He turned away, slipping into the shadows, hoping to avoid any confrontation.

However, Meera was informed by the school that a man claiming to be Ameera's father had come to see her. This unexpected news sent a ripple through her day, stirring something in her that she hadn't felt in a long time. She tried to reach out to Aditya, but he had vanished, his phone numbers disconnected, his whereabouts unknown.

In her frustration, Meera reached out to the one place she knew might have answers, R&AW Chief Ashok Awasthy's office. She knew how deep Aditya's work ran within the intelligence world and figured they would have information on him.

What Meera didn't know was that her inquiry opened a door that should have remained closed. Aditya's secret visit to India was exposed. His superiors had no idea he was in the country, let alone in Delhi, and the revelation triggered immediate concern. His clandestine return, especially without any official clearance, was a violation that could have catastrophic consequences.

Soon, Aditya received an anonymous message. It was blunt and final: 'Stop. Immediately.' He knew what it meant. The higher-ups were watching now, and any more personal moves could cost him everything. His visit had not only jeopardized his career but also his safety.

The walls were closing in on him. What had begun as a desperate attempt to reconnect with his daughter had turned into a catastrophic misstep, one that might cost him far more than he was willing to lose. But he had to try one last time, regardless of orders or consequences.

Aditya stood outside Meera's house, hesitating for a moment before knocking. It wasn't the first time he'd been here, but everything felt different now. This wasn't the home they once shared. It was hers, with someone else.

Meera opened the door, surprised but composed. Without a word, she stepped aside to let him in. Aditya scanned the living room, the warmth of the space unsettling him. It was filled with traces of a life he no longer belonged to. Ameera's dolls and stuffed toys scattered across the floor, framed photos on the walls, and signs of another man's presence, subtly woven into the environment.

They sat in the living room, hostility crackling between them. Ameera was in school.

Aditya broke the silence first. 'You didn't need to contact Awasthy, Meera. Do you even realize what you've done? You've put everything at risk.'

Meera sighed, her patience thin. 'I didn't know what else to do. You just showed up at Ameera's school without a word. They had no idea who you were, Aditya. It scared them and it scared me. What did you expect me to do?'

Aditya's voice tightened, a mix of frustration and hurt. 'I was trying to see my daughter. I didn't want to involve anyone else, least of all my superiors.'

Meera leaned back, arms crossed, her expression resolute. 'That's exactly the problem. You never want to involve anyone, not even me. You come and go as you please, slipping in and out of Ameera's life like it's one of your missions.'

Aditya's eyes flashed with anger. 'You think this is about me slipping in and out? You don't understand the stakes. I'm trying to protect you and Ameera, more than myself. You contacting Awasthy ... it's reckless.'

Meera's voice softened but held firm. 'You're still hiding, Aditya. Even now, after everything, you're still wrapped up in your secrets. That's why I had to leave. You don't live in the real world ... you live in the shadows. You lie for a living. And that's no way for Ameera to have a father.'

Aditya clenched his fists, the weight of her words cutting deep. 'I had no choice, Meera. I can't just walk away from the life I have.'

Meera's gaze softened, but she didn't relent. 'I never asked you to walk away from your life. I asked you to be honest with me. With us. But you chose the work over everything else, over me, over Ameera. That's why I moved on.'

Aditya's voice faltered for a moment, the pain of her words sinking in. 'You don't think I tried? Every day I wake up with the weight of what I've done, what I've lost. And seeing you with him …' he trailed off, his voice barely above a whisper, 'I had thought maybe, just maybe, we could fix things.'

Meera's face softened, and for a moment, there was only silence. 'Aditya, it's too late. I've moved on, and Ameera needs stability. You showing up unannounced, like this … it's not fair to her …or …or to you.'

Aditya looked away, his heart heavy. 'I know.' His voice cracked with resignation. 'But it doesn't change the fact that I'll always be her father.'

Meera sighed deeply, conflicted but resolute. 'I know you love her, Aditya. But you need to figure out how to be in her life in a way that doesn't put her at risk.'

They sat there, the silence between them stretching out, filled with everything that was unsaid, both knowing that the life they once had was irreversibly gone.

'I need the phone back,' Aditya said quietly, breaking the silence. Meera couldn't follow his line for a moment. Then she remembered. Aditya was talking about the phone he had given her long ago, stripped of all functions except to receive calls. It had once symbolized something more, a lifeline to him, to a life of danger and uncertainty. But now, it was just a relic.

She went inside to bring the phone; handed it to him without a word, their fingers brushing for just a moment before she pulled away. The phone had served its purpose, and so had whatever unspoken connection it had held between them.

Aditya slipped it into his pocket, the weight of finality settling in. There was nothing more to say. Whatever remained between them was now in the past, and they both knew it.

'Thank you,' he said softly, turning to leave. Meera watched him go, her vision blurring as she fought to hold back tears, her trembling lips pressed tightly together, unwilling to let the emotion spill out.

∽

The early morning of second week of July 2023, the sun light had barely touched the horizon when Aditya arrived in an app cab at the NSD's high-walled, heavily guarded residence in Lutyens' Delhi.

The security detail barely gave him a second glance as he entered, unaware that technically he was grounded. Aditya's mind was racing. He knew he had made mistakes, critical ones, but he wasn't ready to give up. Not yet. Everything was gone from his life, including his daughter. What was left was an unfinished task that once his country had entrusted him with. He couldn't let that slip through his fingers. The NSD was the only one who could salvage his life for whatever it was worth.

Once inside, he was greeted by the sight of the NSD in his garden, going through his daily yoga routine. Aditya waited in the visitor's room, watching through the window as the NSD moved calmly through his stretches, his focus unwavering. It was a stark contrast to the tension building inside Aditya, but he knew better than to interrupt.

After what felt like an eternity, the NSD finished his routine and entered the house. Aditya was immediately summoned.

The NSD didn't waste time with pleasantries. Still fresh from his yoga session, his eyes were sharp, his attitude as firm as ever. He gestured for Aditya to sit, but the tension in the room was palpable.

'Give me one reason why I should trust you again, Aditya,' the NSD said, settling into his chair, his post-yoga calm masking the intensity of the moment.

Aditya exhaled, gathering himself. He knew this wasn't going to be easy, but he also knew that the NSD was a man of logic, someone who could be reasoned with.

'Because I've never failed you before this,' Aditya began, his voice steady. 'I know I botched the last mission, and I went against protocol. But I've delivered time and again when it mattered.'

The NSD's eyes narrowed. 'This isn't about your past successes. You've jeopardized an entire operation by going rogue. This isn't a personal vendetta, Aditya – it's national security. You acted like it was all about you.'

Aditya felt the sting of those words but kept his composure. 'I acted because no one else could. I went dark because I had no choice. My personal life, yes, it bled into the mission, but that's over now. I know what's at stake. Let me clean up my mess.'

The NSD leaned forward, his expression unreadable. 'You put yourself above the mission. That's a line you can't cross in this job.'

Aditya's voice hardened. 'I didn't cross the line to protect myself. I crossed it to protect this country. Panjwar's death sent shockwaves through Pakistan's intelligence network, and Sukkhi … well, that mistake cost more than just a life. But no one knows their network better than me now. I've been inside, and I can still dismantle them from within.'

The NSD's gaze was fixed at Aditya, trying to read if he was making up anything. Aditya spoke again, 'Sir, let me finish what I started.'

The NSD, with the weight of the decision clear on his face. 'And what makes you think you can pull it off this time? You've gone rogue once; what's stopping you from going off the rails again?'

Aditya met his gaze, unwavering. 'Because I've lost everything else, sir. My family, my child … they're gone. The only thing I have left is the mission. You have my word … I won't fail again. Give me one more shot, and I'll bring them down.'

The NSD leaned back in his chair, silent for a moment. He was weighing the risks, assessing whether this man who had once been one of India's best operatives could still be trusted. Aditya could feel the tension, the unspoken question hanging in the air.

The NSD stood up without a word and left the room, leaving Aditya to wait in uneasy silence. Moments later, he heard the muffled sound of a phone call, the NSD was speaking to Awasthy. The minutes ticked by slowly, Aditya's mind racing as he pieced together possible outcomes. He knew the stakes were high, and there was no room for error this time.

When the NSD returned, his expression was unreadable. He sat down, his tone calm but decisive. 'Forget Pakistan,' he said. 'You head for California. You'll know the details when you land.'

Aditya didn't need more explanation. He had been in the game long enough to understand what awaited him in America. The pieces were already falling into place in his mind. He was being sent to neutralize new threats, ones with greater global implications.

But Aditya wasn't going to make the same mistakes twice. He knew what he needed: a team. He had learned from Sukkhi's death that every mission needed a carefully calculated plan and people to carry it out.

Four names came to mind – men like Sukkhi, each hardened by their own pasts, each with their own debts to pay. Aditya had built quiet connections with them over the years, just as he had with Sukkhi. He reached out, sending word for them to prepare for their new roles. They were to infiltrate the US under the guise of hitmen working for South American drug cartels, entering the country through Colombia and Mexico. Their cover was airtight, and they would arrive in America as ghosts, just as Aditya once had.

The plan was already in motion. Aditya's new team would be his eyes and ears, and when the time came, his hands. The mission might be in a distant land, but the stakes were just as high. This time, he was playing smarter, colder and with nothing left to lose.

But what Aditya didn't know was that America had its own complications waiting for him. Another operative – a woman, someone entirely unlike him – was already deep in the mission. He had no clue he'd soon have a partner, nor did he know the challenges ahead. For Aditya, the unknown was about to become his greatest test.

17

Two Plus Two Makes Five

July 2023.

In the third week of the month, Aditya's first meeting with Mridula took place in a quiet café tucked away in Santa Fe Springs, California. He had come straight from Los Angeles International Airport (LAX), the ride barely taking half an hour. Travelling light, he carried only a duffel bag slung over his shoulder. Dressed in his usual blue denim jeans, a crisp white shirt and a tan cotton jacket paired with well-worn brown boots, he exuded a casual confidence. Mridula took in his appearance, noting each detail with curiosity, sensing that he might be trying to make a subtle impression. Though they were aware of each other's presence in the same organization, it was only 24 hours ago that they learned they would be working together.

Awasthy's call to Mridula was brief but packed with implications. 'Aditya will be joining you in California,' he had said, his tone betraying no room for negotiation. It was not the news Mridula had hoped for. From what she had heard about Aditya, he was anything but a team player, and she had been looking forward to running this mission on her own terms, with assets carefully chosen by her. But a call from Awasthy was not a suggestion; it was an order wrapped in diplomacy. And in a government job, especially in R&AW, the one thing you couldn't do was say 'no'.

She accepted his instruction with a sigh. 'Understood, sir. But are you sure about him? From what I've gathered …'

Awasthy cut her off gently, but firmly. 'You won't regret his company, Mridula. Chalk and cheese can sometimes make the most dangerous team. You two complement each other in ways you might not see yet.'

Mridula wasn't convinced, but she knew better than to argue. 'I suppose we'll find out,' she said, her voice lacking the enthusiasm she knew Awasthy was expecting.

He chuckled, sensing her hesitation. 'Trust me. You both have equal footing. No one's the boss here, except whoever can convince the other. You have your strengths, he has his. Together, you're a lethal combination.' There was a pause before Awasthy added with a teasing edge, 'Besides, it's good practice for life – learning to get along with someone you can't stand.'

Mridula sighed inwardly but maintained her composure. 'As long as I'm not the one cleaning up any mess created by him.'

Awasthy laughed lightly. 'Oh, there'll be messes all right. Just make sure they're the kind that bring results. Have fun, Mridula.' And with that, he hung up.

Mridula stared at her phone, her fingers tapping it absentmindedly. Fun, she thought dryly. Sure, if her idea of fun included babysitting a loose cannon.

Around the same time, Aditya was just about to board his direct flight from Mumbai to LAX when his phone buzzed. It was Altaf. The news, as expected, wasn't all that thrilling. 'You're teaming up with Mridula on this one,' Altaf had said, his tone as casual as if he were announcing the weather.

Aditya paused mid-step, processing the information. 'Mridula?' he asked, though the name was already ringing bells. He knew of her as someone sharp, efficient and notoriously headstrong. A solo player, just like him. The idea of partnering didn't exactly sit well.

'Yep, the same Mridula. From what I hear, she's not too thrilled either,' Altaf added with a chuckle, clearly enjoying the prospect of two alphas being forced into a shared cage.

Aditya sighed, rubbing the back of his neck. 'Well, this should be fun.' The sarcasm in his voice was unmistakable. He didn't mind working with others, but being saddled with someone known for being as stubborn as he was? That was another story.

'Look,' Altaf continued, his tone dropping a little more serious. 'Awasthy has his reasons for pairing you two up. And you know how these things work. Just … play by ear.'

Aditya smirked. 'Play by ear, huh? Isn't that what I always do?' He shifted the duffle bag on his shoulder and glanced at the boarding gate. There was no turning back now.

'Just try not to butt heads too soon,' Altaf advised, though it sounded more like a warning.

'No promises,' Aditya said dryly, before ending the call and heading toward the gate. He was prepared for the mission ahead, but teaming up with Mridula? That was going to be a challenge of a different kind.

Mridula had heard whispers about Aditya's messy divorce and the bitter custody battle over his daughter, the one he lost. As she carried the tray with two steaming cups of coffee from the counter, her mind lingered on the weight he must still carry. She set the tray down on the small round wooden table outside the French café, its quaint charm contrasting the sharpness of their conversation to come.

Taking a seat across from him, she glanced up, her voice soft but probing. 'How have you been, Aditya?'

He didn't need to ask what she meant; it was written plainly between the lines. His gaze stayed on the swirling coffee in front of him as he replied, his tone flat, guarded. 'I can't erase my child's memories from my mind … but the rest, it's all good.'

There was a quiet pause as Mridula absorbed his words, sensing the depth of the wound. She met his eyes, offering a genuine response. 'Time is the healer, Aditya. Don't you agree?'

He let out a short chuckle, leaning back in his chair. 'Are we about to dive into the philosophy of life now?' There was a hint of a smirk playing on his lips, but the tension in his voice lingered. 'I wouldn't mind,' he added, 'as long as this coffee turns into something a bit stronger ... like some form of alcohol.'

Mridula noticed the subtle slip in his last remark 'some form of alcohol'. She filed that observation away, letting it hang in the air for a moment before responding with a half-smile. 'Maybe after we've earned it.'

Mridula's sharp instincts didn't miss the implication behind Aditya's casual remark about alcohol. It was clear to her that he was drinking more than he should, a habit perhaps worsened by the weight of his personal battles. Sensing the need to steer the conversation away, she smoothly shifted gears. 'You know,' she began, her voice warm but measured, 'the work you did in Pakistan ... it's incredible. I've never seen an operation where one operative eliminated so many targets in such a short span. It's ... almost unimaginable.' There was a flicker of admiration in her eyes, genuine, though calculated.

Aditya gave a faint smile and nodded. 'Thanks for the kind words,' he replied, his tone formal, almost dismissive. Inside, however, he couldn't help but appreciate the effort Mridula was making to create a comfortable space between them. She was easing the tension, maybe even trying to win him over in this environment, one that clearly felt more like her territory than his.

But Aditya wasn't naive. He knew how this worked. Mridula had the beauty and the charm to soften anyone's guard. It wouldn't be surprising if this was part of her strategy to lure him in, make him feel comfortable and keep him within her control throughout the mission. He studied her for a moment, wondering if this was just a prelude to the larger game they were both about to play.

'Flattery works wonders,' he remarked with a slight grin, 'but I think I'll keep my wits about me.'

They finished their coffee in silence, each lost in their own thoughts. Mridula paid the bill quickly, and soon after, they were back on the road. She drove him to a modest yet well-kept Airbnb, the kind of place that offered just enough anonymity without drawing attention. As they reached the destination, Mridula handed him a sleek new cell phone along with a small bundle of SIM cards, her eyes meeting his briefly.

'Switch to this,' she said, her tone professional but with a trace of warmth. 'Multiple SIMs, use them wisely. I'll schedule our next meeting after you've had some rest.'

Aditya nodded, pocketing the phone. 'Thanks,' he muttered, his mind already calculating the next steps. Mridula drove off in her gleaming BMW 7X, disappearing into the California night, leaving him standing alone by the curb.

As Aditya entered the Airbnb and completed the formalities of checking in, he glanced down at his passport. It no longer bore the name Hassan Raza, the alias he had carried for so long. This time, he was 'Rahul Dutt', UK citizen, yet another identity, another layer to the intricate game of deception. He ran his fingers over the passport's smooth cover, a quiet reminder that no name was ever permanent in this line of work.

Aditya woke just past six in the evening, the room bathed in the deep hues of twilight. Through the window, the horizon was a stunning mix of crimson red, streaked with vibrant shades of orange and yellow, a striking image of nature's high contrast. For once, Aditya felt compelled to capture the moment, snapping a photo with his new phone before setting it aside. The mood of the sky, intense yet fleeting, felt oddly fitting.

After changing into fresh clothes, he headed down to the reception, craving a quick beverage from the vending machine. As he approached, the woman at the desk looked up and said, 'You've got an incoming call to your room. Would you like to take it here or leave a message?'

Aditya paused, already knowing who it would be. 'I'll take it here,' he said, his tone casual but expectant.

The receiver felt cool in his hand as he brought it to his ear. 'Aditya,' came Mridula's familiar voice on the other end. Her tone was business-like, though there was an underlying note of urgency. 'Let's fix a dinner meeting. I'll send you the address.'

'Go ahead,' Aditya replied, grabbing a pen. As she rattled off the details of the restaurant, he noted them down, mentally preparing for what this next meeting would bring. It wasn't just dinner. It was the start of something bigger.

Mridula had chosen an Indian restaurant for their dinner, a place known for its traditional vegetarian fare. It suited her well as she was a strict vegetarian, and the menu reflected her preferences. Aditya, on the other hand, didn't care much about food. He had never been a foodie, and at this point, the choice of what to eat was the least of his concerns. Anything would do.

His mind was elsewhere, preoccupied with the mission ahead, and the thought of sitting down for a meal was just another formality to get through. He knew this dinner wasn't about enjoying food; it was a calculated move by Mridula. Another step in the dance they had to perform together.

The restaurant's warm, golden lighting cast a soft glow over the room, creating an intimate atmosphere despite the tension simmering beneath the surface. The faint scent of spices – coriander, cumin and dry chillies – floated in the air, but neither Aditya nor Mridula seemed interested in the food. The conversation between them was far from casual; the plates were secondary to the real reason they sat across from each other.

Mridula leaned forward slightly, her expression serious yet controlled, as she briefed Aditya on the latest intel. 'Rinda's disappearance has hit Takkar's operations hard. Without him, Khalistan Tiger Force might still be holding on, but they've lost a major source of funds and weapons.'

The soft hum of the restaurant and the distant clatter of dishes seemed to fade as Mridula continued. Her voice lowered, almost conspiratorial. 'Takkar's camp is in disarray. The Khalistani extremists suspect India's hand in the recent killings in Pakistan, especially over the last year. But here's the gamble … Delhi's strategy seems to have worked. They believe India's focus was solely on removing those wanted by us from Pakistani soil, including PoK.'

Aditya's eyes flickered with interest as he took in the information, but his face remained impassive. The flickering candlelight between them reflected in his eyes, adding to the tension in the air.

'They don't believe we'll go after them in Canada,' she added, her tone cool but deliberate. 'At least, that's the general consensus in Takkar's camp. But Harinder Singh Dhillon … he's not so easily convinced.'

She paused for effect, letting her words sink in before continuing. 'Dhillon's been pressuring Takkar to take a public stand. He's already forced Takkar to claim that he has intelligence on Indian agencies "taking undue interest" in him and his lawyer Dhillon who's conveniently tucked away in New York City.'

As she spoke, the ambient noise of the restaurant seemed distant, almost irrelevant. The real drama was happening at this table, where every word carried the weight of high-stakes espionage.

As their dinner plates remained untouched, Mridula leaned back in her chair, her fingers lightly tracing the rim of her coffee cup, a subtle gesture of thought. The soft glow of the restaurant's warm light fell over her face, casting faint shadows as she spoke. 'What if I hand over everything I've gathered on Takkar to you?' she suggested, her eyes meeting Aditya's directly. 'You could take over the Takkar matter while I focus on the US and manage the CIA. It's something I've been handling for years. We can converge later, once you've made substantial progress on setting Takkar up for D-day.'

Aditya nodded slowly, absorbing her words. The clinking of glasses and distant conversations faded into the background as the weight of her proposal took centre stage. He couldn't deny that she had a point, as handling the CIA was well outside his scope, and it made sense for her to continue managing that delicate relationship. Meanwhile, he could take care of Takkar, the so-called 'plumber' who, in reality, was a ticking bomb waiting to ignite his war against India.

His lips curled slightly in a dry smile. 'I won't mind dealing with Takkar. The man thinks he's playing in the big leagues, but he's just another terrorist disguised as a revolutionary.' The flickering candlelight cast shifting shadows on his face, reflecting the cold determination in his voice.

Mridula raised an eyebrow, her sharp gaze never leaving his. 'Do you need manpower in Canada?' she asked, knowing that taking down a figure like Takkar wouldn't be a one-man job.

Aditya shook his head with quiet confidence. 'Already covered. I've sent four assets from India to the US,' he said, his voice low but steady. 'They're professionals, highly skilled with guns and explosives. They'll be reaching the US through Colombia and Mexico. Some handlers back in India are taking care of their passage.'

A brief silence settled between them, the gravity of their plans hanging in the air. Outside, the city buzzed with life, but at their table, the atmosphere was thick with the intensity of their covert operation. Each word spoken was a step closer to setting their plans in motion.

The last part of Aditya's remark sparked an idea in Mridula's mind, sharp and sudden like a blade cutting through the air. She leaned forward, her eyes narrowing in thought, the wheels turning. 'You know, the best route to Takkar ... might be through Rinda,' she said, her voice low and calculated.

Aditya's brow furrowed. 'Rinda's dead. I killed him in Pakistan,' he replied, his tone matter-of-fact, as though it was simply another mission ticked off a long list.

A small smile tugged at the corner of Mridula's lips. 'Exactly. But I've had time to figure out something since then – Rinda wasn't just a lone wolf. He had business partners in Colombia and Mexico cartels. They were buying Afghan heroin from him. The best quality in the world.'

The room seemed to close in slightly, the soft lighting now casting a more intimate, conspiratorial glow over their table. Mridula's voice softened but held an edge of excitement. 'What if we meet with these cartel bosses in South America? Use them to give logistical support to the pros you've sent from India. They have the resources, the networks. It could be our way in.'

Aditya didn't respond immediately, his fingers lightly drumming on the table. Mridula watched him closely, puzzled by his hesitation.

Wasn't this the same man who had infiltrated two separate cartels in Pakistan and taken out their leaders without blinking? She couldn't understand his dilemma.

'Aditya,' she ventured, her voice probing yet patient, 'you've done this before. Why the pause?'

He met her gaze, the candlelight flickering between them, his eyes darker now, conflicted. Whatever was going through his mind, it was something Mridula couldn't yet grasp. The silence hung heavy for a moment, filled with unspoken tension, as they both contemplated the dangerous path ahead.

Aditya stared at her for a long moment, his eyes searching hers, trying to decipher whether she was attempting to charm him again or if she was genuinely enthusiastic about the possibilities that lay ahead. The flickering candlelight between them cast shifting shadows on her face, but Mridula's expression remained composed, her excitement tempered by calculation.

Sensing his hesitation, she leaned back slightly, offering a more practical suggestion. 'Look, if it's a concern, you can handle the drug cartels alone. It's not about me being involved; the point is, your pros need solid backup, especially on American or Canadian soil. The South American cartels have a network that stretches all across the West. They could facilitate your operation without drawing any attention from the usual diplomatic channels.'

Her words hung in the air, pragmatic and to the point. Aditya knew she was right. It wasn't just about manpower, it was about having the right infrastructure behind the mission. The cartels, with their deeply embedded networks, could provide that without leaving any trace.

He exhaled slowly, nodding. 'I agree. But the cartels ...' he paused, his gaze hardening, '... they can't know the end goal of this mission.'

A smile appeared on Mridula's lips as she let out a soft laugh, her eyes glinting with amusement. 'Of course not, Aditya. We're not that careless.' Her tone was light, but there was an edge to it, a shared understanding of the dangerous game they were about to play.

The deal was set. Now, all that remained was to bring the South American cartels into the fold without letting them know what lay at the end of the road.

Mridula was, in many ways, an idealist, someone who adhered to the rules, even in the murky world of espionage. She had her lines firmly drawn, knowing exactly when to use lies and deception, but never letting them compromise her core principles. Aditya, on the other hand, was cut from a different cloth. A rogue. He bent rules, broke them even, when it came to dealing with the likes of drug dealers, gun runners and terrorists. It wasn't that he lacked principles; he just believed in leaving no room for mercy when facing those who trafficked in violence and chaos.

That … was what set them apart. Mridula operated from within the boundaries, drawing her strength from controlled and calculated moves. Aditya thrived on unpredictability, bending the world to his will if it meant achieving his target. Neither of them knew what lay ahead, but they were both certain of one thing: they had to complete the mission. The question that loomed between them wasn't about *if* but *how*.

As Mridula sat across from him, delivering her plans with precision, Aditya found himself wrestling with one last, distracting thought. He had heard whispers before, rumours about Mridula's allure. Now, witnessing it first hand, it was undeniable. She was stunning, strikingly beautiful in a way that could command a room without trying. There was an effortless elegance to her, a cool reserve that made it difficult to tell when she was lying, when she was trying to charm him and when she was simply being herself.

It unsettled him, that ambiguity. The last thing Aditya needed was to be distracted by her beauty, yet it lingered in his mind like a dangerous temptation. He had faced down killers, cartels and terrorists with steely focus. But Mridula? She was an enigma, someone he couldn't quite read, and that made her all the more dangerous.

Last week of July 2023.

Francisco Valdez sprawled in his chair, legs wide apart, his gut pressing against the buttons of his tailored suit. He took a long, sloppy drag from his cigar, letting the ash fall carelessly onto the priceless rug beneath him. His eyes, sharp and calculating, flicked between Aditya and Mridula as they laid out their case.

'You're telling me,' Valdez grunted, jabbing the cigar toward them like a weapon, 'that Takkar … some bearded fanatic from Canada … and his lawyer got Rinda killed because they thought he was selling them out? That's the shit you're selling me?'

Aditya kept his cool, though the air between them was thick with tension. 'They forced him to overdose,' he said evenly, 'made it look clean. No mess, no trail. But the fact remains, they betrayed him.'

Valdez snorted, leaning back in his chair with a sneer. 'And here you are, thinking I'm gonna back your little revenge fantasy just because you've got some sob story about Rinda. Rinda was useful, sure. But I'm not in the business of getting emotional over dead partners.'

Mridula, unfazed by his crude demeanour, leaned in slightly. 'This isn't about emotions, Valdez. It's about profit. Rinda's death disrupted your supply chain, whether you admit it or not. We're here to get things back on track.'

He leaned forward now, the smile fading, his voice a low, menacing growl. 'So, you … you're asking me to jump into bed with you two, risk my neck, so you can play hero and take out Takkar? What's in it for me?' Valdez raised an eyebrow, his mouth twitching into a smirk. 'You think I give a shit what Rinda did with the cash? I didn't care if he funnelled half of it into some crackpot terror group. He moved product, made me money. Simple as that.' Aditya exchanged a brief glance with Mridula, sensing the shift. 'We're not asking you to get your hands dirty,' he said, his tone measured. 'All we need is your network. Let us handle Takkar and Dhillon. You get your product moving again, and we deal with the traitors.'

Valdez let out a harsh laugh, grinding the cigar into the ashtray with a twist that seemed almost violent. 'You think I'm stupid, huh?

That I don't see the game you're playing? You two come in here, offer me a sweet little deal and I'm just supposed to sit back while you run the show?'

Mridula's gaze remained steady, but her voice lowered, firm. 'We're not here to play games, Valdez. This is business. You back us, and your supply line stays secure. We do the heavy lifting, and you get richer.'

Valdez's eyes narrowed, a wicked glint flickering in them. 'Yeah, well, I'm not interested in getting rich slow, sweetheart. I like quick money. So here's what I'm thinking ... if I'm gonna help you, I want more than just my supply back. I want a cut of whatever you get from taking down Takkar. And you don't get to say no.'

Aditya's jaw tightened, but he kept his voice level. 'That's not how this works.'

Valdez leaned back, spreading his arms with a crude grin. 'Then it ain't working for me. You want my help, you give me a reason to care. Otherwise, I'll sit here and watch you two crash and burn.'

Aditya's eyes flicked to Mridula, reading her calm exterior. They both knew Valdez was trying to squeeze them, playing his game of greed and brutality. But they also knew they needed him.

Mridula spoke first, her voice a soft but deliberate threat. 'You push too hard, Valdez, and you'll end up with nothing. We're offering you a clean deal. You back us, and we'll make sure your supply flows faster than before. Cross us, and you'll be dealing with more than just the loss of one partner.'

Valdez's grin widened, crude and knowing. 'That's the spirit, darling. Now you're speaking my language.'

~

Two days later, under the cover of night, the four assassins moved like shadows through the bustling port of Mexico, stepping off a merchant ship that had quietly slipped in from Morocco. The sounds of bustling sailors and dock workers mingled with the distant hum of the city traffic, masking their presence. There was no fanfare, no sign of their arrival, just another anonymous docking in a place where secrets were currency, and whispers carried more weight than gold.

The cartels' indirect support worked like a well-oiled machine. As the assassins disembarked, they were whisked away in unmarked trucks, slipping through the chaotic underbelly of Mexico unnoticed. Their path was paved with favours called in, debts repaid and a network of shadows that ensured no one stayed in one place too long. It was a system designed to leave no trace, a hallmark of the cartels' mastery in evasion and secrecy.

Two of the assassins were bound for Canada, the other two for the US. The split was deliberate as they had strict instructions not to travel or arrive together. Each route was designed to mislead any surveillance that might trace their movements. The pair headed for the US were tasked with a preliminary reconnaissance in and around New York and Washington, studying potential choke points, safe corridors and local contacts that might later aid their escape. Once their recces were complete, they would quietly slip across the northern border to rejoin the others in Canada. Upon arrival, each assassin found a safe house waiting – a run-down warehouse, a boarded-up apartment or an abandoned farm. All seemed to be chosen to keep them invisible until the signal came.

'We move like smoke. No one catches us,' one of the handlers had said, his voice laced with the quiet confidence of a man who had helped smugglers, criminals and killers slip through borders for years. 'You'll get the guns, the ammo, whatever you need. Just stay quiet.'

In both Canada and the US, local cartel contacts greeted the assassins. Hardened men who spoke little but delivered everything necessary with brutal efficiency. Arms, ammunition, explosives, everything they required was waiting for them, concealed in crates disguised as everyday goods. In Canada, the weapons were hidden in a forgotten shed on a deserted property, while in the US, they were tucked away in an old industrial yard, masked behind piles of rusting containers.

One of the assassins had asked during the drive, 'What if we get heat? What if the locals start sniffing around?'

The cartel handler merely smirked, not breaking his focus on the road. 'You're covered. We've got eyes in places you wouldn't believe. Just don't make noise, and you'll be invisible.'

The assassins hadn't been briefed on the specifics of their mission yet. They knew only that the cartel would supply everything they needed. It was enough for now. Discretion, patience and silence were their weapons until the time came. They were cogs in a much larger machine, and their moves had been perfectly orchestrated to keep them off the radar.

For now, they lay low, waiting in the safety of their shadowy hideouts. Soon, they would meet Aditya and Mridula. Soon, the real mission would begin.

In the days that followed, each assassin received a hefty sum of money transferred through a labyrinth of secretive transactions from accounts in Dubai. The money, clean and untraceable, arrived like a silent promise, fuelling their purpose while keeping them under the radar.

From a distance, Mridula and Aditya discreetly monitored their movements. Two of the assassins were still in New York, completing reconnaissance in and around the city and Washington as instructed, while the other two had already crossed into Canada to prepare the next phase. Those in the US blended seamlessly into the everyday bustle, posing as tourists with cameras slung around their necks, traders negotiating deals, or students navigating unfamiliar streets. Each role was carefully crafted, a mask of normalcy hiding the deadly intent beneath.

Their movements were calculated, every step, every interaction chosen with care. The lies they told were effortless, slipping into conversations like routine small talk, making it impossible for anyone to suspect their true purpose. The stories they spun about their travels, their reasons for being there were airtight, built to hold up under scrutiny.

In the parks, cafés and quiet corners of the city, they appeared harmless, invisible. But beneath the surface, the tension was building. Mridula and Aditya watched as their operatives worked through the world around them, waiting for the perfect moment to strike. The assassins knew the plan was far from complete, but the groundwork was being laid patiently, meticulously.

For now, they were just faces in the crowd, indistinguishable from the masses. Two of them had already relocated to Canada, while the remaining pair continued their reconnaissance in New York and Washington before crossing the border to join the others. Their anonymity was their greatest asset, each move calculated to appear ordinary. Mridula had built her own network in America over years of careful groundwork, and it was essential for both her and Aditya to test these operatives in this new environment. If they could operate undetected on US soil, success anywhere else would be within their grasp.

As Aditya and his four men moved into Canada, Mridula, based in California, ran the operation from afar with surgical precision. The four operatives Aditya had recruited from India were already in place in Canada, so Mridula did not want them exposed on US soil. For the American leg she therefore enlisted a fresh team of Cuban hitmen, procured through Valdez in Miami. It was a tactical choice: separate teams, separate footprints. To the Cubans and to anyone who might overhear, the story given was simple: the target was an Indian-origin drug dealer living under political asylum in the United States. That lie was deliberate; Mridula could not risk letting the true objective be known. Aditya understood the logic and let her take the lead on her own turf.

Each operative moved with deliberate care, their actions meticulously tracked through a covert network that Mridula had quietly set in motion. Over the years, she had cultivated local contacts, hidden allies who were now activated to provide discreet support. Secure, undetectable locations were arranged for the operatives, ensuring they could remain invisible yet ready for action. This shadow network offered constant surveillance and backup at every step.

A meeting unfolded in a modest Airbnb tucked away in a quiet corner of Queens. It was a safe house, discreetly maintained by R&AW, far from the bustling glamour of Manhattan. The apartment was unremarkable, a perfect choice for an operation of this magnitude. The furniture was sparse: a worn sofa, a small table with mismatched chairs and heavy curtains that blocked out the city's lights. Outside, the neighbourhood was quiet, the sounds of distant traffic the only reminder they were in New York.

Mridula sat at the table, her focus entirely on the operatives gathered before her. Tonight her usual elegance was replaced with a no-nonsense black turtleneck, dark jeans and sneakers. Her long hair was tied back in a simple ponytail, and she wore no accessories, nothing that would draw unnecessary attention. She blended into the background, as someone in her position had to.

Across from her sat the four Cuban operatives, each dressed casually but wearing an unmistakable air of danger. Their leader, a tall, muscular man with cropped hair, wore a leather jacket over a plain t-shirt, his sharp eyes tracking every move she made. Next to him, a lean man with tattoos running up his arms, dressed in a worn denim shirt, leaned back in his chair, tapping a finger impatiently. The only woman among them, small but fierce, wore a bomber jacket, her dark hair pulled into a bun, her expression unreadable. The last, a younger man with a shaved head and a nervous energy, fidgeted in his seat, glancing at the others as though waiting for a cue.

Mridula's fingers swiped across her iPad, displaying the briefing material. 'Your target is Singh,' she began, her voice calm but firm. 'He's not just a drug dealer. He's been funnelling money to terrorists ... people who pose a direct threat to India.'

The leader of the group, leaning forward, broke the silence. 'Why him? Why now?'

Mridula's gaze didn't falter. 'Because he's vulnerable now. Singh's cheating of Francisco Valdez has made him reckless, and his operations are starting to crack. This is our chance.'

The tattooed man raised an eyebrow. 'And what kind of protection are we talking about here? This guy's got to have some serious backup.'

'He's careful,' Mridula replied, swiping to show surveillance photos of Singh's safe houses and movements. 'But we've identified weak points. He's been using his dual citizenship in the US and

Canada as a shield. But his dealings with the cartel have exposed him, and he's gotten sloppy.'

The woman in the bomber jacket finally spoke. 'If he's so dangerous, why isn't the cartel taking care of him themselves?'

Mridula allowed a small, knowing smile. 'Francisco Valdez prefers not to get his hands dirty. That's where you come in.'

The operatives exchanged glances, the tension in the room rising with each new revelation. They had been briefed before, but now the stakes were becoming clearer. Singh wasn't just a random drug cartel target. He was a man deeply entangled in something much bigger, much more dangerous.

'You'll have full support,' Mridula continued, her voice sharp and to the point. 'We have safe houses ready, and you'll be watched from a distance. But make no mistake … this has to be clean, and it has to be fast. Singh can't see you coming.'

The younger man shifted in his seat, still fidgeting. 'And if something goes wrong?'

'It won't,' Mridula said firmly, her eyes locking onto his. 'Stick to the plan, and everything will go smoothly. You've been chosen for a reason.'

With that, the room fell silent again, the gravity of the mission settling in. They were just faces in the crowd now, but soon, they would strike and Singh wouldn't know what hit him.

Next, Mridula knew she had to bring her CIA counterpart, Brian Green, on board. Years of experience dealing with the agency had taught her one thing – the CIA operated with a strict 'my way or the highway' approach. They didn't take kindly to other nations adopting similar stances, which meant she had to handle this conversation with precision. Gaining Brian's trust would also offer her valuable insight into what the CIA was thinking regarding India's extrajudicial actions.

The two met in a series of discreet locations, each one more secure than the last. Brian was sharp, cautious and always probing beneath the surface.

In one of their conversations, Mridula leaned forward slightly, her voice steady and calm.

'Your president and our prime minister discussed this directly,' she began, watching for Brian's reaction. 'The situation with Dhillon leaves us no choice. We can't afford to wait any longer.'

Brian's eyes narrowed. 'And yet you're pushing an extrajudicial solution. You know how we feel about that, especially on US soil.'

Mridula didn't flinch. 'This operation wasn't conceived overnight, Brian. Both sides understood the necessity of dealing with Dhillon. Your president knew it wouldn't be easy, but he also knew the stakes.'

Brian leaned back in his chair, assessing her. 'There's a difference between understanding necessity and endorsing it. What happens when this blows up in your face? You're on American turf, and you're playing with fire.'

Her expression didn't waiver. She had expected this pushback. 'I'm not asking for permission, Brian. I'm simply reminding you that, like the US, we prioritize national security. Think back to how your government handled Saudi Arabia after Khashoggi. There was outrage, but in the end, strategic alliances prevailed. The bigger picture always matters.'

Brian's eyes flickered. 'You're drawing parallels between India and Saudi Arabia?'

She smiled slightly, leaning in as she lowered her voice. 'Not directly. But the principle is the same. India is a vital player on the world stage. What we're doing isn't just about Dhillon. It's about protecting sovereignty and securing our national interests. If it ruffles feathers, we'll deal with that. But we can't afford to be passive.'

Brian was silent for a moment, his fingers tapping lightly on the table. 'You're asking us to look the other way while you carry out an operation on our soil. That's not exactly how partnerships work.'

'I'm asking you to understand the stakes,' Mridula said, her tone firm but calm. 'Dhillon has been using the US legal system to protect himself while funding groups that threaten India's security. You know as well as I do that we have to act.'

The silence stretched, both of them sizing each other up. Brian's gaze softened slightly, but his voice remained firm. 'If this goes sideways, it's on you. The CIA won't cover for you.'

Mridula met his gaze, unwavering. 'We're prepared for that.'

Brian leaned back, exhaling slowly. 'Just make sure you know what you're getting into.'

The conversation hung in the air, heavy with the weight of unspoken consequences. Mridula had made her case. Now it was up to Brian to decide how much he would let slip through the cracks. But for the CIA, even too much information was never enough.

Over the next few days, their exchanges became an intricate dance of persuasion and caution. Each meeting was a tug-of-war, tentative agreements followed by moments of hesitation, the negotiations clouded by bureaucracy. The official stance from the CIA stayed non-committal, but beneath the formality, Mridula sensed a shift, a quiet understanding that the groundwork had already been laid by their national leaders.

Brian's eyes narrowed as she spoke again. 'We both know what needs to be done,' she said calmly.

'Set the stage for what exactly?' Brian asked. 'You're talking about an extrajudicial killing on US soil. That's not a conversation we take lightly, Mridula.'

She didn't flinch. 'I understand the gravity, Brian, but Dhillon's actions go beyond domestic politics. He's been using your legal system to shield himself while funding separatist movements that threaten India's security. We can't ignore that risk.'

Mridula's tone didn't waver. 'I'm not asking for permission. I'm asking for understanding. This isn't just about India; it's about preventing a larger crisis. Dhillon isn't merely hiding behind his citizenship. He's exploiting it to fuel a global threat. You've dealt with similar dilemmas before, and you know what's at stake.'

Brian leaned forward, his tone hardening. 'And if this goes sideways?'

'We're prepared for the consequences,' Mridula replied without hesitation. 'This operation is necessary, and we both know it. Dhillon has been radicalizing youth, funding violent separatist movements, and destabilising regions that matter to both of us. This is about preventing a crisis before it escalates.'

Brian's eyes stayed on hers, searching for any sign of doubt, but her conviction held. She had made her case. Now it was up to Brian and the CIA to decide how much they were willing to let slide.

'We'll see,' Brian finally said, quiet but resolute. 'But don't expect us to clean up the mess if it blows up.'

Mridula nodded, her expression unreadable. 'Understood.'

The silence that followed was heavy. Both knew the stakes and the fine line they were walking between principle and necessity.

Mridula understood the gravity of the situation with a precision that few could match. Having spent years embedded within the US, navigating the intricate web of the CIA, she knew their inner workings better than most officials in Delhi. This wasn't just another mission, it was a high-stakes balancing act between power, diplomacy and national security. Each move had to be exact, every word measured.

With this awareness, she meticulously briefed the NSD back in Delhi. No detail was left to chance. Her report didn't just cover the tactical aspects; it emphasized the delicate intricacies of operating under the watchful eyes of the US government, where one misstep could have severe diplomatic repercussions.

The NSD's response came with calm reassurance. 'Your concerns are valid,' his voice steady through the encrypted line. 'But our ability to fully control the narrative on American soil is limited. For now, continue your surveillance of Dhillon. Track every move he makes, and be prepared to strike when the opportunity presents itself. I'll handle the rest.'

Mridula nodded silently, understanding the subtext as much as the words spoken. The NSD was likely manoeuvring behind the scenes, negotiating through diplomatic channels and preparing contingency plans. But the burden of execution would fall squarely on her shoulders.

As she ended the call, her mind was already racing, methodically planning the next steps. This was the life she had chosen – quiet, calculated actions in the shadows. And when the time came to act, as always, she would be ready.

∽

Beginning of August 2023.

Dhillon moved through the streets of New York in his black SUV, flanked by three bodyguards who were tough, loyal men from

Punjab, handpicked for their loyalty and street smarts. The weight of their presence surrounded him, and Dhillon exuded an air of confidence. He felt untouchable, knowing that beneath their jackets, his men were armed, ready to defend him at a moment's notice. They blended effortlessly into the city's chaos, their eyes scanning the crowds, hands inches from their concealed weapons.

But he hadn't accounted for Mridula.

Every turn of Dhillon's SUV, every step he took, was already in her sights. His sense of security was a mirage, and she could see through it with chilling clarity. While he believed the streets were his playground, Mridula saw them as her hunting ground. She had mapped every corner, every blind spot, for weeks.

As the SUV negotiated through the narrow streets, Mridula moved in sync, her steps deliberate yet unnoticed, her presence a ghost among the masses. The bodyguards were good – alert, observant. But they had no idea they were already in the crosshairs of her plan. Their vigilance only served to sharpen her strategy.

She watched from a distance, always one step ahead. Her eyes followed the vehicle as it slid through the traffic, her mind calculating every move, every contingency. This was more than just surveillance; it was a game of patience, and Mridula played it with cold precision.

Suddenly, her phone buzzed softly. A message from one of her Cuban operatives: 'Eyes on target. Ready for the next move.'

Mridula didn't flinch. She calmly tapped a response. 'Stay in position. Wait for my signal.'

Her focus returned to Dhillon's convoy. It had been weeks of meticulous planning which included mapping his routes, analysing his habits, identifying his weaknesses. Now, as his SUV rolled down the avenue, she knew the noose was tightening. Every move he made brought him closer to the moment when all his layers of protection would collapse.

From a corner café, Mridula sipped her coffee, blending into the buzz of the city. Behind her sunglasses, her eyes never left the black SUV as it pulled up to Dhillon's office building. Her hand slipped into her pocket, fingers moving swiftly across her phone.

A voice interrupted her thoughts. One of the Cuban operatives on the other end of the line. 'Are we going for it now?' His voice was taut with anticipation.

'Not yet,' she responded smoothly. 'Timing is everything. Let him settle, let his guards drop their guard.'

There was a pause, then a low chuckle from the other end. 'You play a dangerous game, lady.'

Her lips curved into a smile. 'That's the only way to win.'

Dhillon's bodyguards exited the vehicle first, scanning the area with a careful gaze, but to them, Mridula was just another woman in a café window. She watched silently, her fingers hovering over the screen. The moment was approaching, the tension building. Every fibre in her being was prepared.

The clock was ticking. The endgame was near. Dhillon may have felt invincible, but Mridula, calm, methodical, unstoppable was always one step ahead.

Her fingers tapped out a message, but instead of giving the go-ahead, she smiled slightly and typed: 'That's enough for today. We'll resume on another day.'

The game would continue, but today was about patience; knowing when to pull back was just as important as knowing when to strike.

The operatives were scattered across New York like chess pieces, poised for action. Each one had blended seamlessly into the city in flawless disguises, their roles carefully chosen. One, posing as a tourist with a camera, trailed the SUV in a taxi at a safe distance. Another, disguised as a student, sat casually at Dhillon's favourite lunch spot, eyes constantly scanning the crowd. The third, dressed as a businessman, loitered near one of Dhillon's usual meeting places, blending into the sea of professionals. The fourth operative, always calm and watchful, monitored the unfolding scene from a distance, ready to relay real-time updates.

The choreography was flawless. The guards, vigilant as they were, couldn't sense the invisible net tightening around them. Their sharp eyes scanned the streets, fingers brushing the weapons hidden beneath their jackets. But in the bustling crowds, they missed the threat that moved silently in their midst.

The next morning dawned much like the last. From her discreet vantage point, Mridula watched the routine unfold below and allowed herself a faint smile. Everything was proceeding according to plan. The SUV, the guards, the operatives. All were in place, the tension simmering beneath the surface as each day passed in the same rhythm, edging them closer to the moment of action.

New York moved on, oblivious to the deadly game unfolding beneath its surface. With every step Dhillon took, he unknowingly moved deeper into a carefully laid trap. Soon, he and his bodyguards would realize that this wasn't just another day navigating the city. It was a journey into the jaws of a trap about to snap shut.

Dhillon's routine had been dissected, every detail scrutinized. Mridula's team moved like phantoms through the city's chaos, using the hustle and bustle as cover. Crowded streets and busy corners became their greatest assets, concealing the deadly choreography in motion. Tiny cameras, discreetly hidden in lampposts and café awnings, recorded every movement, feeding the live data directly to Mridula.

The pieces were in place. The game was on.

From the nondescript apartment that served as her nerve centre, Mridula sat hunched over her laptop, the glow of the screen reflecting in her eyes. Her fingers danced across the keyboard, directing the operation with an eerie calm. On her monitors, Dhillon's path was laid bare, his movements caught from every angle. The encrypted earpieces kept her assassins connected, their low voices barely audible in the city's relentless noise, which drowned out any suspicion.

Mridula's assassins moved like shadows, invisible yet ever-present, merging seamlessly with the throngs of people going about their lives. Tourists snapping photos, businessmen on hurried calls, students lost in their thoughts; these were the faces they wore, disguises that allowed them to get close without a second glance.

Dhillon, wrapped in the false security of his armed guards, moved with the confidence of a man who believed himself untouchable. The guards, with their eyes scanning the streets, their hands resting on hidden weapons, were sharp but not sharp enough. They couldn't see the invisible hunters tracking their every step. They couldn't feel the noose tightening around them.

Mridula watched, her focus unbroken, as her assassins closed in. Their precision was terrifying with each assassin in place, each move coordinated, their silent conversations flowing through encrypted channels. The city, in its constant rush, became an unwitting accomplice, masking the sinister intent that threaded through its streets.

The next day. From her vantage point aboard a sleek boat anchored discreetly at the riverfront, Mridula directed the operation with precision. The boat, its lights dimmed to blend into the shadows of the pier, was the perfect command centre. The soft lapping of the water against the hull added a layer of quiet tension. She sat at the helm, her laptop glowing in front of her, casting sharp reflections on the surrounding windows. The screen displayed a live feed of Dhillon's movements through the city, every turn tracked, every step monitored.

Her team of operatives moved like ghosts through the streets, slipping unnoticed into the fabric of New York. One trailed the black SUV from a taxi, another lounged at Dhillon's favourite lunch spot, while the others strategically placed themselves at key points around the city. To any passerby, they were just more faces in the crowd, but Mridula knew better. They were her eyes and ears, connected by encrypted earpieces, their low voices crackling over the radio waves.

Dhillon, shielded by his guards, moved with confidence. His men were sharp, always alert, their hands never far from the weapons concealed beneath their jackets. But they were looking in all the wrong places. The threat was already upon them, hidden in plain sight.

Mridula sipped from a cup of coffee, her eyes never leaving the screens. She could see everything – the SUV winding through the city, the bodyguards scanning their surroundings, her operatives moving with the city's flow. The tension was palpable, rising with each passing second. From her boat, she pulled the strings of the operation, watching as the net began to close around Dhillon.

She tapped a message into her phone, sending a brief command to her team: 'Hold positions. Wait for my signal.'

The city moved on, oblivious to the deadly game playing out in its streets. But on this boat, anchored quietly on the riverfront, Mridula controlled the flow of events. The endgame was approaching, and when it came, she would strike with precision.

Dhillon moved through the city, blissfully unaware of the deadly game playing out in the shadows. The silent hunters tracking him were invisible, their eyes on him at every moment, scrutinizing his every step. What had once been routine, a source of security for him was now the very thing sealing his fate. Each movement was anticipated, countered before he even made it. The trap was set.

From her command centre aboard the boat, Mridula allowed herself the briefest moment of satisfaction. The hunt was reaching its climax, the city itself becoming part of the game. Its chaos, its noise and its incessant movement were the perfect cover for what was about to happen. The strike was imminent, and she knew, with a cold certainty, that when the time came, they would hit their mark.

Away in India's capital, both Ashok Awasthy and the NSD understood the stakes. This operation wasn't just about eliminating a threat; it was about doing so without triggering an international crisis. Their role was to ensure that, while Mridula's team operated in the shadows, the diplomatic front remained calm. Behind the scenes, they worked tirelessly to anticipate potential blowback, to smooth over the cracks before they could widen into fractures. His chessboard was the geopolitical landscape, and each move was made with meticulous precision.

Mridula along with Awasthy and the NSD made a strong team, each using their unique strengths. While she focused on executing the operation with precision on the ground, the other two handled the political side, ensuring India's security goals were met without upsetting the global balance of power. It was a high-wire act, but they had mastered it, using the tools of espionage, strategy and diplomacy to achieve a shared goal. And with each step, the mission inched closer to its inevitable climax.

18

The Last Prayer

18 August 2023.

The early summer evening settled over Surrey, the long June day slowly giving way to twilight. Aditya sat in his car, parked inconspicuously along a tree-lined street, the air electric with anticipation. Surrey's suburban calm was deceptive – behind the neat lawns and quiet streets, a storm was brewing. His eyes moved with practised precision, taking in every detail around him. This wasn't the type of operation where chaos revealed itself in obvious ways. Here, danger wore the mask of normalcy.

His mission was clear, but the air of uncertainty hung over him. He had spent days blending into the quiet rhythms of this neighbourhood, watching, waiting. There were no whispers of criminal intent, no shadows lurking in the alleyways, just a public figure, revered by some and hated by others, living his life under the protection of this serene façade.

Aditya adjusted his earpiece, the faint static breaking the silence. This mission was unlike anything he had undertaken before, far more delicate, far-reaching and politically explosive than what he had done in Pakistan. Failure here could trigger repercussions beyond borders, something Delhi could never afford to be traced back to

India. For that reason alone, he was not operating entirely alone this time. A special intermediary had been brought in, someone who served as the conduit between Aditya and the unseen decision-makers back home. The arrangement ensured total deniability for those in power while keeping Aditya connected just enough to stay aligned. The voice that came through was calm, almost detached. 'You still good? Anything moving?'

He tapped the earpiece twice, signalling silence. He needed full concentration now because in this game, the slightest misstep could mean the difference between success and catastrophe.

Even as his target, Takkar, always surrounded by his loyalists, believes he is untouchable in his stronghold, Aditya knows the truth. Surrey's calm doesn't fool him. Takkar's safety is a fragile illusion, built on the belief that his supporters and network make him untouchable. But Aditya is playing a different game.

He has four hitmen, highly skilled operatives, who have infiltrated Canada with the aid of Mexican drug cartels. These men are ghosts, blending seamlessly into the urban landscape, invisible to anyone not looking closely enough. Each of them is trained to perfection, waiting patiently, tailing Takkar's every move from a distance. They strike like shadows in daylight, ready to move when the timing is right.

From his mobile command post, Aditya orchestrates the operation with the precision of a battlefield general. His phone remains his only connection to the hitmen, communicating through encrypted channels that leave no trace. Every instruction is carefully timed, every detail calculated to ensure his operatives remain undetected.

One hitman, posing as a delivery driver, has stationed his van just far enough from Takkar's residence to avoid suspicion. His task is simple – monitor Takkar's movements, track the ebb and flow of visitors, and keep a watchful eye on the security team's shifts. Another hitman, blending effortlessly with the locals, has taken up the guise of a morning jogger. Each run through the quiet streets sharpens his understanding of Takkar's daily routine – when he leaves, how long he's gone and the patterns of his protection detail.

Aditya watches the data stream in, piecing together Takkar's life, his vulnerabilities. The clock is ticking, and his team is always one step ahead.

The third hitman, disguised as a handyman, has secured employment at a neighbouring house. From this vantage point, he can observe Takkar's home without drawing any unwanted attention. He fixes gutters and mows lawns, all the while keeping a close eye on the target's movements, his seemingly mundane tasks providing the perfect cover for surveillance.

The fourth hitman blends seamlessly into the neighbourhood as a local store clerk, the kind of face everyone recognizes but no one truly notices. He watches Takkar's interactions with the community, every purchase, every casual exchange. Each fragment of information is swiftly fed back to Aditya, forming a complete picture of Takkar's routine. No detail is too small, and nothing goes unnoticed.

With eyes on Takkar from all angles, Aditya's network is as tight as it is invisible. The operation is running flawlessly, the pieces moving in perfect synchronization, all building toward a single, decisive moment.

Takkar's movements were always unpredictable, a tactic that kept him safe, or so he thought. Tonight, though, his guard seemed to drop just a little. The evening air was cool, with the kind of serenity that would lull anyone into a sense of security. He left his home with his usual entourage, heading to the local gurdwara where besides prayer, meetings often took place, followed by discussions of politics, religion and power. He moved with the calm confidence of a man who believed he had nothing to fear, surrounded by those who would protect him at all costs.

In his command post, Aditya watched it all unfold. The second Takkar stepped outside his house, the wheels of the operation began to spin. The hitmen, scattered like chess pieces, moved into their roles with quiet precision.

'Target's on the move,' the delivery driver murmured into his earpiece, blending into the flow of traffic. His van trailed Takkar's car at a safe distance, navigating the quiet suburban streets with ease. His job wasn't just to follow; it was to anticipate. A sudden turn, an unexpected stop, he had to be ready for anything, a ghost in the rearview mirror.

Meanwhile, the jogger altered his usual route, slipping into position. His breaths came in a controlled rhythm, and his pace was steady. To anyone passing by, he was just another fitness enthusiast, pushing through his final run of the day. But his eyes were constantly scanning. Every corner, every car parked for too long, every person standing still a beat too long. It was all logged in his mind. Takkar wouldn't see him, but he saw everything.

The handyman, tending to his chores at a nearby house, kept his ears open. The faint crackle of voices in his earpiece was hidden beneath the hum of power tools. He had a direct line of sight to Takkar's house and the street beyond, blending into the scenery with ease. If the plan took an unexpected turn, his proximity made him the first line of reinforcement.

Back at the corner store, the clerk, seemingly bored behind the counter, was anything but. Every interaction, every stick of gum bought by Takkar's loyalists, was a piece of the puzzle. The men who hovered around Takkar were his real protection – his human shield. They laughed and chatted, seemingly at ease, but the store clerk knew better. They were always alert, their eyes scanning for threats, their hands ready for action at the first sign of trouble.

The men rarely accompanied him beyond the lane; once Takkar stepped into his car, he preferred to drive alone, confident that no one would dare strike him in his own neighbourhood.

Aditya monitored everything from his post, the tension building as each piece slid into place. 'Hold your positions,' he instructed, his voice calm but commanding. Takkar believed himself secure, tucked into the folds of his community, surrounded by loyalists. But Aditya knew that even the most fortified fortresses had cracks, and his team was trained to find them.

Aditya's eyes flickered across multiple live feeds displayed on his screen, the hidden cameras giving him a view from every angle. Each feed was a window into the unfolding operation, capturing every movement of Takkar and his security detail. They were vigilant, as always, scanning their surroundings with trained eyes, but they had no idea they were walking into an invisible net, one carefully woven by Aditya and his team.

The hitmen moved with silent precision, communicating through subtle gestures, a raised eyebrow here, a tap on the wrist there. No words were necessary. Their coordination was flawless, each man knowing his role and executing it without hesitation. They were professionals, shadows moving within the calm of Surrey's evening, unnoticed by the casual bystanders who saw only normalcy around them.

As Takkar's car rolled to a stop in front of the gurdwara, the team sprang into action. The jogger, sweat glistening on his brow, slowed his pace and effortlessly merged into a group of worshippers entering the building. His breathing remained steady, his body language relaxed, but his eyes stayed fixed on Takkar.

The delivery driver parked his van strategically nearby, the engine idling for a moment before shutting off. He remained inside, his view of the gurdwara perfect, ready to track Takkar's every move if things went off course. The van's rearview mirror reflected a scene of quiet serenity, but behind it, the driver's gaze was sharp, waiting for the signal.

The handyman, a fixture in the neighbourhood by now, positioned himself just right, tools in hand, with a clear line of sight to the gurdwara's entrance. He blended into the background of the street effortlessly, invisible to all except those who knew where to look.

Inside the gurdwara, the store clerk moved through the crowd with practised ease, offering greetings, exchanging nods, but always keeping his peripheral vision locked on Takkar's security team. They were tight, clustered around their leader, but the clerk wasn't worried. He had eyes in every corner, each movement, each shift in posture feeding back to Aditya.

Through their earpieces, Aditya's voice came through like a lifeline. 'Stay sharp. Wait for my signal.' His tone was calm, almost unnervingly so. The calm of a man in control, watching the pieces fall into place.

The hitmen held their positions, hearts steady, nerves of steel. The crowd moved around them, unaware of the silent storm gathering in the air. In the stillness of the moment, it felt like the world was holding its breath, waiting for that final command to set everything into motion.

The evening sun dipped behind the skyline of Surrey, casting long shadows across the streets. At the Guru Nanak Sikh Gurdwara on 120 Street, the scene was one of quiet reverence. Worshippers, draped in colourful turbans and scarves, moved with a sense of calm purpose, greeting one another with respectful nods and hushed voices. The soft hum of prayers and the scent of incense filled the air, adding to the peaceful ambience that enveloped the temple grounds.

Among them, Gurdeep Singh Takkar, a towering figure both physically and within the community, made his entrance. As the president of the gurdwara and a known leader of the local Sikh diaspora, his presence commanded respect. Clad in his usual kurta–pajama and turban, Takkar moved with a deliberate calm, his face etched with the weight of responsibility and years of leadership. He was a man revered by many, yet controversial to others – his advocacy for the Khalistani cause had drawn both loyalty and ire.

The atmosphere remained serene, almost sacred, as the worshippers prepared for the evening prayer session. For most, this was just another peaceful gathering, but beneath the surface, unseen forces were at play. A deadly game had already begun, though none in the crowd could sense the approaching storm.

In his mobile command post, Aditya's eyes flickered from one screen to another, analysing every detail with surgical precision. Each camera feed offered a different angle: Takkar greeting familiar faces, his security detail scanning the room, the hitmen subtly blending into the background, their eyes locked onto the target. Every movement was under scrutiny, every shift in posture weighed for signs of vulnerability.

The hitmen were perfectly positioned, their hands steady, their eyes never wavering. The jogger stood in the back, casually watching the proceedings, while the delivery driver remained parked outside, engine off, ready to respond at a moment's notice. The handyman adjusted his position ever so slightly, ensuring a clear view of the entrance, while the store clerk maintained his role, moving through the crowd like a ghost, unnoticed but ever-watchful.

Aditya's mind raced, but outwardly, he was a statue of calm. His breath barely audible, his heartbeat steady. He knew that this operation required more than precision. It required patience. The timing had to be perfect. One wrong move, one premature action, and the entire mission would unravel. Takkar's reign of terror had to end here, but only if the strike came at the exact right moment.

Aditya leaned back, his fingers tapping lightly on the console as he sent a message to the NSD. 'Traffic is smooth. Waiting for signal.'

The reply was immediate but succinct. 'Stand by.'

The weight of those two words hung in the air. Every second felt heavier, the pressure mounting as Aditya's operatives maintained their positions, ready to act but knowing the time wasn't yet right. Takkar, still oblivious to the deadly surveillance surrounding him, continued with his meeting, exchanging quiet words with his inner circle.

In the back of the gurdwara, the jogger wiped a bead of sweat from his forehead, his senses heightened, waiting for the signal that would unleash the storm.

As the final echoes of the evening prayers faded into the stillness, Gurdeep Singh Takkar gathered himself, offering a few parting nods to familiar faces before making his way towards the parking lot. As his bodyguards gathered around him, he gestured to them to leave him and go home. They nodded and departed. Takkar lingered a little to chat with a few acquaintances and then stepped out.

The night air was cool, the remnants of twilight casting a faint glow over the asphalt. The murmurs of the departing crowd filled the space, blending with the distant sound of footsteps and car engines humming to life. For Takkar, it was another routine evening, the comfort of his Dodge Ram waiting at the edge of the lot.

But in the soft shadows of the dispersing crowd, two figures moved with quiet precision. The assassins, camouflaged by the ordinary evening bustle, had been trailing him unnoticed. Their colleagues smoothly advanced to their own positions. Their movements were a masterclass in stealth – calculated, deliberate, yet unremarkable to the untrained eye. Each step was carefully taken, their gazes never straying from their target, waiting for the perfect moment when the crowd's awareness would wane and Takkar's sense of safety would betray him.

The evening air, filled with the sounds of rituals and murmured conversations, masked the true danger closing in. The killers, hidden in plain sight, had already begun their deadly countdown.

The parking lot was a mosaic of motion with families piling into cars, conversations lingering in the cool air and the glow of headlights cutting through the fading light. Despite the bustle, it was the perfect stage for the assassins. The constant movement, the casual chatter; it all provided cover for the two figures slipping closer with each passing second.

Takkar, unaware of the silent predators behind him, approached his Dodge Ram with a sense of routine. He pulled his keys from his pocket, his footsteps slow but steady, the kind of deliberate pace of a man with no reason to hurry. The assassins, however, were swiftly but discreetly moving into position, every movement practised, every step calculated to stay just outside the periphery of his awareness, shadows in his blind spot, drifting closer to the appointed spot like a tightening noose.

The crowd, absorbed in their own lives. Children being buckled into cars, prayers still murmured under breaths, people remained blissfully unaware of the lethal choreography unfolding before them. The assassins' dark intent moved silently beneath the surface, unnoticed, as if the danger itself was hidden in the very air they breathed. The parking lot, alive with routine, unknowingly cradled the threat, moments away from erupting into chaos.

Takkar reached for the door of his grey Dodge Ram, his fingers brushing the handle, unaware of the danger inching closer. The assassins, their hearts steady, eyes locked on their target, advanced with every step, the weight of their mission palpable. Aditya's weeks of meticulous preparation had led to that exact moment, and now it was all about execution.

A white Toyota Camry had been parked inconspicuously across the street for over an hour, its driver pretending to scroll through his phone. He was part of the outer ring of the operation, eyes on Takkar's movement, waiting for the go-ahead. A second vehicle, a silver sedan, idled two lanes away with its engine running – the designated getaway car, manned by a pair of silent professionals ready to vanish at a moment's notice.

As Takkar pulled his truck out of its parking space, the Camry eased into motion, driving parallel to him. Initially separated by a narrow walkway, the truck began to speed up, and the Camry matched its pace effortlessly. Then, as if part of a choreographed routine, the Camry merged into the lane with Takkar's truck. For a brief, ominous moment, the two vehicles moved side by side. Then the Camry pulled ahead of the Dodge Ram and slowed to a crawl, forcing him to slow down too as a perfect setup for the attack.

At that instant, two hooded men emerged quietly from under the covered waiting area near the lot. They moved like shadows, unnoticed by the crowd, positioning themselves where the parking lane met the exit. Their hands stayed tucked inside their jackets, fingers already wrapped around the pistols hidden beneath. They didn't draw yet. Timing was everything. The moment Takkar's truck rolled out of the slot and began to edge toward the main road, they would move. For now, they waited in silence, blending into the background as worshippers drifted past, oblivious to the storm about to break.

The Camry braked hard in front of the Dodge, forcing Takkar to slow down sharply. For a few seconds, his truck crawled forward, boxed in by traffic and unable to accelerate. That was the opening. Two hooded men broke cover from the shadows of the parking lane and advanced with chilling precision. Their faces were hidden beneath sweatshirts, their hands gripping firearms concealed until the final moment. As they closed in on the driver's side, both weapons came up together. The Camry, its job done, accelerated away and vanished into the traffic, leaving the assassins to finish the job.

As the first shot spat out, muffled by the silencer, time seemed to slow. Takkar barely had time to react before bullet after bullet tore through the air, the cold precision of the attack hidden beneath the ordinary hum of the evening. The murmurs of conversation and the soft shuffle of footsteps all continued around him, masking the violence that had just erupted.

The lead assassin, concealed beneath a hood and face mask, moved with deadly calm. With a silenced pistol now aimed directly at Takkar, he squeezed the trigger. The shots came quick, precise and efficient. Fifty bullets fired, thirty-four finding their mark. Takkar's body jerked violently with the impact of each shot, the shock and pain registering in his wide eyes as he staggered back against the seat in his Dodge Ram. Blood spattered across the vehicle, each new shot painting a grim portrait of the attack's efficiency.

Takkar sat crumpled in his truck, a lifeless figure slumped in the very car he had thought would carry him home.

The assassins didn't linger. Exchanging a quick glance to confirm the job was done, they retreated, slipping effortlessly into the surrounding chaos. As screams of horror erupted, they darted toward Cougar Creek Park, their footsteps echoing in the rising panic. Malkit Singh, a committee member at the gurdwara, caught sight of the two hooded men running, their small pughs and bearded faces partly visible beneath their disguises. He gave chase, but as they vanished into the park, he saw them climb into a waiting silver sedan. Three men were already inside, the driver and two lookouts forming the support crew. Within seconds, the car sped away toward the highway. The white Camry, which had set up the ambush, was already gone. A delivery van remained parked near the gurdwara, its driver, Aditya, watching from a distance as the plan unfolded exactly as intended.

The once-peaceful grounds of the gurdwara had transformed into a scene of pandemonium. The serenity of evening prayers was shattered, replaced by screams of terror and the sound of rushing footsteps. Worshippers and bystanders surged towards Takkar's truck, their faces a mixture of disbelief and horror. Some instinctively dialled emergency services, their hands trembling as they fumbled with their phones, while others stood frozen, struggling to comprehend the brutal attack that had unfolded in front of them.

In the midst of the chaos, Bhupinderjit Singh, another gurdwara volunteer, was the first to reach Takkar's truck. He wrenched open the driver's side door, his hands grabbing Takkar's shoulders. But there was no sign of life. 'Help! Help! He doesn't seem to be breathing,' he screamed, his voice shrill with shock.

The crowd's panic escalated as worshippers scattered in every direction, unaware that the killers were already long gone. By the time emergency services arrived, the killers were ghosts, leaving behind nothing but confusion, chaos and the body of a high-profile figure, now silenced forever.

The irony was that Takkar, despite his high-profile status and the danger surrounding him, was in a rush to leave the gurdwara that evening. It was Father's Day, and his family was waiting for him at home. As he exited the gurdwara, he made a quick call to his 21-year-old son. They had prepared pizza, which he loved, and seviyaan, his favourite dessert.

'Have dinner ready,' Takkar said casually. 'I'm coming home.' He had no clue that outside the gurdwara, his killers were already in position, waiting for the perfect moment to execute their plan.

Less than ten minutes later, the phone at the Takkar household rang again. The voice on the other end delivered a chilling message: 'Did you hear? Something happened at the gurdwara. I am so sorry ... Your dad was attacked ... I am afraid it is bad news.'

What was meant to be an evening of celebration had turned into the moment of his demise, with his killers having acted with the precision they had planned for so long.

As sirens blared in the distance, closing in on the scene, the assassins were already far from the chaos they had left behind. The only exception was Aditya. He was hanging around the crime scene until the police vehicles arrived. As the wail of sirens filled the night and emergency responders swarmed the scene, police moved swiftly to cordon off the area, Aditya quietly walked up to his car that was parked a block behind the gurdwara and left. Flashing lights had painted the gurdwara in an eerie glow as officers began their investigation, but they were already too late.

~

Takkar's assassination sent shockwaves beyond Surrey, igniting a full-blown diplomatic crisis that plunged relations between Canada and India into an unprecedented abyss. His killing had led to a series of protests outside the Indian consulate in Vancouver and across Canada, as well as calls and a petition demanding the federal government investigate his death and determine whether foreign interference was at play. The Canadian prime minister accused India of orchestrating the killing on foreign soil, an allegation that India vehemently rejected as 'absurd' and 'motivated'.

In a swiftly convened meeting at South Block, the Indian prime minister assessed the latest developments. Present in the room were the minister of external affairs (MEA) and the NSD, both seated across from the prime minister, who radiated his usual decisive energy.

The prime minister turned his sharp gaze toward the NSD and the MEA as he laid out his directive. 'How we deal with the United States and Canada must remain distinctly separate,' he stated firmly. 'Extend full cooperation to America without hesitation, but don't hold back in striking back at Canada when necessary.' He paused, his tone growing sharper as he explained the rationale behind his stance. 'The reason for this difference is simple: if the United States employs hard diplomacy with us, my Canadian friend will take it as a cue to attack India. We cannot allow that to go unanswered.'

The MEA nodded, acknowledging the complexity of balancing diplomatic ties with the two nations, while the NSD silently processed the implications of the prime minister's words, already considering how best to operationalize the dual strategy.

Attempting to draw a distinction between the United States and Canada, the MEA took the prime minister's point further. 'You are absolutely right about America's hard diplomacy,' he said, his tone measured yet firm. 'The US, unlike Canada, doesn't justify separatism, terrorism and extremism under the pretence of freedom of speech.'

He leaned forward, emphasizing his next point. 'In fact, the social media pages of *Australia Today* were blocked in Canada just hours after it covered my meeting with my Australian counterpart. This alone undermines Ottawa's claims of commitment to free speech.'

He went on to explain that the outlet was not an isolated case. It was merely one among many, including Canadian publications, whose pages on Meta platforms had been rendered inaccessible within Canada. The MEA clarified that this was the result of a disagreement between the social media giant and Canadian legislation, further exposing the hypocrisy in Ottawa's stance on freedom of expression.

The prime minister listened to his MEA carefully, a faint smile playing on his lips as he leaned back in his chair. Turning to the NSD, he pointed at him and, with a mischievous glint in his eye, remarked, '*Bharat ke 007 ne naak mein dum kar diya hai sab ke.* [India's 007 is a pain in the neck for everyone.]' The NSD, visibly taken aback, shifted uncomfortably in his seat. He had long learned that it was no easy task to discern when the prime minister was being serious and when he was simply in a playful mood.

Attempting to read his superior's intent, the NSD cleared his throat and responded carefully. He noted that while the United States had shared specific intelligence inputs with India, Canada's approach was more ambiguous. The narrative suggesting that senior Canadian officials had presented evidence to him during a meeting in Singapore, which he allegedly rejected, was a story shaped largely by media reports and selective interviews.

The NSD continued, explaining that after the meeting, some Canadian officials had privately claimed to have shared evidence with him, but he had firmly dismissed the material as insufficient. What followed, he added, was a breach of understanding. 'Journalists I trust reported on that meeting,' he said, 'despite the agreement between our officials to keep it under wraps. That wasn't just poor diplomacy, it was deliberate.'

The prime minister almost jumped out of his seat, laughing as he pointed again at the NSD. 'See, I told you! I told you how … *humare NSD sa'ab sabke naak mein dum kar detey hai!* [Our NSD sa'ab is a pain in the neck for everyone!]' he exclaimed with mock exasperation. 'How else would such confidential matters find their way to his media friends? No wonder the Canadians decided to go public, piling on even more embarrassing details about New Delhi for the world to see.'

The NSD offered a faint smile, unsure whether to defend himself or take the comment in stride. He knew the prime minister's humour often carried a sharp edge, but this time, it seemed to be a subtle warning.

The prime minister glanced at the clock, aware of another meeting fast approaching. Sensing the need to bring the discussion to a meaningful close, he shifted his tone to one of gravitas. His eyes swept the room as he delivered a pointed reminder to his two key players in shaping India's external image and security. 'Let us not do anything that appears juvenile,' he said firmly. 'We must act with restraint and maturity while pursuing what needs to be done.'

Turning specifically to the MEA, the prime minister added, 'Make sure no other members of my cabinet, especially the home minister, get dragged into this controversy.' His emphasis was unmistakable, the weight of his directive underscoring the need for careful management of the situation.

With that, the prime minister rose, signalling the end of the meeting, leaving both the MEA and NSD to reflect on their next steps in handling the delicate geopolitical tightrope.

Soon tensions reached boiling point when Canada suspended trade talks with India, halting what had been weeks of sensitive negotiations. The crisis escalated further when Canada's foreign minister ordered the expulsion of India's top intelligence officer, who led operations for the country's external intelligence agency. India responded immediately, expelling the head of Canada's intelligence office in Delhi, fuelling the standoff between the two nations.

India lashed back with accusations of its own, stating that Canada had become a safe haven for extremists and terrorists threatening India's sovereignty. A spokesperson for India's foreign ministry branded the country as a breeding ground for organized crime, worsening the war of words. Politicians from both the ruling party and the opposition in India condemned Canada's leadership, accusing the prime minister of using the crisis for political gain.

India raised the stakes by issuing a stern travel advisory, warning its citizens to exercise caution when travelling to Canada due to growing anti-India activities and politically condoned hate crimes. Canada's public safety minister dismissed the warning, affirming that the country remained safe while reiterating the ongoing investigation into the assassination.

The diplomatic rift grew even wider when India suspended the processing of visa applications for Canadian citizens, citing security threats at its high commission and consulates. Although citizens with valid visas remained unaffected, the message was clear: relations between the two countries had plunged to a new low.

India's foreign minister escalated the rhetoric, accusing Canada of allowing extremism and violence to fester for years. He highlighted how Indian diplomats were consistently intimidated on Canadian soil. By October, India had taken an extraordinary step, ordering Canada to remove forty-one of its diplomats from its embassy in Delhi, an act that underscored the deepening divide.

Takkar's lawyer, Harinder Singh Dhillon, didn't hesitate to go public after Takkar's assassination. He claimed that the Canadian Security Intelligence Service (CSIS) had warned Takkar about threats to his life due to his political activism. This wasn't just any activist work. Takkar had been helping organize a referendum for local Sikhs on the creation of Khalistan, a controversial and unofficial vote led by the group SFJ.

Delhi, however, had made it clear: Takkar was no mere activist. He was a man they had labelled a terrorist in 2020, wanted in nearly two dozen cases ranging from sedition to terrorism. By September, Indian authorities had seized his properties in Amritsar and Chandigarh, cementing their stance against him. Dhillon, fiercely defiant, dismissed the charges as fabricated and politically motivated.

Dhillon, a Sikh, a minority making up about 2 per cent of India's population, held firm to his beliefs. He called himself an activist, a man who simply wanted self-determination for Sikhs through

Khalistan. But his ideology clashed with the Indian state, which had crushed a violent Sikh insurgency in the 1980s and 1990s. While the movement had lost much of its support within India, it had found new life in the Sikh diaspora. Dhillon and the SFJ were among its most vocal advocates.

Born in the village of Nathu Chak in Punjab, Dhillon's journey was marked by defiance from the start. As a young boy, he moved to Khankot village in Amritsar with his family. He went on to study law at Panjab University in Chandigarh in the early 1990s, where he first tasted the power of student politics. According to a former Punjab police official, Dhillon had been investigated for a brawl and accused of raising pro-Khalistan slogans. Though he was cleared, the incident marked the beginning of a long and contentious relationship with authority.

In the years that followed, Dhillon relocated to the United States, acquiring degrees in management and law. He worked on Wall Street as a business analyst until 2014. But Dhillon wasn't content with a quiet life. In 2007, he co-founded SFJ with a singular goal: to keep the world's attention on the 1984 anti-Sikh riots, a tragedy that had left deep scars on the psyche of the Sikh community following the assassination of Indian prime minister Indira Gandhi by her Sikh bodyguards.

It wasn't until 2012, however, that Dhillon began to make headlines. His legal strategy became his weapon of choice – using a centuries-old law called the Alien Tort Statute, he sued prominent Indian politicians and celebrities, accusing them of involvement in human rights abuses during the riots. Sonia Gandhi, admitted to a New York hospital for cancer treatment, was served legal papers. The then-prime minister of India, Manmohan Singh, faced a lawsuit during his visit to the US to meet President Barack Obama.

But it was his 2015 case against Bollywood megastar Amitabh Bachchan that catapulted him into global headlines. Dhillon accused the actor of inciting anti-Sikh mobs during the riots, a claim Bachchan denied vehemently. Though the case never advanced, it served its purpose, turning the world's gaze toward Dhillon's anti-India campaign.

Emboldened by the attention, Dhillon took his mission further. In the same year, he announced a global Sikh referendum to push for the creation of Khalistan. Since then, he organized several symbolic, non-binding referendums across the Western world – in London, Toronto, Melbourne. And next on the list was California. The stakes were rising, and Dhillon knew it.

'The Indian government wants me dead. They want to eliminate me for running the global Khalistan referendum voting campaign,' he told *Time* magazine in an interview, eyes unwavering, voice steady.

New Delhi, meanwhile, had no intention of backing down. Even amidst the international outcry over Takkar's assassination, the Indian establishment remained resolute. Behind closed doors, India's top intelligence agency chief and the NSD had made it clear to Mridula and Aditya that the mission was far from over. Takkar was just one piece of the puzzle. Their next target? Harinder Singh Dhillon.

Aditya was already being prepped for his next move – relocation to the US, where Mridula was waiting. Together, they would spearhead Operation Dhillon. The hunt was still on, and the game was only getting deadlier.

19

Mission Never Truly Over

November 2023.

But Mridula hadn't been waiting for Aditya to join her in the US to deal with Dhillon. In fact, as events unfolded, her conviction in the mission began to waver. The aftermath of Takkar's assassination had shaken the international stage, with the Canadian prime minister directly accusing India of being behind the killing of a prominent Sikh on Canadian soil. Despite India's firm denials at every platform, no one seemed to believe them. Not the global community, not even the Indian media.

Yet, back home, it was a different story. For supporters of the Indian prime minister, the assassination was a cause for celebration. Opinion makers and key influencers trumpeted the notion of a 'New India' that was decisive, fearless and willing to take extreme measures on foreign soil. The prime minister himself seemed to embody this stance, proudly presenting it as a hallmark of his leadership.

But within India's security agencies, a heated debate was underway. The Canadian prime minister's allegations had sparked outrage among officials, despite the government's denial. Many criticized what they saw as Western double standards.

'When the CIA or Mossad eliminates targets abroad – or MI6 in its heyday – nobody bats an eye,' one official argued. 'But when

India does the same, those same countries are quick to throw the rule book at us.'

For these officials, the allegations weren't just an attack on the government but an affront to India's sovereignty and its right to defend itself.

Some security officials countered that this argument ignored a crucial distinction: none of these countries carry out operations within the territorial jurisdiction of friends, partners or allies. Further, while foreign intelligence agencies may be tolerated for targeting their own citizens abroad, there is a clear line when it comes to targeting the citizens of host nations.

For instance, India could eliminate suspected Khalistanis or Jaish and Lashkar terrorists in Pakistan or PoK without causing a ripple in the West. Even Pakistan's repeated accusations that India was behind a bombing outside Lashkar chief Hafiz Saeed's home failed to gain any serious attention. But the calculus shifts when the killing of a Canadian citizen on Canadian soil is linked to an Indian intelligence agency. It directly challenges the unwritten rule that friendly nations do not target each other's citizens, a norm that even the most powerful intelligence agencies like the CIA or Mossad are careful not to breach.

This, they argued, was the real reason the West reacted so sharply – it wasn't about the act itself but the perception of a breach of trust between allies.

They pointed out that the CIA's hit jobs during the Cold War or in Afghanistan and Pakistan were carried out in enemy territory or in conditions of armed conflict, where such operations were seen as part of larger geopolitical struggles. Targeting individuals in friendly nations, however, was an entirely different matter.

Despite this, a significant section of senior officials in India's security agencies supported the act of extrajudicial killing. They viewed it as a necessary tool in an evolving geopolitical landscape where the United States and other Western governments struggled to address rising repression globally. India, they argued, had faced few consequences for its actions against dissident groups, largely because the West, particularly the United States, prioritized closer ties with India amid its strategic competition with China. This geopolitical reality, they believed, provided India with the latitude to act decisively when its security interests were at stake.

Cross-border repression manifests in various forms, including violence, harassment and surveillance. India, which surpassed China in 2023 as the world's most populous country, has joined an expanding list of nations employing such tactics to target dissident groups abroad. This trend is not unique to India; it reflects a growing global phenomenon where governments extend their reach beyond borders to silence critics and perceived threats. Consequently, sanctuary for dissident groups is rapidly shrinking, with nearly every continent witnessing the encroachment of such practices. For many, the notion of safe havens is becoming an illusion, as state-sponsored actions continue to erode the boundaries of sovereignty and asylum.

Even as security officials shared their views, disbelief echoed among analysts. Many argued that foreign killings had never historically been a hallmark of India's intelligence playbook. 'If these allegations are true, then this marks a radical reimagination of Indian intelligence and its operations beyond national borders,' remarked a research fellow at the Institute of South Asian Studies, National University of Singapore. The suggestion that India had crossed this threshold left analysts grappling with the implications, viewing it as a significant departure from traditional practices rooted in restraint and discretion.

Yet, he emphasized, under the prime minister and his Hindu nationalist government, India's global stature had reached unprecedented heights. As both a geopolitical counterweight to China and a rapidly growing economic powerhouse, India had never been more prominent or influential on the world stage. This newfound clout allowed India to aggressively pursue a foreign policy that often diverged from Western interests, while still being actively courted by leaders from the US, UK, Australia and Europe.

'This is not the India of the 1980s or the 1990s,' he remarked. 'It's a rising India, driven by a political dispensation that unapologetically believes in the use of force to advance national interests.'

Mridula was not against Dhillon being taken care of; she wanted a gap between India's last major strike, Takkar, and the proposed one on Dhillon. She believed that after the assassination in Surrey, it would be wiser to let the dust settle before moving forward with another high-profile hit.

Mridula was aware, through her sources, that US intelligence agencies had assessed any operation targeting Dhillon to have been greenlit by the head of R&AW. She also knew that Awasthy was operating under immense pressure from the highest office in New Delhi to neutralize the perceived threat posed by Sikh extremists abroad. Her sources further indicated that US spy agencies suspected the NSD was likely privy to R&AW's plans to target Sikh activists. However, they emphasized that no definitive proof had surfaced to corroborate these claims, leaving the accusations shrouded in ambiguity and speculation.

Her sources in the CIA had revealed that India's willingness to pursue lethal operations in North America had stunned Western security officials. But the NSD had no such doubts about the path forward. He pointed Mridula towards the profound shift in global geopolitics. After decades of being treated as a second-tier player, India now viewed itself as an ascendant power in an era of intensifying global competition, one that even the United States could ill afford to alienate. This shift, he argued, was evident in the candid admission of a senior CIA official, who had told her, 'India knew they could get away with it,' when she had voiced her concerns about the risks of attempting an assassination on US soil.

Mridula sought to convince New Delhi that her reservations were not about taking decisive action against an American citizen on US soil but rather about the timing. She argued that her concerns were rooted in strategy, not hesitation, emphasizing the need to carefully assess the potential fallout before moving forward.

But R&AW pushed back with a compelling argument: it would only become harder to target Dhillon once the global outcry over India's alleged role in Takkar's killing reached its peak. In fact, the NSD had earlier proposed a more audacious plan – two simultaneous hits. Takkar in Surrey and Dhillon in New York, both taken out on the same day. The logic was clear: Aditya had eliminated Takkar despite the heightened security around him, and Dhillon, lacking any such protections, would have been an easier target. Now, as New Delhi saw it, if they could strike a well-guarded Takkar, what was stopping them from going after Dhillon, a man living without any public attention or security detail?

Yet the second strike never happened. Mridula had opposed the idea of two hits on the same day from the very start. She cited operational prudence and timing, arguing that too many moving parts could expose the entire network. But there were deeper reasons she never shared. Her personal compulsions that shaped her judgment in ways no one around her could fully grasp. When the diplomatic temperature spiked in the aftermath of Takkar's killing, her argument found unexpected support. The Dhillon operation was quietly shelved, at least for the time being, its file marked for review when the dust settled.

In step with New Delhi's directives, Aditya landed in New York, fully prepared for his next mission. What he didn't know, because neither New Delhi nor Altaf had mentioned anything about it, was Mridula's reservations regarding Operation Dhillon. This silence was deliberate. First, R&AW's policy dictated minimal sharing of divergent opinions within the ranks during active operations. Second, the R&AW chief, Ashok Awasthy, had flatly rejected Mridula's proposal to delay the strike. For New Delhi, the decision was clear that the operation was moving forward, with or without Mridula's full agreement.

Buoyed by a series of successful hits, including the most recent one on Canadian soil, Aditya was confident he could pull off another operation. This time on American soil. Yet, he knew well that the security apparatus in the US was an entirely different beast. His initial plan, based on sporadic intelligence reports from R&AW, offered little insight into Dhillon's daily life. The reports focused more on Dhillon's efforts to push the Khalistan agenda than on his personal routines or vulnerabilities. Aditya understood that to fill in the gaps, he would need to rely heavily on Mridula's surveillance, her knowledge of Dhillon's daily movements, his social circle and his patterns.

Despite the challenges, Aditya wasn't fazed. He had been gradually honing his skills, learning to operate within some of the world's most secure environments. In Pakistan, he had successfully neutralized four targets in a weak security setup. More recently, he had managed to outmanoeuvre Canadian intelligence, which, though far superior to Pakistan's, still hadn't been able to stop him. Now, with America's impenetrable security system standing between him and his target, Aditya saw this as the ultimate test of his abilities.

The following day, Aditya sat back in his seat, quietly observing as Mridula responded to his plan for Operation Dhillon, which he had laid out the day before. The car's engine hummed softly, filling the silence between them, an intentional choice to avoid any risk of eavesdropping. Mridula's gaze remained fixed on the road, her hands gripping the wheel as they navigated through New York's crowded streets. Two Indian operatives meeting in the city, especially after the high-profile assassination of Takkar in Surrey, was sure to trigger alarms within the American intelligence community. This wasn't just a routine drive, it was a calculated move to stay beneath the radar, ensuring their conversation stayed private.

Mridula gave a quick glance at Aditya, unimpressed. 'This feels … theoretical. Like something anyone could pull from old operation files and case studies,' she said, her words sort of dismissive. It wasn't just a critique, it was her way of cutting him down, reminding him of the boundaries. Aditya saw it coming. He knew he'd stepped into her domain, where she expected him to play the sidekick, not the strategist.

Unfazed, Aditya leaned into the moment. 'Fair point,' he said with a small shrug, 'I know I'm coming off a bit textbook. I'm not as tuned into New York's ground realities as you are.' His tone was easy, almost conversational. 'But that's where you come in. You've already got the lay of the land. Together, we can turn those "theories" into something that actually works.'

Mridula's eyes flickered with suspicion as she sensed Aditya's subtle manoeuvring into her space. She shot him a sarcastic glance, her tone biting. 'So, are you looking for an assistant on this operation? I could recommend someone with a proven track record. Indian, former R&AW … might be more your speed.'

Aditya didn't take the bait. He met her sarcasm with a calm smile, steering clear of confrontation. 'I'm not after an assistant,' he replied smoothly. 'I'm looking for a partner … someone I can learn from and apply that knowledge on the ground. That's all.' His words were measured, sharp, but with just the right touch of humility to keep the tension in check.

Mridula began to enjoy the verbal ping-pong they were playing, each move calculated, each reply an attempt to outmanoeuvre the other. The real game, after all, was about who would come out on top. She decided to play along, leaning back slightly with a sly smile. 'I could hand over everything I've done on Dhillon so far,' she said, her voice casual, almost teasing. 'That should be more than enough for you to just wrap it up – one clean strike. Won't take you more than a day.'

She paused, watching Aditya for a reaction before continuing. 'Meanwhile, I can finally be free of this operation and head off on that long overdue holiday with my mother.' Her tone turned more pointed, though still with that air of lightness. 'Of course,' she added, 'I'm not convinced this is the right time to take down Dhillon anyway.'

It was a masterstroke, offering him the work and subtly questioning his judgement all in one move. The match was heating up.

Inside, Aditya felt a flicker of irritation, but his expression remained neutral. His tone calm as he asked, 'Why do you think that?'

Mridula didn't miss a beat. 'For starters, it's way too close to Takkar's assassination. My contacts in the US government are convinced India was behind it, and there's no way they'll let something like that happen again, especially on their turf.'

She let that sink in for a moment before continuing. 'And then there's the timing when India's prime minister is about to visit Washington, DC. How's he supposed to explain another high-profile hit, this time on American soil? What's he going to say to his counterpart, or worse, to the press?' Her voice was sharp, confident. She knew she had made a solid point, and she was watching closely to see how Aditya would handle it.

Aditya kept his voice steady, not allowing her logic to shake him. 'I don't quite see it that way,' he said, leaning forward slightly. 'Like my bosses, I believe Dhillon needs to be neutralized before Takkar's assassination grows to something bigger. We're not exactly sitting on a lot of time.' He deliberately mentioned 'bosses' as a subtle political move, hinting that his stance had the backing of those higher up, adding weight to his argument.

He paused, gauging her reaction before addressing her second point. 'And as for the prime minister facing his counterpart or the media here in America … denial is easy. Every nation does it. The US included, unless they can turn an extrajudicial hit into some kind of public win for themselves. Otherwise, it's business as usual.'

His tone sharpened slightly. 'Let's not forget that the Indian prime minister and the American president already have an understanding on Takkar and Dhillon, don't they?' He watched her carefully, knowing he'd just pushed the conversation into a higher-stakes game.

Mridula glanced at Aditya with a hint of amusement, like a teacher indulging a student's naive ideas about war and revolution. But outwardly, her tone remained composed. 'Aditya, you're missing the point,' she said coolly. 'The CIA couldn't care less about whatever "understanding" the Indian prime minister has with the president. Politicians make promises they rarely intend to keep.'

Her gaze sharpened as she continued. 'The CIA, on the other hand, operates on facts, logic and solid decision-making. You might not like their methods … hell, they can be ruthless, yes … but you can't deny their track record. They don't play political games, they don't care about diplomatic handshakes and photo ops. They play to win.'

There was a quiet certainty in her voice, as if she was reminding Aditya of the real power at play, the one that ignored political grandstanding. Aditya understood Mridula was hinting at the Indian prime minister when she said 'handshakes and photo ops'.

He chuckled softly, sensing Mridula's irritation. 'I must say, your love for the CIA is admirable,' he teased, a playful glint in his eye. It struck a nerve, and she shot back, her voice sharp, 'Easy for you to talk like that … you've clearly had the luxury of distance from the realities I deal with.'

Realizing they were drifting off course, Aditya shifted his tone, offering a sincere olive branch. 'Look, we're on the same side here. Let's not get caught up in this back-and-forth.' He paused, acknowledging her lead. 'You're already deep into this, ready to strike. So why don't you decide when we make the move? I'm here to follow your lead.'

His voice softened, though it carried a subtle undercurrent of challenge. 'Just say the word, unleash the beast in me, and I'll handle the rest. I'll play by your rules.' It was a surrender wrapped in cooperation, a way of telling her she had control, but with the clear understanding that when the time came, he wouldn't hold back.

Mridula's face remained impassive, but inside, a subtle distaste began to form. She had never seen herself as a 'beast' or some kind of untamed operative. That kind of macho posturing belonged to a different breed of spies, especially those who liked to flaunt their victories, to wear their aggression like a badge. She was the opposite, and suddenly, sitting across from Aditya, she realized how much she was starting to dislike him.

His self-assuredness grated on her, more so the way he seemed to think taking down a public figure in Canada had elevated him beyond reproach. He was playing a role she found tiresome, and it only deepened her resolve.

Quietly, without giving anything away, Mridula made a decision. She'd speak to New Delhi, express her growing concerns about working with Aditya. If it were up to her, she wouldn't team up with him again unless, of course, her boss left her no choice. But even then, she would be cautious. This man was not what she wanted in a partner.

Aditya couldn't pinpoint exactly what was running through Mridula's mind, but he had a strong sense that she wasn't keen on a joint operation. She clearly wanted total control, and if he were to be involved, it would only be as the muscle, the striker and not the planner.

Deciding to clear the air, Aditya leaned in slightly, his tone sincere but measured. 'Look, I get it. You run the show. I'm happy to step back and just be the striker. Everything else ... planning, strategy ... that's your call. I'll follow your instructions to the letter.'

Mridula had a quick glance at him. The word he used – instructions – made her think. Was it deliberate to make her feel that she was the boss? Was he playing a game deeper than she had anticipated? Or she should consider the possibility that, for once, she might be dealing with someone who had set aside his ego?

Whatever the case, the ball was in her court now. And Aditya knew she was weighing her options carefully.

The car idled at the traffic signal, its engine humming softly. Mridula's gaze lingered on Aditya, still studying him, trying to read beneath the surface. But Aditya, sensing her scrutiny, threw an unexpected curveball.

'Stop looking at me like that,' he said with a half-smile. 'The last thing I need in this operation is any distraction.'

Though his tone was light, there was an honesty in his words that caught her off guard. But Mridula, ever cautious, suspected he was just teasing, testing her boundaries. She raised an eyebrow, her tone dry. 'What are you, a fan of Bollywood now?'

Aditya grinned, leaning back in his seat. 'By all means,' he replied, playing along with ease.

The signal flicked from yellow to green, and with a firm press of the gas, Mridula pulled the car forward. The brief exchange had broken the tension, but the undercurrent of their power play remained, simmering just beneath the surface.

~

The White House spared no effort in welcoming the prime minister of India on his state visit, a calculated move to solidify ties with a burgeoning power and a strategic partner in the ever-evolving global chessboard, particularly against China. On the South Lawn, tables were adorned with lotus blooms, a symbolic nod to the prime minister's roots. A renowned chef was flown in from California to craft a meticulously designed vegetarian menu, reflecting both culture and diplomacy. The American president, standing beneath the iconic columns, spoke of shared democratic values, underscoring the bond built on trust, candour and mutual respect.

But while the applause echoed through the gardens of Washington, 224 kilometres away in the heart of New York City, a different kind of tension gripped the night. Mridula and Aditya stood in the shadows of a underlit room, their faces illuminated only by the dull glow of computer screens. The air was thick with anticipation as they relayed the final instructions to the Cuban hit team. The target was clear: a persistent adversary of the prime minister, a man who had relentlessly accused him of 'suffocating the dreams of Sikhs' and fuelling the fire for an independent Khalistan.

But the path to this moment had been anything but smooth. It was paved with meticulous planning, heated debates and a clash of egos within India's highest ranks. Officials were sharply divided on the legality of the operation, and personal sacrifices had already been made by R&AW agents, whose loyalty to the nation pushed them to risk their very lives.

The night before, a tense, drawn-out debate unfolded between the NSD and Awasthy during a video meeting in the dim confines of a secure briefing room. The NSD and Awasthy joined from Delhi on an encrypted feed, their faces projected on the large screen, while Mridula and Aditya sat shoulder to shoulder in the New York secure room. Delhi was pushing hard for the hit despite the risks, while Mridula, her voice calm but steely, opposed it. Her argument was clear: the assassination could not be sanctioned while the prime minister was on US soil.

The room had been crackling with tension, and Aditya, though present, had played the role of the quiet observer, a fence-sitter in a war of conviction. In private, he'd had numerous discussions with Mridula, and while he respected her caution, the opportunity to take down the enemy, Dhillon, was too tempting. Even with the Indian leader's presence looming over the operation, Aditya didn't flinch at the risk.

In fact, Mridula had tried to pull Aditya into her corner during the debate, subtly suggesting that he had agreed to wait until she determined the right moment to strike. Her concerns ran deeper than the operation itself, as she couldn't ignore the looming threat of America turning against India if one of their citizens were killed on their soil. Years of careful diplomacy had brought the prime minister to a point where the US favoured India, but one misstep, one miscalculated assassination, could destroy it all.

Mridula's caution, however, wasn't shared by everyone on the call. From the secure room in Delhi, the NSD, a man not known for tolerating hesitation, took sharp offence. His eyes narrowed on the screen as he cut her off mid-sentence. 'You're crossing a line,' he warned, his voice cold and clipped through the encrypted link. To him, her hesitation wasn't caution; it was a challenge to authority, a sign of weakness at a moment that demanded decisiveness.

Mridula, maintaining her calm, attempted to reason with the room. 'We've already seen this pattern ... killings in Pakistan, PoK, Afghanistan and, most recently in Surrey, Canada. The CIA is watching closely. They see it as an expanding wave of aggression, where home governments are more willing to cross borders and subdue political enemies, disregarding the sovereignty of other nations.'

But the NSD wasn't having it. His expression hardened, and he leaned forward, his voice cutting through the air like a blade. 'You're equating terrorists with dissidents? Is that what you're suggesting?'

Mridula straightened, meeting his gaze without flinching. 'I'm quoting from a CIA cable,' she countered, her tone measured but firm. She wasn't backing down, but she knew the weight of her words was hanging in dangerous territory. The room seemed to hold its breath as the tension between them thickened, the divide between caution and action more evident than ever.

Both Awasthy and the NSD exchanged glances, sensing that Mridula was underestimating New Delhi's deliberate and calculated stance on the matter. Hadn't they already weighed every possible outcome? The pros and cons had been studied extensively and, good or bad, right or wrong, the decision about Dhillon's fate wasn't hers to make. That call had already been taken, higher up the chain. The room grew colder as the NSD's voice took on a hard edge.

'Let's not forget,' he said, locking eyes with Mridula, 'America needs us now more than ever to counterbalance China. This is India's moment.' His tone softened into something almost condescending as he leaned back. 'We know we can get away with it. So, relax, Mridula.'

The room felt even more charged, the unspoken truth hanging heavy: no matter the risk, this operation was already in motion.

Mridula didn't push the argument further; it would have been pointless. Deep down, she understood what this was really about. The men sitting comfortably in Delhi were angling for political points, trying to craft their own version of a 'Balakot' ahead of the 2024 general elections. The thought of using extrajudicial killings as political leverage left a sour taste in her mouth. She didn't endorse the idea at all.

Yet, as much as she disagreed, Mridula was a loyal soldier, bound by duty. Defying orders wasn't in her nature, no matter how conflicted she felt. Still, the troubling question gnawed at her: what was the point of fighting a war when the outcome had already been decided? It was a thought that lingered as their tense meeting the night before came to its inevitable conclusion, with the NSD making it clear that the assassination of Dhillon was the top priority for the following day.

As Dhillon moved about the city, following his routine from home to the office, then lunch at an Indian restaurant, a visit to a gurdwara and finally back home, the Cuban operatives tracked his every move. Their eyes never left him, and every update was swiftly relayed to Aditya and Mridula. Aditya remained close to the operatives, shadowing the operation on the ground, while Mridula, miles away in her California apartment, watched it all unfold on her mobile screen, her fingers clenched around the device.

The plan was clear. Aditya wouldn't be pulling the trigger himself – that had been settled from the start. His role was to give the final green light. As the target moved closer to his home, nerves stretched tighter. The operatives' voices buzzed in Aditya's ear, waiting for his signal. Mridula's pulse quickened as she stared at the screen, knowing that the moment was fast approaching. Once Dhillon was safely inside his home, Aditya would make the call. The countdown had begun.

The operatives, masters of discretion, seamlessly rotated in their roles, blending into the city's fabric as they tailed Dhillon. One posed as a business consultant, mingling effortlessly with professionals near his office, while the lone female operative, masquerading as a student, spent hours in coffee shops and libraries, eyes discreetly following his every meeting. The rest adopted the guise of tourists, snapping photos of landmarks while discreetly noting each move Dhillon made, never missing a beat.

'Target is leaving the gurdwara,' one operative whispered into his hidden mic, eyes locked on Dhillon as he emerged from the temple, his gait unhurried, his posture composed. The message reached Mridula and Aditya instantly. Aditya, sitting in his car with a clenched jaw and a cold focus, gave the terse order: 'Stay on him.'

Miles away in Delhi, Awasthy monitored the situation with silent approval, his head nodding slightly in acknowledgement of the progress. The pieces were falling into place, and he knew they were closing in. The tension rippled through every channel, but the execution had to be flawless.

As Dhillon made his way toward his car, the operatives smoothly fanned out, keeping a measured distance, careful not to attract attention. Mridula, her eyes locked on the live feed from her screen, remained in constant contact with the team, her voice cool and commanding. 'No mistakes,' she cautioned, her tone carrying a quiet authority. 'We can't afford to spook him.'

Dhillon's car pulled away from the curb, and one of the operatives quickly hailed a cab, blending into the flow of city traffic as he followed at a distance. Another operative, already positioned near the subway entrance, descended the stairs, ensuring they had eyes on all potential escape routes. Mridula's focus sharpened, her mind calculating every possibility as she coordinated their movements with seamless precision, keeping the operation tightly controlled.

Every second mattered now, and they were closing in. Silently and invisibly.

But the streets of New York were as unpredictable as ever. Just as Dhillon reached a bustling intersection, he made an unexpected turn, abruptly changing his route. The operative in the cab tensed, caught off guard by the sudden shift.

'He's altering his path,' the operative hissed into the comms, his voice tight with surprise. In an instant, Aditya's and Mridula's voices crackled through the earpiece, sharp and urgent.

'Adjust immediately,' Aditya commanded, his tone leaving no room for hesitation.

Mridula's steady voice followed, barely concealing the rising tension. 'Stay close. Don't lose him.'

The team adapted quickly, their movements fluid but taut with pressure. The chase had taken an unpredictable turn, and the stakes were higher than ever. Every second, every decision, felt like a tipping point.

Dhillon finally arrived at a nondescript building – a safe house, tucked discreetly among the city's endless rows of similar houses. The operatives, summoned by their colleague in the cab, swiftly took their positions, blending into the urban chaos like seasoned ghosts. One pretended to browse through a newspaper at a nearby kiosk, his eyes flicking over condiments, soft drinks and cigarettes, but his focus never left the target. Another casually browsed the wares of a street vendor, her posture relaxed, yet her gaze sharp, locked onto the building's entrance.

Every movement was deliberate, every action calculated. Dhillon's safe house was now under their silent surveillance, and as the moments ticked by, the operatives tightened their invisible noose around him.

Inside the safe house, Dhillon gathered with key members of his group. The air inside crackled with intensity, their conversation heated as they laid out plans for a demonstration in Washington, DC, aimed at making a final statement before the Indian prime minister's departure. Strategies were debated, voices raised in urgency.

Outside, the operatives remained in their silent vigil, the minutes stretching into what felt like an eternity. The weight of the operation pressed down on them, every second ticking slower than the last.

Then, out of nowhere, Mridula's eyes sharpened as she caught something on her screen. It was a car, unmarked but unmistakably out of place, had pulled up a short distance from the safe house. Her heart skipped a beat, her voice cutting through the comms with sudden urgency.

'We have a potential complication,' she alerted, her tone steady but laced with concern. 'Stay sharp. Eyes open.'

The atmosphere shifted immediately, the operatives stiffening, ready for whatever came next. The tension, already thick, escalated this unexpected variable threatened to collapse everything.

The occupants of the suspicious car remained inside. Mridula, her fingers flying over her screen, quickly cross-referenced the license plate. Her breath caught as the result flashed back.

'It's a local undercover unit,' she muttered, frustration creeping into her voice.

Aditya, sensing the shift, went on full alert. 'We can't risk exposure,' he said sharply, his decision immediate. 'Abort the mission for now. Fall back and regroup.'

The command was relayed without hesitation, and the operatives, well-trained for such contingencies, smoothly disappeared into the bustling cityscape, blending effortlessly with the crowd. They retreated to their designated safe points, the mission temporarily suspended but far from over.

Meanwhile, inside the building, Dhillon, still completely unaware of the danger swirling around him, continued his meeting. After an hour, he stepped out, making his way back home. The operatives, now maintaining a more subtle cover, kept their distance but never lost sight of him, patiently awaiting further instructions.

In the heart of the American capital, the president stood at the podium, addressing the distinguished guests with his trademark warmth. He spoke eloquently about the deepening bond between the United States and India, describing their relationship as 'built on mutual trust, candour and respect'. His words carried weight, resonating with the assembled dignitaries, as they nodded in approval, the future of global cooperation seemingly brighter.

Yet, as the president's words echoed through the grand hall, the unspoken complexities of global politics loomed large beneath the surface. Behind the veil of diplomacy and formalities, shadows of covert actions flickered, unseen by the public, but felt by those who knew. The delicate balance of power, alliances and secret missions cast a long shadow over the evening.

Meanwhile, back in New York, the operatives had discreetly returned to their positions, stationed strategically around Dhillon's house. Their patience was unwavering, eyes sharp, waiting for the next signal. The calm façade of the evening stood in stark contrast to the storm brewing in the shadows.

As the night wore on, the tension outside Dhillon's house deepened. A knock on the door, and a guest arrived, holding a bottle of expensive whiskey, a clear sign that Dhillon wasn't planning to leave for the rest of the night. The operatives exchanged glances. This could mean the opportunity was slipping through their fingers after coming so close. But they needed him outside, away from his fortified sanctuary, at any cost.

Aditya swiftly repositioned the operatives to strategic points around the house, eyes scanning every exit. But the real challenge now loomed – how to lure Dhillon out of his nest. The longer they waited, the slimmer their chances became.

Aditya made the call. His voice was low, determined. 'I'm making a move,' he told Mridula, the decision already made.

Mridula's response was immediate, sharp. 'No! That's a suicide mission. He's got armed bodyguards inside.'

Aditya's jaw tightened. 'I'm not leaving here without blood on my hands,' he said, his tone cold and resolute. He had come too far, and the thought of retreat wasn't an option. The line went silent as the weight of his words settled in.

The night was closing in, and with it, a dangerous gamble.

Aditya's words hung in the air, striking Mridula with the force of a blow. His passionate resolve had left her momentarily speechless. To her, it was as though he were contemplating a suicide attack, an impulsive move that could reveal everything they had meticulously planned. The thought gripped her with dread. If Aditya went rogue, the consequences would be catastrophic. The CIA, FBI and DEA would come crashing down on them, especially with operatives linked to a drug cartel. The political fallout, she feared, would be a storm New Delhi was far from ready to weather.

But Aditya's mind was already made up. He was indeed on a path that seemed suicidal. There was a hard finality in his voice as he issued new instructions to the operatives, detailing their next piece of action. His calm in the face of what was coming unnerved her more than anything.

Mridula's instincts screamed to stop him, but she knew once Aditya set his sights on something, there was no pulling him back. Inside, Dhillon remained oblivious, his mind solely focused on the casual evening unfolding before him, his attention captured by the amber liquid swirling in his glass. He sensed nothing of the storm brewing just beyond his doorstep.

Outside, the first operative moved toward the entrance, his hand steady as he prepared to breach it. The others silently took up their positions, ready to execute the plan with precision. But in California, Mridula's heart pounded in her chest as a creeping dread washed over her. She dialled a number with trembling fingers.

Dhillon answered, his voice relaxed.

'Hitmen at your doorstep, Dhillon. Scoot,' Mridula warned, her words cutting through the air like a knife. She was clearly trying to sabotage the mission. Aditya's pledge, *'I'm not leaving here without blood on my hands'* was a far cry from the ordered precision such an operation demanded. For him, this mission wasn't just about duty;

it was personal. He had already lost everything that gave his life meaning, and somewhere deep down, he knew this might be his last assignment. Success had to be absolute, no matter the cost. If it meant dying in the process, so be it. He would not return home defeated.

In no time, chaos erupted. The operatives, poised for action, suddenly spotted gunmen emerging from Dhillon's house and then from the neighbouring houses, their eyes scanning the streets for any sign of suspicious movement. It became clear that Dhillon wasn't as unaware as they had hoped. Their cover was on the verge of being blown.

The operatives relayed the escalating situation to Mridula, addressing her by name. Her response was immediate, urgent. 'Abort. Get out of there. Now.'

The mission was falling apart, and the operatives, once so close, were now in a race against time.

But Aditya had already arrived at the scene, positioning himself like a 'stand-off weapon' prepared to strike from afar, just as the Iranian mercenaries had done in Pakistan. From his vantage point, he could see the situation unfolding, but his mind was set. He was determined to complete the mission, no matter the cost.

For the first time since this operation began, Mridula felt a deep sense of helplessness. Aditya had gone rogue, and she knew it. He was about to undo everything she had just tried to salvage. Her mind raced, but she remained calm. There was no room for panic.

She quickly dialled the leader of the operatives, who were already in retreat. The gunmen who emerged from Dhillon's house didn't immediately recognize them as part of any Indian operation. For a few tense seconds, both sides hesitated, unsure who the other was. The men outside looked like ordinary passersby, not trained assassins. The cartel henchmen, wary of drawing police attention in a foreign city, chose not to open fire. It was a dangerous misunderstanding, but it bought the operatives precious time to slip away.

The leader of the operatives, already retreating with his team, received her call. His phone buzzed, and he answered, a smirk playing on his lips as he heard her voice.

'Stop Aditya,' Mridula ordered, her tone cold and authoritative. 'By any means necessary, even if you have to use force.'

There was no hesitation in her voice, but deep down, she knew this was the most dangerous moment yet. She was betting everything on the hope that Aditya could be stopped before it was too late.

The operative complied without hesitation, swiftly closing in on Aditya. Despite his determination, Aditya wasn't physically strong enough to fend off four operatives at once, and within moments, he was subdued. They retreated together, the weight of what had nearly unfolded heavy in the air between them. The leader calmly but firmly relayed the situation to Mridula.

'Aditya's been contained. We're pulling out,' he reported. In the background, Mridula could hear Aditya's fury, his voice rising as he railed against their actions. Knowing she was on the other end of the line, he shouted that he wouldn't forgive her for sabotaging the operation. She ended the call.

As the operatives melted back into the shadows, blending seamlessly into the night, Mridula exhaled, her pulse still racing. But she wasn't done yet. With a steady hand, she made one more call.

In a nondescript office within the CIA, an alert flashed across a monitor, bright against the under lit room. Analysts, ever vigilant, swiftly connected the pieces. Rajan Swamy, a name that had surfaced in their intelligence reports, flagged by Mridula's tip-off, was en route to New York. The significance of this move sent shockwaves through the team. Urgency gripped the room, propelling the analysts into immediate action. Within minutes, the information was escalated up the chain of command, the threat level rising.

The game was far from over.

Within hours, Rajan Swamy was apprehended at the airport. A thorough search revealed $250,000 in cash and two passports which could be undeniable proof of his involvement in a covert operation. He was swiftly taken into custody, and the interrogation began immediately, the atmosphere tense and relentless.

Under the harsh lights of the interrogation room, Swamy finally cracked. 'I did it for the money,' he confessed, his voice weary but matter-of-fact. 'Like I always do.'

The interrogators pressed him further, trying to peel back the layers of deception, but Swamy remained frustratingly vague. 'I don't know the target,' he claimed, shaking his head. 'Or the mastermind behind it. My job was simple … deliver the cash. The money came from a Mexican cartel. I had to hand it over to some guys in New York. That's it.'

The frustration in the room was palpable, but it was clear Swamy was just another cog in a much larger, more dangerous machine.

The CIA's swift apprehension of Rajan Swamy sent ripples through the agency. As analysts pieced together his arrival with Mridula's tip, the gravity of the situation became crystal clear. India's bold, near-reckless move to eliminate Dhillon on American soil was undeniable. High-level meetings erupted, buzzing with the weight of the revelation, as officials weighed the delicate balance between national sovereignty and critical geopolitical alliances.

Back in Delhi, the atmosphere was equally tense. The NSD and Awasthy sat in urgent deliberation, both on edge as they analysed the unfolding chaos. The arrest of Swamy sent shockwaves through their operation, forcing them into hasty strategy sessions. The contrast was stark: while the assassination of Takkar had been executed with surgical precision, the failed attempt on Dhillon threatened to bring to light everything.

Awasthy leaned forward, his voice insistent. 'We've still sent a powerful message.'

The NSD's gaze was cold and calculating. 'At what cost?' he asked, his voice heavy with the weight of potential consequences.

Awasthy acknowledged that the assassination plots had placed the current US administration in a precarious position, forcing them to weigh their professed values against strategic interests. Having spent three years fostering closer ties with India, Washington found itself navigating a delicate balance. He was acutely aware that senior White House officials had begun convening high-level meetings to determine a response that wouldn't jeopardize the broader relationship with India. The head of the CIA, along with other senior figures, had even been tasked with confronting Indian officials and demanding accountability. Yet, despite the diplomatic posturing, the

United States had refrained from imposing expulsions, sanctions or any significant penalties. The NSD listened intently to Awasthy, choosing not to respond immediately, his silence revealing nothing of his thoughts.

Awasthy attempted to assert that any charges potentially levelled against India's alleged involvement would likely be confined to Rajan Swamy. He argued that much of the chatter surrounding Rajan pertained to his links with arms and drug trafficking and his alleged connections with contract killers. 'Those killers,' Awasthy reasoned, 'could just as easily have been hired to eliminate one of Rajan's rivals in the drug or illicit arms trade.' The NSD finally broke his silence. In a measured tone, he advised Awasthy to ensure that Rajan categorically denied all charges when presented in court, emphasizing the importance of keeping India's name insulated from the unfolding controversy.

The room fell silent as they considered the precarious situation, their minds racing to anticipate the fallout.

Mridula's heart raced as she monitored the unfolding situation. Every second felt like an eternity, but slowly, her risky decision was beginning to pay off. The CIA's interception of Rajan Swamy had created the buffer she desperately needed, shielding the operation from what could have been a catastrophic diplomatic fallout.

Rajan Swamy, an old asset of hers, had become her wild card. At the eleventh hour, she struck a deal with him that he would surrender with the cash, pretending it was meant for the assassins. Swamy, of course, knew nothing. He had never been involved in the actual plot, and thus, he was in no position to divulge any information that could implicate India in the attempt on Dhillon. He would go to prison, but only for a time. Mridula had ensured she had the means to get him released later, once the heat had died down.

Her heart still pounded, but there was a grim satisfaction in knowing she had averted disaster. Whatever the fallout, she had saved Aditya. The CIA's focus was now squarely on Rajan Swamy, not on the operative who had nearly crossed the line. For the moment, Aditya was in the clear.

As the dust began to settle, Mridula let out a tentative sigh of relief. Her carefully calculated, last-minute decision had averted an immediate disaster, but the unsettling implications still weighed heavily on her. Killing an American citizen on US soil, while the Indian prime minister was at the White House, would have been catastrophic. Years of diplomatic efforts to secure US support against China would have been jeopardized. With no other option to halt the operation, she resorted to sabotage. It wasn't that she was unaware of the consequences of defying her superior's orders, but she was prepared for them. She had no regrets, knowing that, like her seniors, she too had acted in the national interest.

Though she had resorted to sabotage something she had never done in her life or career – she executed it in a way she believed wouldn't appear as sabotage. After all, no one knew about her last-minute phone call to Dhillon. However, the real loose end was Aditya. While he might not have known about her secret call to the target, he was fully aware that it was her unilateral decision to withdraw the Cuban operatives just as they were about to pull the trigger. Mridula anticipated that Aditya would take some action, though she couldn't predict exactly what it might be.

She was staying in a hotel in New York City, and Aditya had no idea where she was. By now, his communication with R&AW Chief Ashok Awasthy and the NSD had been discreetly revived through secure channels after his arrival on American soil. Mridula, however, had always remained in contact with New Delhi. Regardless, he needed to call New Delhi and speak to either his boss, Ashok Awasthy, or the NSD about Mridula's last-minute withdrawal. Knowing Aditya, Awasthy had already anticipated the call. Similarly, the ever-vigilant NSD had begun to suspect that something was amiss, something had slipped through their control. Awasthy wondered if the situation had unfolded due to a conflict between Mridula and Aditya, while the NSD was more direct in his suspicion – Mridula had defied his order to eliminate Dhillon. Any doubts were dispelled once Aditya made the call. He also wanted to know where Mridula was.

Both the NSD and Awasthy quickly realized something was seriously wrong. Aditya and Mridula were both part of the operation and both were in NYC, so why would Aditya be asking New Delhi where to find her? It was clear there had been no communication between them. Wasting no time, the NSD directly asked Aditya what had gone wrong between the two. Unexpectedly, despite his inner fury and burning desire to confront her, Aditya made no complaint against Mridula.

Aditya explained that Dhillon's security team had detected the presence of operatives outside his house. They were positioning themselves inside, ready to retaliate, which could have escalated into a gang war, something no one wanted. Worse, it might have led to his capture by the NYC police on patrol. Aditya also mentioned that Mridula had suddenly gone incommunicado, and their post-operation analysis was still pending. Additionally, he had one of her bags, which he needed to return before leaving the US, making it necessary for him to meet her.

Awasthy shared a few addresses where Mridula might be found. He believed that a face-to-face encounter between Aditya and Mridula, likely a heated one, could help shed light on what had gone wrong. Both would present their defences, and Awasthy was eager to hear their sides of the story.

Mridula stepped out of the clinic, gently supporting her elderly mother as they made their way to the car. She moved with care, offering her arm to help her mother into the passenger seat. The sun was beginning to dip, casting a soft glow over the street. Mridula closed the car door, pausing for a moment to check on her mother before getting into the driver's seat.

She drove off, navigating the California streets in silence, her thoughts preoccupied. Little did she know, another car had pulled out from a distance. Aditya, at the wheel, watched them carefully, keeping his distance but never losing sight of her car. He had followed her all the way from the clinic, his mind a storm of controlled fury.

Aditya's patience was wearing thin. Every second that ticked by only stoked the fire inside him. Mridula had crossed a line, and he needed answers. He wasn't going back to India with a failure in hand, not after everything he had sacrificed. Not after the success in Surrey.

When Mridula finally pulled into her apartment complex, Aditya parked a little further down the street, watching as she helped her mother inside. He waited, his gaze fixed on her door. When he was sure she had settled her mother in, he made his move.

Aditya walked to the entrance phone and dialed. His voice was steady, but the tension was unmistakable. 'It's urgent. We need to talk.'

There was a pause, then Mridula's voice came through, calm but knowing. 'I'll be right down.'

She told her mother she needed to step out for a moment, then headed downstairs. She already knew why Aditya was there. She had expected this confrontation.

They drove together in silence, heading to the waterfront. The tension in the car was suffocating, both of them bracing for the inevitable clash. When they arrived, they sat facing the water, the cool breeze doing little to dissipate the heat between them.

Aditya didn't waste time.

'You sabotaged the mission,' he said, his voice cold and sharp.

Mridula's expression remained calm. 'I did what had to be done. You can't see it, but I saved us from a diplomatic disaster.'

Aditya scoffed, his fists clenched. 'Diplomatic disaster? I put everything on the line for this operation. My life, my career, my personal life, all of it. This wasn't some game for me. Do you have any idea what's at stake here? You've ruined it all.'

'You don't get it, do you?' Mridula shot back. 'Killing an American citizen while the Indian prime minister is still in the US? It would've been catastrophic. You think you can just bulldoze through without considering the consequences? This isn't war, Aditya. This is bigger than that.'

Aditya's voice grew colder. 'That's exactly where you're wrong. This is war. And in war, there are casualties. Sometimes innocents die, but that's the price we pay. You've forgotten what the mission was about because you're too busy playing moral compass.'

Mridula's eyes narrowed. 'And you've forgotten that this isn't about your ego. This is about protecting national interests. You're a rogue, Aditya. A thug in the name of espionage. You think by killing a few targets, you're saving the country. But you're reckless.'

Aditya's anger flared, but he kept his tone measured. 'I don't defy orders, Mridula. That's what makes me good at what I do. I follow the mission through, no matter how tough it gets. I've already been through this. In Surrey, I took out Gurdeep Singh Takkar, and I succeeded. You know why? Because I didn't let my ethics get in the way. I did what needed to be done. But you … you called off the operation. And you did it unilaterally.'

Mridula leaned forward, her voice sharp. 'You don't get to decide that your way is the only way. I've seen what happens when people like you take control … bloodshed, chaos and international backlash. I wasn't about to let you destroy everything.'

Aditya shook his head, his frustration mounting. 'You don't pull the plug when we're seconds away from taking the shot. You made a choice, and it wasn't yours to make. You went behind my back and spoiled the mission. If you couldn't handle it, you should've quit.'

Mridula's voice was steady, but there was an edge to it. 'I did what I thought was right to avoid a crisis that could have gone out of control. If you want to call that sabotage, fine. But I'm not here to take orders from someone who doesn't understand the bigger picture.'

Aditya's eyes locked on hers, unflinching. 'You ruined this. Our methods may be different, but the mission was the same. The target was the same. And you chose to call it off because you were too afraid of what might happen. I will never approve of what you did.'

Mridula's face hardened. 'I'm not looking for your approval, Aditya. I made the call because it had to be made. You may not like it, but this time, you were wrong.'

Aditya leaned forward, his voice low and cutting. 'You should've had the guts to quit if you were so worried about your ethics and morality. But you didn't. You played it your way, and now, you've cost us everything.'

Mridula's expression tightened, her voice cutting. 'I don't play politics with people's lives, Aditya. I'm not here to dance to the tune of politicians like you. You're like part of that new right-wing lobby in New Delhi, aren't you? The one that's saffronizing even our intelligence agencies. You're turning India into another Pakistan –

where everything is weighed down by religion, and spies like you conspire with politicians to create and manipulate events. I refuse to play to that gallery.'

Aditya's eyes darkened, his fury barely contained. 'I am saffronizing intelligence? You're delusional, Mridula. You sound just like those left-wing liberals who love to eat out of the hands of the establishment, enjoy the perks, but never miss a chance to tear it down. Hypocrites, the lot of you.'

Mridula stood abruptly, anger flashing across her face. 'I don't need to justify myself to you. Unlike you, I don't sell my soul for a mission. I did what I had to do, and I stand by it.'

Aditya rose to face her, his voice low and simmering with rage. 'You'll never understand what's at stake because you're too wrapped up in your own self-righteousness. We had a chance, and you ruined it. Don't think I'll forget that.'

Mridula glared at him for a moment, her jaw set, before turning on her heel and walking away, leaving Aditya fuming by the water's edge.

~

In Delhi, the thrill of eliminating Takkar had quickly been eclipsed by the looming uncertainty of the diplomatic storm brewing just beyond the horizon. The initial victory now felt fragile as doubts swirled among the officials. How severe would the diplomatic backlash be? Would America stand by its unspoken support, or would mounting international pressure force them to reconsider their alliance with India? The diplomatic fallout had started.

India's bold shift to a strategy of 'defensive offense' had over the past decade triggered a cascade of confrontations between R&AW and Western domestic security services, igniting a shadow war that spilled into public view. The consequences were swift and stinging.

In Britain, tensions reached boiling point. R&AW's activities, particularly its surveillance and harassment of the Sikh population around Birmingham, had escalated to such a degree in 2014 and 2015 that MI5 was forced to intervene. The British domestic security agency delivered a direct warning to Awasthy, then serving as R&AW's station chief in London. The encounter was anything but cordial, with MI5 officials making it clear that such actions were pushing the limits of what Britain could tolerate, threatening to strain Indo-British relations.

In Australia, two R&AW officers were expelled after authorities uncovered what the head of the Australian intelligence service publicly called a 'nest of spies'. The revelation sent shockwaves through diplomatic circles. According to the intelligence chief, foreign operatives had been caught infiltrating diaspora communities, attempting to penetrate local police forces and stealing sensitive information about Australian airport security systems. While he refrained from naming the agency involved, it was an open secret that R&AW was the target of his accusations. The press had a field day, splashing headlines that rattled New Delhi.

The drama extended to Germany, where federal police made high-profile arrests, dismantling an alleged R&AW network embedded within the Sikh diaspora. Among those detained was a husband-and-wife duo who had operated a website masquerading as a platform for local Sikh news and events. Behind the scenes, however, they were on R&AW's payroll, funnelling information back to handlers in India.

Each clash underscored the stakes of India's audacious new strategy. For R&AW, it was a high-risk game of influence and infiltration; for the West, it was a challenge to the unspoken rules of the intelligence community. The fallout was becoming harder to contain, and Awasthy knew all too well that the price of this cat-and-mouse game could escalate further.

As Aditya disembarked from the aircraft, the sight of two R&AW men standing inches from the aerobridge confirmed what he already suspected. There would be no chance to head home, no quick shower or moment to unwind before facing the inevitable debrief. They were there to escort him directly to Ashok Awasthy's office. It was routine, but it didn't make it any less frustrating.

He sighed internally. After a failed mission, it was standard procedure that superiors always wanted immediate answers. They needed to understand what went wrong, especially when a high-priority target like Dhillon was still alive. Aditya felt the weight of the mission's failure pressing heavily on him, but what really stung was the knowledge that the entire operation had been compromised by internal conflict. He wasn't the type to make excuses, but he wasn't about to shoulder the blame alone either. Mridula's decision had altered everything.

Aditya followed the two men silently, mentally preparing for the meeting. There would be questions, accusations and dissection of every decision made on the ground. But Aditya had his own questions too. Questions that the higher-ups needed to answer. And questions that he might not like to answer.

Aditya sat quietly in the waiting area, sipping his coffee and eating the egg sandwiches that had been brought to him. He was trying to settle his thoughts, but they kept circling back to the events in New York. Ten minutes felt longer than usual, as he replayed the mission in his head. He had made his peace with the operation's failure, at least externally. Internally, he was still fuming, especially about Mridula's abrupt and unilateral decision to abort. But that was something he wasn't planning to get into just yet.

When Awasthy finally called him in, he was greeted with a concerned glance. The customary questions about his health came first, and Aditya answered them mechanically. Then, as expected, Awasthy asked for a detailed reconstruction of the operation.

Aditya began recounting the mission with precision, starting with the initial setup, their surveillance on Dhillon, the coordination with the Cuban operatives. Everything about it. But as he approached the critical moment, when Mridula had pulled the plug, he chose his words carefully. He wasn't ready to throw her under the bus just yet, despite his anger. He left out the part where she had said, '*Abort. Get out of there, now,*' and also the moment when he had vowed he wouldn't leave without blood on his hands. Instead, he focused on the operational details and the challenges that had led to the mission being compromised.

As he spoke, Awasthy watched him closely, nodding occasionally but not interrupting. Aditya knew that eventually, the real questions would come.

As Aditya finished recounting the events of the failed operation, Awasthy leaned back in his chair, his gaze more intense than before. Aditya expected follow-up questions about logistics or gaps in the plan, but Awasthy asked something entirely unexpected.

'Mridula,' Awasthy began, his tone careful but probing, 'she's not like the others. You know that. She's always had a bit of a rebellious streak.' He paused, watching Aditya's reaction closely. 'Did she do anything that could've impacted the operation negatively?'

Aditya hadn't anticipated such a direct question, and it caught him off guard. But instead of showing his surprise, he used it to his advantage, leaning into his response as though genuinely taken aback by the suggestion.

'Mridula?' Aditya said, raising an eyebrow. 'With all due respect, sir, she's a senior operative with a solid track record. I'm ... honestly surprised you'd ask that.'

Awasthy wasn't swayed by the defence. He had seen enough deflection tactics in his career to recognize one. His tone became more direct, cutting through the pretence. 'I'm asking you if she could have sabotaged the operation. Yes or no, Aditya.'

For a brief moment, there was silence. Aditya could feel the weight of the question hanging in the air, but he was firm in his response, despite everything that had happened.

'No,' he said, his voice steady and clear. 'She didn't sabotage the mission.'

Awasthy's eyes searched for his a beat longer than usual, then nodded, seemingly satisfied with the answer. At least for now.

Awasthy, more seasoned and perceptive than most, quietly analysed Aditya's response. He didn't need a direct confession to get to the truth. In his experienced eyes, Aditya's firm 'No' about Mridula was as good as an admission that she had indeed sabotaged the mission. But Awasthy kept his conclusion to himself, filing it away for future use.

He looked at Aditya with a slight smile, an expression that was hard to read but carried a hint of appreciation. 'No wonder you're a great operative,' he said, his tone light but with an undertone of acknowledgement, 'and an even greater team player.'

Aditya held his gaze, unsure of the exact meaning behind the compliment, but he wasn't about to offer anything further. In the spy world, sometimes silence was as valuable as the truth.

Awasthy leaned back in his chair, eyeing Aditya thoughtfully. 'Would you care for some more coffee?' he asked, as though they were discussing something mundane. Aditya, still processing the conversation, nodded, 'Yes, please.' Awasthy signalled to his personal kitchen, and within moments, freshly brewed coffee was on its way. The silence between them was comfortable, but Aditya sensed that something else was coming. And it did.

'Mridula sent in her resignation,' Awasthy said casually, as if dropping a routine piece of office news.

Aditya froze for a second. Genuine surprise flickered across his face. 'Resignation?' he echoed, his mind racing. Why would she resign? She had years left in the organization, and despite their recent fallout, leaving seemed drastic.

'Seems like an impulsive decision …!' Aditya said, more to himself than to Awasthy.

Awasthy sat back, his tone carefully neutral but with a hint of amusement. 'That's something only she can answer. Time will tell … though I sometimes wish time was a bit more punctual.' He let the words hang for a moment before continuing with a slight smirk, 'She hasn't shared her side of the story with us yet. Until then, she's as valuable to the organization as you are … possibly even a bit more interesting.'

Aditya's next words took Awasthy by surprise, catching him off guard for the first time in their conversation.

'I want to quit, too,' Aditya said, his tone more reflective than defiant. 'I need a break.'

Awasthy leaned forward, his expression shifting from surprise to curiosity. 'You need a break, that's fine,' he said, his tone casual but probing, 'but why does that mean you have to quit?'

He paused for a moment, observing Aditya closely. 'Just a few moments ago, you seemed surprised by Mridula's decision to quit. Now you're saying you want to do the same. What's happening?'

Awasthy chuckled softly, trying to lighten the mood. 'Were you two in some kind of pact?' His eyes glinted mischievously as he added, 'She is, after all, an extremely pretty woman. You wouldn't be the first officer to fall for her. Plenty have, you know.'

The remark, though casual, hung in the air and Aditya felt the weight of the implications. But Awasthy's chuckle suggested he wasn't entirely serious. Just curious enough to gauge Aditya's reaction.

Aditya listened to Awasthy's teasing comments about Mridula, but they barely registered. The weight of his life, the failed marriage, the separation from his daughter and the relentless missions was crushing him from the inside. The extrajudicial killings, even of high-profile targets, had only been a way to prove to himself that he was still alive, that he hadn't lost his edge. But everything else? It felt hollow. The thrill of the mission was all that had kept him going.

Awasthy's words barely stirred any reaction in him. Linking him to Mridula was meaningless; none of it mattered. What mattered now was the break he so desperately needed. A long break, away from everything, where maybe he could sit in the mountains and meditate. Maybe then, he could find something that still made sense.

Awasthy, seasoned in dealing with operatives reaching the end of their tether, recognized Aditya's state. He had seen it before, the weariness, the mental fatigue. He knew how to handle it. Confident that Aditya wasn't lost to the agency yet, Awasthy leaned back and said, 'Alright, Aditya. I get it. You need a break, and you'll get one. Send me an email asking for a sabbatical. We'll make it happen.'

Aditya nodded, grateful for the understanding but still feeling the weight of everything bearing down on him.

As Aditya left Awasthy's office, his mind still heavy with thoughts of the break he desperately needed, Awasthy wasted no time. He picked up the phone and dialed the NSD.

'All's well with Aditya,' Awasthy said calmly. 'He's fine.'

There was a pause on the other end of the line, then the NSD's voice came through. 'And Mridula?'

'I'll discuss that with you in person,' Awasthy replied, keeping his tone neutral. He knew there was more to unpack with Mridula, but that conversation needed to be handled carefully.

The NSD shifted gears. 'Will Aditya be available for the next mission?'

Awasthy didn't hesitate, his voice resolute. 'Why not?'

He knew Aditya was fatigued, but the man had a resilience that couldn't be dismissed so easily.

~

The atmosphere in the conference room was tense as the NSD addressed a group of high-ranking officials, including Awasthy, the foreign secretary and the director of the Intelligence Bureau. His voice was steady, but the gravity of the situation was unmistakable.

'We knew this wouldn't be easy,' he began, his eyes scanning the room. 'Our objectives were clear, and the mission was necessary. But now we must face the consequences, which will be delicate and unpredictable.'

He paused, letting the weight of his words settle over the room. 'Please note,' he added, his voice firm, 'the mission is far from over. The storm is just beginning.'

The officials exchanged uneasy glances, the reality of what lay ahead sinking in. They had crossed a line, and now they would have to walk a razor's edge in the diplomatic world that had just been upended.

The tension in the room was palpable as the NSD continued, reminding everyone of the high-value targets who still posed significant threats to India's security.

'Rasool Azhar,' the NSD began, his voice hard as steel. 'Fourth on India's most-wanted list. He runs the militant organization JeM out of PoK. His group is responsible for the 1999 hijacking of Indian Airlines flight IC-814, which landed in Kandahar, then under Taliban control. Azhar's group orchestrated the 2001 Parliament attack in India and continues to hide in Pakistan under ISI protection.'

As the NSD spoke, in another part of the world, Mridula was driving down a quiet highway in America. The night was calm, but unease clung to the air, her thoughts swirling with the weight of the mission and the uncertainties still to come.

'Next, Syed Salahuddin,' the NSD continued, his tone unrelenting. 'Leader of Hizbul Mujahideen, a pro-Pakistan militant group. Salahuddin seeks to integrate Kashmir with Pakistan, working hand-in-hand with the ISI. He's the second-most-wanted criminal in India, and his group is responsible for a string of terrorist attacks in Jammu and Kashmir.'

Mridula glanced at her rear-view mirror, noticing a truck gaining on her from the distance. Her mind raced, not about the mission she had left behind, but about what came after. In their world, resignations were rarely accepted, and even when they were, freedom was an illusion. She knew she would be watched, perhaps for years. The CIA and the FBI had already pieced together more than they should have. In a game where yesterday's ally could become tomorrow's enemy, Mridula wasn't sure who to trust or what her next move should be.

'And then,' the NSD's voice dropped to a near-growl, 'Masood Ibrahim. The mastermind behind the 1993 Mumbai bombings, killing 350 and injuring over 1,200. He has close ties with terrorist networks, including Al Qaeda. He's also linked to the 2008 Mumbai attacks and has been involved in numerous illegal activities, from drug trafficking to match-fixing scandals. Bringing down Masood is a national priority.'

At that moment, the truck behind Mridula rammed into her car. The impact was brutal. Her vehicle spun violently out of control before crashing into the guardrail. Metal groaned, glass shattered – the scene was utter chaos.

Back in Delhi, the NSD's gaze swept the room, locking eyes with each official. 'We will not rest until all of these threats are neutralized,' he said with unwavering resolve. The team, though shaken by the enormity of their task, steeled themselves. The mission had only just begun.

Meanwhile, back on the highway, emergency responders arrived at the wreckage of Mridula's car. The scene was grim. They pulled out her lifeless body from the twisted metal. Her role in the mission had ended in tragic silence.

After the mission to eliminate Dhillon was sabotaged, Aditya had faced the grim reality of the situation. But failure was never an option for him. He was angry and disillusioned, and had taken a sabbatical, meaning to walk away for good. Then came the news about Mridula. Her death hit him harder than he expected. It wasn't just grief; it was the cold reminder that in their world, no one was untouchable, not even from within their own circle.

For nights, Aditya couldn't sleep. He kept thinking of his daughter, of Meera, of what could happen if the same unseen hand ever reached for them. Mridula's death had changed the rules. It told him that loyalty offered no protection, that trust was a luxury he could no longer afford.

But out of that storm came clarity. He understood that the real enemy was still out there, and the only way to stay alive was to finish what had begun. He took it upon himself to ensure that Mridula's sacrifice and the larger mission did not go in vain. He went rogue, this time with absolute precision and purpose. No longer bound by bureaucracy or trust, Aditya planned his own covert operation, stepping into the shadows as a one-man army. His first target would be Rasool Azhar.

As Aditya closed in on Azhar, the lines between victory and uncertainty blurred. In the world of espionage, there were no definitive endings, only pauses in the endless pursuit of threats that loomed in the shadows. The moment hung in the balance, the outcome unknown. For a spy, the mission was never truly over; it merely shifted, evolved, waiting for the next move. Aditya's path had brought him to the edge of something monumental, but what lay ahead remained shrouded in darkness.

In this life, the answers might not come easily, and neither do the endings. The chase would continue, with new battles on the horizon, and only time would reveal the cost of the choices made.

A Note on the Author

Anirudhya Mitra is a bestselling author, acclaimed screenwriter and award-winning former journalist. His debut book, *Ninety Days: The True Story of the Hunt for Rajiv Gandhi's Assassins* (2023), became a national bestseller and was adapted into the widely acclaimed SonyLIV series, *The Hunt*, directed by Nagesh Kukunoor. He has also written *The Enforcer: An IPS Officer's War on Crime in India's Badlands* (2025).

A former investigative journalist with *India Today* and *The Times of India*, Mitra is credited with breaking some of India's most high-profile stories – from the Rajiv Gandhi assassination and Bofors scandal to the South Asian drug wars and the shadowy world of godmen and political fixers.

Over the years, Mitra has transitioned from journalism to storytelling for the screen, having written original series for leading OTT platforms. He has also produced and written internationally recognized films in Southeast Asia, including *Under the Protection of Ka'bah*, Indonesia's submission for Best Foreign Language Film at the 84th Academy Awards in 2012, and Habibie & Ainun, Indonesia's blockbuster biopic on President B.J. Habibie.